NIGHT ATTACK

Vicki came awake, felt the strange hands on her. Hot hands. Not Garrison's.

"Richard!" she would have cried, but couldn't.

It made no difference. Garrison "heard" her anyway.

Garrison's body rolled over and sat up, its eyes flying open. Their light filled the room with golden lances of fire. Palazzi released Vicki and gazed across the room into the blazing eyes of hell.

"Go to sleep, Vicki," said an icy voice. "Forget this—it isn't happening." And she collapsed back onto her pillows.

The naked man seated upon the bed smiled. "Go," he said.

Palazzi felt himself shot out of the window in a great invisible hand. He soared up into the night, up and away across the great rock of the Acropolis, and the lights of Lindos glowing far below.

And out across the sea sped Palazzi. A mile, two—stationary now, floating and spinning a mile high in the air, and the deep, deep sea below.

"Mercy, have mercy!" he screamed. But no one was listening, and the great hand now hurled him down . . .

PSYCHOSPHERE

BRIAN LUMLEY

A TOM DOHERTY ASSOCIATES BOOK
NEW YORK

This is a work of fiction. All the characters and events portrayed in this book are fictitious, and any resemblance to real people or events is purely coincidental.

PSYCHOSPHERE

Copyright © 1984 by Brian Lumley

Cover art by Jim Thiesen

A Tor Book
Published by Tom Doherty Associates, Inc.
175 Fifth Avenue
New York, N.Y. 10010

Tor ® is a registered trademark of Tom Doherty Associates, Inc.

ISBN: 0-812-52030-0

First Tor edition: October 1992

Printed in the United States of America

0 9 8 7 6 5 4 3 2 1

For AB²

Chapter
1

TWO PAIRS OF EYES WATCHED RICHARD GARRISON and Vicki Maler leave their holiday residence and disappear into the maze of steep narrow streets leading down into the heart of the Greek island village; two pairs, neither one aware of the other. One pair belonged to a thief, the other to an assassin.

The latter, Joe Black by name, was seated at a table on the raised patio of the taverna where the pair he watched normally breakfasted—a taverna they were obliged to pass on any excursion away from their accommodation—whose open-air eating area presented Black with a distant but unobstructed view of the door to their courtyard, seen above rising tiers of flat white rooftops. The village, dropping down into a valley or bay, seemed to have been built on much the same lines as an auditorium or amphithea-

1

tre; for which kindness Black gave the ancient architects a generous ten. It made his task as observer that much easier.

Black wore *Lederhosen* and braces, a wide-brimmed straw hat and an open-neck shirt loud with red and yellow flowers. He was not German—despite his dress, his fat face and cigar—but Cockney: the hired hand of a middling Mafia boss, Carlo Vicenti, who once owned a quarter-share of one of London's less reputable and far more profitable casinos. Richard Garrison now owned that quarter-share, a fact which irked Vicenti more than a trifle. Hence Joe Black's presence here in Lindos, Rhodes, the Aegean.

Black was not alone on Rhodes: a second hit-man, his brother Bert ("Bomber Bert Black," to his dubious circle of friends), waited in Rhodes town itself. Bert was the "hard" part of the team on this occasion. That is to say, his was the hand which would directly terminate Garrison's life. Brother Joe's role was simply to tell him when to do it.

Just a minute or so after 11:00, the subjects of Black's covert surveillance emerged from an alley into the narrow "main" street, crossing it to climb wooden stairs to the breakfast patio. He waited for them to seat themselves close by, waited again until they engaged the waiter's attention and started to give him their orders, then folded his shielding newspaper and left.

He glanced only once at the pair as he went, his eyes lingering momentarily on the black-as-night lenses and frames which Garrison wore. A blind man, this Garrison, allegedly. Black

2

snorted as he descended the stairs to the street and made his way towards the open village square and coach-and-taxi booking office. *"Huh!"* The damnedest blind man he had ever seen! And his mind went back to the first time he ever came into contact with Garrison . . .

That had been at the Ace of Clubs, where on occasion Black had used to do bouncer (or "floor attendant" as the dealers and their minders preferred it). The "blind" man had come in one night with his woman, also blind, the first time they had ever visited the place. The last, too, if Black's memory served him correctly. As patrons, anyway. He snorted again: *"Huh!"* Well, and hadn't once been enough?

That had been, oh, six or seven months ago, but Black remembered it like yesterday . . .

. . . Remembered Garrison buying one large pink chip worth fifty pounds sterling, and the way he had casually crossed to the central roulette wheel to toss the chip onto the table's zero. And how with the next spin the ball had dropped, as if pre-ordained, directly into that very slot—how in fact it had fallen into that slot *twice* in succession. And how Garrison had let the spoils of his first incredible gamble ride!

The gasps of shock, astonishment and appreciation that went up then had been the summons which brought the boss, the raven-haired Carlo Vicenti himself, hurrying up to the table, his face darkening under brows already black as thunder. "Mr, er, Garrison? Yes, your custom was recommended. The club's misfortune, it appears." He forced a smile. "Well, sir, you have won a great deal of money, in fact a fortune, and—"

"And I want to let it ride one last time," Garrison had unsmilingly cut him short.

"On the zero?" Vicenti's jaw had dropped.

Garrison had frowned thoughtfully, only half-seriously, almost mockingly. "Certainly, on the zero, why not?"

"But sir, you have already won over sixty thousand pounds, and—"

"Sixty-four thousand and eight hundred, to be exact," Garrison had cut him short again, "—including my stake, of course. But please do go on."

Vicenti had leaned towards him then, staring up into his dark, heavy lenses and stating in a lowered tone, but perfectly audibly, "Sir, unbeknown to you, the operator of this wheel has already been obliged to ask the house for permission to cover your second bet. Normally, you understand we would have a limit of one thousand pounds on this wheel. And besides, the zero cannot possibly come up a third time."

Garrison had stood rock still, apparently frozen to the floor by something Vicenti had said. His answer, when finally it came, was delivered in a voice steady, firm and chill: "Am I to understand that this wheel is fixed?"

Vicenti was astounded. "What? I said no such thing! Of course the wheel is not fixed. I did not mean that the—"

"Then it can 'possibly' spin a third zero?"

"But certainly, sir—except it is most unlikely, and—"

"Unlikely or not," Garrison cut in for the third time, "I wish to bet."

A half-apologetic shrug. "We cannot cover it. And sir—" this time Vicenti's voice had been almost conspiratorial, wheedling, "—aren't you being just a little frivolous with your money?"

"Not with mine," and now Garrison smiled broadly. "With yours, perhaps, but not mine. I only started with fifty pounds."

All of this Joe Black had witnessed from a position close at hand. Also the way Vicenti had turned an explosive purple at Garrison's last remark. At that moment Joe had known, whatever the apparent outcome of this confrontation, that the little Sicilian would take a terrible revenge on the blind man—in one way or another. The one thing Vicenti had never been able to stand was to be laughed at—and here he stood, an object of ridicule. Certainly in his own eyes. Possibly in the eyes of half of the club's regular clientele, who now gathered about the table in various attitudes ranging between awe and delight. In fact it was mainly Garrison's lucky streak which had fired their imaginations, not Vicenti's discomfiture; but the Sicilian had taken their smiles, their subdued laughter, chuckles and excited whispers as being derogatory to himself.

"Wait!" he had snapped. "I need to confer." And the wheel had remained stationary for a full five minutes until he returned.

"Well!" Garrison had remained cool, smiling—

at least with his mouth, for of course his eyes had been invisible.

And now Vincenti had seemed eager that everyone should hear him. "Mr—er, Garrison?—I am a part-owner of this club. Indeed I own one quarter of all its assets. Even so, I personally could barely cover tonight's losses. Your winnings, that is. But . . . I am a gambler." And he had paused to smile a shark's smile, teeth white and gleaming in a veritable death-grin. "Since you, too, are a gambler—a most extraordinary gambler, obviously—I have a proposition which might interest you."

"Go on."

Vicenti had shrugged, continued: "I have been authorized to take full responsibility in this matter. Responsibility for the current, er, damage, shall we say?—and for my, er, proposition."

"Which is?"

Vicenti had then taken out his personal checkbook, written a check for £64,800, folded it neatly and delicately placed it on the table's zero. "Take my check by all means, or—we spin the wheel. But on this understanding: since the club does not have that sort of money, if you win you accept my share of its ownership by way of payment."

Which was where, if Garrison was a normal, sober man and in his right mind, he should have backed down and taken his winnings. Everything was against him: namely the incredible odds against the zero and the fact that he could win no more real cash. And at the same time Vicenti stood to gain immeasurably. For despite the fact that all the odds were on his side, still he had shown that he was indeed a gambler—that he personally was willing to risk his all on this one spin of the wheel—and that Garrison was up against a man of equal verve, daring and determination. But more important by far to Carlo Vicenti, there was no longer any laughter from those patrons crowding the table, no more amused sniggers and whispers. Instead the mood had become one of tense excitement, of breathless suspense. Quite simply, it was now Vincenti against Garrison. This had become a very personal matter.

Then—

Joe Black remembered a very strange thing, something which even now, six months later, made him shudder in a thrill of almost supernatural intensity. Garrison had seemed—to change. His very shape inside his evening suit had seemed somehow to bulk out, to take on weight, solidity. He had become—squarer. His face, too, had taken on this squareness, and his smile had completely faded away.

No one else appeared to notice these things—with perhaps the one exception of the blind man's woman, who backed off from him a little, her hand going nervously to her mouth—but Joe Black was absolutely certain of what he had seen. It was as if, in the space of only a few seconds, a different man stood in Garrison's shoes. A man with a different voice. A harsh, arrogant, authoritative, somehow Germanic voice:

"I accept your gamble, my little Sicilian friend. Let the wheel spin. But since so very much rests upon it—in your eyes at least—please be so good as to spin it yourself."

"That's most . . . unusual," Vicenti had grated in return. "But so is everything tonight, it appears. Very well—" and in utter silence he had moved through the throng, which opened to let him pass, spun the wheel, raced the ball against the spin—and waited.

Rock steady he had stood there as the wheel gradually slowed and the ball skittered and clicked, ramrod straight at the head of the table, his face split in a frozen, almost meaningless grin. And the ball jumping, rolling, skittering, and the wheel slowing. And a sea of faces watching the wheel—except Garrison's which, blind or not, seemed turned upon Vicenti's face—and Joe Black's, which watched only Garrison.

And the wheel still turning but the ball now firmly lodged in its slot. Vicenti's eyes bulging. A touch of foam at the corner of his madly grinning mouth. Concerted gasps, sighs, amazed little utterances going up from the onlookers—and all of them drawing back from the swaying Vicenti to give him space, air.

And his half-gasp, half-croak, as the fingers of his left hand clawed at the table's rim, giving him support: *"Zero!"*

"You have my address," Garrison's voice was still the new, cold Germanic one. "I shall expect the documents delivered in the near future. Goodnight to you." And he had picked up Vicenti's check and pocketed it, and without another word had led his wife across the floor, out of the room, out of the club and into the night.

Oh, yes, Joe Black remembered that night. How rage and utter hatred had blazed in Vicenti's fever-bright eyes as he watched Garrison leave; how he had then switched off the table's overhead light and given the dealer and his assistant the rest of the night—indeed the rest of their lives—off, telling them never to return; and how he had retired rubber-legged to the club's offices. There he had consumed large amounts of alcohol, being quite drunk later when, after the club had said goodnight to its last patron, he staggeringly returned—returned with a fire axe and great gusto to reduce the table, wheel and all to very small fragments.

Not a night Black might easily forget . . . it was the night Vicenti had offered him the contract on Garrison's life . . .

The second pair of eyes watching Richard Garrison and Vicki Maler belonged to a gentleman from Genoa named Paulo Palazzi. A gentleman, that is, to unacquainted eyes. Unlike Joe Black, Palazzi had no prior knowledge of Garrison beyond the fact that he was a very rich man. Anyone with his own chartered aircraft sitting idle in a hangar at Rhodes airport would, of necessity, be very rich. This had seemed indisputable to Palazzi; nevertheless, he had made several discreet, local inquiries to prove the point; and if further confirmation were needed there was always the fact that Garrison and his lady had paid for and were now enjoying the luxury of

9

rooms large enough to accommodate three to four times their numbers. Privacy costs money. A lot of money . . .

Paulo Palazzi was small, slim, immaculate in a white, lightweight Italian suit and patent leather shoes, and bareheaded to show off his mop of curly black hair. Light-skinned, clear-eyed and fresh-faced, he could be anything between twenty-five and forty years of age. A cheerful, fairly well-to-do Italian tourist—to anyone offering him less than a very close scrutiny. And indeed he was fairly well-do-to, on the spoils of various illicit occupations, including his very successful summer trips. This was one such: a week on Rhodes which, with a bit of luck, would pay for itself many times over.

He had been watching Garrison's comings and goings for three days now, sufficient time to acquaint himself quite intimately with the man's humors and habits. Only one thing continued to concern him: Garrison's blindness. For plainly Garrison was *not* blind, despite the heavy dark glasses he constantly wore. Or if he was, then his four remaining senses had expanded out of all proportion—or, more likely, he was richer than even Palazzi had reckoned. For who but an *extremely* rich man could possibly afford the very special and miniaturized aids he would need to make so light of so serious an infirmity?

Not that Garrison's blindness—real or assumed—gave Palazzi any sort of moral pause, on the contrary. The thing was a positive boon, or might be if Palazzi's plans needed to be altered. No, it was just that Garrison seemed to see so very well . . . for a blind man. Well, doubtless he had his own reasons for the subterfuge, if indeed it was such. And for Palazzi . . . it must remain simply a curiosity, one of the idiosyncrasies of a victim-to-be.

Palazzi sat upon a spread handkerchief, his slim legs nonchalantly crossed, his back to a merlon of the ancient battlements, high over Lindos on the precipitous wall of the Acropolis itself. He held a pair of powerful binoculars to his eyes in slender, highly articulate and well-manicured hands, his gaze fixed upon the vine beneath which he could just make out the light blue of Garrison's T-shirt and the coolly contrasting greens of Vicki's skirt and top. He smiled to himself, idly reflecting upon his own cleverness.

His *modus operandi* was simplicity itself, perfected over the last three seasons. Three seasons, yes, for he had discovered Lindos three summers ago. Lindos and its mighty rock.

From the old battlements, courtesy of the crusading Knights of St. John of Jerusalem, he could see virtually all of the village. Not a single house or home, shack or taverna was hidden from his scrutiny. Sitting here, warm in the brilliant sunshine and breathing the sweet, clean air of the Aegean, he could study any victim's to and froings at will, picking and choosing the perfect time to strike. And occasionally, just occasionally, there would be enough in it to keep him in luxury for . . . well, for a little while at least.

As for the way it worked:

Tomorrow evening, for example, Garrison and his lady would very likely go out. They would eat, drink, talk a little in one or another taverna late into the Lindos night. Their movements would be languid, leisurely. They were on holiday, in no mood to hurry. Later they might go to a disco, burn off a little excess energy. But whatever they did, it would make little difference. Palazzi, having seen them leave their rooms, would have plenty of time to get in, discover their hidden valuables (they all did that, hid away their jewelry and spare cash), take what he wanted and get out.

And of course Garrison would not be his only victim tomorrow night. There was also a fat, rich Frenchman and his mistress, who Palazzi knew were booked to see a show tomorrow in Rhodes; and finally there was a Swiss playboy and his girlfriend, who invariably danced and drank the night away. And all of them would be leaving their accommodation at approximately the same time, their movements entirely visible in the magnifying lenses of the thief's binoculars. And the cost of remaining up here when the crowds of visitors were finally ushered out of the place and the Acropolis locked its door? Oh, a few hundred Drachmas, enough to keep the gnarled old watchman in ouzo for a night or two.

And in the early hours of the following morning—with the sun not long up and the local constabulary still rubbing the sleep from their eyes—why, Paulo Palazzi would be gone! Lone passenger in a taxi headed for Rhodes town, where he would change his suit, his style, unload a few choice items for cash and re-adopt his real name. Under which, four or five days from now, he would fly back to Genoa and business as usual. And if what he had seen of Mrs. Garrison's jewelry alone was anything to go by ... it would be quite a long time before he needed to do any "serious" work again.

Which was probably why he was so cheerful, nodding a bright good morning to a couple of pretty British girls with Birmingham accents where they leaned out over the wall close by and *oohed* and *aahed* their awe at the scene spread below. Yes, it was a very pretty scene, and a *very* good morning. Hopefully tomorrow would be just as good, and especially tomorrow night.

Putting his binoculars away, snapping shut the catch on their case and standing up, Palazzi smiled at the girls again. One of them had the most exquisitely jutting breasts. He licked his lips. A pity this was a purely business trip, but—

Well, business is business . . .

Five minutes after Joe Black left the elevated patio where his intended victim now breakfasted, Garrison paused with a forkful of scrambled egg raised halfway to his mouth. Suddenly upon his mind's eye, leaping into view from nowhere, he had viewed—something. A scene. Not a true memory but something else entirely. Just what . . . he couldn't say, except that for a moment all of his senses had seemed electrified into a tingling defensiveness. The scene had been dim and smoky and had depicted a male figure, seated, his hand spinning a small rou-

13

lette wheel which he held between crossed legs. The thing had lasted no longer than a split second. Now it was gone, beyond recall.

"Richard?" Vicki's voice reached him. "Something with your egg?"

He unfroze, relaxed shoulders grown too tight, and lowered his fork. "No," he smiled, "it's fine. I've had enough, that's all."

"You looked so strange just then," she was concerned.

"Did I? Oh, I was probably miles away."

She tilted her head questioningly. "Is it nice there?"

"Um?" He was still distant.

"What were you thinking?"

"Thinking?" He shrugged, shook his head, said the first thing that came into his mind—something which mildly surprised even him. "Did you notice the man who left a few minutes ago? With the leather pants and flowery shirt?"

"Yes, a German like me. Or rather more typical—or at least how you English believe a typical German should be." She smiled. "A bit loud, really. You were thinking about him?"

"Too loud," Garrison answered, "and not at all German. And yes, I suppose I must have been thinking about him."

"Not German? But he looked so—" She stopped smiling. "You were eavesdropping? Listening to his thoughts? But why, Richard?"

"Actually, I wasn't," he said truthfully. "Hell, I hardly noticed the bloke. But—oh, I may have seen him before somewhere. He's not German, though, you can be sure of that."

"And does it matter? His nationality, I mean?"

He wrinkled his nose, gave her question perfunctory consideration, grinned and said, "Shouldn't think so."

Now Vicki relaxed, reached across the table and took his hand, laughed out loud. "Oh, Richard, you really are the strangest man!" And because it had been spontaneous, she failed to see the significance of her words.

Garrison continued to grin outwardly, while inside:

Oh, yes, he thought, *I really am. But there are stranger things in heaven and earth, Vicki, my sweet. Stranger by far.*

And he knew that one of those things, those oh-so-strange things, was even now beginning. Or perhaps it had started long ago and only now was coming to a head, like pus gathering in a boil.

All about Garrison the Psychosphere eddied and swirled, pulsing endlessly, apparently ordered and serene. But occasionally it carried the ripples of far, distant disturbances beyond his understanding. Such ripples were there even now; they did him no harm, but they troubled him. He felt like a fish swimming in the Great Sea of the Psychosphere, and like a fish he sensed the presence of some mighty predator. Out there, somewhere in the fathomless deeps— a shark!

That was an interesting thought:

A shark in the Psychosphere, and Garrison not so much a fish as a spear-fisherman. While he preyed on smaller denizens of the deeps, some-

15

where close at hand a large predator circled him. But he wasn't afraid, or at least not wholly afraid, for he had his spear-gun. Except . . . if a confrontation was in the offing, would his gun be powerful enough? Its once-tough rubber hurlers were getting old, growing weaker from continued stretching.

Worse than this, would he even see the enemy if it came—or would it coast up silently behind him, jaws agape?

Suddenly fearful, lost in his fantasy, Garrison cast about with his mind. Terror was the spur, boosting his ESP even as it boosted his adrenalin. Searching, he peered deep into the Psychosphere. Somewhere, somewhere . . .

. . . There!

That mottled, marbled shape, silent as a shadow, intent upon the pursuit of some other prey, showing no interest in Garrison whatsoever. Until—

—The shark-shape turned suddenly in Garrison's direction, came at him in a blind, head-on fury, a dull-gray bullet snarling through the matterless stuff of the Psychosphere.

It was close, looming closer . . . it sensed him!

"Richard?" Vicki's voice reached in to him, causing him to start as if slapped—which in turn made her jump. "Wandering again?" she nervously asked.

Garrison's face felt drained of blood—but he forced a grin, rose and reached across the table to draw her up with him. He hoped she couldn't feel the trembling in his arms. "Good idea," he said. "To wander, I mean. Let's walk down towards the beach . . ."

But even as they set out she could tell that he was still not entirely with her . . .

Chapter
2

MORE THAN FIFTEEN HUNDRED MILES NORTHWEST of Rhodes it was midday and brilliant with sunshine. London was abustle—but in Charon Gubwa's mind-castle all was cool, shaded and calm as a somnolent beast. The Castle did *not* sleep—it never slept—but Gubwa had been alone all morning in his private quarters and not to be disturbed; which was about as close as the Castle as an entity might ever get to the stasis of slumber.

The Castle's staff, Gubwa's "soldiers," went about their tasks almost robotically, corpuscles in the Castle's veins; the machines and computers and support systems throbbed and pumped, rustled and ticked and whirred, organs by which the Castle lived; but Charon Gubwa himself—rather, the Gubwa consciousness, the id, the mind of the place—he had in part removed himself.

Physically he was there, for he was also the Castle's pulse, without which it could not function and would have no purpose, but mentally . . .

This was one of those days when Gubwa practiced his arts, when he exercised his mind as more orthodox men might exercise their bodies; except that where the latter were bent upon physical creativity, the structural improvement of themselves, Gubwa's exercises were designed for the mental degradation and eventual destruction of others. And they were in truth "exercises": training tasks he set himself to carry him to the very threshold of an objective—but not to cross it. Not yet. Not until the time was ripe, when the result could only be total victory.

And in this respect Gubwa was a general, whose weapons were the telepathic and hypnotic powers of his own mind. The Castle and its staff: they were merely his armor. The world outside, the world of common men: that was his objective. Eventually.

But Gubwa was tiring now. His exercises had lasted for close on three hours and he was beginning to feel that mental strain which ever accompanied such excesses of mind.

He was seated in a massively padded armchair before a great glass tube which reached vertically from floor to ceiling. Within the tube a large globe of the world, with its continents and oceans etched in realistic bas-relief and color, hung in electro-magnetic suspension. Gubwa's eyes were closed; he sat completely relaxed—physically. Indeed he might well appear to be asleep, but he was not.

19

Upon his lap lay a computer remote, its tiny screen glowing with this word and coordinates:

MOTH: 3°95' —64°7'

"Moth" was the codename of one of Britain's Polaris submarines and the coordinates told her location: midway between Iceland and Norway, roughly halfway along an imaginary line drawn due North between the Shetlands and the Arctic Circle. On Gubwa's globe this location showed as a steady point of light in the western reaches of the Norwegian Ocean, a telltale glow which served purely as a guide, a focal point, for his intense telepathic transmissions.

The coordinates had been snatched from the unsuspecting mind of the Duty Officer at the pen in Rosyth, roughly corroborated by a similarly unwitting mind in the Admiralty, and given final definition by Moth's Captain himself where he went about his duties 400 feet beneath a sparkling, choppy, sun-flecked surface. And that was where Gubwa's mind was at this very moment, seated astride the mind of Moth's commander.

The Castle's master was well pleased with the way the morning's exercises had gone—so far. But this was his last "visit" of this session and it was the most important; it would determine his mood for days to come—it might one day determine the fate of the world.

As for the rest of the morning's work, work already completed:

Strategic Air Command had been a hard one. The Americans—especially their military elements—had a rigidity of mind difficult to crack; they were mentally obstinate. USAD's pilots were no exception. The United States Airborne Deterrent had often been described as a never-ending flirtation with disaster, but it was also the symbol of a nation's security-consciousness carried to the nth degree. Never a moment of the day or night went by without some of those planes were in the sky, and the minds of their pilots were never easy to find and had proved singularly difficult to penetrate.

Be that as it may, Gubwa knew most of them by now; and yet not one of them knew him. His knowledge was the result of over three years' covert surveillance, a gradual insinuation of himself into their minds. This was a continual process which he must forever update and change to suit circumstances. Air patrol routes were changed from day to day (deliberately, of course, to confound the Russians; but as often as not to Gubwa's confusion, too) and pilot turnover was fairly frequent. Because of the nature of the task, however, pilot substitution or replacement never occurred *en bloc*; there were always half-a-dozen easily recognizable, susceptible minds open to him, most of which he had learned to control in one degree or another. For control was the real object of these exercises. To control minds such as these was to control world destiny. Literally.

This morning Gubwa might well have started World War III, and it was his intention one day to do exactly that. For example: he might have caused one or more of the supersonic, nuclear-armed American bombers to enter into Russian airspace, ignoring all commands to turn back. Simultaneously he might have bombed or "nuked," as current jargon would have it, Detroit, Boston and Ottawa. And if he had also managed to maintain radio silence there would have been no way to convince the Pentagon and US authorities that such an attack had been carried out by their own planes! Even had they accepted the unacceptable, conditions worldwide would by then have been rapidly disintegrating, with every country of major military capability elevated to or accelerating towards a "red alert" situation. At which stage . . . a little pressure applied to a certain jittery mind controlling the firing-buttons of a nest of missiles in their silos at Vytegra, USSR, and—

—And then there had been the Chinese.

Gubwa had been there, too—to a selected location in the scattered chain of silos along the border of the North Sinkiang Desert. The Chinese still did not have the West's or Russia's targeting technology, but what they lacked in sophistication they more than made up for in muscle. And their bombs were incredibly dirty. A chain-reaction of hysterical button-pushing there could well result in a thousand-mile wide band of nuclear destruction and desolation reaching from the Aral Sea to Siberia!

All very gratifying, and Charon Gubwa might well congratulate himself on the success of the morning's exercises so far. He had broached these various thresholds without breaching them, which remained a step for the future. But now, in the mind of Moth's commander, he desired to apply one last test before terminating today's training session. And this was a test which would require a delicate touch indeed—or a brutal one, depending on the point of view.

Gubwa had long since learned all of the atomic submariner's habits and idiosyncrasies, and he was well aware of Captain Gary Foster's wont to catnap. The sub's commander was one of those people who work best under pressure, the more extreme the better; whose mind and body performed at their highest levels of efficiency under a workload others would deem crippling. And when called upon he could perform under such stress for long hours at a stretch, even days. His secret (or so he himself believed) lay in an equally impressive ability to fall asleep, however briefly, at the drop of a hat.

This he was given to do as often as three or four times in any period of twenty-four hours, always to the amazement and occasionally the consternation of his immediate subordinates and crew; for while they themselves would normally sleep for six or seven hours at a stretch between duties, their Commanding Officer rarely went down for more than two hours and often made do with as little as fifteen minutes! In the middle of a watch—or a good read of *Playboy*, or a hand of poker—when by all rights Captain Foster should be deep in slumber, he would silently, unexpectedly appear in a hatchway or through a bulkhead door, his sardonic, humorless grin cold as the wind from the pole. So that

Moth's company was aware to a man that there was never a time, nor even a moment, when they could guarantee that their Captain was "off-duty." It made, he was in the habit of reminding them, for a "very tight ship." It was good for discipline.

And it made Charon Gubwa's task that much easier.

Sleeping minds were far simpler to penetrate; in sleep a man's mental defenses are down, where often a mere suggestion may carry the weight of a command. Using his usual technique of gradual insinuation over many short visits, Gubwa had found that he could slip in and out of certain minds as easily as unlocked rooms, inhabiting and using them as he saw fit. And from the sleeping mind—where certain deeply embedded post-hypnotic commands could be left to take root and germinate—it was usually only a short step to the waking mind, when Gubwa's unwitting host would become quite literally a zombie working to his command. Thus it was with several of the USAD pilots, and thus he intended it to be with Moth's commander.

It is, nevertheless, a rare brand of hypnotism indeed that can cause a man to do that which his nature would not permit at its normal level of consciousness. And this was the purpose of today's test run: to see if it were possible so to manipulate Gary Foster's mind that he would perform *contrary* to the fundamental elements of his own nature, ideals, and training. In short:

to see if he could be made to press the button! Not to actually cross that threshold, no, but certainly to stand upon its doorstep.

Gubwa had found Foster taking a catnap, a habit of the Captain's around midday, and had crept into the unguarded, sleeping mind. There had been no dreams as such, merely an awareness of the great gray metal shape surrounding mind and body as it cruised in the deeps, powerful as the atomic engine which propelled it and semi-sentient with its computer-controlled "mind" and sensors. With no dreams to usurp, Gubwa had simply inserted a phantasm of his own:

IT'S COLD OUTSIDE, BITTERLY COLD. WE ARE THREE HUNDRED MILES INSIDE THE ARCTIC CIRCLE, EDGE OF THE BARENTS SEA, LYING STILL ON THE BOTTOM AT THIRTY FATHOMS. MOSCOW IS 1300 MILES AWAY. THIS IS NO EXERCISE. THE ALERT STATE IS RED. IT IS RED ALL OVER THE WORLD. THIS IS WHAT YOUR TRAINING WAS ALL ABOUT, GARY. THIS IS WHAT IT WAS FOR . . .

NOW YOU CAN ONLY WAIT. YOU WAIT IN THE OPS AREA. YOUR RADIO OP HAS JUST RECEIVED INFO THROUGH THE DECODER. HIS FACE IS WHITE, DRAWN . . .

In his tiny cabin, Foster moaned and turned over on his narrow bunk. Droplets of sweat stood out suddenly upon his brow. He mumbled some incoherent query, but in his dream his words were sharp-etched, brittle with tension. "What is it, Carter?"

"Russian bombers are on the edge of our airspace. Others are coming over the roof, closing on Canada. American bombers are already inside Red airspace. And . . . and . . ."

"Yes, Carter?" Foster snapped. "Come on, Sparks, what is it?"

Carter nodded, gulped. "We're to initiate NUCAC 7."

NUCAC 7: first phase of a missile launch! Following which there would be NUCACs 8, then 9 . . . and finally 10. And 10 would signify the launch itself!

Foster almost said: "No, I don't believe it," but he held the words back. Instead he said: "Action stations, all. NUCAC 7 op immediate. Other NUCACs . . . imminent. Mate?"

His 2IC, Mike Arnott, nodded briefly, grimly. NUCAC required both of them: in the hands of one man alone it would be too dangerous. Unthinkably dangerous.

Carter called out: "Coms cut between Moscow and Washington . . ."

The keys code had come through with the NUCAC 7 order; Carter had already punched the code into Moth's ops computer. Twin red lights were flashing on panels in the curving walls; the panels slid open. Foster reached up and took out a bunch of harmless looking keys from one recess; likewise Arnott from the other.

To one end of the ops area, built into the bulkhead, stood a booth only slightly larger than a telephone kiosk; its windows were dark, tinted; its sealed door bore the legend:

NUCAC CELL

Foster and Arnott crossed to the booth, inserted duplicate keys in locks on opposite sides of the door, turned them. The seals snapped open, interior lights flickered into life. Foster slid the door aside and they entered, cramming themselves into tiny padded seats and facing each other across a table whose center was a screen. Foster reached up and pulled the door shut. Outside in the ops bay Sparks plugged in their audio system and gave them direct access to all incoming signals.

GOOD! said Gubwa, fascinated by the progress of the dream he had instigated.

Foster glared across at Arnott and barked, "Good? What the hell's good about it?" The other stared blankly back. Both men put on headphones.

NUCAC 8, said Gubwa.

"Jesus Christ!" Foster hissed through clenched teeth. "It's all coming apart!" Almost automatically, he and Arnott pressed twinned buttons, fed coded coordinates into the computer for its translation, watched the illuminated, reticulated table-screen coming to life between them in lines of red and blue light, glowing with figures, times, ever-changing computations.

Gubwa was now the voice of incoming signals. He painted a scenario of chaos, madness:

SEVEN RED BOMBERS INTERCEPTED AND TAKEN OUT OVER MANITOBA. SATELLITES REPORT INCREASED ACTIVITY ROUND SILOS IN RUSSIA AND INTERMEDIATE MISSILE BATTERIES IN EAST GERMANY. FRENCH SILOS SABOTAGED

27

BY 5TH COLUMNISTS. PARIS NUKED! ICBMS FIRED IN USSR! AND IN USA! CRUISE MISSILES LAUNCHED ON USSR FROM EUROPE! INNER LONDON NUKED!

"Jesus! Jesus! Jesus!—" Foster was whispering over and over.

NUCAC 9, said Gubwa.

"No!" Foster gasped. "It's all wrong! It has to be wrong! We would've been the first to know, not the last. They're blowing up the world out there—bombers, ICBMs, Cruise—and we're only on NUCAC 9?" Sweat dripped from his chin, plastered his shirt to his back. Outside his dream, Foster's body struggled out of his bunk, staggered from his tiny cabin.

NUCAC 10, said Gubwa.

"It's all yours, Captain," said Arnott, feeding the final code into the computer. A tiny panel snapped open in the table's surface beside Foster's right hand. In the recess, a large red firing-button blinked on—off—on—off—on—

"Captain?" said Arnott.

NUCAC 10! Gubwa snapped.

For a moment Foster's right hand hovered over the button—then shot across the table and grabbed Arnott's throat. "Dream!" he was babbling. "Dream—nightmare—it has to be—!"

NUCAC 10! Gubwa squeezed Foster's mind.

But Arnott was dissolving away in Foster's grasp, the outline of his face and form melting down. And the NUCAC cell's lights and fittings were blurring, shifting like melting wax. Foster was waking up!

Despite Gubwa's every effort to restrain him,

the man was breaking free. His situation had been *too* nightmarish, the ultimate nightmare, and he must—

—"Wake up!" Foster gasped.

NO!

"Must!"

Failure! Gubwa was furious. There must be a fault in his scenario. He hadn't built it carefully enough.

Foster was almost awake. And his mind was agitated, a whirlpool, crowded with terror, confused and yet resolute. Grimly determined to . . . *to wake up!* Useless in this condition. Useless to Charon Gubwa.

The exercise was over. The Castle's master withdrew from Foster's mind.

At which precise moment, in Lindos, Rhodes, Richard Allan Garrison was fantasizing about the great mottled mind-shark . . .

"Captain! Captain Foster! *Gary!*" someone was yelling. The voice was Arnott's, but choked, strangled. Foster felt his grip broken, was hurled back. The slender thread which remained, linking him to the world of dreams, snapped. The last revenant of Gubwa's hypnotic scenario vaporized as Foster felt the pain of slamming backwards into a bulkhead . . . but hands were there to grab him and hold him up. He shook his head, stared about through eyes which refused to focus, shrugged off the two crew members who stood gaping at him.

"What in hell—?" Then he looked down at himself where he stood trembling in shock, dressed in loose, sweat-soaked issue pajamas! He remembered now: he had intended to sleep for an hour, maybe a little longer.

Across the ops area Mike Arnott was perched on a table, massaging his throat. Foster moved unsteadily towards his 2IC. "Mike, what—?"

"You tell me, sir," said the other hoarsely. "You floated in here like a ghost just a minute ago. You were gabbling something—don't ask me what. I only caught one word, NUCAC—then you grabbed me by the throat!"

Foster wasn't yet oriented. "I grabbed you? You're on watch?"

"Of course."

"And nothing . . . unusual? No incoming signals?" Foster's eyes were wide now, staring.

"Only . . . well, this!" Arnott answered. "The rest was routine." He grabbed the other's trembling arms, held him steady. "Gary, what is it?"

"Where are we?" the Captain's breathing was slowing down, regulating itself. He peered at location charts, sighed his relief. "An hour from turnabout. Thank God!"

"Where did you think we were?" Arnott was incredulous. "Were you asleep, dreaming?"

Foster nodded. "Only explanation. Sleepwalking, too, apparently." He almost fell into a chair, reaction catching up with him. "It was the Big One—NUCAC 10!"

Arnott's eyebrows went up. He nodded to the crewmen. "You two wait outside a minute." They left. "Sir, that's a funny sort of dream you've had." He shrugged. "Understandable, considering our job, but . . . been pushing it too hard, perhaps?"

Foster looked at him, narrowed his eyes. "That could be the answer, I suppose. Don't concern yourself, I'll have a checkup. But . . . I'd like it if this didn't go any further. Speak to those two, will you?" He nodded towards the hatchway.

"Of course."

"Good. Now I'd better get some clothes on." Foster turned away, glad that his cabin was close by. As for the checkup: he would speak to the ship's doctor. And he'd see another doctor later—just as soon as Moth got back to Rosyth . . .

Thwarted, on leaving Foster's mind Gubwa should have soared instantaneously back to his own seat of consciousness in the Castle, but something intervened.

Another mind moved in the Psychosphere, was close, almost on a collision course. There was no real contact but an awareness—from which Gubwa recoiled no less sharply than the other. Two wary forces facing each other, drawing back, finally fleeing in mutual panic—

—And Gubwa snapped open his eyes in the Castle, starting at once to his feet. If he had been furious before, now he was doubly so—and not a little worried. Now what had *that* been? *Who?*

Of course there were other minds in the Psychosphere: the Psychosphere was the essence of all sentience, of mental intelligence. But the vast majority of minds were no more aware of the Psychosphere than a bird is aware of air. *This* mind had been aware, or had seemed so. And Gubwa had sensed . . . fear? Perhaps. In which case the close brush had probably been accidental.

The Castle's master knew that the Russians had their own telepaths, as did the Americans. They had a certain raw talent, these ESPers, but they were amateurs compared with Gubwa. Fifty percent of what they learned was guesswork, none of it could ever be trusted. Polaris submarines were almost impossible to detect through technology, so it could have been a Russian mind Gubwa had come up against—even an American for that matter. And because it had been unexpected, Gubwa had panicked.

He snorted. Obviously the USA and USSR—one of them, at least—was making some progress in the training and use of ESP-endowed surveillance agents, telepathic spies. It was something which would bear looking into.

But meanwhile, there was the other problem, the fact that Foster had broken free of Gubwa's control, had refused to press the NUCAC button. Oh, in a genuine crisis he would respond to training, of course he would—but even then he would have to be absolutely certain of the nature of the situation. This *was* his training, had to be; the world could not afford that kind of mistake. Given the smallest loophole or blind spot in even the most perfect scenario, Foster would reject it. Gubwa couldn't win!

The Castle's master cursed vividly. It was a problem. If he could not control Foster's single mind, how could he hope to control both his and his 2IC's simultaneously? Trust Great Britain to build these sort of dual-control, failsafe systems into its hardware!

Well, facts must be faced up to. Moth was out of the question. The other Polaris subs, too—
—Unless.

Slowly a poisonous transformation took place in Gubwa's gross features. Suddenly smiling, he cursed again—cursed himself for a fool. The easy way is always the simplest way. Why even attempt to control two minds simultaneously— or four, or six—when you can control the mind *which controls those minds?*

After all, Moth got her orders by radio, didn't she? And the operator who sent them was only one man, wasn't he? One mind! And if there was trouble there, why, Gubwa could always take it higher! He laughed out loud. Of course he could . . .

. . . Right to the Admiralty itself!

Chapter

3

Vicki Maler, red-haired and marvellously golden-eyed (her eyes had once been green and blind), her slim elfin face cocked a little to one side—Vicki Maler, once-dead and cryogenically suspended at Schloss Zonigen in the Swiss Alps, returned to life through the will of her lover, Richard Allan Garrison—stood now beside the bed where Garrison tossed and turned in the throes of nightmare. She did not wish to wake him, despite the occasional spastic twitching of his limbs and the starting of salty droplets from his neck and the hollow between his shoulder blades; no, for one could never be certain of his mood when first roused from sleep. Not these days. Not any longer.

Vicki's thoughts were her own; they were as private, vital and original as any she had conjured in her previous life (or, as she thought of it now, in that "earlier" time), before the final, hideous acceleration of the creeping cancer which had ravaged her body to its painful death. And because she was intelligent, because she knew Garrison to be the instrument of her revival, her reincarnation, the fact that her mind retained its individuality vaguely surprised her. For not only had Garrison replenished her body and driven out the killing cancer, but also her mind; he had revitalized it intact, inquiring and unique as any mind, and not at all a product or substructure of his own expanded multimind.

She was, in short, her own person. No, she corrected herself, she was Garrison's person; for he had left her in no doubt as to her fate should any accident befall him, when she must surely return to her previous state, whose clay shell, however vital now, must crumble as a centuried mummy exposed to air and light. Oh, yes, for if Vicki seemed bright and unflickering, an electrical glow in life's filament, then Garrison himself was the light switch. And if he were switched off . . .

As a girl in her teens Vicki had read Poe, Lovecraft and Wilde. She well remembered the horrific demise of M. Valdemar and that of Dr. Munoz: *her* fate, too, should Garrison die. But she was more inclined to associate Garrison himself with the terrible fate of Dorian Gray. Not that Garrison had ever been a man of great vices, he had not. But . . . things had happened to him. Things . . .

Vicki supposed she should be grateful for those things, but still she preferred to remember Garrison as he had been in that "earlier" time. Then he had been, well, just Garrison. But that had been before the changes, before her rebirth.

Odd, but despite the fact that she was the same girl she had been "earlier," Vicki nevertheless felt . . . yes, reincarnated. After all, eight years had gone by without her active, physical presence in the world, when she had lain—dormant?—in her cryogenic crypt at Schloss Zonigen; but for Garrison they had been real, waking years. And strange ones. Moreover, Vicki's body had all the vitality and strength of her pre-cancer years, or at least of those years before the disease had commenced to drain her. So that in a sense she had been born again into a younger body than the one she last remembered.

She shuddered at the thought: the body she remembered.

The husk. The pain-riven shell. The bewildered flesh whose contamination had bloated and burned and filled her veins with the fire of stricken cells in ravenous, monstrous mutation. A body full of cancer. Livid with pain. No, with agony!

Vicki shuddered again. She not only remembered the cause of her death (for she *had* died) but Death Itself—or Himself. She had actually known His touch, the cruelly constricting fingers of the Grim Reaper; and not merely His touch but His iron grasp. And in her case those bony fingers had been of fire—or of acid.

Death. The Old Man. The oldest man in the

world, who could not die Himself until He had snuffed out the very last life.

Immortal, therefore. Immortal, and . . . cruel.

Certainly in the worst of her pain-racked days Vicki had felt that someone enjoyed her agony, else why should she suffer it? If all were to balance, then there must be an enjoyment equal to her suffering. Well, finally she had the last laugh, for Death the One Immortal now had a second immortal to contend with. The Old Man must now wait on the demise of one Richard Allan Garrison, and Garrison did not intend to die—not ever.

Garrison stirred and mumbled something in his sleep, then flopped over on to his back. He was through the worst of his nightmare and the sweat was drying on him. Vicki listened to his near-inarticulate mouthings. He mentioned Schroeder, she thought, and Koenig, the sounds coming out in a jumble. Vicki allowed herself a third, this time quite deliberate shudder and peered intently into his face. It seemed calm now, resigned almost. But beneath those closed eyelids . . .

She straightened and stepped silently to the room's gilt-framed mirror. The gold of her eyes matched the yellow glow of the frame, burning in the reflected fire of the day's last ray of sunlight. She marvelled at her own eyes—those golden eyes which had been blind in that earlier time, blind for many years—their sight now restored through the will of Garrison. His own eyes, too, blinded by fire and blast, repaired miraculously in glowing, uniformly golden orbs.

Eyes which saw more, much more, than those of other men.

Miraculous, yes. Garrison performed miracles. His powers were very nearly . . . infinite? They had seemed so at one time, but . . . he himself did not know—had never fully explored—the extent or limitations of his powers. In fact of late he had kept an uneasy silence on the subject.

She turned to him again where he lay, her movements edgy, nervous. And silently she repeated to herself. *Miracles* . . .

But wasn't that a God-given gift? The power to work miracles? And if there really was a God (Vicki had always doubted it) why should He so reward Garrison? Or any human being for that matter. Or perhaps there actually *was* a God—now.

Had there been others with Garrisons's powers, Vicki wondered? What of the old legends? What of Merlin and the great wizards of immemorial myth? Her thoughts became blasphemous. What of Jesus Christ? He too had restored sight to the blind, raised up the dead, walked on the water. Hadn't He?

But no, cases were different. *His* miracles were generally accepted as having been all to the good. Garrison's were sometimes . . . other than that.

Her thoughts turned abruptly to their whereabouts . . .

The decision to go to the Aegean had been made, as were most of Garrison's decisions, on the spur of the moment. His pilot (he owned an executive jet aircraft) had been on holiday and so not immediately available, which was why just one week ago he had chartered a private plane and crew to fly them out to Rhodes airport. There was a second route he once might have taken—a rather more esoteric route—but in the world of passport controls, a world where "miracles" would doubtless attract attention, he had chosen the much more cumbersome and, in his own words, "mechanical flight" method.

The house they had hired in Lindos consisted in fact of a nest of three holiday villas or apartments with their own secluded courtyard. They occupied only the largest room, leaving the other two standing empty. They had eaten out with only one exception, when Garrison had cooked a pair of large gray mullet, self-caught on the trident of a rubber-powered spear-gun purchased in Rhodes. Garrison was an excellent swimmer and spear-fisherman, his prowess in the latter deriving from three sun-drenched years in Cyprus as a Corporal in the Royal Military Police. Here in Lindos, however, he had quickly lost interest in the "sport." He had soon realized that there was little skill involved and no thrill whatsoever when one might simply command the fishes to impale themselves upon the tines of one's harpoon.

And so in a matter of days they had settled down to an existence of hot, idle days and balmy nights, of not unreasonable wines and cheap island brandy (another legacy of Garrison's soldiering), and of good local meats and fruits in the village tavernas. And yet even in this near-exotic, idyllic setting of Lindos—with its narrow white labyrinthine streets, church towers, elaborate archways, its drain-dwelling, night-venturing frogs and tumult of cats—even here they had not felt totally at ease. The problem, as most of their problems, had its roots in Garrison's multi-personality.

Usually the Schroeder and Koenig facets took a back seat or were subsumed in Garrison's far stronger seat of consciousness—but on occasion they would come bursting to the forefront. Often, Vicki thought, unnecessarily and far too forcefully. Her thoughts took her back to an incident as recent as yesterday, one which perfectly illustrated her point . . .

After their open-air, patio breakfast, Garrison had suggested they walk. They had taken the path that led out of the village to a quiet, sheltered bay of yellow sand between white flanking rocks and looming perpendicular cliffs. Feeling the heat of a suddenly breathless midday, they had wandered from the path to seat themselves on tumbled boulders beneath the overhang of scree-shod cliffs that reached up to the mightier, precipitously concave Rock of the Acropolis itself. At their feet where they sat lay a large bed of cabbage-leaved plants sporadically decorated with small yellow flowers much similar to the English primrose; with many green, oval fruit-pods some two inches long, each pod hanging heavily from its own individual stem.

As they had sat down, so Garrison's leg had brushed against one of these fruits which, with a quite audible squelching or popping sound, had at once jet-propelled itself from its stem to go bounding about amidst the thick leaves until it found a gap and fell through to the shaded earth beneath. At the moment of the explosion Garrison had jerked away from the plant, but not before feeling a splash of liquid on his hand and forearm.

"You should wipe your hand," Vicki had been a little concerned. "That juice is mildly caustic—or poisonous, I can't remember which. But I've read about it somewhere or other."

Garrison had sniffed at his wrist, wrinkled his nose and grinned. "Catspiss!" he snorted—but he had nevertheless used his handkerchief to clean the affected areas. And Vicki had laughed at his exclamation, for of course this had been Garrison pure and simple. Garrison himself, the man she had loved in that earlier world. A natural man and unself-conscious.

A couple of Greek youths had taken the same well-trodden route to the beach, walking a little to their rear. Neither Vicki nor Garrison had attached any significance to this; it was a free world. In any case the youths seemed little more than kids, fifteen or sixteen at most and brothers by their looks. And by far the great majority of Lindos people were kindly and utterly charming.

There had been few people about—one or two couples slowly negotiating a rough ramp cut in the cliff's face down to the beach, and a scattered handful on the beach itself—but that was just exactly how Garrison had wanted it. This had been his prime purpose in coming out to Rhodes in the first place: an escape from the rush and bustle and pressures of a life which, for the last year at least, had seemed to catch him up like an insect in the cogs of some vast machine. But an insect of carbon steel, which could not be crushed and without which the machine itself could not function.

For Garrison controlled—no, he *was*—that machine. Not quite self-made but certainly self-sustaining, self-servicing. Even the finest machine needs a little oil, however, and this holiday was to have been just that: light lubrication for the gears of a life suddenly grown vastly complicated. More than that, it was to give him time to consider his future. To ponder what best to do with the powers his multimind controlled—those powers which, with each passing day, he felt weakening in him, draining from him like the slow trickle of sand from the glass globe of an hourglass.

Vicki had been silent, dwelling a little introspectively on her life with Garrison, happy just to sit beside the calm, apparently greatly relaxed and benign figure of her companion—at least until she heard the clatter of pebbles and the indolent *slap*, *slap* of sandals which announced the arrival of the two Greek boys. At that she sighed.

She had known then why they had been followed, taking little pride in the knowledge that her own brown and beautifully proportioned body was the magnet which had drawn these adolescent islanders after her. She felt only a niggling annoyance. She was skimpily dressed, true, in a tiny green halter, green figure-hugging shorts and white sandals—but surely these lads could find themselves a pair of girls more their own age to ogle? While it was still fairly early in the tourist season, still the village was full of just such apparently unattended young ladies: English, German, Italian, Scandinavian. Or perhaps the youths had mistakenly suspected that Vicki and Garrison had something other in mind than merely sitting in silent contemplation in the shade of the rocks?

Garrison, too, had noticed the approach of the boys and for a moment he had grinned good-naturedly. He had of course immediately guessed their motive, and a glance—the merest peep—inside their minds had confirmed it. Well, boys are boys and Greek boys are Greek boys, and no complaints there. But then, as the youths had taken seats upon rocks in the middle of the pod-bearing plants and openly stared at Garrison and his lovely companion—particularly and pointedly at Vicki—the grin had quickly slipped from Garrison's face.

One of the minds his own had touched upon was a distinctly unpleasant one, whose strong sexual overtones were warped and vicious. He was full of animal lust. In Garrison's brief glimpse inside the youth's head he had found him savagely assaulting Vicki. Slimy with sweat and sex, the attack was unnatural as it was murderous. Nor were these mind-scenes mere fantasies but repeats of an earlier assault, a real assault, but with Vicki's face and figure superimposed. The youth was, or had been, the author of a rabidly cruel rape!

And as Garrison's face had hardened and taken on a grimmer aspect, so he had slowly risen to his feet. Drawing Vicki up with him, he had hissed in her ear: "That older boy's a rapist!"

"What? But how could you possibly—" she began—and paused. For of course she knew that if anyone in the world could know such a thing, that someone was Garrison.

"And when he can't do it he likes to think about doing it," Garrison's voice had turned to a snarl. "Doing it to you!" His face had twisted in rage, its color rapidly draining away.

Vicki knew that behind Garrison's heavy sunglasses with their built-up sides, his golden eyes were burning bright. "Come," he said. *"Wir gehen!"*

He half-dragged her from beneath the shade of the rock, hurriedly picking a way through boulders and coarse shrubs and grasses back to the path. Stumbling behind him, she had known fear. His being was in flux, its change betrayed by a voice which retained very little of Richard Garrison's true nature. There was a certain harshness about that voice, and those words he had spoken in German—

He paused to fill his lungs, drew her up alongside him. His fingers tightened on her side, digging into the flesh of her waist. He glanced back—and his face was no longer Garrison's. Not quite.

"Thomas!" Vicki whispered.

Her companion's eyebrows formed a frown, drew together, dipped down in the center be-

44

hind his special glasses. His gaze was upon the pair of youths where they stood now amidst the patch of pod-bearing plants. For their part they stared back, the face of the older one wearing a contemptuous grin.

"Swine!" Garrison/Schroeder said, but the word had sounded more like *Schwein* to Vicki. She had known instinctively that he scanned the youth's mind. More deeply now.

"Richard," Vicki had clutched his arm. "It's not your business."

"But it has to be somebody's!" he told her harshly. "And *you* are my business—and that bastard's thinking things about you! He needs a lesson." And again his eyebrows had drawn together.

At that very moment Vicki had heard the sudden yelping of the youths. She had followed Garrison/Schroeder's gaze—and behind her own special sunglasses her golden eyes had gone very wide. She gasped at what she saw.

The younger Greek was stumbling jerkily out of the patch of pod-plants, backing away from the other youth until he came up against the white rock of the cliff. The older boy, the unwitting subject of Garrison's manipulation, stood as if rooted to the spot—while all around him the sprawling bed of vegetation went totally insane!

It was a scene of madness, an alien scene, or one perhaps from Earth's prime, when the *flora* could more ably match the *fauna* in ferocity. The plants tossed and churned, each leaf violently flapping, pods straining, swelling and bursting

45

from their stems with sounds like muted machine-gun fire. And their juices—concerted, *directed*—fell upon the Greek youth where he stood wildly windmilling his arms, his feet apparently mired in the now sodden earth. Then, in a final frenzy, a last burst of vegetable violence, the entire patch ejaculated into his eyes.

The youth screamed and clapped his hands to his face. His hair, the skin of his face, his entire upper torso was drenched in plant fluid—but at last he could move, and now he commenced a grim, hopping dance of agony.

"No!" Vicki had cried. "*Nein*, Richard! *Bitte, blind ihm nicht!*"

Garrison had glanced down at her. In his face she had seen something of him, also a lingering trace of Thomas Schroeder—but mainly the blunt hardness of Willy Koenig. Garrison's third facet had surfaced, the most ruthless facet of all.

"As you will," Garrison/Koenig's voice rasped. "And you're right, of course, Vicki—for we know what it's like to be blind, don't we? But—" His gaze fell once more upon the terrified youth.

The pod-bearing plants were dead now, wilted and shrivelled, black and stinking. Their stench wafted to Garrison and Vicki on a breeze suddenly blown up from the sea. The Greek youth's agonized dance had slowed to a moaning stagger, his feet stumbling in the slop of decaying vegetation. He still clutched at his face but, in another moment, stood still and tentatively took away his hands, peering gingerly, unbelievingly all about him. The pain went out of his eyes and blotched face and he began to laugh hysterically. But only for a moment.

"A lesson," Garrison/Koenig repeated—and with his words the Greek youth's eyes suddenly stood out from their sockets. He gave a great howl, threw his hands down as if to protect his groin, bent forward and fell face-down in the rot of decay. And there he lay, his body threshing spasmodically upon the putrid earth.

Garrison climbed up on to the path and turned towards the village. Vicki ran after him, her red hair flying behind her. "Richard, you didn't—?"

"No, I didn't," he answered her unspoken question. "I didn't ruin them, merely kicked him in them. A sort of forever kick."

"A forever kick?" she caught him up, grabbed at his hand. He paused in his striding to put an arm around her. The strength in his fingers was hard, rough, in no way the gentle, firm grip of Richard Garrison. Not of Garrison alone.

He nodded. "I simply put another kink in his mind—a kink to counter those already there. From now on, whenever he looks at or thinks of a woman that way, like a beast, he'll feel like he's just been shot in the balls!"

"But in effect that's—"

"Castration? Right! But it's less than what I'd have done to him if you hadn't stopped me . . ."

Chapter
4

THAT HAD BEEN YESTERDAY, AND BY THE TIME THEY
got back to their rooms Garrison had been
himself once more—or as much himself as he
ever could be. There was an aftermath, however,
inevitable in the wake of any resurgence of his
Schroeder and Koenig facets: a scratchy, unrea-
soning irritability.

Vicki, totally aware of Garrison's Jekyll and
two Hydes existence and as well versed as could
be expected in such matters, had coped with the
problem in a manner tried and trusted. Namely,
she had plied Garrison's senses with a bottle of
dirt-cheap brandy!

Strange how this simple device always seemed
to turn the trick, or perhaps not so strange when
one thought about it.

Bad brandy had been Garrison's tipple ever
since his Cyprus "initiation," when on occasion,

usually after several losing hands of three-card brag, a bottle of one-star had been all he could afford to buy! And so he had actually come to like, even to prefer the stuff.

On the other hand, but of equal consequence, bad brandy had certainly *not* been Thomas Schroeder's drink, whose taste had always been impeccable and therefore far more expensive. Nor had Koenig, a born Schnapps drinker (though when the mood was on him he could generally drink anything), ever greatly fancied Garrison's favorite.

The way brandy worked, Vicki suspected, was simply as a stabilizer: it helped him stay "in character"—or helped his character stay in him. On this occasion Lindos, too, had helped, for the old Garrison had been very "Med-conscious," had loved the Mediterranean from first sight; and a third stabilizer (Vicki liked to think of it as the most important) was their sex.

Even though their affair in that earlier time had been brief, it had been intense. She had remembered his preferences and, in the two years flown since her resurrection, had practiced pleasuring him until she was expert. No woman knew or had ever known Garrison's body or the way it responded to sexual stimuli better than Vicki Maler. As for the Schroeder and Koenig facets: their tastes were entirely different. Moreover they respected Garrison—so far, at least—and they had *never* intruded or in any way attempted ascendence in this respect.

For that Vicki was naturally glad; but in another way, and however paradoxically, she was not so glad. She was fairly sure that Garrison *himself* was faithful to her, but there had been more than a few occasions—always when he had found it necessary to let one of his alter-facets take ascendency—when *his body* had absented itself from her bed, often for two or three nights at a stretch. Twice she had found evidence of his visiting high-class London call girls; and she was well aware that a onetime "secretary" of Thomas Schroeder, one Mina Grunwald, now lived in Mayfair where Garrison (or rather Garrison/Schroeder) was in the habit of seeing her.

This then was Vicki's problem, the reason for her . . . yes, jealousy: that while she knew that the Schroeder/Koenig facets respected Garrison's privacy, she could not be one hundred percent certain that he respected theirs. After all, his was the original, dominant facet, and it remained housed in its own body. Vicki was not yet quite used to the idea that when the subsidiary facets were in ascendence they could use that body to sate their own sexual appetites. Fortunately neither one of the subsumed or adopted characters had been overtly sexual in their own bodies, else Vicki might not have been able to live with her own feelings and emotions. But then again, what could she have done about it? She knew for a certainty and quite literally that she could *not* live without Garrison. Or so she had been led to believe . . .

At any rate, her ploy had worked yet again, when the cheap brandy, her own body, and the Greek island atmosphere had all combined perfectly to dampen Garrison's excitability and bring about a complete resurgence of his true identity. At eight in the evening he had desired to go out; they had eaten in the village's best taverna, where he had consumed a little more of the local brandy; following which they had found a disco and danced the night away, so that the stars had already started to fade in the sky by the time they had returned to their rooms.

Garrison had been tired by then, perhaps too tired to sleep, and it was plain there was something—perhaps many things—on his mind. Things he must talk about.

Having changed into cool night clothes, the pair had sprawled themselves upon a wide, raised Lindos bed to talk and sip coffee. And after a while Garrison had asked: "Vicki, how much have I told you? Ever, I mean? You never asked me a hell of a lot—never pushed it, anyway—but how much have I really told you?"

"Some things you told me, Richard. Some I guessed. After I woke up—I mean when I lived again—you told me a lot of things. You didn't really say anything, not in words, but I was made to understand a lot. You remember?"

"Oh, yes," he nodded. "I was kind of a god, wasn't I? I could just get into your mind and make you understand." For the first time since her reincarnation, Vicki definitely felt his uncertainty. Amazingly, Garrison seemed to be displaying insecurity! His words were all past tense. I *was* a god. I *could* get into your mind.

"Your powers are still godlike, Richard," she told him.

51

"You mean demoniac!" he replied, but without venom. "*My* powers, when *I* use them, are . . . safe."

"Safe?"

"They don't hurt anyone, not much anyway. Not deliberately. But Vicki—" he caught up her hand almost pleadingly, "—when *they* use them . . ."

"Oh, Richard, I know!"

"But you don't know, not everything. Some of the things they've done . . . they go way over the top. They protect me, yes, but they over-protect. They won't let me run my own life, my own body. Hell, it's not 'my own body'—it's theirs too!" He was nervously massaging her fingers, drawing comfort from her presence.

"How did it come about?" she eventually asked. "I mean, at the beginning."

Garrison sighed. "Let's see if I can break it down for you. Thomas Schroeder wanted to be immortal. He was deep into parapsychology, augury, transmigration—all that stuff. 1972, we were in Northern Ireland. Him on business, me as a soldier. I'd been having this recurring dream, about bombs. That wasn't odd in itself, lots of the boys over there dream about bombs. It's all part of the job. But my dream, my nightmare, was different. It wouldn't go away. It came to me night after night. A warning about something I could neither escape nor even avoid.

"So . . . it happened, my first glimpse of ESP in action. The first hint that maybe my mind was different from the minds of other men. There was a bomb blast. I saved Schroeder's life, the lives of his wife and kid. They were OK, but he was badly chopped up inside and I was blinded. Afterwards—well, it worked out that he thought he owed me."

"He *did* owe you, Richard. I remember all of that like it was yesterday: you coming out to the Harz. How proud you were, how smart in your uniform."

"Oh, yes, all of that," Garrison grunted, "but before I got out there things had happened. For one thing, Schroeder knew by then that he was dying. And he didn't want to stay dead. Reincarnation—in me!"

She nodded. "I knew something was going on, that his interest in you should be so—consuming."

Garrison smiled wryly. "Consuming, yes," he repeated her. "Anyway, I had always had a quiet interest in Schroeder's sort of thing, the paranormal I mean, and I admit he fascinated me. But at the same time I didn't believe he could do it, you know? It was too weird. I might just have washed my hands of the whole thing. But . . . there was a carrot for the donkey. That carrot was a friend of Schroeder's, a guy called Adam Schenk. He predicted Schroeder's death, yours too, a lot of things. And for me: he predicted I'd see again. This would be made possible through Schroeder himself, and through a machine. What sort of machine . . . ?" he shrugged. "I didn't know, not then . . .

"Anyway, out there in the Harz, things were happening to me. Schroeder had a lot of tricks up his sleeve. A whole building full of them. Gear for testing a man's ESP potential. He tested mine and it was high. Very high. And all the time I was becoming more and more convinced that he really had something. And anyway, how could I lose? All the dice were loaded in my favor.

"I was blind—he offered me sight!

"I was an ex-soldier, crippled—he offered me money. Money beyond my wildest dreams.

"I was a nothing, a nobody with nowhere to go—and he offered me power and position.

"How could I refuse?"

"You couldn't," Vicki answered.

"I didn't. We made . . . a pact," Garrison shrugged again. "Simple as that. No big deal. We just agreed that when he died, *if* something of him remained and *if* it could find its way to me, then that I'd receive it. He could live again in me.

"In return there was the chance, however remote, that I'd see again; meanwhile there were a couple of tricks to help me find my way around the blindness.

"I had special 'spectacles' that worked on sound instead of vision. I had bracelets for my wrists, too, which worked the same way. And I had Suzy. My dear, wonderful Suzy. She's getting old now, but I look after her. Hell!—and hasn't she looked after me?" For a moment he grinned. "Damned right, she has!" The smile slipped a little and he nodded. "And of course there was Willy Koenig.

"Willy looked after me, too—just as he'd always looked after Thomas, his beloved Colonel." The smile slipped away completely. "Just as he's looking after us even now—damn him!"

"Richard!" she gripped his hand. "Don't! You only make it easy for them."

He relaxed, grunted: "You're right, of course. I do make it easy for them, and I really can't afford to. Not any longer." Again the insecurity.

"What is it, Richard?"

He shook his head. "Let me tell it my own way, in my own time . . .

"Schroeder made me rich before he died. After he died I was incredibly rich. Now—? Even I don't know how rich I am. You see, since coming back he's opened up sources only he had the keys to, funds which had doubled and sometimes trebled during the years passed between. His interests were worldwide. Even in his lifetime he made some of your so-called 'tycoons' look like penniless paupers by comparison! And all of that is mine now—or ours. His, mine, Koenig's. Thirty guys have a big office in London—more a block of offices, really. They look after my interests. Some of my interests, anyway. There are other people in Zurich, Hamburg, Hong Kong— you name it. But none of them knows what I'm really worth.

"Suddenly the world of international finance was open to me, and I couldn't resist it. And no risk involved. With my ESP powers working for me I couldn't pick a loser. I was a Midas. Everything I touched turned to gold! And then . . . then one day I heard about the machine. I stumbled across Psychomech."

As he paused Vicki said: "You've missed something out, Richard. What about your wife?

You never did tell me about her." Vicki's voice was soft, low. "Or does it hurt too much?"

He shook his head. "It doesn't hurt at all, not now. Terri was something that had to be—she'd been 'foreseen' by Adam Schenk—and without her I'd never have found Psychomech. You might have remembered something about Terri and her lover, something unpleasant, but I made you forget. I removed it from your mind. Believe me, it really doesn't matter now." Again he paused, then continued in a burst:

"Anyway, I found Psychomech. A machine that could blow up a man's darkest fears to giant size—until they're about to crush him or drive him insane—and then give him the strength to fight back, to defeat them. A tremendous boon to psychiatry. A mechanical psychiatrist. A tin shrink.

"But think about it:

"What happens if you totally liberate a man's mind, if you rid it of all its fears? Would there be any limits to the scope of such a mind? And what if that mind were already rich in psychic energy, powers almost beyond imagination?"

Vicki's golden eyes were wide behind dark lenses. "That's what happened to you," she sighed. "The birth of a god!"

He nodded. "Or a demon, yes. But on my own I wasn't ready for it, wasn't big or strong enough. I had to have help, had to let Schroeder in, fulfill our pact. Then . . . *we* let Koenig in."

Vicki shuddered. "I seem to remember something of that. Willy was there, and you told me

56

not to be afraid, and then—he wasn't there any more."

Garrison said: "It was the only way. He wasn't like Schroeder and me. He was clever in his own way, but not in ours. And I *was* a god! Psychomech had blown me up into something awesome. I was bigger than myself, bigger than Schroeder and myself, bigger than Psychomech—or so I thought. My powers seemed immeasurable. God!—I brought you back, didn't I? Took away your agony, gave you life, sight?

"Absorbing Willy was—" he shrugged, "—a mere nothing. Ultimate power, ultimate ego, infinity stretching away and out before me. Infinity, Vicki, with all its infinite possibilities! Until—"

"Yes?"

"Until something went wrong. I'm not sure what . . . Or maybe I am. Maybe I'm ready to admit it now." For a moment he was silent, his mind miles away. Then: "Anyway, I destroyed Psychomech." He sat up and took her hands. "With Psychomech I was, could have been, immortal. Without Psychomech? I'm a man, a three-dimensional body, flesh and blood. How could I hope to contain all of that power in this little battery? I couldn't. The battery leaks. The power is leaving me, more every day. And now? Each time I use—each time *they* use—that power, I grow just a little weaker.

"Do you remember my gambling phase: London, Monte Carlo, Las Vegas? Do you know what that was all about? I mean, didn't you ever ask yourself what I got out of it? Me, rich as Croesus, playing cards and roulette? Winning money on the horses, the football pools? Hell, I would've enjoyed that sort of thing when I was in the army, but with my sort of money? So why did I do it? I'll tell you why: at first it was the sheer excitement! Oh, I knew I couldn't lose, but still it was exciting to win! Do you see? Every gambler's ultimate fantasy.

"Maybe my powers were wasted, eh? Fantastic, beautiful, wonderful powers, all locked up in an ordinary, greedy, conceited little body. But in the end I stopped gambling. I realized that the thrill had gone out of it—that I was doing it now for an entirely different reason—doing it because I *had* to! No, it wasn't a vice, I wasn't hooked on it. Not that way. But I had simply been testing myself. Because I knew that if ever the day came when I should lose . . ."

"Then that your powers would be failing you," she finished it for him, nodding.

"That's it," he said. "That's it exactly. I mean, after Psychomech I was a god—for a fortnight, a month? Then I was a godling—for how long, a year? Now a superman. And tomorrow?"

She wrapped her arms around him. "I would be satisfied with you as a man, Richard. Just a man. That's all you were when you first loved me, when I fell in love with you, and—"

His laughter, brittle as ice, choking itself with its cold bitterness, cut her short. "No, Vicki, no!" he finally shook his head. "You don't see, do you?" Now his words sounded strangely hollow, and yet full of a sadness. "You would not be satisfied because you simply *would not be*! You

58

are—you exist—because of my power, because I commanded it."

"But I—"

"I've tried to explain before, Vicki. What would become of you if I were simply a man? What *will* become of you if that day should ever arrive when my commands go unheard, unheeded?"

She had no answer, only a memory. The memory of acid in her veins, a burning current in her blood, the white-hot grip of Death's bony fingers.

"Yes," Garrison had nodded grimly, "that's it exactly . . ."

After that . . . there had been little more to say, and then it had taken them a long time to get to sleep. When finally they did, Garrison had dreamed . . .

Chapter
5

*G*ARRISON'S DREAM BEGAN, AS HAD ANOTHER DREAM
*some ten years earlier, with a Machine. The
Machine. The Machine known as Psychomech.*

*It was not a car or a motorcycle or an airplane,
that Machine, not any sort of conveyance one
might readily imagine, and yet Garrison rode it.
His journey or "quest" was symbolic, for sym-
bolism is one with the very nature of dreaming,
but like any ordinary dreamer he was not given
to know that. He had not known it in that earlier
dream, neither did he know it now—nor indeed
that this new dream would be equally prophetic
and much more of an omen.*

But . . . he rode the Machine.

*He rode it through weird, alien valleys where
tall, lichenclad rocks cast ominous ochre shadows, flew it high over dazzling furnace deserts*

*and vast tundras of yellow marshland, sailed it
across strange gray oceans whose giant squid-
like denizens rolled up their saucer eyes to gaze
unblinkingly upon him, and with it threaded previously unvoyaged paths through the mazy
gorges and passes and precipitous needle-peaks
of scarlet mountains.*

*He rode effortlessly, with authority, towards
quest's end . . . without ever knowing what the
end of the quest would be. But for all his apparent mastery of the Machine—that Machine which,
while it seemed almost omnipotent for the moment, he nevertheless and naggingly suspected
to be slowly failing, gradually leaking its energies and wasting them uselessly—still he knew
there would be obstacles in the way. In this
world, as real to Garrison as the dreamworld of
any dreamer, there were always obstacles. Had
he not faced them before?*

*Oh, yes, he had been here before, several times.
This much he knew. But he could not remember
when or why. Or what his quests had been on
those previous occasions. He did know he had
not been alone. There had been—friends.*

Friends, yes. Suzy had been one such.

*Suzy. The name was warm in Garrison's mind,
a comfort to him. Suzy the dog, the black Doberman bitch. And almost as if he were a magician, as if remembering her had conjured the
physical Suzy out of midair, he became suddenly aware of her presence. She was there even
now, seated on her haunches, close behind him
on the broad back of the Machine, one great paw
firm on his shoulder, her warm breath on the back*

61

of his neck and her occasional, muted whining a reassurance in his ear. Suzy, Garrison's familiar spirit.

How long she had been there he could not say. Perhaps he really had conjured her out of thin air, for certainly he controlled stange powers. He remembered that now: how he was gifted with powers far beyond the grasp of mundane men. A magician? Garrison smiled at the thought. Yes, a magician, a wonder-worker, a warlock; and Suzy his familiar. But what sort of warlock who could not remember the nature of his quest or how he came to be here . . . or even where he came from?

Or perhaps some other warlock, more powerful yet, had robbed him of his memory . . .

Garrison became wary. Were there enemies here, close by?

In his mind he began to check off points in his favor. He was strong and he had powers. He had the Machine (for all his anxiety about its ebbing strength) and he had Suzy. And—

He frowned, forcing himself to concentrate. There had been other—friends? Their names came to him in a sudden, vivid flash of memory.

Schroeder and Koenig.

Strange names—and stranger friends!

Now he remembered. Schroeder had been the man-God, and Koenig his familiar. But that all seemed so very long ago, and where were they now, these two? Garrison shuddered as a tiny voice from within seemed to whisper: "Closer than you think, Richard. Much closer . . ."

The images of Schroeder and Koenig burned bright a while longer in the eye of Garrison's memory: the former lean and pale, small and balding; older than Garrison and wise in the ways of men, wise as the bright eyes that gleamed huge behind thick crystal lenses. And Koenig, huge and blocky, bull-necked and pig-eyed, his sandy hair cropped in a crew-cut, with hands and feet and body and head all honed to a perfect razor's edge in death-dealing arts. Their images burned bright before flaring up and blinking out like snuffed candles. They were gone, but their names remained.

Schroeder and Koenig.

And again that tiny voice seemed to whisper in Garrison's mind—or perhaps it laughed? Or maybe it was not one voice at all but two . . .

A sudden chill drew him from his reverie, that and Suzy's great paw insistently scratching at his shoulder. Lost in thought as he had been, his mechanical mount had continued to forge ahead under its own direction. The Machine had negotiated the maze of mountainous needle-peaks and now paused at the rim of a canyon whose sides sank sheer into a haze of mist and depth and darkness. It was a canyon whose deeps were unplumbed, whose secrets remained unfathomed, and whose name—

—was Death!

Death has many shapes and sizes, colors, creeds and guises. Garrison knew that. Also, instinctively, he knew that this canyon was one such guise. He jerked his body back from the yawning gorge, hauling on mental reins—and the Machine reared beneath him like a startled horse. Cold and afraid, he yet gentled his metal and

*plastic steed; while behind him Suzy's breathless
barking and pawing warned him that his fear was
not unjust.*

Garrison felt it in his guts like an icy blade. He
feared Death.

But how so? He was a wizard and immortal,
and—

Immortal? His mind grasped at the word, the
concept, crushed it and held it close, examined
it.

Immortal. Undying. Why then should he fear
Death? Unless . . . unless he was mistaken.

Perhaps he was not immortal after all. Perhaps
that was the nature of his quest: to seek out and
seduce the Goddess Immortality? And to do
that—why, naturally he must first overcome
Death himself, in whichever guise he found him!
Very well, the canyon was one such guise and so
he must cross it. But—

What if he should fall?

He nodded and smiled, however wryly. Fall?
He could not fall. The merest command, by word
or thought, and he would be buoyed up. He remembered the word for it: levitation. And himself a
master of the art. How then might he fall?

Consciously he could not. Unconsciously? The
fall would crush his body and so kill him. A large
stone banged against his head would break it and
also kill him. Left alone he might just be immortal, but if some accident should occur—or an unsuspected hand directed against him . . .

Oh, yes, a clever enemy could kill him. He could
be made to die.

Perhaps that, then, was his quest: the search

for true immortality. And only Death standing between himself and quest's end. Death and his minions.

Motionless the Machine stood in air, with evening on the one hand staining the far horizon, and on the other a sinking sun whose rim showed like a scythe above far purple hills. And directly in Garrison's way this canyon, whose gaping maw split the land as far as the eye could see.

No way round it, Garrison knew now. It was here to test him.

A moaning wind came up and stirred the dry dust of the canyon's rim into spiralling devils, whipping at the legs of Garrison's tattered trousers. It was a chill wind, reminding him of night, which drew closer by the minute. No good to be caught out here, exposed, in the open, when darkness fell.

He scanned the far side of the chasm: a flat expanse, wooded in places, reaching back to low hills beyond which a darkening horizon merged with a darkening sky. He must cross. And soon.

He felt a sudden urge to ride furiously forward, now, out over the rim, without another second wasted—but Suzy seemed to read his mind and whined afresh in his ear, her paw digging insistently into his shoulder. He turned to her. "Where are they, Girl, eh? Where do they hide, Death's soldiers?"

She licked at his ear, her moist eyes anxious, then pointed with her muzzle down into the gorge. The loose flesh of her mouth drew back in a snarl, exposing sharp ivory fangs, and her ears lay flat upon her head. Left and right she gazed, and up into the high sky, and her black coat bristled into a million spines that stood out stiff from her body.

Then . . . the spell was broken. She lay down, panting, offering up a series of baffled, curious short yelping barks.

Garrison smiled grimly. "Everywhere, eh? Well, I suppose I knew that." Then his grim smile became a frown and he grew angry again—at his own frailty, his indecision, weakness. And him with such powers to command.

"Fool!" he cursed himself. "Wasting time like this!"

He quickly set the Machine to rest upon the canyon's rim, climbed down from its back and stretched his limbs. Suzy jumped down beside him, easier now, her tongue lolling, her eyes gazing at him inquiringly. He patted her great black head. "Let's see what's in store for us, eh, Girl?"

And placing his hands on his hips he lifted up his head and arrogantly threw out his voice across the darkening gorge:

"Death," his voice was strong, echoing loudly, "I know you seek to claim me. Well, that won't be so easy. I'm no ordinary man simply to die at your command, be sure. And now I command you! Show yourself, Death. Show me your soldiers, your devices, your pitfalls, so that I'll know them and give you a better fight. Or are you really the great skulking coward I suspect you to be?"

He waited expectantly—perhaps just a little nervously, despite his bold stance—but . . .

No answer.

The wind from the gorge moaned louder and Garrison felt its chill more keenly. He shivered, his flesh shuddering as shadows started to creep.

And what now? For plainly he had been correct in the first instance: not only had some greater warlock robbed him of his memory, but also of his powers. There once was a time when he might have drawn strength from the Machine, but now—?

It was worth a try.

He laid his hands upon smooth metal flanks, searching for those weird energies which had sustained him through so many strange adventures. Nothing. The Machine was cold, lifeless as an old log.

"Steed?" he snarled, snatching back his hands in frustration. "You, a steed? A beast of burden? A burden, sure enough. An anchor! Carry me? On the contrary, I carry you! Yes, and you weigh me down." He turned his back on the Machine and roared his rage and defiance out over the shadowed gorge:

"Death, I'll not be denied. If you won't show yourself then I'll not come to you. Why should I meet a challenge I don't understand? Fight opponents I don't know, can't see? No, I'll simply wait here, or go back the way I came—and to hell with questing!"

"Richard," came a faint whisper, seemingly from within his own mind. "Richard, I can help you—if you'll let me."

Garrison's hair bristled on his head and his flesh grew clammy. He knew that voice, soundless except in the immense caverns of his own mind, that insinuating whisper from within. It was the voice of the vanished man-God Schroeder, who in another world he had called his friend.

"Is that you, man-God?" he sought confirmation. "Or are you in fact Death, seeking to make a fool of me? If you really are Thomas Schroeder, then show yourself."

The voice within chuckled, however drily. "Oh, you know me well enough, Richard. And you know I cannot show myself, not in the flesh. Not any more. But I can still help you, if you will let me."

Garrison was still suspicious. "You, help me? True, you were a man-God, Thomas—but no more. How would you help me, ghost? I am flesh and blood, and you—a mere memory, a voice in my head."

"More than that, Richard," *the whisper was stronger now, gaining in confidence.* "And if your memory was whole you'd know it. Myself—and Willy Koenig, too—we're more than mere voices in your head. And we can still help you, just as we helped you before."

Garrison listened to the whispering voice and frowned more darkly, and at his side Suzy whined and tugged at his trousers with her teeth. Finally he said: "I do remember something of it. That you helped me, yes—but also that your reward was greater than your effort warranted."

"But you paid readily enough in the end," *the voice in his head answered.* "Else your life, your sanity, your survival were forfeit."

"That's a lie!" Garrison snarled. "I paid grudg-

ingly, despite the fact that I bought my mind, my life. But you had tricked me into a pact, and I would not break it . . ." He calmed himself down before continuing. *"This much I remember, at least: that you sought to serve yourself, not me."* He shrugged. *"Still, I suppose that's in all of us. As for Koenig: he was my true friend. But you—"*

"I, too, was your friend, Richard. I am now. I seek only to help you. And night draws on . . ."

Garrison turned up the collar of his ragged jacket. Schroeder was right, for the sun was almost down and the shadows advanced visibly. But still he was suspicious. *"I paid you once for your help, and didn't like the price you asked. Oh, I can't remember what you took from me, but I know it had great value. I know that it was worth . . . too much. What fee is it you'll demand this time, eh?"*

The whisper grew stronger, almost eager, and its reply was instantaneous. *"Equality!"*

"Equality? Explain. You want to be my equal?"

"Yes."

Garrison pondered it. What did it mean? What's in a word? Equality? Is a stone equal to another stone? And men? A man is a man, after all.

"But I," came the whisper, knowing his inmost thoughts, "am little more than a revenant. A ghost, you said so yourself."

"You desire flesh for your thoughts, is that it?"

"I'll explain no more. I desire equality. Nothing else."

"And for Koenig?"

In answer to that Garrison sensed a mental shrug. Then, as if an afterthought: "Koenig is

69

Koenig. I am me. Or desire to be . . ." *The echoes of the whisper faded away, and Garrison suspected that the unseen whisperer had almost said too much.*

But . . . equality. What did Schroeder the ghost who was once Schroeder the man-God mean? This was very important. If only Garrison could remember all of it. But—he could not.

"How can I promise what's not mine to give?" *he asked eventually.*

"Simply promise it," *came the eager whisper.*

"Very well—" *(a sigh inside)* "—on one condition."

"Name it."

"That you'll aid me wherever you can, to quest's end."

And now laughter, welling up from inside. Pealing laughter from within, subsiding slowly into a dry chuckling and finally petering out. "My friend, how can I deny you? Yes, and you shall have Koenig's help, too."

"Agreed!" *said Garrison.* "And now—show me what you can of the way ahead. Show me my enemies, the soldiers of Death. Show me—the future!"

"Ah!" *the whisper was thin now, receding.* "Not so long ago you would not have needed me for that. It would have been a very small magic. But your powers are deserting you, Richard. You are their master still, but for how much longer?"

"You're right!" *Garrison snapped.* "The Machine is dead or dying, and my powers are failing along with the Machine. But—" *his anger went out of him in a great sighing breath,* "—why are *these things happening, Thomas? Do you know the answer? If you do, and if you really are my friend, you'll tell me."*

Faintly, a mere tremor in his mind: "Don't you remember, Richard? You stopped the Machine. You killed the beast. This thing you carry with you is only a cold metal and plastic carcass. Even more of a revenant than I am. Psychomech is dead!"

"Don't go!" Garrison cried, afraid once more. "The future—you promised."

"Indeed," came the very sigh of an answer. "Very well, let's see what we may see . . ." And the whisperer was gone.

Garrison blinked his eyes, started, gazed wildly all about. The Machine sat there, leaden, dead; Suzy whined and cringed at his feet, her tail tucked between her legs; crag-cast shadows crept closer still and the vanished sun shot up a few last beams to lend a dying glow to the distant horizon. Soon that horizon would be black. Soon night would spread her blackest cloak upon the land. And the canyon still to be crossed. And the tale of the future as yet untold.

Then, when Garrison had all but given up hope—

A spark in his mind. A glowing point of light emanating from that inmost region where Schroeder's ghost held dominion. A light growing brighter by the second, expanding, blossoming into—a vision!

A vision so dazzling that the earth seemed to reel under Garrison's feet, sending him staggering, stumbling, falling to his knees. A vision so real that he not only viewed it but lived it, was part of it. A dream within a dream, seeming more vital than the dream itself. A dream of the future. His future.

A dream . . . and a nightmare!

But in the first instance, the dream. The beautiful dream . . .

Chapter

6

GARRISON SAW THE GODDESS IMMORTALITY. BE-
yond any doubt, even though Her back was
towards him, he knew that it was She. And he
believed he knew why Her face, as yet, was denied him. For who might guess the conse-
quences of gazing unprepared upon such a face?
But certainly it was, could only be, the Goddess
Herself.

The beauty of Her form was . . . undying. Her
figure, Her posture, the incredible garment She
wore—the very throne upon which She sat,
carved from the rock of Life Everlasting—all offered mute witness to Her immortality. But Her
face was something which, for the moment,
mercifully, Garrison could not see.

Of Her flesh, however, of thigh and shoulder
and neck where they showed: they were of the
misted Marble of Eternity, the softest and yet

73

most durable surface imaginable, so that Garrison's entire being seemed to sigh and sway forward, drawn by the magnet of Immortality's flesh. Her hair was the jet of Deepest Space; the nails of Her fingers and toes were crimson as the Blood of Time; and Her garment: it was of the shimmering silver micromesh of Unbreakable Continuity. But Her voice—that *voice* when it came—must surely be the final proof positive of Her Identity.

Who might describe it, that voice? Whose texture, if ever Garrison should later attempt its recall, was or would be all things to all men. Soft as winter snows, warm as summer suns, pure as purest gold and yet earthly as living loam:

"Someone seeks my seduction. The million millionth man would live forever," the voice laughed. And slowly, majestically, She rose up from Her throne, turned and allowed Garrison to gaze upon Her face. And framed by those blackest tresses of space he saw—a void!

The void. The Great Void, which is filled with all things. The roaring rushing reeling sucking space-time continuum itself—into which, in a single instant, he was irresistibly drawn! Sucked in, rushed like a mote across the vault of the universe to gaze down upon—THE ALL!

The sight was blinding, unbearable, and Garrison closed his eyes. Not in terror or horror but at the sheer awesome beauty of it. And the thought occurred to him: "If there is a place I would be, this is that place. If there's wine I might drink, this is the wine. If for every man there's a destiny, then let this be mine. And if I am not to be immortal, if I am to die, then let it be at once, here and now . . ."

But that was not to be. In another moment, whirled and hurled out into a cold and cruel reality, he cried out his agony and vainly grasped at that which was already beyond his reach. He grasped, clutched—

—and the nails of his fingers split open where they scrabbled uselessly at stone made slimy under a beating rain.

Garrison cried out again—howled his frustration this time—as crazed lightnings beat all about him, amidst the roaring of tumultuous waters and the earth-shaking pounding of great hammers, or of engines built by gods. He made to rise, found himself upon a steep, slippery slope, slid and rolled and clattered down the face of a scree-littered decline to a jutting rocky ledge.

Finally he came to a halt and lay there in the mud and the downpour, all the wind knocked from him, soaked and sucking at sodden air. Here, in the partial lee of black rocks where they balanced on this precarious ledge, at last he dared open his eyes fully and drag himself wearily to his feet. And now he gazed out upon a bleak and monochrome scene, a scene of wild desolation—and of man's imposition on raw nature—a scene monotonous in its power and wearying to the eye. With one exception.

Lightning crashed again, lending the air a momentary brightness and causing Garrison to shrink down and shutter his eyes. But the scene of a moment ago still burned on his retinas. His location was halfway down the wall of a small valley perhaps a mile across, dammed at one end where a man-made lake reached back its wind-tossed expanse of dark water into the cliff-guarded recesses of a forbiddingly gloomy re-entry. Water arced in six enormous spouts from the dam's face, its thunder the mighty hammering Garrison had mistaken for the engines of gods. He gazed out from a position almost directly above the great wall of the dam, and the trembling of the earth was the vibration of its mighty generators, and the rain which soaked him was that thrown up by the controlled eruption of pressured waters.

Shielding his eyes against stinging spray and cold mist, Garrison peered across the valley at a wild skyline, where once more he spied an unmistakable mark of man: a platoon of titan pylons carrying ropes of cable, marching double-file away across the hills. But while both dam and pylons were certainly human artifacts, in the valley itself, towards the far wall and in a timbered belt higher than the course of the old dammed river, there stood that sole exception to the scene's almost awesome drabness: a hemisphere of golden light like the bulge of some small sun half-sunken in the earth, whose pulsating dome rose tall and dazzling over the tall pines it dwarfed.

Lines, altered by ego, crept into the observer's mind from some forgotten source: *In Xanadu did Garrison a stately pleasure-dome decree . . .*

But—was this really a pleasure-dome? Or might it not be a temple? A temple to a goddess.

The Goddess of Immortality! The thought persisted: that this was indeed that temple wherein a moment ago (or a month, a year?) he had come face to eternity with the goddess of his desire. But why here, in this desolate spot, with the works of mere mortals so much in evidence? And the throbbing golden glow of the dome: why should it tug at his memory so? Of what did it remind him?

A good many questions and no time to explore them; time barely to pose them before—

The scene shrank, grew small as Garrison was drawn out of himself, his spirit snatched up in some great unseen fist and lifted at breathless speed into the sky; until he looked dizzily down upon valley, dam, dome, *himself* and all, from a windy aerial elevation amongst the boiling clouds. Except—

Except that, even as he watched, the scene grew dim, and under his eyes the valley, dam and dome disappeared, were replaced by a parched plain of bones and skulls and hot white sands—and himself, ragged and desiccated now, gaunt as a starveling, with puffed, cracked lips and red, staring eyes. And behind him, dragged inch after interminable inch across those burning sands, the Machine, all rust red and trailing frayed cables and crusts of corrosion.

And now Garrison felt his aerial observer-self being set down upon a floor, and he saw that the desert of bones and the starveling Garrison and the crippled Machine were only images trapped in an otherwise milky sphere. A scene viewed in a shewstone, a crystal ball; and he himself (or his spirit) now sat cross-legged in a circle of wizards or demons, all intent upon the struggles of the Garrison in the shewstone. And the place where they sat was like the floor of a great pit, with smoky flambeaux to give a little light, and the atmosphere of the place was full of the reek of death and the sting of sulphur. Then, knowing these seated beings for his enemies, Garrison gazed upon them each in turn and fixed them as best he might in his mind's eyes, so that he would know them if ever he saw them again.

And he saw that they were dressed in the various robes of wizards and that they carried the wands and charms and injurious devices of such. One of them wore a black, immaculate evening suit and bow-tie, and his features were dark and greedy. And he spun a small roulette wheel between his crossed legs, occasionally pausing to deal sharp-edged cards at the shewstone, as if to pierce its crystal and so harm the struggling Garrison within. And his wand was a heavy one and hung unseen in his armpit like a familiar toad, causing the breast of his jacket to bulge where he sat among the wizards.

Another was tall and slender and gray as a night cat, covered head to toe in a zippered suit, with bandolier and belt, grapples and grenades and all; and this one's eyes were steel in his face (what little of it could be seen) which was pale, cold and emotionless. And he toyed with a string of dark prayer-beads (except that its cord was of steel and carried no beads at all!) sometimes slipping its noose over the shewstone, as if to snare the beleaguered man within.

Yet another was small and yellow, with slanting eyes set in a face inscrutable as that of the sphinx, and he sat motionless as carved from yellow stone—except for his eyes, behind whose slanting slits the feral pupils followed each tiniest action of the miniature Garrison trapped in the crystal ball. And there were others, all at odds and different in dress and mode of application; but all of them muttering runes of destruction, so that Garrison's fear grew in the face of their massed enmity.

And he started slightly as he noted a pair—seated close together and a little apart from the rest, where shadows obscured them—whose looks were as the looks of two he remembered from a former time. The looks of Schroeder and Koenig! But he could not be certain, for their forms and faces were made lumpish and vague in the flickering light from the pit's flambeaux. Their interest did not seem inimical, however—rather the reverse, for they shied from the others and their occupations about the shewstone—but still he gained the impression that their business here was a sly one and more in their own interests than in those of the tiny Garrison.

One other he especially noted there in the gloom. This one stood, arms folded, well back from all the rest, and overlooked them. And his outline was very wavery and unsolid, so that Garrison thought perhaps he gazed upon a ghost. A ghost cloaked in a Robe of Secrecy, whose face and eyes, even as Garrison strained to see them more clearly, turned full upon him.

And beneath the cowl of the Secret One's robe . . .

. . . Gray eyes of a keen intelligence, set in a face of stone! A very solid ghost, this, or a most mysterious and secretive man. But certainly not an enemy, Garrison could sense that much. Rather a covert watcher: a guard, perhaps. And perhaps a friend.

A Secret One indeed, this man of stone.

At that very moment it seemed to Garrison that following the lead of the Secret One, all of the other pit-dwellers slowly began to turn their faces towards him. It was as if, for the first time, they sensed that he was here. And such was the malignant effect of this concerted movement—this awful *awareness*—that he sprang to his feet in a terror; in which same moment he felt himself drawn up as if on invisible strings, out of the pit to hover, light as air, over the concentric tiers of a great amphitheatre of the gods.

Gods, yes, and the amphitheatre full of them about their pursuits—but false gods, Garrison quickly saw, who used their powers entirely to their own ends and not those of their followers. And occasionally one such false god would go to the pit's rim and look into it, and nod his satisfaction or frown his disdain or disappointment, so that Garrison knew that the false gods controlled and approved the vile sorceries of the pit-wizards.

For these gods were worse than the sorcerers and demons they governed, and in their supreme arrogance and insolence they had put on such robes of honor and wisdom as were never theirs rightly to wear. They wore the great wigs of judges and the bowlers of politicians, the learned aspect of leaders and scholars and the airs and manners of gentlemen—but behind their backs they carried the whetted knives of assassins, and in their mouths were words of treachery, and one and all they wore in their eyes the monocles of jewellers and did obeisance to One who was everywhere present in the amphitheatre, whose name was Avarice.

And Garrison knew them now, that they were the false gods of High Finance, and occasionally of Justice and Power, and sometimes even of Law and Order and Government. So that even as he was taken up yet again in the fist of the unseen giant—taken up and whisked aloft into a darkness from which to gaze down upon the amphitheatre of false gods—Garrison took note of them and nodded grimly, and vowed never to worship them.

But even peering upon them from on high, suddenly he sensed that he was not alone, that some Other was here who also observed and took note. And hovering there in darkness over the amphitheatre, over its central pit of wizards, over shewstone and all—buoyed up and suspended in air by some force or power beyond his knowledge and great (he suspected) as any power of levitation he had ever controlled—Garrison strained his senses to locate the whereabouts of that Other, whose presence was like a dark omen.

And he heard . . . the *breathing* of the Other, slow and measured and deliberate. And he sensed the slow pulse of blood through the Other's veins, like a throb of power. And he felt the very eyes of the Other, burning *through* him and unaware of his spirit, as they too gazed down upon the works of the beings below. And in the silence of that high place these signs of the Other caused Garrison's hair to rise up on his head, so that he shrank down into himself and grew afraid.

But he grew angry, too—at his own fear, partly, but also angry that the things he had seen, which could only be of that future he had desired to know, had not been shown to him more clearly. For which omission, having no one else to blame, he illogically blamed the Other. And so he deliberately turned his eyes upwards to seek out the Other's form—and what he saw was strange beyond all strangeness.

Above him the darkness writhed, was filled, brimmed over with evil! A diseased evil insidious as cancer, gray as leprosy and warped as insanity itself. A vast octopus of evil, whose countless tentacles twisted and twined, with many sucker mouths that gaped and showed their sharp hooks, whose tossing flesh was livid with inimical energies, and whose eyes—

Whose eyes burned feral with a bestial lusting beyond any lusts Garrison could ever imagine as existing in the mind of man.

The mind of man? The thought was icy in its utter terror, freezing his brain. But surely what he saw was not, could not be, a man? And yet

Garrison drew breath in a gasp. For his every instinct told him that it *was* some sort of man, this creature of evil. A man whose true form lay hidden behind or had been overwhelmed by the massive evil within him, so that Garrison saw only the evil itself. But what sort of man, whose aspect must needs carry this monstrosity of a mask?

Garrison called upon his own powers, the ESP magic he controlled (or which, in another world, he had once controlled) to seek beyond the octopus guise he saw. He closed his eyes and concentrated his will upon the discovery of the octopus-obscured Evil One, and . . .

. . . And in a flash—one brief instant of clear-sightedness—he viewed upon the surface of his mind's inner eye the being behind the monster. He saw him—*and in turn was seen!*

Two minds touched, Garrison's and that of the Other, touched and explored—however briefly—and drew back in mutual shock and astonishment! And both knew that this was not the first time they had met, and despite their shock both were equally curious.

But though Garrison might have attempted to look again, that single glimpse was all that he was allowed; for in the next moment he felt himself snatched up yet again and . . . transferred. His spirit melting down into his body . . . *his body starting to shuddery life where it kneeled at the rim of the canyon . . . his brow cold where it rested upon the metal flank of the Machine.*

And in the fast-fading light he saw streaks of rust like fresh-dried blood upon those same flanks. And he heard Suzy's whining where she tugged at his ragged sleeve. And he saw that night walked the land and touched the stars into cold, glittering life.

Then Garrison sighed and gathered shaky legs beneath him and stood up, and before that last vision could escape him utterly he gave thought to what he had learned of the Other, that Evil One who wore the guise of a bloated, diseased octopus. Neither white nor black, that Other—neither man nor woman; neither sane nor insane—and yet all of these things. And human!

Human, yes. How?—Garrison could not say, could only shake his head in wonder.

And finally he sighed again and climbed wearily up on to the Machine's broad back, calling Suzy to jump up behind him. Then, lifting the now pitted Machine into the air, he pointed its prow out over the canyon and with a gradual acceleration moved out beyond the rim and started across. And he knew no fear.

For if what he had seen of the future was real, then he knew that the canyon could not stop him. No, for there was a long, long way to go yet before his eyes would light upon Immortality's temple, and—

And why then was he falling, curving down into the throat of the gorge like a hurled pebble at the end of its flight?

Faster and faster the Machine plummeted into blackness; and Suzy howling like a banshee where she crushed to Garrison's clammy back; and the chill air of the canyon whistling through his hair and ragged, billowing clothes; and Gar-

rison straining to bring the rushing descent to a halt, straining to use powers seemingly defunct in him, of which he had once been master.

And his own voice screaming his desperation, his hatred: "Liar! Schroeder, you lied! You showed me a false future!"

And in his head Schroeder's whispered denial: "No, no, Richard—I told you no lie. There is a future, our common future—but this is merely a warning . . ." *And a throaty chuckle fading and becoming one with the bluster of rushing air.*

And man and dog and Machine, falling, falling, falling . . .

Chapter
7

CHARON GUBWA HAD ALSO DREAMED, BUT AT THE moment of contact he had been shocked awake. A minute later—a mere minute to allow for orientation—and he lay still in his vast bed, listening to his own pounding heart. A dream, yes, but more than just that. Gubwa's defenses had been down, breached. And such turbulence when the barriers were broken! A potential enemy, a *powerful* enemy, had located him, had penetrated his mind-castle.

But how? It had never happened before, should not even be possible; but . . . yesterday's incident was still fresh in Gubwa's mind, took on a new significance in the light of this latest incursion. He had thought the Polaris encounter an accident, but now. . . ? No, whatever had gone wrong, it could hardly be accidental. Once, maybe—but twice?

Which meant—Gubwa must now assume that Garrison had been looking for him, had actually sought him out.

"Richard Allen Garrison," Gubwa whispered the name to himself, his thoughts darkly seething and more than a little awed. "Oh, I've sought out *your* mind on occasion—or rather, the minds of those close to you—but I hardly suspected you would ever come looking for mine! Not twice in twenty-four hours!"

Garrison, yes—it could only be him. Who else could create such a turbulence in the Psychosphere? Only two men in the whole world had that sort of power. Garrison was the other one.

Gubwa heaved his great trunk upright and rested for a moment, panting from the exertion, until he could exercise his will upon himself and take command of his huge, obese and obscene body. Then, as the blood began to course more freely in his veins and his respiration regulated, he peered about in the dim glow of a tiny red ceiling light.

8:20 A.M. Gubwa stretched, yawned.

On his right lay a sleeping white woman who should have been beautiful, her face almost perfect but a little too thin. Her chest rose and fell evenly, smooth and unscarred despite the absence of breasts surgically removed. Perfect plastic surgery, it could almost be a male chest. Except there were no nipples. Not even the perfunctory nipples of a boy. And yet she was not sexless. On the contrary.

She lay on her back, shapely legs spread wide, exposing a huge and gaping vulva that vanished into her body like a tunnel. In sleep her mouth was wide open and even as Gubwa looked at her gaped wider yet. Utterly toothless, it was the entrance to a second tunnel: the ribbed vault of her throat. Her master knew both entrances intimately—yes, and a third for the moment hidden.

On his left lay a young male, black, entirely naked of hair. He was heavy-lipped, squat-nosed, slope-headed, utterly ugly—but his breasts were a woman's breasts, with great square ebony nipples. His penis was a flabby pipe, without the support or benefit of testicles. A eunuch, but hardly the harem guard. Rather an intimate, a favorite at the Court of Gubwa.

Yes, both of them were of The Flock. Both "man" and "woman" (if such terms were at all applicable), "wives" to Charon Gubwa. Two among many.

Gubwa eased his bulk down the bed until he sat, feet upon the floor, at its foot. He stood up, his great flaccid penis reaching close to halfway down his thigh, its glans like the head of some dead cobra dangling in the shadow of his great belly. Folds of flesh heaved as he crossed the room, the effort quite literally more mental than physical. He *lightened* himself as he went, the closest he could come to actual levitation. His forte was of course telepathy, with hypnotism coming a close second and the other ESP abilities trailing behind. And while he was greatly practiced in his powers, still he knew their limitations.

As for Garrison's limitations: Gubwa would

give a lot to know them. They were what made the man so dangerous to him, and to his cause. Too dangerous. But . . . Gubwa was satisfied that the contact had been too brief to constitute a real breach of his security. He had after all been asleep and presumably dreaming. And it was not impossible that he, Gubwa himself, had subconsciously sought out Garrison. It wouldn't be the first time he'd visited the minds of others in his sleep. Oh, it was unlikely, but . . . the man *had* been on his mind a lot lately. But even that couldn't explain yesterday, and it certainly didn't explain the failure of the mind-guards. Not this time . . .

Gubwa donned Eastern-styled slippers and a red, voluminous knee-length robe. Doors opened for him with a pneumatic *hiss* as he billowed towards and through them, out of his bedroom and into his general living quarters. This room was spacious: high-ceilinged, with resilient rubber-tiled floors, its dimly lighted decor almost industrial in slate-gray and silver tones. To one side stood a great heavy metal desk above which, carved into the striated bedrock of the wall, the squat, angular bas-relief figure of a naked man, arms akimbo, stared stonily down into the room.

The carved figure was that of Gubwa as he had been fifteen years ago when first he took up residence here, and closer examination of its stony features would show that he was not—not entirely—a man. Or perhaps something more than a man, depending upon the mental perspective of the viewer. For like Gubwa himself, and like the eunuch still sleeping in his bed, the great bas-relief had pendulous breasts; but there any comparison between Gubwa and the eunuch ended. For between the spread legs of the carving the heavy penis was deliberately shown erect, with bulbous testicles drawn to one side, displaying the parted lips of a female organ, clitoris swollen and extended like a small penis. The figure was hermaphroditic—as was the living creature it depicted. Its feet were set firmly upon a great globe in bas-relief, bearing carved representations of Earth's islands, continents and oceans.

Gubwa crossed to the desk, stabbed at a button with the forefinger of a massive left hand and spoke into the grill of an intercom. "Gubwa to guardroom. There has been a mental intrusion. Check the mind-guards and report to me at once."

He took his finger off the button, moved round behind the desk and seated himself in a padded steel chair. He waited, mused, explored the possibilities of the situation.

The mind-guards were Gubwa's answer to the insomnia of the telepath, a sleeplessness he had suffered at intervals for twenty-five years before discovering the remedy. Awake he could control, channel and direct his contact with outside minds. They were at his mercy, to be read like books and picked clean of information. Most of them anyway. But asleep it was a different story. Asleep they impinged, *infested* his mind with their own innumerable fears and poisons. Or they had used to, before the mind-guards.

There were always four mind-guards "on duty" at any one time, men and women whose narcotic dependence was total. Addicts long departed the real world to dwell in the permanent twilight zone of their own deliriums. Gubwa was happy to let them live this way, to supply the drugs which alone kept them alive. When he was awake their chaotic nightmares could not affect him, and when he slept the mind-guards slept, guarding his mind. That was their sole function.

There was a drug, supplementary to their addictions, which effectively switched them off—cast them into a mental void, created within them what amounted to temporary brain-death—which was the absolute negation of thought. And which created *around* them a barrier impenetrable to the random thought-streams of the outside world. Impenetrable also to any thought-probe. Or so Gubwa had always believed.

And that was important! For there were people who could probe with their thoughts just as Gubwa himself but without his expertise, often without even knowing that they did it. Their minds were simply broadcasting stations, sending out a constant stream of telepathic waves. And they generally ignored or failed to recognize incoming messages. The dangerous ones were those who could actually read the minds of others, and one such was Garrison. Garrison, the world's greatest telepath, whose thoughts—whose *directed* thoughts?—had now seemingly penetrated Gubwa's barriers and shocked him from sleep.

Garrison would not have recognized him (sleeping minds are mere caricatures of the waking consciousness), but he most certainly would have detected something of Gubwa's strength. And if he *had* been probing, *why?*—unless he actually suspected the presence of one whose ESP abilities might challenge his own! If that were so . . . then it was also Gubwa's worst fear realized.

Where was Garrison now? Suddenly anxious, galvanized by an insecurity previously unvisioned, Gubwa typed Garrison's name into his computer. The machine's screen immediately responded:

AEGEAN . . . DODECANESE . . . RHODES . . . LINDOS . . .

Gubwa questioned the machine's authority. It quoted date, time, destination and departure flight number from Gatwick. Its source was the airport computer. Gubwa's anxiety turned to impotent rage. One day the tentacles of his organization would reach out to envelop the entire world, and then—

—He calmed himself. For the present he had nothing on Rhodes. The island was one of the many places as yet beyond even his ever widening technological sphere, which was the best money could buy. As were the completely illegal systems through which that technology was channelled.

He stabbed the intercom's button again. "Guardroom—" his voice was harder now, slightly threatening. "When I say at once I mean *at once!*" He released the button, stood up, took his computer remote and went to his globe in its clear glass cylinder. Seating himself before it, he keyed GLOBE, RHODES and LINDOS on the remote and watched the miniature world rotate until the Greek island came to rest directly before his eyes. A pencil beam within the globe shone outwards upon Rhodes, its center the village where Garrison and Vicki Maler were staying.

Gubwa began to sweat. This wasn't to his liking. There was always the possibility, by no means remote, that he might reveal himself. But he had to know.

Vicki Maler's thought patterns were familiar to him. Very well, since he dare not carry out direct mind-surveillance on Garrison he must go instead to the girl. He stared once more at the Aegean island, the point of light, the location of the tiny village. He pictured the girl and allowed her image to swell large in his mind's eye. His physical eyes he slowly closed, sending a telepathic probe out, out, searching the ether, searching . . .

. . . until he found her . . .

. . . touched upon her mind . . .

. . . a touch, nothing more . . .

. . . no awareness of his presence. Innocence. Innocent thoughts . . .

. . . mildly worried thoughts . . . worried for Garrison . . .

. . . he entered, unsuspected, less than a ghost in her head . . .

. . . and in the next instant Charon Gubwa

gazed out through Vicki Maler's eyes at the sleeping Garrison . . .

. . . sleeping for the moment, yes, but in the throes of nightmare . . . and even now she was reaching to wake him!

Gubwa withdrew at once, soared back into the Castle, into himself and opened his eyes. Garrison was asleep, or had been asleep at the moment of contact some minutes earlier. Garrison and Gubwa both.

Gubwa sighed and sank down heavily into his chair. What he had seen made for an easy, acceptable explanation. It seemed that Garrison had not sought out Gubwa but that indeed the reverse had been the case. Because he had been concerned about Garrison, in his sleep he, Gubwa, had unconsciously, involuntarily sought *him* out!

All well and good—but what if the other had been awake? Garrison's telepathic ability was in a word fantastic! Gubwa hated to admit this even to himself, but it was so. The man might easily have trailed him back here, back to the Castle itself. And what then? Gubwa did not want to kill Garrison, not yet. There might be a great deal he could learn from the man, but secretly.

Which brought him once again to the question of the mind-guards. For just as their mental negativity kept unwanted thoughts out when Gubwa wished to sleep, so should they keep his in, or at least suppress them, when he was in fact sleeping. That is if they were operating with their accustomed efficiency. And four of them

94

had always been sufficient, until now. Yesterday's "meeting of minds" had occurred, as it were, *outside* the Castle—but this morning's intrusion . . .? It was most suspicious.

As if to confirm Gubwa's doubts, his intercom suddenly barked: "Number Three mind-guard has pegged it, sir. She's dead."

Gubwa quickly crossed to the desk and pressed his button. "Stay there!" he snapped. "I'm coming."

Gubwa's Castle was *not* the most heavily fortified inhabited retreat in the world, but it was one of the most secret. Indeed its ramparts were not at all in evidence.

Small by any ordinary castle's standards, the Castle had but one level. It was square in shape, some thirty by thirty yards, with one perimeter corridor and two diagonal corridors; in plan, a square with a cross in it, forming four triangles equal in size and area. One of these contained Gubwa's personal living quarters, his Command Center and (set quite apart and forbidden to all but The Flock and Gubwa himself) his "harem"; another held his extensive library, study, mind-lab and swimming pool; a third contained the "barracks," accommodation for his two dozen "soldiers," also a gymnasium and other recreational facilities; and the fourth was the utility area, housing the Castle's air filtration, heating, electrical and general life-support systems. The four mind-guard cells were located in the Castle's "turrets," that is to say at its four corners, which could only be reached along the perimeter corridor.

The corridors were better lighted than Gubwa's private rooms, so that he was obliged to squint his eyes as he made for cell Number Three. His eyes were weak, unable to cope with any but the dimmest light; for which reason, here in the Castle, all lighting was subdued. Not even the corridors were bright by normal standards, but they were still too bright for Charon Gubwa. Outside the Castle, there Gubwa wore tinted contact lenses, but such trips as he was obliged to make were extremely few and far between. Being physically agoraphobic (mentally to the contrary) he went out only when he *had* to go, which had become virtually never. With the exception of food and stores, which Gubwa's "quartermaster" must of course periodically replenish, the Castle was to all intents and purposes self-sufficient.

Moving his bulk along the perimeter corridor whose outer wall was solid rock and whose inner wall was plastic-coated steel, Gubwa arrived at the cell in question. There a white man named Gardner, one of his most trusted lieutenants, waited for him, coming to attention at his approach.

"What took so long, Mr. Gardner?" Gubwa's voice was cold.

Gardner was dressed in the Castle's gray T-shirt and slacks uniform, his left breast emblazoned with a silver "G." He stood himself at ease before answering. "Guard on duty was showering, sir. It's his right, a shower before knocking off, as you well know, sir. I chivvied him up, sent him to check the mind-guards. He checked this one last, couldn't get any readings. He unlocked the cell, entered, checked, found she was dead, contacted me. I contacted you at once."

Gubwa nodded. "Who is this guard and where is he now?"

Gardner inclined his head towards the heavy metal door of the cell. "Inside with the girl."

Gubwa pushed by him and entered the cell. The girl lay upon her bed dressed in the attire of the mind-guard: a short, sleeveless shift that reached halfway down her thighs. She was—had been—quite pretty. Her breasts were small beneath the material of the shift, but firm; her legs were long and shapely; her mouth was full in a young/old face which showed all too well the stresses and strains of her addiction. Gubwa looked at her, laid his great hand upon her breast, drew his forest of white eyebrows together in a grim frown. Then he looked at the guard.

His glance this time was cursory, apparently disinterested, flickering from the features of a nervous young black to Gardner's own impassive face. "Gardner, I want to speak to you in private. You—" again he glanced at the young Negro, "—go and fetch one of your fellows—for disposal duties. And a stretcher."

"I'll call one up, sir," the guard answered, his Adam's apple bobbing. He unclipped a tiny walkie-talkie from his waist-belt.

"I said fetch," Gubwa stopped him, his thick voice suddenly icy. "Now go and *fetch*!"

The young man nodded, gulped, turned on his heel and went out. His footsteps echoed away down the corridor. "Close the door, Gardner," said Gubwa, his voice now soft. "And now—help me get her shift up."

Gardner lifted the dead girl's hips while Gubwa hoisted her single garment. Then the two stood back. "Ah!" said Gubwa, a word which carried all the menace in the world.

Gardner glanced again between the girl's legs. "It could only have been him," he said. "Jackson."

"Or you," Gubwa told him.

Gardner shrugged, knew better than to argue. "Or me, yes, sir."

Gubwa probed his mind, discovered no fear. At least, not in connection with this. "But it wasn't you who attacked this girl, no—it *was* Jackson. Or . . . what about the others on duty?"

"Seven of them, all sleeping—but I was awake, of course. And they'd have to get past me. They'd all done their stint. Jackson's was the last. He'd finished, was getting ready to knock off for the day, showering when you called. He's not usually so particular, but this explains it. It was Jackson, all right."

Together they pulled down the girl's shift.

"My orders are clear enough, wouldn't you say?" Gubwa's voice had grown softer, more dangerous yet.

"Yes, sir."

"The mind-guards are not to be disturbed in any way, isn't that so?"

Again: "Yes, sir."

"And I pay enough, that my orders should be obeyed?"

98

"More than generous, sir," Gardner nodded.

"Yes," Gubwa mused, "and I also keep the men well supplied, with all of their personal little needs. So—why?"

"A bit of illicit crumpet," Gardner shrugged. "You know what they say, sir: stolen apples are always the sweetest? Even the sour ones . . .?"

Gubwa smiled grimly, nodding his agreement. He pursed flabby lips. "I shall . . . dismiss him, of course. Today, personally. Will you be able to recruit a replacement?"

"Of course, sir. Any time. As many as you like, within reason."

"Good!" Gubwa answered as footsteps sounded in the corridor. "Then recruit . . . two." He turned away from the bed. "I shall attend to the, er, disposal arrangements myself. As for you, Gardner: as soon as your shift is relieved you may fall out. No need to wait for these two . . ."

"I understand, sir."

The lift cage descended from the Castle into black bowels of rock and earth. At its lowest extremity the shaft bottomed out on to a ledge over a natural chasm. A single red fluorescent tube flickered into life, illuminating the shelf and, as it came down the shaft, the cage. The doors folded back and Gubwa stepped out, followed by the stretcher-bearers, Jackson and Smith.

"Put her down," said Gubwa, his voice echoing in the unseen but felt subterranean vastness, where the dim red light of the fluorescent tube covered and colored them with its ruddy wash. He stood on one side of the stretcher, facing across it and out over the rim of the fissure. "Stand there," he pointed, "and there."

Smith was white, a little older than his colored colleague. With nothing on his conscience, nothing to fear, he was quick to obey; Jackson moved a little slower. They positioned themselves, as indicated, opposite Gubwa and facing him, their backs to the chasm. Gubwa steepled his fingers, forearms horizontal in front of him. He lowered his head and its great round bush of white hair until his forehead rested upon the tips of his fingers. Jackson and Smith glanced at each other, their eyes puzzled, questioning.

"We have come," Gubwa kept his head bowed, his voice deliberately sepulchral, "to send this poor girl to her last resting place. It is her due. She was a faithful servant." He put down his hands, lifted his head, straightened up. He nodded, then:

"Put your hands between her body and the stretcher and lift her up," he commanded. They did as they were instructed, holding the girl's corpse before them like some grisly offering. She was surprisingly light.

"Good!" said Gubwa, towering over the men and the dead girl they supported in their arms. He lowered his head again, reached out across the empty stretcher and laid one great hand on the girl's thigh, the other on her shoulder. It was as if he were about to bless her.

Perhaps in that last moment Jackson and Smith—especially Jackson—sensed Doom's rushing approach; but they were much too late to avoid it.

"Go to your rest, my *children!*" said Gubwa, his sepulchral tone sharpening on the last word. And with that last word he pushed with all the weight of his great body.

The two men shouted their alarm, were forced back, off balance. They flailed their arms, their cries turning to screams. The rim crumbled beneath their feet . . .

They were gone, the body of the girl, too. Only their echoing screams remained, fading.

Seconds later there came a clattering of dislodged rocks and stony rubble, followed by three distinct splashes and the sounds of lesser debris striking deep water. Then silence.

Gubwa stood for a moment at the rim, then bent down and dragged the stretcher into the lift. His face was without expression. The cage doors closed on him and the lift climbed its shaft. The red fluorescent light flickered out . . .

As Charon Gubwa rose up through the strata of centuries, so a second lift moved in another shaft, carrying Gardner and the six remaining members of his team. Gardner's cage moved slowly, would take all of fifteen minutes to pass through two hundred and seventy feet of shaft; but this was not inefficiency. On the contrary, the slow-running cage was necessary to the *complete* efficiency of Charon Gubwa's operation, his organization. For these fifteen minutes were the minimum required for the "debriefing" which occurred whenever his people left the Castle; and that debriefing was in progress now, perfectly synchronized with the monotonous creep of the cage.

The cage itself was in near-darkness, its gloom barely relieved by the regular pulsing of a single electric-blue ceiling light. And in that strangely ethereal atmosphere the seven men leaned against the walls and listened to Gubwa's deep, even, sonorously hypnotic voice. Although it was only a recording, still that voice was not one to be ignored, denied or in any way defied, for Gubwa was a hypnotist without peer and his words merely reiterated and reinforced previous orders.

This was the third and last time that the seven men would hear those orders on this occasion, for the lift was slowing more yet as it approached its terminal. This was what the voice of Gubwa said to them:

"Your work is done," (the monologue began) "and you are now free of duty. You will next report for work at the time shown on your duty roster. Only genuine sickness will prevent such reporting, in which case your immediate superior will be informed in advance. Of the work you have performed and the things you have seen you will remember nothing. You will take nothing, neither material nor memory of the Castle with you. When you return you will bring nothing, neither material nor intent with you into the Castle. Your only intent will be to do my service.

"You will know only those things I require you to know, and your answers to questions concerning myself, my organization, the nature of the Castle itself or anything at all concerning the work you perform for me will be the prepared answers I have ordered you to learn.

"You will keep your minds open and receptive to mine at all times. You will obey without question or hesitation any and all commands I care to issue, spoken or telepathic, except the occasion arises when to do so would not be to my benefit. At any such time you will offer explanation and I will decide the outcome.

"You will do no deliberate wrong outside the Castle but obey the common laws of the land, causing no unwanted attentions to be focussed upon yourselves; neither will you proceed furtively or in any manner likely to arouse suspicion. You will in short live your lives normally within the periphery of my beneficence, and you will be satisfied.

"In the event that you are compromised and that any enemy of mine seeks to subvert you or extract from you information whose divulgence I have forbidden, and further that you are in any way made incapable of refusing such information—then you will simply cease to function. You will die.

"These are the words of Charon Gubwa. I have spoken, so let it be . . ."

The lift came to an almost unnoticeable standstill and the pulsing blue light went out. The doors opened and Gubwa's zombies stepped out. They were in a dim basement room. Behind them the doors closed and the lift sank from sight.

Gardner took out keys, went to the room's single metal door, unlocked its twin locks. He and the others passed through and he locked the door behind them. Now they were in what looked like an underground car park, thick with dust, in which no cars were parked. From somewhere overhead came the dull rumble of traffic.

Footsteps echoing, the seven crossed the concrete floor and entered another lift, and Gardner thumbed its single button. Three levels up they walked out into sunlight, crowds and a street full of heavy traffic. The lift's doors closed automatically behind them. An outer door closed over the inner doors. A sign above the outer door said:

NOT FOR PUBLIC USE.

And down below, more than three hundred feet straight down, the Castle lay hidden, mysterious and . . . forgotten. For them, at least.

Silent until now, Gubwa's men yawned, blinked their eyes in the light of day, nodded farewells and went their own ways. To all intents and purposes they were ordinary citizens about their business, clad in the ordinary clothes and wearing the ordinary expressions of common, everyday life.

Gardner's way took him a couple of streets to where he would catch his bus. Waiting at the stop he lit a cigarette and engaged himself in conversation with a sweaty fat lady in a feathery hat. Just across the road, a sign on the corner of a building said:

Oxford St W1

Chapter

8

NINETY MINUTES EARLIER IN LINDOS, VICKI MALER had awakened, stretched, and checked the time: 10:30 A.M.

10:30 A.M. local, and the sun was high in the sky and blazing over the great Rock of the Acropolis. Vicki yawned and stretched again. She had had, oh, maybe six, six-and-a-half hours' sleep? The same for Richard. It was almost time to wake him up. While he didn't particularly like being awakened, neither did he care to sleep too long. He had begun lately to complain that things "passed him by" while he was asleep.

In any case, now would be a good and sensible time. He was nightmaring again and had started to moan. She had heard him mention Schroeder and Koenig, and he had cursed once or twice. His temperature was up, too; sweat gleamed on his brow and in the hollow of his collar bones; he shook his head from side to side as if seeking a way out of some terrible predicament. Yes, she should wake him. After all, *he* had awakened her, with his tossing and turning.

"Liar!" the word suddenly gurgled from between his clenched teeth, seemingly in denial of Vicki's last thought. And: *"Falling! Falling!"*

She went quickly to his side and laid a hand upon his shoulder. But as his frantic jerking and tossing grew still more pronounced, she shouted, "Richard! Richard, wake up! It's all right!"

He came awake in a moment, his golden eyes flashing open, his body jerking upright from the waist, back ramrod straight on the raised wooden bed. As his hands flew into a defensive position in front of his face and chest, so Vicki stepped quickly back out of range. Then . . . his wide, molten golden eyes blinked, focussed, and he saw her.

He licked bone-dry lips, lay back trembling. "God, a *bad* one!" He angled his head to stare at her, managed a shaky laugh. "A beauty!"

"It must have been," she told him. "You were shouting."

"Oh? What was I shouting?"

"Something about a liar—and falling?" She deliberately left out the other bits of mouthing, about Schroeder and Koenig.

"Falling? Oh, yes," he frowned. "I remember that. Something of it anyway. But a liar?" He shook his head.

"Do you remember anything else?" she asked.

He got up, still shaky, and put his arms around her. Then he released her, tugged open her robe and hugged her again. She held him tightly, feeling something of her old love for him flooding her veins, her body.

Her "old" love for him? Had something changed, then?

With her face buried in his shoulder, she bit her lips, controlled her thinking. Occasionally (unconsciously, she liked to believe) Richard eavesdropped on her mind. He was not doing so now, but he nevertheless felt the tension in her body. "Something wrong, Vicki?"

"Only that I worry about you. What we talked about last night, and these dreams of yours . . ."

He released her and began to pull on his clothes. "I know," he said. "But you know they're not entirely my own. I mean, I am dreaming for three of us. Do you understand?"

She nodded. "Yes, I do. And surely *you* understand why I worry."

He returned her nod. "Of course—" he paused, frowned, then pulled on a T-shirt. "Only this time—with *this* dream—"

"Yes?"

He shrugged. "This time I believe I was dreaming for myself. I only wish I could remember more about it. I feel it was special, important."

"Important? A dream?"

"I've had dreams before, Vicki, and some of them were damned important. But—" and again he shrugged. "—Maybe it'll come back to me later."

But for all his shrug, as he finished dressing

and slipped his feet into his sandals, she could see that the dream continued to preoccupy him. She tried to drive it from his mind, asking: "Aren't you going to wash?"

"Eh?" he looked up, half-smiling. "Oh! No—I won't bother now. A dip in the sea, a shower on the beach—it's today we're to visit the Acropolis, isn't it?"

"Oh, yes!" she was enthusiastic. "We'll have a wonderful view from up there. As long as you promise not to go too close to the edge . . ."

His smile disappeared completely and she bit her lip again, knowing she had erred. "I only *dreamed* I was falling, Vicki," he reminded her. "Awake . . . it simply can't happen. You know that."

Oh, yes, she knew it. "Of course. I only—"

"Get dressed now, won't you?" He turned away from her, gazed out of the window into the vine-shaded, black and white cobbled courtyard. "We can have brunch in the village on our way down to the beach."

Some nine hours later, right on cue, Paulo Palazzi's fat Frenchman departed Lindos. He and his much younger mistress—a nymphet with big loose breasts which she loved to bounce about all over the lesser of the village's two beaches—left town in a local taxi, their faces glowing shiny-red from too much sun. The girl wore a loose evening gown, presumably for the sake of her sunburn. Palazzi was pleased to note that she didn't seem to be wearing too much jewelry; doubtless the weight of gold and stones would constitute a great irritation against rapidly roughening skin. How then, he wondered with a grin, could she possibly cope with the far greater weight of her lover? The poor, rich fat slob! But, where there's a will . . .

Then, a nervous twenty minutes later, he saw the Swiss party appear from the doorway of their spacious high-priced villa, laughingly making for the village center where already the tavernas were growing boisterously raucous. Happily the pair left an upper window hanging ajar. True, it was unseasonably warm even for the Aegean, but . . . there would be more than the breeze off the sea and a couple of mosquitoes going in through that window tonight! Palazzi grinned again, this time at his joke and at the thought of the mosquitoes. The buzzing little vampires would have to wait their turn for rich Swiss blood tonight. He, Paulo Palazzi, would be taking first fruits—and his sting was far more painful.

And then there was Garrison. At the thought of the so-called "blind" man Palazzi's eyes narrowed. This one was more problematic, erratic, less likely to adhere to any sort of regular schedule. He might not even go out tonight, which would be bad news but not necessarily an insurmountable problem. The man probably slept quite heavily, certainly *would* sleep heavily if the amount of local brandy he consumed was anything to go by. Or perhaps he drank the brandy because he slept badly? Whichever, only time would tell. And time, for the next few hours anyway, was on the side of the thief.

It was growing dark now, would be quite dark

by 9:00 or 9:15. Palazzi had promised the night watchman he would be off the rock by then. That promise had been made as he returned from his midday meal in Elli's Taverna toting a small, cheap bottle of ouzo to reinforce their friendship. But still, Palazzi didn't wish to outstay his welcome—or give the old boy any reason to question his motives.

He picked at his well-groomed fingernails for a little while, then took up his binoculars one last time and found Garrison's courtyard where it was lighted by the glow of shaded lamps above the inner doors. And even as he watched, so the lights went out one by one, and straining his eyes he saw a pair of dim figures moving amongst the courtyard's shadows. Then—

There they were! Hand in hand, their pace leisurely as they descended into the maze of streets. And dressed for dancing, yes! Garrison in a paper-light white suit and open-neck shirt, his woman in a halter and culottes.

His woman . . .

Palazzi's eager, wolfish grin slipped a little. Another enigma: she, too, was supposed to be blind. At least she, too, wore a blind person's spectacles. Well, blind she may or may not be— but beautiful she most certainly was. And her figure . . .!

Palazzi allowed his thoughts to wander back to the topless girls he had watched on the little beach. Funny how binoculars, bringing those naked breasts so close you could almost pucker your lips and kiss them, seemed at the same time somehow to set them in another, alien

111

realm. Much more exciting to actually be within reach, even if one mustn't touch. And the pretty English girls he had seen two days ago: they had been close, especially the girl with the *big* ones. Braless, her nipples stiff with excitement, shaping her blouse as she leaned out over the ramparts . . .

Palazzi suddenly felt himself erect, his penis huge in his pants. Nothing new. The thrill of anticipation. Not sexual (he told himself), rather environmental. But pleasing anyway. He stroked his hard through his trousers—then jerked guiltily alert as he heard a rattle of stones, a jingle of keys, and a wheezy, boozy, inquiring Greek voice.

"Coming!" he called out, his Greek only so-so. "Just coming." He scrambled from the wall, dusted himself off, made for the great stone arch which would lead him to the steep, winding descent. "But such a lovely night. I quite forgot the time. It's the solitude I like, you know? Just sitting up here on my own." He wasn't sure the old fellow really understood him. "You enjoyed the ouzo? Good! And yes, thank you, the sunset really was quite beautiful."

From far below, music and the sounds of muted revelry began to drift up into the darkening air. Lindos was rising from its evening torpor. Palazzi could feel its spiced lamb and retsina breath in his face, beckoning him to the feast . . .

All through the day Garrison's mood and morale had gradually deteriorated. Vicki had sensed it, had seen how he tried to keep a rein on feelings and emotions he himself did not fully understand, and she, too, had grown restless in sympathy with his near-schizophrenic mood. She had known (mercifully) that it was his *own* schizophrenia, springing perhaps from a delicate suppression of the two "live-in" mentalities which were now permanent facets of his id, his psyche—had known that neither Schroeder nor Koenig had outwardly manifested themselves during the course of the day—but the mere thought of the effort of will he must exercise simply to remain ascendant was chilling. She doubted if she would ever become accustomed to it.

She traced the source of the trouble back to this morning's dream, possibly as far back as their encounter with the Greek youths. Until then all had seemed to be going well, their holiday had been doing both of them a great deal of good. But now, tonight—?

Now he fidgeted and frowned a lot. He had toyed with his food and argued over the bill, then stomped angrily out of the taverna where they had eaten. He had also consumed too much brandy, had allowed himself to get upset too easily when the music of a particular taverna (they had tried several) wasn't just exactly to his liking, and had complained bitterly of "rowdy, drunken grockles," when in fact the holiday-makers were as yet quite sober and extremely well behaved. He was, in short, on the point of boiling over, blowing up to release the tensions

113

seething within. And that was the last thing that Vicki wanted.

Oh, no, for she knew that just beneath the surface of the Garrison she had so loved (again that doubt, that niggling past tense) there lurked others only too ready to spring into being. Vicki knew that she—and Lindos, too, for that matter—could well do without the advent of Herr Willy Koenig, late of the Schutzstaffel and personal bodyguard to his beloved Colonel Thomas Schroeder. And her sentiments, or lack of them, applied just as well to the Colonel himself. Oh, she had been fond of both of them in life, in the flesh, but now that they dwelled in Garrison's head, in his very being, she was afraid of them and hated them. Neither one of them must be allowed to surface tonight.

Which was why, at her first opportunity, she allowed Garrison to "catch" her frowning and stroking her brow.

"Oh?" he was quick to query, leaning towards her across their wicker table.

"Nothing. A headache coming on, I think."

Garrison was immediately sympathetic, reaching to touch her brow—and his face clouding over in a moment, knowing she lied. "*If* you had a headache," he told her quietly, "I could cure it in a moment. You know that."

"Tired, then," she tried desperately to cover up. "Perhaps I'm just a little—"

"Tired?" he shook his head. "No, not that either. We slept for an hour or two this afternoon after our climb." He pursed his lips, breathed deeply, began to look angry—then let out all of his air and anger in one great sigh. "What the hell—it's me, eh?"

"Oh, Richard!" she gave his hand an urgent squeeze. "It's just that you seem to be working yourself up to something. And I don't know what ... to ..." She let the sentence taper off, her voice breaking a little.

He stared at her for a moment, and it was as if she could feel the warmth of his golden eyes right through the dark, heavy lenses of his glasses. A warmth that drew something of her anxiety right out of her. "I don't know either," he admitted. "It's a feeling, that's all. That I'm missing something. That something's wrong. With the world, with me. Hell, you *know* what's wrong, Vicki!"

"Look," she squeezed his hand again, "why don't we call it a day, have an early night? We can sit in the courtyard. I'll make coffee—a lot of it. Coffee and brandy—and a cigar for you. You'll like that. We don't have to do anything except sit there and relax, and listen to that little bird singing his one sad note."

Garrison nodded, smiled however wanly. "Yes, he is sad, that little bloke. With his *poop!* ... *poop!* ... *poop!* I wonder what he looks like?"

"Maybe he's ugly," Vicki said, rising and putting down money on the table. "Perhaps that's why he only comes out at night."

And later, as they climbed through the narrow streets and rose above the babble of bright, crowded taverns, Garrison added: "And maybe that's why he's so sad, eh? Being ugly, I mean, and only one note to sing."

"But such a beautiful note," Vicki answered as they reached the door to their courtyard. "Like liquid moonlight."

Garrison caught her round the waist, kissed her hungrily and gently fondled her breasts in the darkness. "Listen, what do you say we forget the coffee and brandy, eh? Why don't we help the little guy out and make some music of our own?"

Together they stepped over the threshold, closing the door quietly behind them . . .

Palazzi had started with the Swiss pair. Staying only one narrow street—or rooftop—away from his own less than splendid accommodation, they had seemed the obvious choice.

On leaving the rock of the Acropolis he had spent a few minutes on the lower slopes of the climb, talking to the old Greek lace ladies where they tidied away their wares for the night, finally telling them goodnight and ensuring that they were watching him when he entered his accommodation at the foot of the rock. Then—

—Five minutes to change into his "working clothes" and climb out through a window high in the rear wall of his room, and a few more to flit across the flat, shadowy roofs. And ah!—how the adrenalin had flowed in Paulo Palazzi's veins.

Night was his element, in which he was less than a shadow, and the sheer excitement of the night was an almost physical force within him.

But . . . his excitement had quickly ebbed. The

Swiss couple were a bitter disappointment; pickings in their rooms wouldn't even cover the cost of Palazzi's holiday. A fistful of cheap jewelry, some Drachmas, a few Swiss Francs. Miserable!

Disgruntled, he was out of the burgled room only a little after 10:15 P.M.

Now he was tempted to go after Garrison, the Big One—but he resisted. He knew that his urgency was spawned of disappointment and greed. No, better first to do the French job and let the Garrisons settle into their evenings' entertainment. Besides, the Frog's accommodation was closest. Also . . . well, Palazzi still had a sort of feeling about Garrison and his woman. Something about them that made him nervy.

The thief's instinct served him well, for at 10:25 as he entered the darkened courtyard of the French couple's villa and began silently to pick their lock, Garrison and Vicki were just having their conversation about the music of a different sort of night-venturing bird and entering their own accommodation. Had Palazzi gone there first he must certainly have been disturbed as he went about his business.

Of course he was not to learn this until some thirty minutes later when, coming at a crouching, gliding lope across the roofs, he saw the lamp over their door glowing yellow and heard their muted voices from within. At that Palazzi cursed long, vividly and silently—before resigning himself to a serious revision of his plans. And while his mind worked he stretched himself out on the roof almost directly above the pair on their raised wooden bed, listening to the sounds of their lovemaking.

Of their actual conversation he could hear very little: breathless, hoarse murmurs, panting sighs and moans of pleasure. But the soft *slap*, *slap*, *slap* of perspiring bodies in loving collision was very distinct—and protracted! They knew how to do it, these two.

Despite the necessary revision of his plan, Palazzi began to feel excited—sexually this time—and his penis grew fat, elongating itself within the zippered confines of his jump suit. For he could picture that beautiful body down there, the body of Garrison's woman, all open and soft and pinkly moist, her thighs spread wide, inviting, as Garrison rode in and out of her, in and out. And those breasts of hers, nipples erect, slippery with perspiration and spittle as the blind man's mouth worked on them and sucked them into a life of their own.

Blind man. Jesus! The poor bastard didn't even know how good she looked! How good and ripe and golden. Not if he really was blind. Palazzi licked his lips, stifled a lump rising in his throat, forced himself to concentrate upon the plan's revision and gradually calmed down.

Actually there wasn't a great deal to revise. If he was to be out of Lindos tomorrow he must do the job tonight. He didn't like the idea of doing it while they were asleep in there, but—they must at least be part-blind, mustn't they? And certainly they'd be exhausted and sleeping like the dead.

In any case, he had no choice, for the Froggy

too had disappointed him. Less than ten thousand Drachmas, no French currency at all, only an old gold-plated Rolex Oyster and some bits of jewelry worth maybe three hundred thousand Lire in the right market. Terrible!

But Garrison . . . Ah! He was different. His woman's jewelry alone—no, half of it—would be worth a small fortune. If only they'd get finished with their rutting and get to sleep. 11:20 already, and they were still at it.

Five minutes later the noises began to come faster. For a moment or two they grew frantic and then: a little cry, sharp and sweet, gurgling down into a sigh, and Garrison's hoarse panting gradually subsiding. And finally silence.

Silence for a few minutes. Then the weary slap of naked feet upon the floor, and the lights blinking out. The courtyard light, too, and again silence. The rustle of a sheet. A sigh. And Palazzi patiently waiting on the roof . . .

Neither Garrison nor Vicki dreamed anything of any importance that night. Not before Palazzi's visit, and certainly not afterwards.

As the thief had expected, their lovemaking had drained them. Except for their deep, regular breathing, they lay still and silent as he went about his business of discovering and pocketing their money and personal valuables. And there was plenty to find. More than enough to make up for all other disappointments.

But it hadn't been all that easy; there had been a point when the thought had crossed Palazzi's mind that perhaps he had better turn back. That had been shortly after entering through an open window—to discover Garrison's woman stretched out at his very feet!

Palazzi's night vision was trained to a marvellous degree. Gloomy as the large room was and the moon in the wrong quarter of the sky (the right one for the thief), and only starlight ghosting through the small windows, still he had been able to make out every object in the room with clear definition. The faint beam of a pencil-slim torch had supplied what little extra light was needed for the serious work.

But the girl, Garrison's woman sprawled there at Palazzi's feet. With her face turned to one side and a handkerchief loosely knotted over her forehead, its folds covering her eyes. Her chest rising and falling, rising and falling.

Naked under a sheet, the points of her breasts sticking up and forming peaked hillocks of white linen on her chest. Her arms thrown wide, legs open under the sheet, feet protruding. An attitude of unconscious abandon . . .

Across the room Garrison had the large bed to himself—the bed where the two had made love. It was typical of the raised Greek beds much in evidence throughout the village; but the woman's bed was also raised, higher in fact. Lying upon a sort of square landing or platform, its deep mattress rested upon the ceramic-tiled roof of the tiny bathroom, shower and toilet unit. And spread-eagled, the woman's form almost filled the railed-off bed space; so that the thief had to step carefully indeed to avoid touching or disturbing her. Careful, too, to avoid the possibility of his shadow falling on her face. Even with her eyes covered by the handkerchief, still she might sense his presence.

And then the wooden stairs to negotiate (without making them creak), and upon the floor the jumble of their discarded clothing, piled where they had stripped their bodies naked. A little heap of the woman's jewelry lying on a tiny casual table—her open purse hanging from the knobbed newel at the foot of the stairs—and Garrison's wallet in the inside pocket of his coat, flung casually across the back of a chair.

And the jewelry, not half but *all* of a fortune! Palazzi was tempted to whistle, tempted again when he saw the contents of Garrison's wallet. A fat wad of crisp English £20 notes, at least thirty of them, and an equal amount of high denomination Drachmas. The woman's purse also bulging.

At that point some of the pieces of jewelry had moved and chinked dully in Palazzi's pockets. Garrison too had moved. Only a slight movement, true, accompanied by a little grunt of discomfort, but sufficient to freeze Palazzi to the floor as if taken root there. He waited, watching, listening. Garrison, lying face-down, was starting to snort a little, blowing air into his pillow. He threw out an arm and automatically adjusted his position, stopped snorting. Palazzi waited.

Starlight silvered and softened the room's sharper edges.

All was quiet once more . . .

Palazzi waited no longer. It was time to get

out. The night was moving on. When they had finished making love, he had waited on the roof for over an hour before making his first move, since when he'd been in here with them for a full fifteen minutes. The time now was exactly 1:08 A.M. The Swiss couple would still be dancing; the Froggies on their way back from Rhodes, unless they had decided to stay over for the night; and Palazzi was still one hundred percent safe, but he knew he couldn't afford to waste any time now. And nothing to waste time on, not really. Nothing to linger over . . .

Climbing the open stairs back to where Vicki Maler lay stretched out on her back, Palazzi found himself glancing across the room at the sleeping form of her lover. The man must be wearing a luminous watch on his wrist, its dial glowing close to his face, for there was a distinct patch of yellow light on the pillow where he lay face-down. A sort of golden luminescence.

Suddenly Palazzi's desire to be out of there swelled up strong in him. He foolishly allowed a stair tread to creak as he crept higher, which caused him to freeze again for a moment and hold his breath before he dared to continue. He was allowing himself to become spooked. But why? What was there to worry about?

He had removed light bulbs as he went, putting them all safely out of the way. Even if Garrison and his woman woke up and hit the switches the room would remain in darkness. And of what use bright lights to their eyes anyway? No, nothing to worry about here. Why, they didn't even have a telephone! The entire village could only have a dozen or so.

Palazzi stepped over the sleeping woman's form and seated himself on the marble sill of the open window. As he swung one leg over the sill onto the flat roof outside, she stirred. Her right knee bent, straightened; the sheet got hooked up on her foot, sliding down her perfect body. Her brown, beautiful breasts were exposed. Starlight gleamed on the round globes of flesh, increasing their desirability tenfold.

Palazzi's hands were free, and so was his personal demon. He slowly, carefully unzipped the front of his jump suit, took out his suddenly stiff penis, gripped it and stroked the taut skin to and fro; then released it and raised his hand over the girl's right breast. He readied his other hand over her mouth, and—

—lowered both hands simultaneously.

She came awake, felt the strange hands on her mouth, her breast. One hand clamping, the other squeezing, molding, pinching. Hot hands. Feverish. Not Garrison's.

"Richard!" she would have cried out, but couldn't.

It made no difference. Garrison "heard" her anyway.

Three of them heard, struggled to come awake, to take command. And in situations like this—for all that Garrison had been a soldier in his own right, with lightning reflexes—Willy Koenig, ex-Schutzstaffel specialist, had always been the fastest. And by far the deadliest!

Garrison's body rolled over onto its back and

sat up, its eyes flying open. Their light filled the gloom with golden lances of fire. Palazzi released Vicki, gurgled some inarticulate thing as he gazed across the room into the blazing eyes of hell.

"Go to sleep, Vicki," said the icy voice of the owner of those eyes. "Forget this—it isn't happening—it's all right. *Schlafen Sie.*" And she simply collapsed back onto her pillows.

Palazzi made to dive through the window but found himself picked up instead—snatched up like a toy and suspended in air, floating towards the center of the room. Now he, too, would have cried out, but couldn't. The zips on his jump suit flew open, his loot tumbling free.

The naked man seated upon the bed smiled—a nightmare smile humorless as that of some ghastly, luminescent zombie—and pointed with a zombie's stiff arm, hand and finger. "Go," he said.

Palazzi felt himself shot out of the window, rushed across the rooftops in a great hand, high over the tavernas where they catered to their late customers. He soared up into the night—mouth gaping, cheeks filling with air—eyes bugging, streaming tears as the rush of his motion stung them—his suit billowing and flapping like crazed black wings. Up and away across the great rock of the Acropolis, and the lights of Lindos glowing far below, and the lanterns of small fishing craft bobbing on the gentle swell of the slumbering Aegean.

And out across the sea sped Palazzi. A mile,

two, and a great jet plane thundering by over-head, its windows like rows of eyes. And—

—And Palazzi floating, stationary now, with only an icy wind blowing on him across the sky. Floating and spinning a mile high in the air, and the deep, deep sea below.

"No!" he screamed, hoping that someone, somewhere, somehow would hear him. "No, I didn't intend to harm her. Mercy! Have mercy!" But no one was listening. Certainly not the owner of the great invisible hand, which now, without warning, hurled him down . . .

Chapter
9

At 6:00 A.M. GARRISON—*ALL* GARRISON NOW, FOR the Koenig facet had retreated once more—drank his fifteenth cup of coffee, smoked his twentieth cigarette and shivered in the light of the new day. It was not cold but he shivered. He sat on the edge of his tumbled bed and gazed out of his window, listening to a frantic cock's crowing and the early morning rumpus of distant donkeys.

His thoughts were confused, in disarray. Lindos, Rhodes, the Aegean . . . what the hell was he doing here anyway? And last night—no, in the early hours of this morning—he had killed a man. No, he gritted his teeth, correcting himself again, Willy Koenig had killed a man. And he, Garrison, had been unable (unwilling?) to stop him or even try to stop him. And Schroeder had a hand in it, too: Thomas Schroeder, protecting not only Vicki (his one-time ward) and Garrison (his present host) but also himself.

Oh, yes, and that was the rub, as Garrison saw it. He, Garrison, wasn't allowed to live his own life because the others lived it for him. What happened to him must also happen to them, and so they must protect him. And the constant conflict (Garrison sighed, his shoulders slumping), the conflict was draining him.

He had to face up to it, he was being drained. Of physical strength, of his psychic energies, perhaps even of his sanity. And no use a stake against vampires such as these; no, for they dwelled within him. Sometimes he felt quite (he shivered again), quite mad. He had felt it just a few hours ago, and even knowing it was not madness but maddening frustration—the frustration which comes of having *no control*, which in itself might or might not be a definition of insanity—made it no less frightening.

He was not his own man. His body was not his alone. He shared his powers, too—and they were being used up. A leaky battery in a communal torch in an eternal night. And no way to recharge. Pretty soon the light would go out. The battery would spill its acids. The whole thing would melt into a rusty mass and become totally useless. And darkness would reign over all.

His mind clung to part of that last thought and examined it. No way to recharge.

And at the very back of his mind it seemed that he heard a tiny whispering voice say, *"Don't you remember, Richard? You stopped the Machine. You killed the beast . . ."* It was Schroeder's voice and he recognized it, but it could only be memory for his alter-facets were incapable of independent communication. He couldn't talk to them and they couldn't talk to him, or to each other. He *was* them, they *were* him. So where had he heard those words spoken? And what did they mean?

Garrison believed he might at least have the answer to the second half of the question, and he paled.

Psychomech!

Oh, yes—that was one beast he really had killed. Out of jealousy. So that no one could ever follow him into . . . into what? This misery?

Misery, yes—born of fear. His powers were failing and he knew it. Right now he felt utterly exhausted, drained (again that word), unable to face up to whatever it was he felt closing in on him. It wasn't simply lack of sleep, wasn't the knowledge that he had killed a man—that bastard had probably deserved it anyway—wasn't even the way Vicki sometimes looked at him now, with something less than her old, customary adoration.

It was simply that he felt—usurped?

Usurped, yes. The incident with those Greek youths, for instance. *His* anger, certainly, but Schroeder's and Koenig's action. And this morning's burglar: the same thing. And Garrison paying for it. *His* energy draining away. A battery leaking its vital spark, or having that spark leeched by parasitic thieves.

And no way to recharge . . .

But maybe there was a way.

He shivered again, stood up and crossed the room, glanced at and caused the water to boil in its kettle atop an unlighted gas ring. He climbed the open, wooden stairs. Behind him the jar of instant coffee poured two perfect measures into a pair of mugs; a carton of milk tilted itself, the kettle, too, until the mugs were filled. The level of sugar in its bowl went down by exactly one spoonful; a little whirlpool raced in Garrison's mug.

There had been a time he would have performed these small feats in front of Vicki, but no longer. She was asleep now, anyway, and so could not see them. But once—

Once, in the beginning, she would have been amazed, would have laughed delightedly. Later . . . then she became apprehensive. And now? Now such magic only served to frighten her.

He sat down beside her where she lay and touched her arm. Warm, alive. And yet once, not so very long ago . . .

He knew that she would remember nothing of the affair with the burglar. No, for he had told her to forget it, that it wasn't happening. Since then she had not stirred. Had not even changed her position. Her chest rose and fell, rose and fell. Garrison stared, looked closer, listened to her breathing, felt his own pulse quickening. Was there something wrong here? Some imperfection? Some . . . deterioration?

Her skin looked paler somehow, despite her tan, and her respiration seemed a trifle jerky. There were previously unnoticed lines at the corners of her eyes, her mouth. Not age lines, no. Not crow's-feet. More the marks of a subtly altered metabolism, of—

—*Of something he did not wish to contemplate!*

With fingers that shook slightly he eased the knotted handkerchief from her eyes, lifting their lids with the pressure of his thumbs. She slept on as he jerked back, horrified.

Beneath those now trembling eyelids, sightless orbs had seemed grotesquely huge and pallid in the frames of their scarlet sockets. The golden glow had been missing from Vicki's eyes!

Garrison's panic fuelled his powers. "See!" he commanded. "Be filled with light, life, warmth, energy. Take of my own energy . . ." And slowly—at first a faint pulse of yellow burning beneath her pale eyelids, then brightening to a glow—the gold returned. The lines faded out, smoothed into her skin. Her pulse and respiration steadied.

"Awaken!" And she came slowly awake, opened those great golden orbs of eyes and smiled at him.

And Garrison leaned his back against the window's frame and tried to control his trembling. "It's morning, Vicki," he managed to tell her at last. "I've made coffee."

Morning, yes, and Garrison had determined that this would be their last morning in Lindos. There were things he must do—and without delay.

While there was still time . . .

Joe Black had left small sums of money in the hands of various unsuspecting informers in Lindos, advance payment for that tip-off which was vital to his and brother Bert's planned hit. One of these informers was *not* the young, pretty, shorts-clad local representative of a small British tour operator who awakened him that morning bright and early, and being only half-awake when he answered her knock Black might easily have given something of his real interests away. He was not dull-minded, however, and quickly caught on to her own interest in Garrison's affairs.

"Yes," he mumblingly admitted, yawning and rubbing sleep from his eyes, his face peering from behind his door. "I am interested in the, er, Adonis Studios? In all three rooms, yes. Far superior to this place. But—" and he shrugged. "To my understanding the chap who has them will be there for another four or five days."

"Not at all, Mr, er, Schwartz?" she smiled. "He's moving out this morning—him and his lady. Flying back to London, I understand. I got the tip from Costas Mekos, one of the taxi drivers here. That was just before he set off to drive the Garrisons into Rhodes—about twenty minutes ago."

Now Black understood all. Costas Mekos *was* one of those into whose eager hands he'd placed a little cash. But—twenty minutes! Black's heart gave a lurch. "I see. And you being a Skymed Tour representative, and the Adonis Studios being Skymed accommodation, you—"

"I hate to see such good rooms go to waste, yes!" she sweetly answered. "You see, Mr. Garrison has paid for his rooms in advance, and the money is non-returnable, and so—"

"You can let me have the rooms at reduced rates?"

"Well, I—"

"Maybe a thirty percent discount?"

"Now I can't be absolutely specific off the top of my—"

"Of course not, I understand. Well, Miss, er—?"

"Just call me Linda. Skymed's Lindos Linda, you see?" She tilted her head and smiled sunnily.

"Of course. Well, Linda, I'd invite you in but behind this door I'm quite naked. Can I contact you later? You see, I'll have to get in touch with friends of mine in Rhodes. And I really can't make any spur of the moment promises. They may have got themselves fixed up by now."

"Oh, I see," she was a little disappointed. "Well, my office is in—"

"I know where it is," Black smiled, thinking: *go away, you silly bitch*! He decided to speed her departure. "Listen I know it's early yet, but I have a very nice bottle in here and I was just going to make myself a little breakfast. If you'd care to, er—?" and he opened the door a fraction wider. She got a glimpse of a muscular hairy thigh.

Black was not a pretty sight. Not any time, but worst of all unshaven and after a night's uneven sleep, with whiskey fumes still heavy on his breath. The trick worked, as he had known it would.

Lindos Linda backed off in the face of his leer,

her smile becoming falsely fixed, her friendly tour operator manner evaporating in a moment. "Thank you, but I've already breakfasted. The early bird, you know?"

"Ah, yes. Pity." He started to close the door.

"But—"

Jesus, what now?

"You're not German. I mean, you know, your name? And I've seen you in the village and I thought—"

"My wife is German," he lied. "I've spent a great many years there." He opened his door wider still. "Of course, my wife isn't with me right now, and—" But Lindos Linda was already smiling her farewell, backing away into the sun-splashed, cobbled village street . . .

Bert was the "suave" one. He had played his part with his usual efficiency, fixing up Garrison's two-man aircrew with booze and birds, worming his way into their confidence and along the way acquiring the affections of their leggy air hostess. It had been one long party ever since he arrived, and he hadn't needed to be too careful about protecting his identity. After all, they weren't going to be talking about him. It had been expensive, true, the masquerade; but the brothers could afford it on what Carlo Vicenti was paying. And anyway, Bert had always liked the good life.

He had played it that way, too: a lucky punter on holiday, looking for pleasant company to help him spend his winnings—but not too fast, for he wasn't quite used to being rich yet. The crew of Garrison's jet, at loose ends and not wishing to blow too much of their earnings on the high life, had proved an easy mark. After a day or two Bert had mentioned his interest in aircraft, they had fixed it to take him out to the airport and see their plane, he had been like a kid with a new toy. Like a malicious kid, who pulls the wheels off. Or in this case the guts, undercarriage and all the major flight-control cables.

The device had been small, deadly, something he could carry in his pocket. A limpet, armed it would cling to metal. It now clung behind a bulkhead in the plane's tiny hold. As yet it did not tick, wouldn't until Bert gave it the remote control signal. Which would be as the plane took off. Then—

Then the bomb would tick away the seconds to disaster. It would tick for one hour. And somewhere over the Aegean, midway between Greece and Turkey . . .

The sea was five, six hundred feet deep there; the plane and its contents—specifically its human contents—would probably never be found. Bodies would decompose, turn to sludge. The plane would rot, crumble away. The sea would roll overhead, as it had for half of time, and Carlo Vicenti would be very happy. And Joe and Bert Black would have earned their bread.

Bomber Bert Black rarely dreamed, and he never suffered from nightmares. He was a man without a conscience, which was just as well in his line of business. Lacking morals, his morale was abnormally high; unlike his brother he could wake up happy, at peace with the world. Even on a day when he would shatter that peace beyond restructuring—for some.

This morning he woke up at the *buzz* of his telephone and lifted the handset smoothly from its cradle before it could awaken the girl curled beside him. It was Joe on the other end, and the other's tense whisper told Bert all he needed to know:

"They're on their way. The word is they'll fly today."

"Sure," Bert answered, giving nothing away, taking no chances that the girl wasn't really asleep.

"You can do it?"

"Yeah, it's done—all but the *coup de grâce!*"

"Oh, yes? And you still in your hotel? Get your arse down to the airport!"

"Be cool," Bert grinned into the mouthpiece. He glanced at the girl and she snored obligingly. Fast asleep, and little wonder after the night they'd just had. "They won't leave without me being there. They can't!"

"What? Listen, what the hell are you—"

"Cool, *cool!*" Bert insisted. "I'll explain later. Just believe me it's all fixed, that's all. Hell—I'll be there to wave them goodbye!" He put the phone down, cutting off Joe's sputtering.

Then he turned over, carefully spilled the girl onto her back, gently parted her legs and kneeled between them. He was drawing up her knees when she awakened and blinked at him sleepily. "Bert? My God! Again?"

"Hey!" he told her. "It's a beautiful day. If we start it right it'll stay right." He eased himself into her. "Enjoy, Baby!"

And to himself: *cop it while you can, Sweetheart. The next guy who takes a bite at your sweet little pussy will have gills and fins and slimy, slimy scales!*

"Who were you waving at?" Garrison asked the stewardess when she came into the plane's tiny, luxurious lounge after the takeoff. "You were all at the hatch, laughing, waving."

"Oh," she smiled, "that was just a friend we met up with in Rhodes. Nice chap. More money than sense—but, you know, nice."

"Ah!" Vicki smiled. "Romance on a Greek island, eh?"

The girl wrinkled her nose. "Well, not exactly. He was pleasant enough, I suppose, but—oh, I shouldn't think I'll see him again. Anyway, there was something about him." She shrugged. "Good fun, yes, but a bit too calculating for my likes. Too cold by far."

She frowned for a moment, thoughtfully, then smiled. "It helped pass the time. Now then, Mr. Garrison, Mrs. Garrison, what can I get you to drink while you choose a meal for yourselves?"

Garrison and Vicki drank a little ice-cold lager, picked at cold meats and salad from the limited menu, finished with ice cream, coffee and liqueurs. While they ate they talked.

"You promised you'd tell me what it was all about," Vicki worriedly pressed him when they were alone, dropping the witty, happy attitude she had adopted for the benefit of the crew. "Why are we going home, Richard? Why now, halfway through our holiday?"

Garrison gazed out of his window for a moment, sipped lager, used his fork to toy with a piece of chicken breast. "Vicki, you remember our conversation the other night? Well, now I'm ready to face up to what's wrong. And I'm ready to start doing something about it—while there's still time."

"And is there something you can do about it?" she asked.

"With a bit of luck, yes. What went wrong was this: I destroyed Psychomech. Simple as that. But that's not an end to it. No, for I'll build the machine again. Or rather, I'll have it built. The man who modified Gareth Wyatt's original Psychomech now works for me. If I give him a helping hand—or mind—there should be no problem."

"No problem," she nodded and sighed. "But you felt it was sufficiently urgent that it couldn't wait." She sighed again. "I really did like Lindos a lot, but—"

"No buts about it, Vicki," he cut her short. "It *is* urgent. I thought you understood that from our conversation the other night. If I told you just how urgent I believe it is, then I'm sure it would frighten you—as it frightens me."

"It frightens me anyway," she answered. "The

137

thought of a mind-expanding machine—and you at its mercy!"

He chuckled, however mirthlessly. "Psycho-mech wasn't a monster," he told her. "Even if the men who built it were monsters, the machine was . . . just a machine. I *was* at its mercy, yes, but only because I placed myself in unscrupulous hands. Anyway, that backfired on the people who would have hurt me. Backfired badly!" Again his chuckle. "My multimind was the result, but that's all history now. Except . . . I have to do it again. For myself, yes—and for you."

She knew what he meant, could suddenly feel it in her bones. She fed on Garrison's power no less than the others, was kept alive by it, and his battery was leaking. She shuddered, cringing as her mind conjured once more the agony she had known in those tortured days before . . . before she had died.

Remembering, she clutched at Garrison and began to say something. Perhaps she had something to say, perhaps not; in any case it went unspoken. One hour had gone by since the plane had taken off in Rhodes. They were now out over the Aegean, heading for the Yugoslav–Bulgarian border.

Beneath their feet, down in the little jet's luggage hold, Bomber Bert Black's device stopped ticking. An electrical connection was made. The floor jumped as from the blow of some mighty hammer, and the plane gave a great shudder in answer to a strangely dull, booming explosion.

Debris flew past the windows as the small craft lurched and shook. Then—

Like a mortally wounded dragon the jet screamed her agony as her nose tilted and she commenced a tight spiral down the sky . . .

Chapter
10

CHARON GUBWA SAT IN HIS STUDY. ALTHOUGH THE
metal-walled room was a large one, with
two great desks and with steel shelves along three
of the high walls, still the place was cluttered. Its
chaotically untidy appearance was, to Gubwa, a
luxury. In his own eyes his life was very ordered,
so tightly ordered indeed that a measure of personal imperfection or imbalance was a necessity.
Books were piled everywhere in apparent disarray, and empty spaces gaped along all of the
shelves.

Those books which were in their places, however, displayed Gubwa's passion for so-called
"fringe" sciences, his consuming interest in that
paranormal of whose powers a perverse Nature,
aided and abetted by the equally perverse Science of man, had gifted Gubwa excessively. But
quite apart from these there were dozens of

works offering mute witness to their owner's other leanings. For alongside books on parapsychology (mainly volumes concerning telepathy but including levitation, prevision, telekinesis and a half-dozen others) there were numerous volumes dealing with politics and political doctrines, world religions and mythologies, war—its causes and effects—aftermath and survival, and a host of biographies of warlords, dictators, kings, emperors and tyrants. There were, too, a large number of books concerning themselves with man's inhumanity to his fellow man, and bulky treatises on the effects upon human beings of narcotics, carcinogens, other poisons, acids and lethal chemicals, and radiation.

A workbench displayed a fantastic array of half-assembled or disassembled instruments and gadgets, some of which—intended eventually for Gubwa's mind-lab—were or would be tools for the measuring of forces and stresses other than those of mass, space and time; and in and about the general clutter stood devices of hypnotic or brainwashing natures, ranging from revolving mirrors and faceted crystals through common stroboscopes to a small pulse-laser. The fourth wall was a melange of large framed photographs depicting sex in all its many phases and facets, from simple love through gross indecency to the lewdest forms of perversion, sadism and bestiality.

In short, the study was nothing less than the den or lair of a twentieth-century sorcerer; and its magics were not white but black.

Amongst all of this apparent disorder, the sole

item kept impeccably tidy was the tall filing cabinet in which Gubwa kept the records of his workforce. From this cabinet he had taken a file whose cover bore the name: Charles Edwin Jackson. The case was now closed, the file dead as its subject. Gubwa felt no sorrow, no regrets, no guilt. Such feelings were for fools. He riffled once more through its pages, scowled, tossed it into a wastebasket.

Waste, yes, as everything and everybody must waste in the end. Unless one were immortal, of course. Gubwa did not pursue that line of thought; it was one which already occupied enough of his time, and time was always a pressing matter.

More than twenty-four hours had gone by since he mind-probed Vicki Maler, and they had been busy ones. The Castle's internal security had been shown to have loopholes and Gubwa had needed to plug them. The rape of one of his mind-guards should not have been possible and that was worrying; it had showed a weakness in the systems Gubwa employed to make and keep his soldiers subservient.

All of them were addicts to a greater or lesser degree, slaves of the common and occasionally not so common drugs available to Gubwa through various markets. Not all of them had come to him that way, however. But . . . their complete dependence upon him was his most powerful ally. Dogs were loath to bite the hand that fed them.

Jackson, apparently, had been a dog of a different color! At least until Gubwa had looked a little closer at the man's records. Then a previously overlooked pattern had become immediately visible.

First of all, Jackson had been partially resistant to hypnosis. But *resistant*, not immune. There were men who could not be hypnotized (Gubwa had come across several in his time), but Jackson was not one of them. His resistance probably sprang from a constant battle of wills between himself and his parents during his teen years, which had made him not only highly argumentative but also very strong-willed and single-minded. There was that in his mind which resisted outside interference or "commands" contrary to his nature or natural desires. This was present in all men but had been more so in Jackson; an additional manifestation of which was his "closeness" of mind, the fact that Gubwa found some difficulty in reading his thoughts. Having for so long been obliged to hide his feelings and thoughts from his parents, Jackson had developed a real resistance to mind-probing.

Secondly, his metabolism had been erratic: the drug he used would take him in a variety of ways. Normally Gubwa could keep a fine control over the dosages his soldiers required—they could not be allowed to become inoperative through their addiction—but again in Jackson's case there had been complications. During the last twenty-four hours outside operatives had discovered at least one external supplier who had admitted catering to Jackson's needs. And how many others? Obviously Jackson had "moonlighted," supplementing Gubwa's drug allocation with privately contracted and often inferior supplies. This meant, quite simply, that he had made himself partly independent of Gubwa's control, had become a rogue in the organization.

Not only was he less likely to listen to Gubwa's hypnotic commands but he might well read or translate them to his own advantage. Especially considering his ghetto background and upbringing. For instance, Gubwa's orders that his soldiers would "do no deliberate wrong outside the Castle" but "live their lives normally," and so on. Jackson had never considered it "wrong" to take drugs; it had been a way of life in the circles he frequented. And his view of "normalcy" was hardly the common one. The ghetto is not a normal place, and it has its own "laws of the land." In this connection Jackson could no more be said to be contemporary with society's majority than Charon Gubwa himself.

And finally there had been the simple fact that Jackson was a rapist. This had not been proven and Gubwa had not seen fit to follow it up, but in 1979 the police had twice connected him with attacks upon women. In enlisting Jackson, Gubwa had merely noted this additional warp in the fabric of his psychology, this additional appetite to be fed; for it was one which, along with drug addiction, must in the end increase Jackson's dependence. Less fortunately, it had also increased his unpredictability. Where sex is free and freely given, the rapist's violent *psychological* need becomes starved!

And so a lesson learned and Charon Gubwa had no one to blame but himself. Indeed he might be seen as more to blame than Jackson. By the simple expedient of allowing his soldiers more knowledge of the purpose and nature of the mind-guards, he might well have avoided the entire incident. In this episode the need-to-know basis he usually employed had failed him; for the fact was that, in the mentally negative condition in which the mind-guards protected him, they were totally susceptible to even the slightest physical movement or exertion. Their condition could be compared to a dreamless, mental hibernation, when all their brains were capable of was the basic control of bodily life-support systems. And they must be allowed simply to sleep the condition off and the drug out of their systems. Just as creatures forced from hibernation will often die, so, too, Gubwa's mind-guards.

Fortunately there was in his harem a woman whose drug dependence fast approached critical. She was useless now except as a sex surrogate, for even her lovemaking was unreal. Well, her fate was decided: she would finish her service to Gubwa as a mind-guard, and at the last . . . the pits beneath Gubwa's Castle were deep and uncaring. For full fifteen years those pits had offered mute, unprotesting service and would continue to do so as long as they were needed . . .

The Castle's master stirred himself from his musing. Time was wasting and that irritated him. More than twenty-four hours on this one investigation, and important things waiting to be done which could wait no longer. Gubwa had set pots boiling all over the world; unless he stirred them occasionally his special brew might lose something of its flavor.

He left his study, passed through the mind-lab, out into the Castle's central corridor junction and made for the Command Center in his private quarters. The entire route was no more than thirty strides from start to end, but as he went Gubwa planned ahead, singling out those garden minds he must once more infiltrate, and the seeds he must sow in them.

Gadaffi, for example. A little pressure there and Gubwa could turn Libya's eyes south to Nigeria, Chad and the Sudan. Not too much pressure, however, for here there was a fine balance to be maintained. The mind was volatile enough without external influences; too sharp a probe might well overbalance the whole thing. Better to keep things on the brink; just keep the pot boiling.

Then there were the generals Chan Tan Masung and Li-pan Dang on the Sino–Soviet border. An incident or two there wouldn't go amiss. And it was time, too, that France offered Argentina the new Excism III air-to-sea missile, with its infallible anti-jamming system. That would give the Falklands and the British government something to think about; for of course Gubwa would see to it that news of the sale was "leaked" worldwide.

Nor must he forget the PLO: since Israel's crippling blow against them almost a year ago, they had been far too quiet. A gentle squeeze or two—an idea implanted—in the minds of the at present low-lying leaders of the organization might just succeed in elevating young Ali Zufta into prominence and power overnight! But *there* was a mind to be watched! Gubwa must be careful not to create that which might grow beyond the measure of his control. But at the same time it would be remiss of him to forego a little mental agitation in certain Israeli power-circles . . .

He reached the Command Center and issued instructions that he was not to be disturbed, then took his computer remote and seated himself before the great globe.

Now where to start?

Gubwa smiled, keyed GLOBE and WASHINGTON DC on the remote. And as the globe spun and steadied he fixed his eyes and thoughts firmly on the North American capital. In his mind's eye he formed a picture of the White House, remote-viewing its inner chambers. The mind he sought was in residence, was . . . taking a nap! Preparatory to a busy evening ahead. That was all to the good.

Gubwa probed . . .

. . . *Dreams of grain, wheat . . . endless conveyor belts carrying countless bags of it . . . buckets and bushels and tons of it . . . golden grain to fill the rambling bellies of the USSR . . .*

. . . *Peace and goodwill . . . and ice splintering and melting from a glass containing cold-war cocktail . . .*

. . . *Leaders of nations smiling, shaking hands*

across a table, embracing . . . their flags side by side on a wall behind them . . .

. . . Money for the farmers, the poor folk . . . work for all . . . peace . . . prosperity . . . votes!

NO! Gubwa insinuated his own thoughts. WOULD YOU FEED THE DEVIOUS BASTARDS AND MAKE THEM STRONG ENOUGH TO GO TO WAR WITH YOU? WOULD YOU REALLY BOW TO THE DIRT-GRUBBERS, PANDER TO THE WORK-SHY FOR THE SAKE OF A FEW VOTES? AND IN ANY CASE, WHO IN HIS RIGHT MIND WOULD VOTE FOR A MAN WEAK AS THAT?

. . . Chaos! . . . A dream growing into nightmare . . . pictures chasing themselves in endless procession . . . grain wasting . . . empty Russian ships turned back . . . thin Russian faces . . . hungry children . . . grain again, heaped in the docks, rotting, rat-infested . . . chaos and horror!

NO!—Gubwa pictured a vast iron hand smashing down, destroying the idle conveyor belts, scattering mountains of foul grain left and right. He pictured Russian factories, workers building missiles; pictured them weakening as they exhausted their supplies of food. Missiles rusting in their silos. Armies of tanks grinding to a halt on the plains of Europe, their skeleton crews leaving them and advancing, arms outstretched, begging for food. A HUNGRY ENEMY IS A WEAK ONE!

. . . A weak enemy . . . Cossacks falling from their mounts . . . Mongol hordes throwing down their weapons, their arms too weak to carry them . . .

STARVE THE BASTARDS!

And again: STARVE THEM!

Yet again: STARVE THEM!

. . . A world map, Russia and its satellites in relief, packed with a sea of gaunt, hollow-eyed, starving faces . . .

AND ONLY FEED THEM IN YOUR OWN GOOD TIME—WHEN THEY COME TO YOU ON THEIR KNEES!

. . . The All-Giver handing out food to a silently bowed multitude . . . the USSR, the entire world on its knees, praising the great, the mighty, the almighty America, A-m-e-r-i-c-a! . . .

. . . The Star-Spangled Banner . . . the White House. . . .

. . . Retreating now in the mind's eye of Charon Gubwa. He opened his eyes, sighed, smiled.

Good! Very good!

Now then, in Moscow the time would be, oh, early morning. Very well, now would be as good a time as any to see what *he* was up to. Gubwa keyed GLOBE, MOSCOW into the remote, his mind seeking the Kremlin, his eyes narrowing as the suspended sphere reacted to meet his requirement . . .

The plane spiralled down out of the sky like a lazily falling autumn leaf, or a great silver moth singed by the candle sun. Ten seconds had passed since the explosion. Inside, the floor tilted at forty-five degrees and G-force held Garrison and Vicki together, crushed to each other and to the curving wall beside Garrison's seat and window. The engines had stopped, their howl replaced by the whispering *hiss* of sliced air. Cabin pressure had somehow been maintained but the main controls were gone. The situation was hopeless; the spiral was tightening as the angle of descent increased.

Forward, the door to the cockpit slammed back on its hinges and a moment later the hostess staggered through billowing curtains, literally dragging herself or climbing up the length of the small lounge. Blood poured from her nose. Her eyes were wide, bright in a face filled with fear. "Going down!" she needlessly gasped.

Garrison half-pushed, half-levered Vicki back into her own seat, said: "How bad is it?"

Before she could answer he had read her mind. Very bad. She was totally panicked, a mind full of chaos and thoughts of imminent death. And yet her training had brought her back here, an automaton working only to the book. "Your seat belts," she gasped, and: "—life jackets . . ."

Garrison shot his probe past her into the cockpit. The co-pilot's mind was blank, unconscious. He must have banged his head. The pilot was fighting with the controls, knowing he must fail but still desperately trying to command some sort of response from the crippled aircraft. A frightened man who knew he was going to die. But brave.

Garrison probed deeper:

Abombabloodybombabloodybomb, over and over again. And, *Nohopenohopenohopenohopenohope!* And, *Bombnohopebombnohopebombnohope!* And, *Shitshitshitshitshitshitshitshitshit!*

Garrison spoke in the pilot's mind: THERE IS HOPE, and was at once denied:

150

Nononononononononono!

HAVE FAITH!

Faith? It was as if the man had suddenly realized it was not his own voice he heard in his head but that of some other. Even above his fear and horror Garrison could now sense awe in him. The man was Catholic, deeply religious, a believer.

FAITH! he repeated. FLY HER.

Can'tcan'tcan'tcan'tcan't! She'scrippledcrippled crippledcrippledcrippled!

Garrison knew he could save himself. And he could probably save Vicki. Teleportation. He could get them out of the plane, set them down on terra firma somewhere, anywhere. But—

—What about these people?

And just how much power could he muster? What if he was wrong? And anyway—damn it to *hell!*—he couldn't just leave them to die. But if they were to be saved he needed the pilot's help, needed his faith.

IT IS NOT YOUR TIME, MY SON, he told him.

MyGodGodGodGodGod! The pilot's hands worked at the controls. Garrison lifted with his mind. Levitation. He squeezed his eyes tightly shut, gripped the plane, levelled out its plunge.

My God! Adrenalin ebbed a little in the pilot's system. His hands shook—but the plane seemed to be answering the controls! *My great heavenly merciful . . . God—!*

CORRECT YOUR COURSE, said Garrison.

Yes, oh yes! Yes, yes, oh yes!

Garrison kept his eyes closed, his mind tightly in control, and spoke to the girl. "We seem to

151

have levelled out. The pilot will need you. If only to make coffee."

She blinked at him, gave him a silly grin, giggled hysterically, then spat, "Coffee!" Her sudden laughter was a cackle. "Fucking *coffee!*" she laughed. And again: "Holy fucking mother of . . . coffee!" Terror had almost robbed her of her senses. Tears were in her eyes, her face a mad white mask stained with blood from her still dripping nose.

"Coffee, yes," said Vicki, standing up and slapping the girl's face, almost knocking her from her feet.

The blow stung some sense back into her. She held her face as hot tears gushed, more freely now, before turning and stumbling back towards the cockpit.

Vicki fastened Garrison's seat belt, half-collapsed into her seat and fastened her own. She knew Garrison was doing this—saving all their lives—knew it and dared do nothing which might interfere.

LIFT HER UP, Garrison told the pilot. TAKE HER UP TO HER NORMAL ALTITUDE.

No power! No engines! Impossible! the pilot was crying, tears streaming down his face. He was talking to God!

FAITH!

The plane began to climb. Powerless, she flew higher, her wings slicing the wind.

"Vicki," Garrison gasped from between clenched teeth. "I need your help."

"Richard, what can—?"

"No, don't touch me!" he shrank back as she

152

leaned across. "Just . . . *lift!* Will the plane to fly, to keep on flying. Repeat over and over to yourself these words: we'll make it, we'll make it, we'll make it. Repeat them and believe them."

Vicki took a deep breath, sat back and closed her eyes. She clenched her fists. *We'll make it, we'll make it, we'll make it . . .*

The co-pilot was coming out of it. Garrison probed him. WAKE UP. WE NEED YOUR HELP. WE'RE GOING TO MAKE IT. WE'RE GOING TO MAKE IT!

Garrison cut the probe and groaned. He could feel his mind beginning to buckle. It wasn't strong enough. He needed help. Much more help. He felt himself beginning to slip, to slide, to fall.

It was as if he fell into a great hole in the earth, a chasm. But even as he rushed down into blackness, others were released to finish what he had started. His mind split. The Garrison facet receded, but the other facets surfaced, were free!

Garrison's body slumped in its seat, his face pale as death, his hands twitching. The body was useless now, except as a shell, a house for three minds. Two of these were now free to fly the plane, but Garrison himself—

—He fought a different battle, flew a different machine. The machine. Psychomech. Except Psychomech wasn't flying but plunging to destruction!

"Liar!" Garrison's yell drowned out Suzy's

howling. *"Liar, Schroeder, liar!"* But Schroeder was gone and still the Machine plunged.

Garrison hung on for dear life—or death?—and bared his teeth in the rush of frigid air from the depths below; and behind him the bitch clung to his back, her fear no less than his own. And suddenly, from nowhere—like a cold cloak thrown upon him by some unseen hand—there was a chilly calmness, a clearness of mind, a feeling which went beyond fear. A desire to know whose design this was, whose hand had brought him to this end.

Who was it down there, down in the depths and the darkness, whose magnet mind drew him like a meteorite falling from the night sky? Oh, yes, for someone had engineered this, be sure of it! This was the work of some dire enemy—perhaps one of those enemies spied in the pit of the wizards! But which one? Garrison must find out. His magic was weak now, true, but not so weak he didn't feel the urge to fight back. He must at least try to fight back.

Garrison sent his mind winging back, back to his dream within a dream. He sat once more in the circle of wizards, and he gazed once more upon them where they cast their strange runes and made their dark magics. And one he saw whose face he knew at once: a dark face and greedy, belonging to a swarthy wizard whose immaculate attire could not conceal the evil that lurked within.

He shuffled cards and occasionally spun a small roulette wheel which he held between his crossed legs, this one, and his eyes smouldered *with hatred where they stared unblinkingly at the tiny Garrison-figure in the crystal ball.*

And sure enough the Garrison in the shew-stone rode a tiny Psychomech, and man and Machine and dog all plunging to their doom in a lightless chasm. And now Garrison knew that this was the one!

Still falling and knowing the fall soon must end, Garrison quit his useless, ineffective levitating and drew his powers in. He wrapped them about himself as a man wraps a robe—or coils a whip! He reached out his mind into another world, another place—the pit of the wizards—and hurled his energies in one final blast full in the face of the wizard with the cards and the wheel . . .

It was business as usual for Carlo Vicenti, and as usual his business was dirty. A thoroughly dirty game. His Knightsbridge penthouse flat was the venue; two of his boys' were bit-part players; the star performer was one of Vicenti's girls, caught once too often taking too much of the ante. She had a lesson to learn, as all of them did at least once in their short working lives, and Vicenti was just the one to teach her.

Now she was held down in a straight-backed dining chair, Fatso Facello on one side and Toni Murelli on the other. They had torn her dress down the front and jerked up her brassiere, so that her normally proud breasts were forced down a little beneath the black material of the bra and made to bulge. Vicenti considered all women cows to be milked dry; and now, the way this little tramp's udders flopped there—swollen and bruised by the rough handling of his thugs, who'd taken turns with her on the thick pile carpet for a warmup—they only served to affirm his conviction.

"Mary," said Vicenti almost genially, waving his thin cigar in the air in an expansive gesture as he drew up a second chair in front of her and hung his arms lazily over its back, "you have given me problems. Things to think about. Now this I don't like. Smooth operations I like. Girls doing as they're told I like. Whores making money and taking their cut, I like. But taking my cut, too—or not even telling me there's a cut to take—this I *really* do not like!" His voice had hardened. "Not one little bit do I like it . . ." He reached out, caught up her bra in one tight fist and wrenched it from her. Its elastic had left a horizontal groove in the flesh of her breasts two inches above her small nipples, just over the rim of her large, prominent areolas.

Scared to death, the girl panted. She was blonde, young—no more than twenty, twenty-one years old—and the perspiration of panic and terror gleamed on her face. She would normally be pretty, but now her eyes were bright darting pinpoints in the bloodless face of a trapped animal. Vicenti thought: why is it that when they're scared they always look so ugly?

Finally she gabbled out: "They were just a few spare tricks, Mr. Vicenti, honest! And in my own time . . ."

He gave a short, harshly barking laugh, which was echoed by amused grunts from the thugs holding her down. "Your own time? Hey—your time's my time, little woman. Didn't anyone ever tell you anything? And my time you've been wasting."

"But I didn't—"

"But you *did!*" He leaned forward, tilting his chair. "Now listen and I'll tell you how it's going to be. You've maybe been working too hard and got kind of confused, forgot your loyalties. You know? So . . . see, I'm a nice guy really. What I'll do is this: I'll give you a couple of weeks off. A holiday. No work. Of course that also means no money, but you'll get by on what you got stashed. And just to make sure you don't work—" he drew deeply on his cigar, blew the white crust of ash from its glowing tip, reached it towards her breasts.

"No, Mr. Vicenti, no! Please don't mark me! Please!" She cowered down, then tried to surge upright. Facello and Murelli grunted as they tightened their grip, holding her rigidly immobile.

"See," Vicenti said again, almost conversationally, "there's not too many guys will suck on scabby tits. You know, they get to wondering how they got that way. They think, you know, maybe she has a bad case, eh?" He reached out his free hand, pinched her left nipple until it stuck out between his thumb and forefinger, brought the hot tip of the cigar closer.

What happened then was too fast and too fantastic for Vicenti, Facello or Murelli to follow. The girl, half-fainting, her eyes shut in a face death-white and quaking, didn't even see it.

Vicenti seemed suddenly to squash down into

himself, as if someone had placed a massive unseen weight upon his shoulders. He crashed through the debris of his splintering chair and slammed against the floor. He didn't cry out, had no air left in him for that; and even as his soldiers let go the girl and went to help him he was lifted up away from them and hurled against the wall. Fortunately for him the wall was of softboard on thin timbers, more a fancy partition than a true wall, with tiny shelves for expensive knick-knacks and odds-and-ends. Fortunately because it gave beneath his weight caving in on him as he went through it. Then—

—For a moment it was as if a howling wind filled the room. Curtains flapped angrily and magazines were scattered in the rush of frenzied air; pictures rocked crazily where they hung on the walls; doors and windows slammed and small ornaments fell from shelves. In all it lasted no longer than three or four seconds. Then the winds were gone, and in their place . . . silence!

Vicenti lay groaning, barely conscious, half-in, half-out of the wall's debris. His soldiers crept towards him, eyes wide, mouths agape, unable to take it in.

The girl, seeing her chances, bunched up the tatters of her dress in front of her chest and fled the room. Facello and Murelli may have heard her go but they made no move to stop her.

"Boss—?" Murelli croaked, shocked almost dumb where he kneeled beside his hoodlum master.

"Get me . . . *uh!* . . . a doctor," Vicenti told him. "And . . . later . . . you can pick up those

. . . *uh*! . . . sons of bitches, the Black brothers. Jesus, I want to see . . . *uh*! . . . those bastards! They were supposed to . . . *uh*! . . . kill the guy, not him kill me!"

"Guy?" Murelli turned bewildered eyes upon the gaping Facello and shrugged questioningly. Obviously Vicenti had banged his head. He wasn't making much sense. "What guy, Boss?"

Vicenti coughed and tried to lie still. He didn't know which part of him hurt the most. "What guy?" he managed to reply. "You have to be kidding! Are you . . . *uh*! . . . blind, you two? Didn't you even . . . *uh*! . . . see him?"

"Who, Boss, who?" Facello kneeled beside Murelli and stuck his fat, scarred pig's face close. "Who do you mean, eh?"

"*Uh*! . . . Garrison, that's who! You two . . . *uh*! . . . you didn't even *see* him? Idiots! I don't know . . . *uh*! . . . how he got in here or what he . . . *uh*! . . . hit me with. But—oh, God! Get me a fucking doctor, will you?—but it was . . . *uh*! . . . him OK. Yeah."

And with that he lay back his head and let the pain roll over him, bearing him swiftly away upon a dark red cloud of unconsciousness . . .

Garrison hurled his bolt of ESP-energy—and in his mind's eye he saw the wizard struck and hurled back from the satanic circle. But—no time to stay and savor the event. No time to wait and see if this wizard lived or died. Time merely for a final glance at the shewstone before returning his mind to the plunging Machine. One glance . . . but sufficient to tell him all he needed to know.

For in the shewstone the toy Machine's monstrous descent was halted and a tiny, triumphant Garrison stood upon its back, howling his victory, shaking his fists and beating his breast!

Garrison thrust the vision away, returned his mind to the Here, the Now, the Chasm and the Plunge. And . . .

. . . The wind no longer howled past his head, Psychomech no longer plunged, Suzy no longer yelped her terror but licked his ear and whined worriedly. The Machine stood still upon the air, held there by Garrison's power returned. And if he had stepped down from the Machine, then he could have stood upon the chasm's boulder-strewn floor.

That close!

He did not step down but stood up, stood tall upon the Machine's broad back and howled his victory and shook his fist—behaving even as the tiny Garrison in the crystal had behaved—and Suzy's sardonic baying gave strength to his own, until the chasm rang to the echoes of their laughter.

Then, upward to the narrow crack of star-scattered sky which was the great rift's mouth, Garrison rode the Machine. Upward and outward, and away upon his quest . . .

Chapter

11

THE MEETING WAS OF TEN MEN; IF NOT THE MOST IMportant or influential men in the British Isles, certainly their representatives. It had been convened secretly, through government channels, and its Chairman was the head of an obscure branch of the Secret Service. Obscure in the sense that it dealt with "obscurities," current jargon for tasks which were too intricate, problematic, sensitive or bloody for the talents and tastes of its contemporaries.

The Chairman was an extremely tall, slim man whose high-domed head and shifty, piercing blue eyes spoke of a foxy intelligence. His hands were very long, delicate and fragile-looking, as were his features, but there was nothing fragile about his mind. That was a steel trap.

Of the others gathered about the long, polished table: with the sole exception of a small and wiry yellow man, they were white, in the main British or of European extraction. Their fields were Finance (mainly banking), Mineral Rights and Mining (oil, gold and diamonds, etc.), Transport (shipping and airlines), Telecommunications (including computers), Weapons (the manufacture, sale and control of such), and Espionage (on a more general or at least more easily recognizable level than that of The Chairman, namely MI6.) There was also an Official Observer, governmental of course, and finally a Man from the Inland Reserve.

MI6 had brought someone along for the ride, his aide, apparently: a silent, gray-eyed, stony-calm wedge of a man whose movements, despite their almost robotic precision, were remarkably adroit, hinting at great speed, strength and coordination. He sat back a little from the table, unobtrusively reading from (or writing in) a file which lay open in his lap.

Some of those about the table knew each other, however vaguely, or knew of each other, but in the main they were strangers and in other circumstances might be more than a little cagey. Though their interest was a common one, still they made strange bedfellows.

The object of the meeting was that which formed this common bond amongst them, making friends or conspirators—for the moment, at least—of otherwise potential antagonists. The venue was The Chairman's country house not far from Sutton, Surrey, and the meeting was set to commence at 2 P.M. on an early June day. No one had been late.

"Gentlemen," The Chairman rose to his feet when all were settled down, "thank you for being here and for your punctuality. I'll try not to waste your time but get straight to the point. When this, er, get-together was planned some months ago it was not projected as an extraordinary meeting but more an overview from which to glean essential facts upon which to act—" he shrugged, "—in whichever ways were considered necessary. In short, while a problem was foreseen, it was not yet known quite what we were dealing with. And . . . we're still not sure." He paused, looked around the table at each face individually, and finally continued in his dry, well-modulated voice:

"Since then continued investigation has lent the matter a deal more urgency, so that we must now consider the subject extraordinary as stated, but with a definite emphasis on *extra*! All of you, with the exception of—" he almost said "our Oriental friend," but at the last second checked himself, merely including his head in the Chinaman's direction and receiving a similar acknowledgement, "—who has his own sources, were furnished with brief details from which to prepare your own points of information. The findings of your preliminary or subsequent investigations are what now bring us together to discuss—again as an overview, but with more positive action in mind—the very serious nature of the, er, possible disruption?" Again he paused.

While his opening address had been couched in terms which must surely mystify any uninformed observer, the circle of faces meeting his own showed no sign of misunderstanding or misinterpretation. Each and every one of them knew what he was talking about.

"To be more specific," he eventually went on, "the problem quite simply is a man. A very strange, immensely talented, highly enigmatic and incredibly rich man. His name, as you are all aware, is Richard Garrison." The assembled personages stirred. Someone cleared his throat. Another shuffled his feet.

"Yes," The Chairman nodded, "you all know his name well enough. Individually, But perhaps as a group you are not aware of the interactions of his . . . influence? His influence, that is, in so many—and such diverse—spheres. Perhaps the Bank of England would like to start us off?"

As The Chairman sat down, B of E (or Finance), a stocky, middle-aged man of medium height whose small-lensed spectacles and jutting jaw gave him a sort of aggressively fishy, pike-like look, stood up. "Nine years ago, *ahem!*" he began, "Mr. Garrison was a customer of ours. A fairly important, respected customer—*ahem!* That is to say we held—er, you understand I am not at liberty to disclose actual figures—some *ahem*, millions of pounds of his money in cash, disposable assets and various investments. A lot of money for one man, yes, but a mere drop in the overall financial ocean. Recently, however . . . well, things have changed somewhat. In fact they have changed a great deal." He paused to take out a handkerchief and wipe his suddenly perspiring brow.

"To illustrate my point I might say that if Mr. Garrison, *ahem*, were to withdraw or transfer his cash—his *cash* alone, you understand—then there could be problems. The 'drop in the ocean,' you see, has become a bucketful, indeed a lake! Oh, we could cover it, of course, but even the B of E might have to call on certain reserves . . ." He paused again to let that sink in, though no one at the table seemed in the least surprised.

"A little over a month ago," B of E continued, "acting on rather special instructions, I contacted friends in Switzerland to confirm their backing in the event of just such a massive withdrawal or conversion. This had become necessary when, in the space of just a few weeks, Mr. Garrison had added, *ahem*, considerably to his account. Various deposits totalled half as much again as his original holdings.

"Well, as a result of consultations in Zurich, it came to my knowledge—and of course this is in the strictest confidence—that Garrison's accounts abroad, *ahem*, make his British holdings seem a pittance by comparison!" The sweat was heavy on his brow now and he had stopped wiping it. "In fact, gentlemen, he is capable of moving millions about like you and I might move pieces in a game of chess, but far more devastatingly—*ahem*! And he never loses a piece!

"Before we sat down at this table I took the opportunity to speak to an acquaintance of mine whose interests also are financial. Perhaps he would care to enlarge upon what I have said?" He carefully sat down, his eyes steady upon those of a red-haired, very fat and florid man seated opposite.

As Financial Friend heaved wheezingly to his feet the general consensus of opinion taken from those seated about the table would have been that if overeating didn't get him, pressure of work would. And at least half of those present would not have minded that at all. Financial Friend was from the Inland Revenue, and he was not in the right job. His shirt and jacket were far too tight, and when he spoke his voice was far too highly pitched:

"Gentlemen," he wheezed puffily, "Mr. Garrison pays his taxes—some of them, anyway. He pays an awful lot. He *would* pay a great deal more except that he has the very best accountants in the land, possibly in the world, working for him. That is no exaggeration: I suspect that he pays them more than he pays us! What he does pay us is . . ." he shook his head and blinked his eyes rapidly in an expression of astonishment, "is an awesome figure! I believe that someone once said of The Beatles, that if we had another ten equally successful groups, then we could abolish income tax for the masses. That was an exaggeration, of course, but if said of our Mr. Garrison it would be much more literally true! Awesome, yes, and yet—as has already been said in connection with him— a mere drop in the ocean. In Garrison's ocean, that is! And getting hold of even that drop might well be likened to squeezing blood from a stone . . .

"I only wish there was a way—and you may

believe me when I say we are working at it—of getting hold of some of the taxes we're sure he has avoided paying. That's all . . ." He continued to wheeze for a few moments more, then collapsed flabbily into his seat.

The Chairman at once rose and took up the thread, redirecting the meeting's course:

"Of course, gentlemen, we must be careful not to allow ourselves to dwell too deeply on Mr. Garrison's considerable—or should we say incredible—wealth. Nor upon his attachment to it, which is only natural. Some might even say laudable. How he *got* it might be much more illuminating, for quite frankly his roots were only very austere. In fact only a little over ten years ago he was a Corporal serving in the Royal Military Police. And he might still be a member of that estimable Corps if a terrorist bomb had not blinded him in Belfast. After that . . ." and he went quickly on to vaguely outline something of Garrison's relationship with Thomas Schroeder, and of the benefits he had acquired upon the German industrialist's death. In all he was on his feet for some twelve minutes, after which he was glad to sit down again and hand over to MI6.

Intelligence was not at all typical, in no way a stereotype. Small, grubby, with badly bitten fingernails and unevenly cropped sandy hair, he more readily portrayed a sleepless, bankrupt greengrocer. Only when he spoke did it become apparent that his appearance was a front. His voice was clear and cutting, his sentences short and void of the usual security or police jargon. He gave the impression, too, that he would have been delighted to avoid the use of the word "alleged," but that in Garrison's case such was quite impossible.

"Gents, the implication of this meeting is that Garrison's a crook. By crook I mean a criminal, local or international or both. Well, if he is then he's the cleverest of them all. Put it this way: he's off and running and already overtaken the hare! He's so far ahead we don't have a hope in hell of catching him. Not yet. But . . . if he *is* a crook then he'll make a mistake. They all do sooner or later.

"Okay, let's assume he is. First of all I'll tell you what he's *not* into—simply because we don't yet know what he *is* into! He's not into gambling, even though he owns a big slice of a London casino. That's not to say he doesn't gamble; he does, and phenomenally well. But there's no legislation against a man's good luck. He doesn't organize gambling, that's all. He's not into drugs; he doesn't use them or push them. He's not into sex—vice, that is. Oh, he occasionally fools around with a couple of high-class ladies, and he has a regular ride in the city—that is to say a mistress, a kept woman—but his heart would seem to belong to the woman he lives with, one Vicki Maler, an alleged German national. Actually, we don't quite know *what* to make of her. Her case is as weird as his, maybe weirder, but I'll explain that in a moment . . .

"Right, so we can strike narcotics, prostitution and gambling. He is not into the protection rackets, not into smuggling or gunrunning or fraud. Not that we can discover, anyway. He has no big deals going with any known crime syndicate, here or abroad. Which means we can also strike the Mafia, extortion, etc." He paused and sighed.

"Garrison would appear, therefore, to be on the up and up, honest as the day is long. Well, maybe not *too* honest. Inland Revenue doesn't like him because he dodges," he shrugged. "But if that's a crime we're a nation of criminals! So what are we left with?

"He doesn't mug old ladies, doesn't even spit on the pavement. A thief? A terrorist? That isn't even in his nature! He's an ex-cop, albeit a military cop. So, to echo our Chairman's question, where did he get his money?

"You'd think we'd have trouble finding out, eh? Well, we had a little trouble, but not a lot. In fact as soon as we stopped hunting haggis and began to accept the facts at face value it was easy. *Everything he has is legitimate!* Everything!" MI6 glanced out of the corner of his eye at Inland Revenue. "With the possible exception of what he is alleged to owe certain parties in certain quarters . . .

"So why has it taken us so long to discover he's legitimate?" Again he shrugged. "Easy. How can any guy with that kind of money *be* legitimate? Is it possible?

"Well, it would certainly appear to be—but not without a few mildly disturbing discrepancies, ambiguities and anomalies. Let me explain:

"I said Garrison isn't a racketeer or terrorist. That seems to be true enough—but there do appear to be tenuous links. As you already know he was blinded by a terrorist bomb. IRA, Belfast 1972. Now let me make a point here and say he *is officially blind*. I've seen the records. Army records, medical records, the lot. Permanently blind." He stood nodding his head for a moment, knuckles on the table. "Blind, yes . . . but I'll come back to that.

"Two years ago the IRA were after him again. At least that's the way it looks. A London-based Irishman with old IRA connections tried to kill him. Something went wrong. The Paddy blew himself to bits instead. That sort of thing happens. But leave it for the moment.

"Then there's a much more sinister sort of organization called Nazism. Thomas Schroeder was an ex-SS Colonel. That's not strange—a great many of their top ranks were set free and lots of them still occupy positions of power. Contrary to popular belief, they weren't all villains. Schroeder, so far as we know, wasn't a villain. Or he was, but not in the usual poisonous, Jew-killing sort of way. Anyway, he wasn't taking any chances. He never was brought to trial. Him and a young SS-Scharführer called Wilhem Klinke—later Willy Koenig—knocked over a truckload of SS bullion and disappeared with it, probably into Switzerland but we don't know that for sure. We don't know that they stole the gold, but it seems a fair bet. That was towards the end, February 1945.

"When Schroeder died some ten years ago Koenig went to work for Garrison. For some reason known only to himself, the old Colonel not only made sure his money was transferred to Garrison but also his main man. So, a link, however tenuous, with Nazism.

"And another link is a guy called Gareth Wyatt. Wyatt was a doctor, a psychiatrist whom many supposed to be a quack. Certain parties tried to tie him in with a British escape route for the type of Nazis who *were* villains.

"Well, when the IRA had their second bash at Garrison, they also had a go at Wyatt. We don't know why, except that Garrison had been undergoing treatment at Wyatt's place. The psychiatrist had a house in Sussex. I say he *had* a house, because when the IRA or whoever were finished there was no more house. They took it out. They also took out Wyatt and Garrison's wife. That is to say, the two died in the explosion—if it was an explosion . . ." He paused and frowned.

"Now this is a funny thing. Funny peculiar, not ha-ha. Wyatt's house was big and old, your old country home sort of place in its own grounds, much like this one. Just what happened there—what *really* happened—will never be known. But the house isn't there anymore. Not a brick. The grass grows green over the place where it stood. Underneath—" he shrugged, "the foundations are fused like blast furnace slag!

"Anyway, about the same time we also have the disappearance of Willy Koenig. Not dead, no, simply . . . let's say 'retired.' Where to, who knows? But definitely not dead. Koenig is a very rich man in his own right, as well you might expect if you remember the SS gold, and he still makes good use of his money. A lot of it is tied up with Garrison's. But 'disappeared' is certainly the right word because no one seems to know where he is. He simply isn't seen anymore . . .

"Let's go back to Garrison's blindness. To put the record straight, and no matter what the old medical records say, Garrison is *not* blind! He hasn't been for at least two years, since about the same time as his wife and Wyatt got hit. One theory in my branch is that his blindness was psychosomatic, and that Wyatt was treating him and was successful. That might also explain the link between them. Anyway he *was* blind, isn't now, but continues to wear a pair of blind-man specs. So does the new woman in his life, this Vicki Maler.

"Now for a long time, apparently, Garrison has had dealings with a German firm of oculists—or not exactly oculists but specialists in mechanical aids to sight. This firm supplied him with a lot of expensive equipment when he really was blind. Their latest job for him is the manufacture of several sets of contact lenses, for both him and Vicki Maler. But these are to be very special lenses. Contact lenses to let light in but not out! Like one-way windows. He wants to be able to see things without his eyes being seen. Okay, but surely ordinary contact lenses would suffice? Or again, maybe it's a special condition of his eyes." He paused, stood for a moment longer, said: "A break, I think, gents. You'll excuse me but I'd like a cigarette; also I'd like to sit a while. Would you mind if I carry on seated and smoking?"

No one minded. All of them were fascinated. MI6 sat, produced cigarettes, lit one and relaxed a little in his chair before continuing. "Okay, we were talking about special conditions, anomalies and such. Garrison's lady, Vicki Maler, is just such an anomaly. She's in the process of becoming British but holds a German passport which says she was born in 1947. That would make her thirty-six years old but she looks ten years younger than that. Red hair, elfin features, lovely figure—beautiful!

"They travel a fair bit, Garrison and the woman, and they use airports. Her passport has been checked out—discreetly. It's genuine and was issued in Hamburg in 1960 when she was thirteen. The only thing is—" he paused, cleared his throat and looked at the faces watching him, "—that the Vicki Maler the passport was issued to died in 1974! Oh, and one other thing. She, too, was blind . . .

"Fine, so for some unknown reason Garrison's woman has 'assumed' an identity other than her real one . . . Or has she? Well, here are a couple of pretty macabre facts for you:

"One—in the early summer of 1974 the body of one Vicki Maler was placed in so-called 'cryogenic suspension' at Schloss Zonigen in the Swiss Alps.

"Two—this was done on the posthumous instructions of Thomas Schroeder, dead since '73 . . .

"And three—two years ago that same Vicki Maler's frozen remains disappeared right out of the Schloss!

173

"As for the Swiss authorities: well they've neatly tied the whole thing up and buried it—and I can't say I blame them. One thing, however, is very definite: Vicki Maler's name has been lifted from the register. That is to say, not only is there no longer a corpse answering to her description in the fridge, but the records say there never was one.

"Now, there's a lot more about Garrison that we know, some of it very interesting, some not so interesting. I don't propose to bore you with trivia, and there are those of you yet to have your say. But there are two more things of major importance. One is Garrison's money, its source. It wasn't easy to dig up all the facts out of their various crevices, and there's doubtless a lot we've missed, but most of his bedrock resources—his bulk cash and holdings—all came his way at that same time two years ago. Through Thomas Schroeder. Now Schroeder had been dead since 1973, but he'd left his executors with clear and foolproof instructions. Garrison got the lot.

"Next, I said he didn't control gambling. That's true. But he does—or did—gamble. Not so much now, not at all that I know of, but he did. This was something else that started two years ago. In fact for a period of something like four months, shortly after the Wyatt business, he seems to have done little else. And very successfully.

"He hit just about every major football pools syndicate in the world—eighteen of them in all, top wins that is—and jackpots every time! But never with any publicity. We were called in by Littlewoods to see how he was fiddling it. He wasn't. But we stuck to him anyway, and what that led us to was literally unbelievable. Gents, when Garrison gambles he doesn't lose. Ever! He doesn't even come close to losing!

"Under various pseudonyms he reduced almost every major bookmaker and gambling consortium in Great Britain to near-bankruptcy. He did the same in the world's greatest casinos, some of the smaller ones, too—and finally he took Las Vegas. And he took Las Vegas like no one ever took it before. So well that overnight he went to Number One on the Mafia hit list! Except that when they got around to it there was no one to hit. He'd simply disappeared, moved on with money and credits totalling some twenty-seven million dollars!

"And all of this done more or less openly, with only a minimum of effort to cover his tracks, as if he had absolutely nothing to fear. And why not? For as an honest, upright member of society what would he have to fear?

"Oh, he went to Vegas in a sort of disguise, with a retinue of his staff also disguised—but can you blame him? My guess is he *knew* he would clean up, knew it for a certainty, and when it was over he simply desired to fade out of sight—which is what he did. Since then he hasn't gambled a penny. It's as if it was something he wanted to try—a system, maybe, or just something in his blood—and having got it out of himself he lost all interest in it. Crazy!"

He sat shaking his head, lit a second cigarette, finally looked up. "That's me finished. My branch is still on Garrison, of course, but at a distance. We don't intend to harass him, and I'm pretty sure we won't get anything on him. He's clean . . .

"One very last thing: I think you'll discover pretty soon, when the rest of you have had a chance to speak, that we've all of us underestimated Garrison. It's just a feeling I have, that's all."

"Underestimated?" The Chairman was on his feet again. "Will MI6 take a moment more to explain?"

MI6 nodded. "Okay. I think that if we could really *see* Garrison, all of him—I mean if we could really get under his skin—we'd find we're fooling about with one of the most powerful men in the world. Powerful in just about any way you care to mention. And barring any accident, any deterioration in his health, shall we say, I think he's destined to be *the* most powerful very shortly."

No one spoke. After a moment The Chairman said, "Thank you." He stood looking round the table, unsmiling, tall and gaunt and strangely cold. Finally he suggested, "A break for coffee, gentlemen? Following which we'll continue. And I think by now that we're all beginning to see just why this meeting was called."

The seated men remained silent. Then one by one they began to stand up and stretch their legs . . .

After coffee it was the turn of Mineral Rights and Mining, followed by Transport, and finally Telecommunications. All told similar tales. In the last two years Garrison had gone from strength to strength; he and/or his companies were the majority shareholders in almost every big business one might care to name; he was the man *behind* the men in control. And no one outside this room knew it. But—

"—That's just the problem, gentlemen," The Chairman took pains to point out, when once more he had the floor. "If Garrison were the Aga Khan, or the Maharaja of Mogador, or some despot oil sheikh—if his name was Rockefeller or Getty or Onassis—if he was the President of the USA or the head of the Cosa Nostra, then we'd know what or what not to do about him. And if he had any of those backgrounds we'd more ably understand him and not need to fear him. But he isn't and he doesn't. What he is is an ex-Military Police Corporal turned big businessman—no, Super-Tycoon—who seems destined to become the richest, most powerful man in the world. And no one knows except us and a handful of others. How he does the things he does is not important—though I'd dearly love to know. What's to be done about him is important. Quite simply, if Mr. Garrison turned nasty he could pull the chairs out from under all of us! He can ruin our economy—the world's economy! He can cripple airlines, shipping, communications, industry . . . may have already begun to do so, if only as an exercise in the manipulation of power. Oh, yes, that's a possibility: already he may have flexed his muscles, maybe more than once or twice!"

"That is very true," said Finance, jumping to his feet. "Look at the recent, *ahem*, fluctuations—supposedly inexplicable fluctuations—in precious metals. Look at the collapse of certain airlines, the much more devastating collapse of entire economies, the shuddery state of banking, of Wall Street and the Stock Exchange . . ."

"My God!" Inland Revenue wheezed, also on his feet. "But I didn't know the half of it! Not the tenth part of it!" He was trembling in every ounce of fat. He ran jelly fingers through his flaky hair. "He's made complete fools of us—must owe us millions. He's—"

"Wait!" The Chairman thumped the table. "Gentlemen, please remain seated . . . Please!" They sat. "Obviously you have seen the light. Yes, Garrison is a potential bomb, and yes he would seem to have his finger on his own trigger. But—"

"—But you'd be advised to stop right there!" MI6 broke in, his voice calm, controlled.

"I beg your pardon?" The Chairman's voice was sharp, his eyes suddenly hooded.

"Before you say anything else," said MI6, "there's another little thing you should know." He glanced at Government Observer, a very young man whose silence throughout had been generally mistaken for lack of understanding or experience, then stared directly at The Chairman. "I was given the option of telling or of holding back. Now I think you'd better know, all of you, before hysteria sets in. It's just one

178

more 'anomaly,' if you like. Simply this: Garrison *is* British and he *is* patriotic."

With the exception of The Chairman, MI6's audience looked blank. The Chairman guessed what was coming and groaned inwardly. He had hoped MI6 didn't have this information . . . but too late now. A pity. It had all been going so well.

"Garrison has made out a will," MI6 continued, pausing to wave the others down as they all began to question at once. "*Please!* His will is simple—within its vast scope, of course—and so worded or constructed as to be quite irrefutable, incontestable. It was received by Her Majesty's Government just a few days ago, before Garrison went abroad on holiday. He also left instructions that he didn't want to talk about it. The government is to be executor in the event of Garrison's, er, sudden demise. And everything—that is, *everything*—is to go to the country, to England!"

There was stunned silence. The Chairman bit his lip. Someone must have leaked this to MI6, as it had been leaked to him. Perhaps Observer, on instructions from above . . .

Finally MI6 went on. "So you see he doesn't intend to pull the chairs out from under us after all. Doesn't want to be King of the World. Isn't bent on chaos, destruction. Which makes me wonder just what we're all doing . . . here . . ." As he slowed and came to a halt, so his eyebrows lowered in a dark frown. He gave a last look around at the staring faces, then turned his eyes down and began to pick at his already ragged nails.

The Chairman decided to take a chance, find out what their reactions would be. "Nothing has changed," he said. "This . . . this will of his could be a blind, a ploy, a safeguard against deeper investigation. The fact remains: while he's alive Garrison is a potential bomb. But—"

"Gentlemen," said the small yellow man. For the first time he was on his feet, smiling, bowing. He straightened up. "Now, if I may speak?" his voice was a whisper, extremely gentle and soothing, exemplifying everyone's conception of an English-speaking Chinaman. Almost a caricature. "My master arrived at these same conclusions some time ago. For which reason he has taken a special interest in Mr. Garrison. Now he wishes it to be said that whatever else may be decided, Mr. Garrison is not to die. That would not be—beneficial?"

Again the stunned silence, or maybe not so stunned. But in another moment the entire room was on its feet.

"What?" The Chairman had watched and was guided by the immediate reactions of the rest and was the first to shout his denial, covering his tracks. "Can I believe my ears? Do you really imagine that I was suggesting . . . that we would even consider . . ."—until even his strident denials were lost in the general hubbub. However, and for all that he continued to protest, his mind was on different things. Such as *his* master's instructions that indeed Garrison was to die. The country would benefit beyond the wildest, most optimistic dreams of any economist—and so would the branch! The potential for the expansion of espionage and counter-intelligence would be enormous. The CIA would soon be small-fry by comparison.

These were the reasons The Chairman's boss, the head of the branch, had supplied—but The Chairman knew there was at least one more. His boss was a man of means, and greedy. He had admitted that he more than merely "played about" with stocks and shares; everything he had was tied up in the game. And he had hinted that he might easily double his holdings in certain areas but for the interference of a couple of large shareholders, namely Messrs. Garrison and Koenig. Thus Garrison's death would be of great personal advantage to him.

As thoughts such as these passed through The Chairman's head, the row taking shape about the great table had increased twofold. Mineral Rights and Mining was also shouting the little Chinaman down. "Who the devil is your master anyway? Does he think the authorities in this country are cold-blooded murderers? Mr. Chairman, I demand to know . . ."—until his voice also became one with the uproar. But in the back of his mind he, too, was already considering the prospect of Great Britain as a major controlling influence in OPEC, and of the advantages of large slices of the South African and Australian mining pies.

It was the same with most of them—with the notable exceptions of the Chinaman himself, MI6 and his 2IC, and Observer. The first of these had merely followed Charon Gubwa's instructions, was not greatly interested in the furor his cautionary words had sparked. MI6 simply sat back and took stock of things; his narrowed eyes were on The Chairman, and his mind seethed with dark suspicions. He had always believed in the Service as a whole, but never in The Chairman's somehow sinister, self-governing branch of that body. Honor among thieves indeed! As for Observer: he sat still, bland-faced, and observed.

After a while the din died down a little. Through it all the Chinaman had remained on his feet, smiling still. Now he took the opportunity to make for the doors, which at that moment opened to admit The Chairman's uniformed man. He went straight to his employer and handed him a note, then turned on his heel and left. He would have closed the doors behind him but the Chinaman stood there, smiling.

For no apparent reason, suddenly everyone's attention seemed riveted on The Chairman. He seemed to be having some difficulty reading the note, but at last he cleared his throat and looked up, the corner of his mouth twitching a little.

"Gentlemen," he finally said, "it seems that any actions we, er, *might* have considered—any further investigations, that is to say—have been pre-empted." His voice was just a little shaky. "By that I mean," he hurriedly went on, "it would appear that some other or others have found Mr. Garrison's, er, talents equally troublesome—even more so."

He cleared his throat again. This had not been of his doing. If it had been then it wouldn't be bungled. As it was it was an embarrassment, but on the other hand it might provide the cover of an authentic precedent in the event of a future, more successful enterprise.

"Mr. Garrison's plane," he went on, glancing at the note, "has recently landed at Gatwick. The landing was—it says here—'a miraculous escape!' The plane was sabotaged. A bomb. No one was hurt, but Mr. Garrison has been taken to a private hospital. Severe shock, it appears . . ."

His words sank in. Slowly their heads turned to stare at the little Chinaman.

He stood at the doors, smiled back at their frowning expressions. Then he bowed and his sighing voice seemed to fill the room:

"Gentlemen, I am sure you will now have other items for discussion. Hopefully one of them will be measures for the protection of Mr. Garrison. My time, however, is limited. I bid you good day."

No one objected as he silently left the room . . .

Chapter
12

T HE MEETING HAD BROKEN UP SHORTLY AFTER RE-
ceiving the news of the sabotage attempt
on Garrison's plane.

MI6 and friend had come up by train from Wa-
terloo, Government Observer in his car. Now,
walking across The Chairman's drive together,
Observer invited the other two: "Can I give you
a lift back into the city? That way I could save
both of you some time, and perhaps we could
have a little chat . . .?"

"Thank you," MI6 agreed at once. All three got
into Observer's old Rover and sat there, waiting
for the rest of the departing delegates to move
their cars. When the way was clear, Observer
drove out of the grounds, down the driveway and
onto the road for the city. From an upstairs window of the house, The Chairman watched them
go.

The Chairman was not happy. He was in fact angry. Angry with MI6 (though of course the man had only been doing his job); with whoever had tried to blow Garrison out of the sky, for failing; but mainly with Charon Gubwa, who for some time had been getting a little too big for his boots.

The Chairman used Gubwa as an intelligence source, had done so for more years than he cared to think about, and in his turn Gubwa used him. Like Garrison, Gubwa was into business, did a little "financing" and etc. The Chairman had never worried too much about the etc., but it had made Gubwa rich. Very rich, The Chairman suspected, though not on Garrison's scale. But then, who was rich on Garrison's scale?

Oh, Gubwa was bent, most definitely, but he was also one superb grass! The Chairman had built his early reputation on Charon Gubwa's tip-offs. What he couldn't understand was Gubwa's sudden interest in Garrison—in his continued good health, that was to say.

It could be, of course, that Gubwa worked for Garrison, but The Chairman doubted that. Gubwa didn't really work for anyone, except himself. In many of their dealings—certainly in recent years—he had always suspected that Gubwa got far more out of their intelligence transactions than ever he did! It had dawned on him, too, that perhaps Gubwa was a double-agent, working not only for The Chairman and his branch but also for a number of foreign agencies. Yes, unfortunately that did seem a strong possibility.

But . . . Gubwa's organization did have a serious weakness: The Chairman knew the location of its headquarters. And he had long ago formulated certain courses of action. This was not a thought he let himself dwell upon too often: Gubwa had an uncanny knack of "knowing" or "predicting" things before they happened. It would not be in The Chairman's interests to have Gubwa discover the axe that he held over him. Not until he was ready to let it fall, at any rate.

As for Gubwa's headquarters:

In early 1944 when it had been rumored that Adolf Hitler might get the A-bomb first, several underground command posts had been built in and around London—subterranean shelters from which the war effort could be directed to the last. These had been kept operational until the late 60s, when costs had gone through the roof. The least viable of these shelters, in Central London, had been due for closedown: an unused, dusty, dark place deep underground, built in a natural cave halfway down a great fault in the bedrock. Charon Gubwa had bought it and turned it into his home and headquarters. The place had always been secret and Gubwa had kept it that way; but The Chairman knew of its existence and had even been down there—once.

That had been all of ten years ago, but The Chairman remembered it well. Now, despite the fact that the house was quite warm, he shivered. The thought of that great steel coffin down there in the bowels of the earth, Gubwa's Castle, always did that to him. He hadn't seen all of the place, but enough. Enough to know that he could have put Gubwa out of business there and then, and that he should have. The reason he hadn't was simple: the man had more leads than a telephone exchange! If The Chairman had wanted to know something about anybody or anything—literally *any*body or *any*thing— Gubwa could usually get that information for him. In return all The Chairman had to do was keep people off Gubwa's back, at least until he was better established.

Well, perhaps he'd done a little bit more than that. The Chairman soured at the thought. No, he'd done a *lot* more than that. When the computer age had come rolling in, he had been instrumental in extending Gubwa's eyes and ears. That is to say, he had seen to it that Gubwa's own computer had access to external sources and systems. He had known of course (he tried to excuse his error) that he could shut down Gubwa's operation whenever he desired, as soon as the man outlived his usefulness. But what he had not foreseen was the massive build-up of computer technology, the extensive use of the damned machine in almost every aspect of life and facet of society. He had in effect given Gubwa an intelligence system second to none, had built a wall of technology about Gubwa's already formidable Castle of Secrets. And that was a weapon which eventually might be turned against The Chairman himself, and against his branch. It would not be used, no—not as long as he played the game with Gubwa; but there had been times recently when he had not wanted to play the game. Like at this very moment . . .

And of course if The Chairman's chief ever discovered that old mistake of his—that old, old mistake with all its implications, including the fact that it had remained unreported, uncorrected through all of these long years—then The Chairman was finished. Then his head would well and truly (and literally) roll! But who was there to tell him? Not The Chairman, and the only other person who knew of it was Charon Gubwa himself.

Of course, the only way to put Gubwa out of business now would be to go down there with a squad of trusted branch heavies and literally rip the place to bits—and in the process destroy any evidence linking Gubwa to himself. Yes, and it just might come to that if the man had any more tricks up his sleeve like this last one!

The Chairman had known of course that Gubwa was sending a representative to the meeting. He himself had agreed to it. But he had certainly not foreseen the idiot demanding that Garrison's life be spared! Not there and then, just like that! The way it had been done had only served to accentuate the fact that The Chairman's branch *had* considered Garrison's removal as a serious proposition. Indeed, only the timely arrival of that note telling that someone else had already tried to kill Garrison had averted what might have proved to be a very damaging scene.

The Chairman's anger began to boil over. He snatched himself away from the window, poured himself a drink, tried to control the heat he felt bubbling up inside. The last of his guests had gone now and the day had grown well into late afternoon. Pretty soon The Chairman's chief would be on the blower demanding an explanation. Or at least asking awkward questions.

The Chairman took his drink down to his study, locked himself in, picked up the telephone . . .

Gubwa was more or less expecting the call. He half-sensed it was coming. If he had attended the meeting—through the mind of Johnnie Fong—then he would have been sure it was coming. But he had not done so. Too frequent or prolonged use of his ESP-talents invariably tired Gubwa, so that wherever possible he used them sparingly. In any case, there had been other things to do.

Therefore, when the telephone in his study buzzed, a precognitive tingle told Gubwa that it was The Chairman. He smiled as he picked up the telephone. "And how are you today, Sir Harry?" he inquired, his voice oily.

"Listen, Charon, you know bloody well that I'm angry!" came the answer. "Have you any idea how much you might have embarrassed me today?"

The "might" puzzled Gubwa; he had been sure that the other *would* be embarrassed. He did not yet know of Garrison's brush with disaster. He decided to play it straight, but without being too inquisitive.

"But it was my intention to embarrass you!" he laughed. "I knew you would be considering Garrison's . . . removal—for 'the good of the country,' and all that—but it doesn't suit me to have him removed. Not just yet. I simply brought it out in the open, that's all: showed how it might serve a variety of purposes if he were eliminated. That's my way of ensuring that nothing does happen to him. For if anything does, now—why! they'll all be looking to you for the answers. And that really would be embarrassing!"

Sir Harry listened to all of this in growing dismay and anger. Gubwa *had* got too big for his boots. He might have to bring his plans for the man forward somewhat. "Now listen, Charon, I—"

"No, you listen! Garrison must not be harmed! There is a lot I have to know about him first. Things which could be of great benefit to both of us. After that—" He let the sentence hang there, incomplete.

Gubwa could almost hear Sir Harry grinding his teeth. "Gubwa, you . . . who works for who around here?"

"Oh, now, Sir Harry," Gubwa's voice was dangerously soft. "You know better than that. Who works for who, indeed! Why, we're partners, you and I! And I've just explained that it's to *our* benefit that Garrison lives—for a while longer, anyway."

"Charon, you're pushing your luck. I have my orders. You can't interfere with that. And anyway, if I don't get him it's likely the others will. They'll make a better job of it next time, you can be sure of it."

Gubwa's pulse quickened. The others? What others? And what next time? He did not want to ask The Chairman what he was talking about, not directly, so—

"Wait!" he said.

He knew where Sir Harry was. He closed his eyes, sent his mind soaring out, entered the other's thoughts. They were guarded, as usual, but Gubwa could get in. He probed, saw, withdrew. Sir Harry didn't even know he'd been there, wouldn't have believed it if Gubwa himself had told him.

"There won't be a next time," Gubwa said, his mind racing. Damn it, who had tried to kill Garrison? And why? It looked like he must now put everything else aside and concentrate all of his energies on this one project, on Richard Garrison. "Not until I'm ready. As for my pushing my luck: if that's a threat, Sir Harry, forget it. I would survive. You, on the other hand, might not be so lucky."

"Now who's threatening, Charon?"

Gubwa didn't like the sudden chill in the other's voice. This was a man you mustn't squeeze too tight. "Look," he said, "why are we fighting?"

"Damn it, you know why! That was a dirty trick of yours, Charon. I'd never have let your Chinky Chappie in the house if I'd known what you were up to. His presence at the meeting would have been difficult to explain away as it was, but now—? People are bound to start asking who and why and what. Don't you understand? I've been told to deal with Garrison. Now I can't—not without difficulty, anyway—because you've screwed it up!"

191

"Then let me do the job for you—but in my own time, when I've got what I want."

This sounded better. "How much time?" Sir Harry was cautious.

Gubwa thought about it, said, "A month, six weeks at the outside. That should be time enough."

"Time enough for what, Charon? What *is* your interest in Garrison?"

"Ah, Sir Harry! Can't we keep a few little secrets to ourselves, you and I? Be satisfied that I'll kill him, that's all."

The Chairman still wasn't quite satisfied. "I don't know . . ."

"And I'll do it in a way that lets you and the branch out entirely. No possible connection."

That sounded much better. Sir Harry lingered over the proposition, letting himself be swayed. And why not? After all, no one had set a time limit on Garrison's life. Six weeks should be quite satisfactory. And when Gubwa had done the job . . . that would be time enough to sort *him* out! Fortunately Gubwa was not probing any of this; fortunately for Sir Harry. "All right," he finally agreed, "we'll do it your way."

"Good!" said Gubwa, "and there's something you can do for me. I could do it myself, but this way is quicker."

"Oh?" Sir Harry was cautious once more.

"Yes, I'll need to know the name of Garrison's minder."

"I don't know if he'll have one yet."

Gubwa laughed. "Oh, I'm sure he will! Proba-

192

bly your friends at MI6. They're a trustworthy lot, in the main. Do find out for me, won't you?"

"I'll do my best," The Chairman growled.

"Fine! Well, that about concludes it, I imagine. Unless there's anything else you'd care to mention? No? Well, then. It was good to hear from you again, Sir Harry, and—"

"Save it for true believers!" The Chairman told him drily. "Six weeks then. And Charon . . . no mistakes, eh?" And without waiting for an answer he put the phone down . . .

On their way back into the city, MI6 and Observer engaged in what was at first a wary conversation. The man in the back of the car, MI6's "aide," sat in silence, apparently little interested.

"Er, what you were saying about Garrison," Observer opened. "Did you mean it? About him being straight, I mean?"

"Oh, yes. Straight as you or I—no disrespect, you understand—and probably a sight straighter than a lot of the others at that little get-together."

Observer grinned, relaxing a little. "I know what you mean. We rub shoulders with some strange ones, don't we?"

MI6 nodded. "All part of the game, I suppose."

"You've little in common with Sir Harry, then?" A tentative probe.

"The Chairman? When I started with MI6 during the war, his branch didn't even exist. It came later. Most of the murky stuff came later. I mean, it's *all* cloak and dagger, you'll appreciate—but with that lot it's mainly dagger! But—I suppose we need 'em. You know what they say: it takes one to know one? Well, they deal with some pretty weird jobs, with unpleasant people and nasty situations. So-called 'obscurities.' " He glanced at Observer out of the corner of his eye. "But you know that, of course."

"Something about it, yes. They're a close-mouthed lot, I know that much. Sort of a law unto themselves. I'll not mislead you—I've a good many colleagues who'd like to see them shut down!"

MI6 nodded. "You don't surprise me. They're a damned sight too heavy-handed for my liking. And as for Sir Harry . . ." he sucked his teeth. "That guy's a snake! Er, my personal opinion, of course. But it's common knowledge he numbers several more than shady characters among his friends and informers. And he probably protects them. That Chinaman, for instance. Who did he represent, eh?"

"Umm," said Observer. "I'd wondered about that myself. But, as I've said, they're pretty close-mouthed—and so far they've had good cover from up top." He let his eyes flick up, brought them down to glance knowingly at his passenger. " 'She' is happy with much of their work. Personally—Sir Harry's being a snake isn't just your opinion, I'm afraid." He chuckled wryly. "That's why I want you to look after Garrison. It really wouldn't do if anything were to happen to him."

"Oh?" MI6 seemed genuinely taken by surprise. "You mean me personally?"

"You—or your best man. We trust you, and that covers anyone you care to recommend. In fact I especially appreciated the way you stuck your neck out for Garrison. Yes, I liked that . . ."

MI6 thought about it. "Of course I'd need authority, orders?"

"You shall have them. In fact you have them, as of now. The papers will come later."

"Okay, I'll see to it. To be truthful I half-expected the job, and I have the very man for it. He's not much known over here. Worked mainly abroad. But he's good stuff. Name of Stone— Phillip Stone—but of course that's strictly between you and me . . ."

Behind him, in the back seat, Stone merely sat and said nothing. He had wondered why he'd been called to attend this meeting today, and now he knew.

"Good!" said Observer, "then get him on the job. Just one thing: make sure he does it with discretion. This Garrison's a funny type. If he was to cotton on that someone was minding him, well he'd be almost sure to make a fuss about it. Which would only make the job that much more difficult."

"Oh, he'll not get wind of this guy, I can safely promise you that. He's one of the best."

"I'll take your word for it," said Observer, easing his foot from the accelerator as they moved into heavier traffic. "Incidentally, do you have any idea who might have bombed Garrison's plane?"

MI6 shrugged. "Could be the IRA are still after him. Or the Mafia."

"Mafia?"

MI6 nodded. "That Vegas job I was talking about. And if he's been holidaying on Rhodes . . . it's their neck of the woods, you know. Close enough to it, anyway." He shrugged. "On the other hand it could be anybody. He must've stepped on a few toes to get what he's got."

Observer grunted his acceptance of that, then said: "Well, let's just make sure—for the immediate future, anyway—that nobody steps on him . . ."

Phillip Stone suited his name well. He was like stone. A crag of a man, seventy-three inches tall and all of it with hard edges. And they had needed to be hard. As an intelligence agent (he hated the word "spy") Stone had several things going for him. No one who looked (and was) so rough and ready could possibly be *that* intelligent. And no one who acted so unconcerned and disinterested could possibly be the data-collecting machine which Stone was. His third asset was his hardness itself, which over the years he'd accumulated like a stalactite collects calcium. Layer upon layer. The hard way.

Nothing had ever been easy for Stone. When you're big and rough-looking there's always someone waiting to knock you down, if only to prove he's bigger and rougher. Stone had been knocked down a good many times, in a good many ways, until at last he'd learned to stay firmly on his feet.

Life that offered neither threat nor thrill was no life for Phillip Stone. At eighteen he'd joined

the Parachute Regiment just to jump out of air-
planes, and at twenty-three he'd been cashiered
out for his persistent disobedience to the orders
of his senior officers, which had culminated in a
brawl with one such where he'd broken the
man's jaw. Stone had never understood how he'd
become an officer in the first place—he hadn't
wanted to be one—but being broken out of the
army hadn't bothered him. Jumping out of air-
planes had bored him in the end, and anyway it
had entailed all that other junk—like doing what
you're told to do.

No, he was a lone wolf and the Regiment had
been just a little too clannish. He still had fond
memories, even now, but . . . there had been
other places to see, other things to do. He had
inherited a little money from an aunt he'd never
known, and the army had given him a thirst for
travel, and so—

His idea had been to work his way round the
world, except it hadn't turned out that way. He'd
got as far as Cyprus before falling in with a
bunch of lads in Nicosia on a drunken night out.
Believing they were squaddies from one of the
local British camps, he'd gone along with them,
had even let them talk him into going through
some form of silly ritual. He'd been drunk and
couldn't remember a lot about it. But they
hadn't been squaddies—regular soldiers anyway—and the ritual hadn't been silly. Not in
their eyes. No, it had been their form of enlist-
ment. And when Stone came out of his drunk he
was somewhere in Africa and someone had
given him a rifle!

Under orders again, this time from Colonel "Crazy" Dave Clegg, also late of Her Majesty's Forces, Phillip Stone had found himself a mercenary in the wildest outfit any man could ever wish to desert from. But he hadn't deserted; instead he'd proved himself worth his weight in gold to Crazy Dave; the business they were involved with came to a rapid and fruitful (if bloody) conclusion; Stone had soon found himself back in Blighty and a civilian once more.

Two weeks had been too much. There was a girl he'd known in Minden. He decided to look her up and boarded a plane for Germany.

Meanwhile . . . Crazy Dave Clegg hadn't forgotten him. Stone's name was soon being whispered in the esoteric vaults of MI6. Connections were made . . .

Stone's reunion with his *fräulein* didn't work out; he fell in with a couple of middle-aged but sprightly American tourists, ex-GIs who'd been through this way during the war; in a few days they'd persuaded him to accompany them to Frankfurt. Shortly after that Stone had mislaid his passport, but a call to the British Consulate soon solved that one—with a speed and efficiency he later had cause to remember! His new passport, unlike the old one, made no mention of him being an ex-Army officer, but since he no longer *was* an officer he'd seen nothing sinister in that. Nor in the next port of call of his American friends, which just happened to be Berlin. Only a few jumps later had seen him ferrying innocuous-looking little letters to and fro between East and West Berlin (his ex-GIs had ladies over there remembered from the war, but they hated tearful and fruitless reunions and besides they were married now), and the jump after that had been straight into jail—on the wrong side of the wall!

Only then had he stopped to add things up— things which, in all his prior experience, had only ever happened in thriller or "spy" novels— by which time he was on his way to Moscow. Apparently he'd asked for political asylum there, or at least that's what the reds told MI6. He was interrogated, brainwashed, became a double-agent without ever (in his eyes) first being a single-agent! Later, having been returned to Frankfurt where he was picked up by the CIA, he was "de-briefed," shipped back to Blighty, inter-rogated by Intelligence and re-employed in Hong Kong. There he "went to school," became a fully-fledged agent, improved his unarmed combat and surveillance techniques, was finally moved on into China as a "student of Oriental customs, architecture and antiquities."

In 1977 the Chinese authorities finally cracked his cover; he was given the full treatment by the nasties in Peking; only the blossoming Chinese love affair with Great Britain and the USA saved him. He was kicked out with a minimum of pub-licity and a fresh-scrubbed mind, had his brain repatriated by MI6, and finally ended up back in Germany as a junior counter-intelligence ad-viser to NATO.

Well (he'd often consoled himself), and he'd wanted to see the world, hadn't he? But the world hadn't quite finished with him yet, nor he with it.

The job in Germany wasn't to his liking—too quiet. He became restless—possibly as a result of hearing a rumor that certain parties were trying to recruit a gunrunner for Afghanistan, supplying the Khash-lun tribesmen with arms to fight the coming Russian invasion. And so Stone had moved on, becoming part of the Afghan underground. The invasion had come; on his own initiative Stone had founded a well-organized guerilla group; London had got wind of this and whipped him out of there. Lawrence of Arabia had been different, they told him: we had been at war then!

Since when he'd puttered round with the idea of selling himself to the Israelis, or of removing to South Africa where several ex-soldier friends had settled, or of moving into industrial espionage in America. Meanwhile MIs 5 and 6 had kept him employed, however low-key, usually on surveillance or in a minder capacity.

Now he was to be minder to Richard Garrison, which Stone had already decided would be far too tame for him. But . . . a job is a job, and at least you could live on the money. This was the last time, though, and after this it would probably be the good old US of A for him. You could still find a little fast action across the Big Pond.

These were his thoughts as he left the MI6 offices in Whitehall, where he'd chosen his cover and been "kitted-up," and made his way across London via the underground for his flat in Richmond. There he'd pick up his car and head for

Haslemere, where Garrison was in a very private and very exclusive hospital. He did not see the small, sturdy, business-suited Chinaman who followed him out of the tube and into the evening at Richmond—Johnnie Fong was an expert at not being seen—and he was not greatly interested in the pushing-and-shoving argument between two hulking, boozy yobs in a shop doorway along his way. But after that—

—The "yobs" were on him like sacks of coal, pinning him to a wall in a moment. And in the next moment, before he could muster either mind or muscle, the little Chinaman was in front of him, unloading the contents of a large hypodermic right through his shirt and into the wall of his stomach! Stone recognized the Chinaman at once—and then he reacted.

He hurled one of his attackers from him and swung his free fist round in an arc, crashing it into the face of the other. But by then he already knew that it was all over. A car had pulled up; the street was melting like soft toffee; his attackers, one of them with a mangled, profusely bleeding face, were levering him into the back of a large black station wagon. He still moved his arms a bit but they felt like rubber, with no bones in them. His legs had long since surrendered and his mind was last to go, or maybe his vision. He would later recall that before passing out he saw the Chinaman's face, close up, and his broad slash of a smile.

That sinister yellow smile receding down a long black tunnel, and Stone's thought going with it: *You just wait, Fu Manchu. I'll be seeing you again . . . you again . . . again . . . again-againagainagainagain . . .*

But in fact, he never would see him again.

Richard Garrison wasn't the only one in hospital: Carlo Vicenti was there, too, in a "gentleman's" ward in a large Central London general. He had been there all afternoon and evening while they fixed him up, and was now mildly sedated where he sat propped up, deep in painful conversation with three sharply-tailored, mean-looking and somewhat swarthy visitors.

"Yeah, yeah, we know," Marcello Pontellari's nasal voice was full of sarcasm. "Three cracked ribs, a busted collarbone, a sprained wrist and a busted pinkie. Oh, yeah, and lots of bad bruising—*wow!*" his sneer was deliberately exaggerated. "Isn't that terrible? Girls we carve with razors or burn with cigarettes; guys we pave roads with or dump in the river; and you. . . ? Somebody breaks a small bone or two and you scream like all hell!"

"Not just somebody," Vicenti snapped, grimacing at the pain his reaction caused in his bandaged shoulder. "Garrison! It was him—must've been him—or his twin brother!"

"Your boys saw nothing," Mario "the Dwarf" Angelli blew rings from his cigar. "They say you acted crazy but nobody was there."

"Idiots!" Vicenti snapped again, and again groaned. "What in hell's *wrong* with you guys? You think I threw myself through that wall?"

"Frankly," said Ramon Navarro de Medici—"Ramon the Rat," as he was known throughout the rank and file of London-based Mafia—"yeah, that's what we think. Least, that's what your boys tell us. A fit, they said. He went nuts, they said."

"Went nuts!" Vicenti snorted. "I tell you I *saw* the guy!"

"Yeah, we know—that's what we came to check. It's why we're here. The Big Guy sent us, you know?"

Vicenti grew silent. The Big Guy? The first successful Mafia Boss in England? He was interested in this? Why?

"See," de Medici went on, "your boys have to be right. Dead right. Garrison wasn't there, couldn't be there. He was trapped in a crippled plane somewhere between the Greek islands and England."

A crippled plane? The Black brothers!

"A bomb," Vicenti nodded his understanding.

"Yeah, *your* bomb!" de Medici answered. "You had him contracted out. The Black boys. We got it from Facello. You did it personal and private, which ain't exactly in the rules, but—"

"But—" Vicenti shook his head, "—but he was *there*!"

"No," Medici was emphatic, "he was on a plane with Bert Black's bomb. But this time Bert fucked up. The plane didn't go down. Anyway, that don't change anything. Garrison *was* on the plane—couldn't have been anywhere near you."

Vicenti's mind was chasing itself in ever-decreasing circles. "I don't understand," he said. "I just don't—"

"Hour and a half after you say he worked you

over, Garrison's plane was coming in on a wing and a prayer at Gatwick. No wheels, controls, no nothing. But a neat landing. Garrison in hospital: nerves. Pilot crazy as a loon, says they were saved 'by God!' "

Vicenti fell back on his pillows, groaning as his shoulder gave him more pain. But his injuries now took second place to his confusion, his disbelief. "What the hell . . .?" he whispered. He squeezed his eyes shut, shook his head again.

"Yeah," said Marcello Pontellari, his tone sarcastic as ever, "what the hell . . ."

"Listen, Carlo," said de Medici, "just ignore Pontellari and listen. The Big Guy is interested in all this. See, you're not the only one who hates this Garrison. The boys in Vegas hate him, too. But see, they don't want him dead."

Vicenti's eyes popped open. "What's that?"

"Yeah," de Medici continued. "You remember Vegas a year, year and a half ago? Something big went down there. Bunch of punters cleaned 'em out good. Took millions and disappeared. And all legitimate, they *won* the fucking money! Can you imagine that? They *won* the mother!"

Vicenti's eyes were narrow now. He ground his teeth. "Jesus! Oh, yes, I can imagine it. Christ! Didn't he do the same thing to me, this Garrison? Didn't he clean me out?" He stared at de Medici and his lips curled back from his teeth. "So the Big Guy and the boys in Vegas think—?"

"Not think," de Medici cut him off, "they know. He did it to Vegas just like he did it to you. They know it was him 'cos they finally tracked him down. A guy with more tricks up his sleeve than a cardsharp! But . . . well, you can see why the Big Guy has to cancel your contract on Garrison, okay?"

Vicenti frowned. "Come again?"

"See, right now this guy is worth a lot more alive than dead. The Vegas mob wants to know how he does it. Yeah, and so do we. We'd like for no one else to do it again—not ever! So, after they let him walk, we're going to pull him in. Then, when we get through with him—" he shrugged. "He's all yours, if you still want him."

Vicenti nodded. "Okay. But what about the Blacks? Can you find 'em, get a message to 'em, call 'em off?"

"Yeah, it's done already. They get back from Rhodes three days from now, Monday, 7:00 P.M. into Gatwick. By that time you should be out of here and on the mend. There's a general meeting Monday 8:30 at the Big Guy's usual offices. The Blacks'll be there. You, too. All of us. Hey!— this is *big*, Carlo."

Vicenti pursed his lips, rolled his eyes and stared up at the ceiling. He frowned. "Yeah, big," he grunted. "But it still doesn't explain how I thought I saw him when he wasn't there. And yet, you know, somehow I had a feeling he wasn't *really* there."

He paused and gazed into the eyes of his visitors, then lowered his eyebrows in reproof. "Hey, don't look at me like that! We're talking about the same guy bust me out of the Ace of Clubs, remember? Tricks up his sleeve? Brother, you can say *that* again!"

Chapter

13

PHILLIP STONE NIGHTMARED, AND WHEN HE WOKE UP he had difficulty deciding just where the bad dream ended and the reality began. He had dreamed of the KGB, of the goons in Peking, of man's inhumanity to man. But he had never in his life dreamed of anything quite like Charon Gubwa.

The man was a hill of pallid flesh!

Standing, he would be inches taller than Stone; he had at least twice Stone's girth, must weigh almost four hundred and thirty or forty pounds; and his arms and hands were like great knotted clubs, making Stone's seem fragile by comparison. As for the pallor of his flesh: it wasn't sickness, Stone saw, but albinism: he was a pink-eyed, mottled gray albino Negro! And that wasn't all he was. Stone's eyes weren't quite in focus yet, and his mind was certainly way out, but he knew a monstrosity when he saw one. Whoever the big man-woman was, he *was* a monstrosity.

The light was pretty dim and Stone's senses were all in conflict with one another. Either he was upside down or gravity had no meaning here—wherever "here" was. But his orientation, chiefly the weight of his own body and the way his clothing fell, told him that he was seated normally and that "down" was where his feet were; while the crick in his neck said that his head was tilted back, which meant that what he was looking at was on the ceiling!

He closed his eyes for a moment, thought about shaking his head to clear it (a mistake, that, for the very thought hurt), and very slowly, carefully opened his eyes again. And this time he understood.

The ceiling was a mirror, or at least a large area in the ceiling's center was a mirror. What seemed to be happening up there was actually happening directly in front of Stone, but for the moment he was content to witness it second-hand. He didn't want to attract anyone's attention, not just yet. First he would like to know where he was; he already knew how he came to be here. More or less.

But . . . he would also like to know why he was tied to his chair. Or maybe he knew that, too. For if he wasn't tied down, then by now somebody, even several somebodies, would be suffering a few choice agonies from Stone's extensive list of such.

All of that, however, could wait—would have

to wait. For the moment he would just sit here and watch the action. And the action was . . . something else!

The great mottled albino freak lay on what looked like a wider-than-average masseur's table, where three girls worked on the doughy obesity of his body. Their punching and pummelling was performed to the tune of the monster's sighing, grunting and moaning, and all four—slaves and master alike—were naked as the day they were born. Time was when Stone would have looked at the girls first, but right now he was more interested in the (man? woman?) *creature* on the masseur's table.

With his white hair forming a huge frizz of a bush upon his head, and his incredible pink eyes—themselves anomalies in a typically negroid physiognomy—and above all else, the sexual organs of both man and woman . . .

. . . Stone's mind reeled!

Not only from the contemplation of this most inhuman of human beings, but also from the effects of the drug which had stunned him and facilitated his kidnapping. Whatever the stuff had been, his head now felt as if it had been kicked twice too often. There again, it *might* have been kicked; he remembered making a mess of the face of one of his attackers—perhaps the man had avenged himself while Stone was out for the count. Whichever, it was like the very worst hangover he'd ever known, and Stone had known quite a few. He fought back the nausea he felt welling up and looked at the girls who were working on . . . on the thing.

Another mistake, another anomaly. Only two of them were girls. As for the other—Stone wasn't sure. It had breasts, small but definitely female, but the rest of the gear was male—again small, like a young lad's, but male. And he liked his work, that one. He had an erection, anyway, what there was of it. And so did the mountain of meat he was working on.

Stone now saw that this was more than simple massage. It was the full treatment. Fascinated despite his nausea, he watched the thing through to its end. One of the girls was plying the hermaphrodite's great penis with one hand, and toying with his opposing parts with the other. The second girl, and the boy-girl, were rubbing warm oil into his flabby body; the latter was also sucking with feminine lips upon the black giant's great swollen-slug nipples.

How long this had been going on, Stone couldn't say. But the end came quickly. The huge body began to quiver and heave; massive hands flopped over the side of the table, fluttering like stunned birds; the hermaphrodite's sperm erupted into the face of the girl working his shaft, who smiled her relief and pleasure . . . obviously it was important in more ways than one that her master should be completely satisfied.

Stone turned his eyes away then, as that swollen knob of muscle emptied itself in long bursts; but not before the hermaphrodite's pink eyes had met his own in the mirror, and not before he had seen the slow smile—of sexual pleasure, yes, but also in recognition of Stone's recovery, his consciousness—which gave the thick, gray-mottled lips the curve of a sharp-horned, leprous moon.

The pink eyes were like magnets: they held Stone's gaze, drew his head round to look again, as a snake draws a bird before striking. Then—

"You're awake, Mr. Stone. Splendid!" It was a deep, sonorous voice, negroid but with its charm and lilt almost cultured out. Possibly an adopted voice, falsified, but Stone thought not. And deep underneath, despite its masculinity, there were strangely feminine nuances, girlish or woman-ish undertones. But the female facet was definitely subservient. Stone found himself wishing he knew more about hermaphoditism in human beings—in anything, for that matter.

"Oh, it wouldn't do you any good, Mr. Stone," said the voice, "believe me. I am in no way typical. Indeed I am not a 'type' at all. I am unique!"

The effect of those words—so casually but fluently composed, so easily spoken—was like an electric shock in Stone's mind. He *knew* his thoughts had been read as accurately as if he'd spoken them out loud, but the concept was simply too incredible for him to accept as fact.

"More accurately," the creature on the masseur's slab smiled again. "And that is a fact! Men don't always *express* their thoughts accurately—but they do *think* them accurately." Now Stone believed. He was stunned, but he believed.

"Precisely the point of the exercise," said the creature.

The proof of the pudding, Stone thought, quite deliberately—

"Is in the eating, Mr. Stone, I agree!"

"Impressive," Stone found himself hard-put to be phlegmatic, "but why bother to show me?"

"It is important that you know. And if I had simply told you, you would not have believed. This way I would hope that you will not try to hide anything from me. The talent is tiring, you see? All of the ESP-abilities are, and I do not wish to tire myself unnecessarily. On the other hand I don't wish to be duped. For which reason I will, from time to time, occasionally read your mind. Do we understand each other?"

So far, Stone thought.

"Well? I am waiting."

"Yes," said Stone, "we understand each other." And he realized he'd learned nothing at all from that last ploy—except that perhaps the freak spoke the whole truth. And why should he lie? After all, he held all the cards.

Stone knew there were ESPers in MI6, but he would never have believed that anyone could reach such heights of perfection in the art. Actually, he'd always considered it a waste of time and money. But now . . .? ESPionage, indeed!

"Good," the other nodded. He held out his arms and his paramours—slaves?—eased him upright until he could swing his legs from the slab. He stood, and a robe of towelling was draped across his shoulders. He fastened it about his vast waist, waved the two girls and the boy-girl away. Stone heard a door open and close pneumatically.

"That must be disconcerting," said the creature, approaching, looming larger in the ceiling mirror. "You can move your head, Mr. Stone. Why not look at me directly? I am not of the Gorgons, you know."

Stone raised his head upright and it hurt. Lights flashed before his eyes and inside his skull, causing him to wince. "Jesus!" he said.

"It will pass," said the other.

Stone winced again, screwed up his eyes, blinked them rapidly. He was glad the lighting was subdued. "Okay, Mr. whoever you are, what's it all about?"

"Gubwa," said the other, "Charon Gubwa. I doubt that you ever heard of me."

"No need to doubt it," said Stone, trying now to be flippant, "I never heard of you. But I'm all ears if you want to tell?" By now he had ascertained that he was securely strapped in his chair, his arms as well as his legs. Apart from his head, he couldn't move by so much as an inch. There was absolutely nothing he could do, no physical action he might take, and so it seemed best simply to sit here and listen. At least that way he might learn something—before the other decided he had learned enough.

"Oh, but I want you to learn everything, Mr. Stone," said Gubwa, proving his point yet again and paying no heed to Stone's wit. "Everything—for reasons which I shall now explain:

"First, when you know all about me you'll stop *wondering* about me. This will leave your mind free to think more clearly about what I require of you. Second, you are intelligent—indeed a member of an 'intelligence' organization—and wily, devious minds have always fascinated me.

Third, your natural curiosity pleases me, as that of a child pleases his instructor. And finally—"

"—Finally, nothing you tell me will do me any good, because I'm never going to talk about it?"

"Correct!" Gubwa agreed, smiling again. "In fact when I'm finished with you, not only will you not talk about it, you might not even think about it."

Stone nodded, flexed his muscles one last time against his bonds, shrugged and gave it up. "I'm very angry, Gubwa, but I'm sure you already know that. You probably also know that if I could get out of this chair I'd wreck you, so *I* don't suppose it does much harm to tell *you*! As for the rest of it: I suppose you could call me a captive audience."

"That is also correct!" Gubwa laughed, but to Stone his laughter sounded like the rattle of a snake. Gubwa was rubbing it in, gloating on Stone's helplessness. And knowing it brought out the agent's mean streak.

"Listen, Your Uniqueness," he growled. "Did you ever stop to think that maybe you're not so unique? That maybe you're just another freak?"

Gubwa moved behind him, surprisingly quickly for a being of his size and bulk. Stone's ears tingled but nothing happened. Then the chair spun silently round on rubber wheels. Gubwa steered it towards metal doors that hissed open. "Oh, but I know I'm a freak," he said. "That's what makes me unique. I was born before my time. Like Jesus, da Vinci, Einstein. And I am no less than them, in my way. Indeed I am more than them. I am the destiny of the

213

human race, Mr. Stone. And I shall remold that race in my own image. Homo Sapiens? Bah! *Hermaphro Sapiens!*"

They passed into Gubwa's Command Center and Stone found himself wheeled to where he could stare up at the massively-carved figure of the albino where its feet straddled the globe of the world. And at last the agent began to know something of awe, and of fear. The man meant it. His aim was conquest, empire—with himself as Emperor of Earth! He was as mad as a hatter.

"Right on the one hand, wrong on the other!" Gubwa snapped. "I dream of empire, yes, but I am not mad. Indeed I am utterly sane."

"Most madmen *think* they're sane," Stone growled.

"I do not intend to argue with you, merely to inform you. Then you shall work for me—at least for a little while, longer if you are sensible—and finally . . . well, I shall leave the end of it up to you. You are, as I have said, intelligent. I could find a place for you in my organization. But do please remember, Mr. Stone, that yours is hazardous work at best, and no one will worry too much if you simply go missing. That is why you are paid so well, after all. The 'X' Factor: danger-money!"

Stone remained silent.

"Very well. Now listen to what I have to say. I shall begin at the very beginning . . .

"My great-grandfather was the son of a South-African chief, of the blood of Shaka and Cetewayo. Unlike those two, he mined yellow metal and blue stones for his white masters. And the earth was also rich in pitchblende, uranium. That was one generation. As a child and a young man, my grandfather worked the same mines, until the precious metals and stones were gone. By which time there was a new interest in the previously useless metal. Finally, my father and mother worked for whites, too, and my father ended his days cleaning the vats in a refinery. He had been bald since he was eighteen and his teeth had fallen out before he was twenty-five. But do not think I hold all this against you white men, for I do not. No, in a way I owe you a debt.

"Perhaps I was meant to be twins, I don't know, but that's not how it worked out. You see, I was really the product of three parents. The one in the middle was radiation!

"I was born neither black nor white but gray— not even a true albino, you see? Unique! I had the parts of both male and female, equally well developed. I do not have a womb, no, but all the rest of the equipment is there—sensory certainly. My breasts are real, not merely cosmetic adornments, and my passions are of both man and woman . . .

"I have pink eyes and they are weak, but in the darkness of a post-holocaust world they would be ideally suited. My size is godlike, towering, and my body has the mass of solidity. My frame, freakish according to you, is a leader's frame, that of a great emperor. And my powers . . .

"What do you know of ESP, Mr. Stone? No, do not answer; first let me tell you what I can do. I am telepathic, as you have discovered. I read minds. But that is only one of my powers. I cannot yet levitate, not yet, but I do have great potential. Here, let me show you . . ." He went to an upright weighing-machine and stood upon its platform. The needle spun dizzily and twitched to a halt at just over four hundred and thirty pounds.

"Now watch!" ordered Gubwa. He closed his eyes. In a matter of moments a fine beading of sweat stood out upon his brow. The needle on the dial crept down, down. Three hundred pounds. Two hundred and ten. One hundred and seventy.

Gubwa opened his eyes, sighed—and the needle shot up again. He stepped off the platform. "And that is a measure of power I must use constantly, Mr. Stone, else movement itself would be cumbersome. Hypnotism is another art of mine, in which I excel. But you will discover that for yourself soon enough. I am also what you might call a seer: I prognosticate. Not, unfortunately, very accurately—but I can see something of the future. The immediate future, quite clearly—the distant future, dimly. Suffice it to say that when I put my money on a horse it usually wins. In all matters of gambling, I am rather unbeatable."

Stone frowned. In all matters of . . . *gambling!* His mouth fell open. Garrison! So that was how he did it!

Gubwa had chosen that very moment to read his mind. His pink eyes became slits in his puffy, leprous face: his version of a knowing smile. "Indeed," his voice was very low, very

216

sinister. "Richard Garrison—and you have been given the task of protecting him."

Stone's mind went back to Garrison's file—all he had read and memorized of the man—but in the next moment he gasped, gritted his teeth and bit his lip until it hurt, deliberately dragging his mind away from that subject.

Gubwa laughed, a deep, almost hearty laugh. "Oh, do not concern yourself! I know more of Garrison than ever you could tell me. Far more, though not yet enough. Sincerely, Mr. Stone, there is nothing I want of you in the way of information. Nothing I want *out* of you at all. Instead, let me tell you something about him." He quickly outlined the relevant facts, even went so far as to mention several things Stone had not previously known, until the agent once more relaxed in his chair. Gubwa was right: there was nothing Stone had that he didn't already know.

"So what do you want of me?"

Gubwa pursed his lips, then shrugged. "Again, it can do no harm to tell you. I have—'a friend'— in a rival branch of your so-called 'secret' services. He would dearly love to see Garrison dead, also to discredit MI6, your branch . . ."

"Sir Harry," Stone scowled.

"Close enough," Gubwa nodded. "Actually Sir Harry's boss, working through him." He smiled again. "But you see, you *are* intelligent! And being so intelligent, perhaps I need explain no further?"

"I'm getting the picture," Stone answered, "but I'd still be happier hearing it from you. I mean, you're the telepath, not me."

Gubwa raised his eyebrows. "You disappoint me. But as you will, I shall explain:

"By using you to achieve my aims, I will kill Garrison—eventually—and at the same time perform a service useful to Sir Harry. MI6 will carry the burden of the blame. Now this is not all-important to me, this 'service' I propose to perform. No, for eventually I will be obliged to deal with Sir Harry, too. That is to say, kill him. But being 'in league with him,' shall we say, does give me a little security in the event that my plans are not immediately successful. It is simply a matter of being careful."

"Let's get this straight," said Stone. "You see yourself as the future Emperor of Earth, right?"

Gubwa nodded. "Yes."

"I see. And you'll bring this about through, er, holocaust?"

"Not 'er' holocaust, Mr. Stone, *a* holocaust. The neutron bomb, chiefly, though there will be other nuclear devices involved, yes."

Stone nodded, very slowly. "And after that you intend that the human race—what's left of it— should become a gang of freaks, *Hermaphro Sapiens*, like yourself?"

"I will see to it that several genetic engineers, clone technicians, etc., survive, yes. They will be the fathers of the New Earth—figuratively speaking, of course. I, in fact, shall be the true father. My own sperm shall be the seed of future generations."

Stone sighed, nodded, slumped down in his chair as best he could. After a moment he looked up. "You really are quite mad, you know that? I mean, surely this is something straight out of James Bond. Just let's suppose for a moment that you can do all you say you're going to do: mentally manipulate the world to disaster, kill us all off and start again with a selected few— yes, and even breed a race of superfreaks to—"

"Ah!" Gubwa stopped him. "No, I said nothing about that. I would never allow the development of another whose powers were as great or greater than my own. That would be strictly controlled."

"I see . . ."

"What do you see?" said Gubwa, looking into the agent's mind. His great gray face grew angry then. He approached, towered over Stone's chair, looked down on him. "You're wrong, Stone, I fear no man!"

"Except Garrison?"

"I said I fear no *man*, Mr. Stone! No m-a-n." Gubwa spelled it out. "You are *Homo Sapiens*; the world I envisage will be a world of *Hermaphro Sapiens*; but if I am right in what I suspect of Garrison—"

"He's not a man?"

"A man—of sorts. *Homo Superior*, I suspect."

"And you want to know what it is he's got that makes him *Homo Superior*, right?"

"Correct. And when I have the answer—then he dies."

"So what it boils down to, man or superman, you *do* fear him."

"You see?" Gubwa hissed, towering closer still. "So very intelligent! Wasn't I right about you, Mr. Stone?" He clubbed one mighty fist and raised it, and for a moment Stone believed he would strike him. Then—

—He quickly turned away and pointed, throwing out the fingers of his fist straight and stiff in the direction of the bas-relief figure astride the Earth-image. "Nothing must be allowed to interfere with that, Mr. Stone—nothing!"

"And Garrison could, is that it?"

Gubwa turned and stared at him. "Perhaps," he nodded. "Yes, perhaps he could. But that in itself is not my dilemma. No, you were right the first time. I want to know what makes him tick. You see, I know where *my* powers come from: they are born of the atom, as were the body and mind that house them. Therefore I will admit to being, as you say, a 'freak,' a mutation. But Garrison is not. How then is *he* what he is?"

"A telepath?" Stone seemed surprised. "Surely lots of people have claimed to be—"

"Claimed!" Gubwa exploded. He threw back his great head and laughed. "Telepath! How little you know! You have no idea, Mr. Stone, what Garrison is, what he can do. Telepathy, indeed! Oh, much more than that. So much more. He is—" he threw his arms wide, forming a great cross, "—incredible! Let me tell you about Garrison. Let me fill in a few more of the gaps in your knowledge. Where to start . . . oh, yes!

"I have always been aware, you see, that certain minds are different. My own, for instance, and those of several others I've come across over the years. There are a great many men—women, too—whose ESP centers are developed away and beyond the norm or average. Indeed, one might grade them as the numismatist grades his coins.

"First there is 'Ungraded' or 'Poor,' common man in all his billions, who knows nothing whatsoever of ESP let alone controls the power. And 'Fair,' who occasionally finds himself whistling some obscure tune precisely at the same time another begins to whistle it, for he has received an impression of it from that other's mind. Then there is 'Fine' who knows 'instinctively' when his father dies—though they are miles apart—or who can 'feel' that something is about to happen. Of him there are many thousands. Do you see the structure?"

Stone nodded. "I follow you. Go on."

"Very well. Above 'Fine' we would place 'Very Fine'—the man who can fairly accurately read the minds of his wife or children, and who usually has a leaning towards the so-called 'occult.' That is to say, this one *knows* he is different. Alas, he is only a little different. But rising through the grades we now find 'Extremely Fine'—the gambler whose chances are far better than average; perhaps the policeman or detective whose 'hunches' always seem to work out. These are few and far between, and with them the power goes far beyond mere blood-ties or friendships. Rarer still, however, are the topmost grades, who can read most minds with little difficulty and whose control of ESP is far more extensive than mere telepathy.

"Recently, in Tibet, I discovered an entire cache of this latter grade—a rare find indeed. I became jealous, caused the Communist Chinese authorities there to suspect them of being Fifth Columnists—which they were—and was directly responsible for their extermination. All of this without once leaving this retreat of mine."

"How utterly charming of you," said Stone.

"Coins," Gubwa continued, ignoring his sarcasm, "and their grading. I wandered there for a moment. Finally I must grade myself . . .

"Well, as I have said, I am unique. I suppose you might say that I have been overprinted—a rare coin made rarer still by having been struck twice on one disc . . . or perhaps I am an exceedingly high denomination mistakenly minted in a base metal. Just so—but this is a far different grading to the one I used to apply to myself, before the advent of Garrison.

"Oh, yes, for there was once a time when I considered myself FDC—that is to say *Fleur de Coin*. But . . . I graded myself too highly. It was a gigantic vanity. Only Garrison is truly FDC, and only he is truly unique. There *is* no other like him.

"Telepathy? That is the most meager of his talents. No, untrue, it is merely one of them. Consider: he was blinded. Now he sees. Consider: his woman was also blind. She sees. Ah, but that is not all: she *was* dead!"

At this Stone snorted his derision. "The body of a certain Vicki Maler was placed in cryogenic suspension at—"

"Not 'a certain Vicki Maler,' Mr. Stone—*the* Vicki Maler. Garrison revived her. I know. I have been inside her mind. She was frozen against the chance—the million-to-one chance—that science might one day discover a means of reviving her. Garrison already has that science. And consider this: she was riddled with the terrible cancer which killed her. Now she is perfect. That, too, is Garrison's work . . .

"Finally there are his most recent—shall we continue to say—works? Occurring within the space of the last twenty-four hours, they are perfect examples of his power. Only yesterday—for you have been unconscious overnight, Mr. Stone—his plane was bombed. That was over the Aegean Sea. He flew that crippled plane to England, to Gatwick, and landed it there safely. Without engines, without any means of aerodynamic control, without wheels! And the plane landed like a feather, the most perfect of perfect crash-landings."

"I know about that," said Stone. "A miraculous escape, a—"

"Rubbish!" Gubwa snapped. "You know nothing. A miracle is in the eyes of the beholder. It is usually the occurrence of a highly unlikely event. The impossible on the other hand cannot occur because it is *impossible*. What will the authorities make of it, I wonder, when they discover that Garrison's plane came in ninety minutes too soon? From the moment the bomb exploded and crippled it, it must have been travelling at a speed *far in excess* of its maximum possible speed!"

Stone's mind was whirling again.

"Now *that* is what I call levitation!" Gubwa continued. "The pilot is still convinced it was an act of God. Oh, the effort tired Garrison, certainly, for which reason he is now resting—but is that difficult to understand? Think of it! Think of what he did! Moreover, he discovered the author of the crime and struck back. Except that here he was much more lenient than I would have been."

"Now you've really lost me," said Stone.

"Ah! Of course, for you do not yet know who tried to kill him. Well, I shall tell you. It was the Mafia—or rather, a small member of that crude and unwieldy organization. His name is Vicenti."

"Carlo Vicenti? We've been interested in him and his pals for some time. Are you sure it was him? How did you get onto him so quickly?"

"I am sure, yes," Gubwa answered. "The bomb could only have been planted in Rhodes; an ugly pair called the Black brothers are there; I have been in "Bomber" Bert Black's mind. It was them. He himself planted the device."

"Wait," said Stone, his gravelly voice suddenly weary. "Too fast. If they are still in Rhodes, how could you have been 'in' Bomber's mind? How do you know they are there anyway?"

Gubwa turned Stone's chair to face his huge desk. "You see my computer there? I know the Blacks are in Rhodes because my computer told me. It talks to the computer at Gatwick. Also to those at New Scotland Yard, and to many others. Even to your own machine at MI6 HQ." His smile was broader now than Stone had ever seen it. "Ah, and at last you begin to see, Mr. Stone! And perhaps I am not so crazy after all, eh?"

"But how did Garrison know it was Vicenti? And how did he strike back at him?"

Gubwa sighed, losing patience. "When the bomb went off he became aware that he was a target. He looked for people with a grudge. Vicenti was one such. A quick look inside his mind—" He shrugged.

"You mean he tackled Vicenti after his plane landed, before he went into hospital?"

"While his plane was in the air, Mr. Stone. Distance is nothing to the true telepath, not if he knows his target. He visited Vicenti's mind as I visited Bert Black's. At least I suppose that is how it was. And he then delivered Vicenti a psychic blow, several of them, but not fatal. Vicenti, too, is hospitalized. He should consider himself lucky; if I were Garrison I would have killed him."

Stone now seemed weary to death. "But you can't be sure that Garrison did it to Vicenti. He might simply have been involved in an accident."

"But I have been in Carlo Vicenti's mind, too. *He* knows that it was Garrison. He doesn't know how, but he knows it was him."

"It's all over my head." Stone seemed genuinely lost. "Maybe I'm not as smart as you think."

"Oh, but you are," Gubwa laughed. "You have a very agile mind. You have soaked up every word I've uttered, even as a sponge soaks up water. Your weariness is an act. You must not take me for a fool, Mr. Stone, for I am not. Nor have you led me on, as you assume. I have told you nothing I did not wish you to know."

Stone wasn't a good loser. "Shit!" he said through clenched teeth. He sat up a little straighter. "Okay, I'll stop pretending. And let's say I believe all you say. Or at least let's say I'm open to suggestion. There are still some things I'd like to know. For one, how did you get onto Garrison in the first place? That is, how did you twig him for . . . an ESP-master?"

"Two years ago," Gubwa answered, "a good many strange things occurred, all centered about him. Until then I had not been interested in Garrison, did not know he existed. The world is full of minds; I visit only those I wish to visit. Garrison was of no interest to me. Since then, however, I have discovered all that I now know of him. Which isn't yet enough. But it will be . . . soon.

"It was then, two years ago, that he regained his sight; then that he returned Vicki Maler to life, cleansed her of her disease, gave her back *her* sight. In other words that was when Garrison first became aware of his power, or gained full control over it. As to how I know it—" again his shrug, "I am a telepath. And every telepath in the world must have felt something of it!"

Gubwa's voice had fallen to a whisper, was filled with awe. "If I believed in God, Mr. Stone, which I do not, then I would have known that God was come down amongst men. Do you know what is meant by the biosphere?"

Stone nodded. "It's what you'll pollute with neutron bombs."

Again Gubwa chose to ignore the jibe. "Then picture a great meteorite rushing through Earth's atmosphere and causing the most violent storm you could ever imagine. Picture the air and the ocean whipped to a frenzy, the elements enraged. Do you have it? Good! Now take it one step further. Picture a *psychic* biosphere—a Psychosphere, if you wish—in which ESP talent and potential takes the place of life in the biosphere. And picture that Psychosphere torn as by some mental meteor! That was Garrison's coming, his awakening, Mr. Stone. And that explains the paradox: why on the one hand I want him dead, while on the other he must not die."

Stone looked blank.

"Numismatics, my friend," said Gubwa. "He is *Fleur de Coin*, the only one in the batch. Where was he minted, by whom? If you were a collector and such a coin came into your hands, wouldn't you ask yourself these questions? Of course you would. And if you checked the metal, discovered that it had been melted down from old stock and re-stamped—"

"A counterfeit!" said Stone.

"Just so," Gubwa excitedly agreed, "but better than any original, the work of a genius! And what question would you next ask yourself?"

"Who made it?"

"Correct!" Gubwa clasped the agent's shoulders in iron hands. "And surely—*how* was it made?"

He looked down, looked deep into Stone's unflinching gaze. "What happened to him two years ago, that gave him powers comparable to those of a god?"

Stone narrowed his eyes, believed for a moment that he had found Gubwa out. "Why don't you ask him?" he said. "Why don't you just get inside his mind and—" He saw his error.

Gubwa's eyes had shot open, were now wide and pink and bulging. "What?" he hissed. "Have you learned nothing? Believed nothing? Man, I would not even *approach* Garrison's mind! I would sooner swim in a pool of piranhas—yes, with the veins of my wrists open and bleeding!"

Chapter
14

"**O**F COURSE I SOUGHT TO DISCOVER THE source of this vast disturbance in the Psychosphere. I had to; the thing was wild, it lured me. And to find it—why, all I had to do was close my eyes and send my mind blindly out, out . . . and the very *aura* of Garrison did the rest! I found myself hurled about like a twig in a whirlpool, a leap in the very maelstrom. Enter his mind . . . ?

"I have been on the threshold. It seethes, boils, crashes with energies. I would be a fly caught up in a high-speed fan. And if I survived—*if*, mind you—he would know me, would follow my limping trail home. And knowing me, he *would* destroy me."

"He didn't destroy Vicenti," Stone pointed out.

"But he hurt him!" Gubwa was quick to return. "And how then would he deal with me, who stands at the back of it all? Charon Gubwa, the grand engineer of all his trials."

"You? How?"

"How? But didn't I set those minds in action which now work against him? It was a testing, don't you see? Only it got out of control! I dared not go against Garrison, not personally—dared not try him out—and so I arranged for others to do it for me. Who else do you think put Garrison in the minds of all those oh-so-interested parties if not me? I *can* influence the minds of others, Mr. Stone, don't forget it. Indeed, I am an adept. Haven't I told you I destroyed those monks in Tibet? Ah, but they weren't of Garrison's mettle!

"Still, the wheels I have set in motion must eventually crush him, one way or the other. Or I will crush him, by discovering his secret. But until I know it he must not be crushed."

Stone slowly nodded his head. "And that's where I come in, right?"

"Correct. Garrison has a weakness, a chink in his armor. The woman Vicki Maler. I believe that she knows his secret. Or if she does not actually know it, then at least the clues to it are buried in her mind. I shall dig them out."

"Why haven't you already done so? If all you say of your telepathy is true, you—"

NO, NO, NO! Gubwa shouted in Stone's mind, electrifying him afresh. "You still don't understand, do you? Garrison is close to the woman. She is like his child. Resurrected her?—why, one might go so far as to say he *made* her! He is never very far from her mind. And if ever he found me there . . ."

"And so you can't really tackle her," said Stone.

"Oh, but I have tried, I have tried. It had seemed to me that recently, within the last six months, Garrison's strength was waning. When chance permitted, I actually found and entered Vicki Maler's mind. There were several such occasions, and I was always lucky. Or perhaps it was not simple luck. Perhaps my ESP told me the best times. But in any case the contact was always brief—never long enough to learn much, no time to be discovered. The last time was only a matter of days ago, while she and Garrison were still in Rhodes—since when he has performed these 'miracles' we've spoken of, proving that he's as powerful as ever. Or at least powerful enough to constitute a real threat."

Stone frowned. "So how will you do it? If you can't get at her, how will—"

"I can't 'get at her' as you have it, while she's out there, beyond these walls. But *in* here there are ways! Here I am the master, and I am not without protection."

Stone saw it coming. "I'm to bring her here?"

Gubwa smiled, nodded. "Indeed you are."

"So you really are crazy after all! If what you've told me of Garrison is only half-true—why, he'll mince me!"

"That is a distinct possibility," Gubwa blandly agreed. "And one to be avoided." He smiled again.

"And through me he'll find you, and—"

"No," the other snapped, his smile disappearing in an instant. "He will not find me. If you are discovered your mind will simply self-destruct. It will burn itself out before telling anything about me. Oh, yes, Mr. secret agent Stone—you would die before talking, or before having the facts extracted."

"—And in any case, I won't do it."

Gubwa's smile was back, growing wider by the minute. He began to nod his great white head. "Oh, yes, you will." He took Stone's chair and wheeled it across the floor. Doors hissed open at their approach. "I'm now going to show you my mind laboratory, Mr. Stone. Being as you are a secret agent, you'll be familiar with the term brainwashing. Yes, I'm sure you are. Well, my mind-lab is a veritable laundry. And of course I've already mentioned my expertise in the field of mesmerism? yes . . ."

Along the corridor the great albino paused for a moment. "Dear, oh, *dear*, Mr. Stone! Why, I'm really quite surprised at you! Those are not very kind thoughts at all, now are they?"

While Charon Gubwa worked on Stone in the mind-lab, Vicki Maler sat by Garrison's bedside in a small whitewashed hospital room in Haslemere, Surrey.

It was an austere place by any standards, but Garrison's private doctor—a much respected man, whose patients were extremely rich and/ or very important persons all—liked austerity. To him sparseness was synonymous with cleanliness, and cleanliness was the basic necessity of all good medicine. At the moment Vicki was alone with Garrison, indeed at present he was the only resident patient, but Dr. Jamieson was about somewhere.

The room's window look out under the branches of willows across a close-cropped, fenced garden. Beyond the fence a stream or beck sparkled in early morning sunlight. In fact the place was not a hospital at all in the accepted sense of the word but Jamieson's home. It was very expensive but not at all an easy place to find, and Vicki was satisfied that Garrison was safe here. Safe from what she could not say. From his own waking fears, maybe. From killers—such as the would-be killers who had sabotaged the plane—that remained to be seen.

Until now their personal security had not been a problem to concern her. Safety usually went hand in hand with Garrison; to be with him *was* to be safe. Or had used to be. She looked at him; sedated, he slept. And he needed it. His face was drawn, his forehead lined. His hands twitched occasionally, however faintly, on top of the bedclothes . . .

Vicki had arrived an hour earlier. She had been greeted by the doctor and his nurse-assistant, probably his wife. Richard (they had told her) would not be up and about until Monday morning. Since today was Friday, that would give him three more full days and nights of rest, and Dr. Jamieson would ensure that they were three full days.

The police had been on the telephone twice, requesting a statement from Garrison in respect of the bombed plane, but the doctor had put them off. His patient could not be disturbed, he had told them. Garrison was physically and mentally run-down, teetering upon a nervous brink, and the only sure way he could be revitalized was by resting.

There had also been the matter of the contact lenses, which had arrived while Garrison and Vicki were in Rhodes. She did not know what Richard had done to Dr. Jamieson, but the business of her own and Garrison's eyes didn't seem to be at all problematic. He had already fitted Garrison's lenses (in accordance with previous orders, apparently), and upon Vicki's arrival he had worn a pair of tinted spectacles to fit hers. After a few minutes she hadn't even known she was wearing them. Then she had been taken to Richard's room and left there, since when she had simply sat here at his bedside.

Very carefully, she now took one of his hands in hers. His flesh was cool, seemed somehow fragile, almost brittle. A plastic hand. She squeezed it, just to reassure herself. But of what? To confirm that Garrison was real? That she was real? Vicki found herself trembling. *Was* she real?

The fact that she no longer loved Garrison suddenly bloated in her mind like some strange orchid. One minute it was absent, the next it had opened, hybrid and scentless. It was not beautiful, but strangely it was not ugly. It was merely there: a fact, not even a hard one to assimilate. For how can one love a constant threat? The axe that hangs over one's head . . . the fraying threads of rope by which one hangs from the cliff . . . the clock relentlessly ticking away one's final hour.

You cannot love that which you don't know. She had once known Garrison, briefly, and through her long illness his remembered beauty had remained with her, buoyed her up; the joy of having had him sustained her to the end. And she had thought that she could have loved him. And she *had* loved—adored him—in the new beginning. Then . . . the rope had started to fray. The axe had seemed so heavy hanging over her. The ticking of the clock had grown incredibly loud, a roar of sound in her ears.

If Garrison died, she died—and this time she would stay dead. Vicki had been there once. It was a fearful place. She couldn't remember the limbo of it and didn't want to, but she had hated it. She hated the thought of it, the *threat* of it. Garrison was that threat. Him she did not hate, but she was even more certain that she did not love him. And how long before she did hate him, and how shortly after that must he know it?

Being Garrison, perhaps he had already seen it coming . . .

She stayed with Garrison for a further half-hour. Suzy, Garrison's black Doberman pinscher bitch whom Vicki had left waiting patiently in the car, sat still until she had the door half-open, then squeezed out. The dog's tail wagged and she lolled her tongue at her mistress but no amount of persuasion, cajoling or threatening could get her back inside the car again. Angry, Vicki followed Suzy back to the door of the doctor's house. Dr. Jamieson stood upon the step, smiling a little awkwardly, waiting for her to leave.

He was a stocky, moon-faced man in a very old tweed suit. "It's all right, my dear, she can stay," he reassured Vicki. "Richard said she'd probably be along."

"Oh!" said Vicki. "Yes, she doesn't like to be too far away from him."

Suzy wagged her tail, came and licked Vicki's hand. She was aware now that she could stay. But her head kept turning in towards the house; she wanted to be with Garrison.

As Vicki finally drove away, both Jamieson and Suzy came down to the gate at the bottom of the drive to see her off; but as soon as the car cornered out of the leafy lane, Suzy left the doctor's side and ran back to the house. In she went and straight to Garrison's room, where she waited until Jamieson opened the door for her. Then she entered and jumped up on the chair beside her master's bed.

She sat there straight-backed, her head slightly forward, ears erect, eyes fixed firmly upon him where he lay. She watched him intently, listened with twitches of her ears to his steady breathing. Then she settled down a little, gave one small whine, lay back her ears and made herself a little more comfortable.

Jamieson left the door open for her. She would come to him when she was hungry . . .

Garrison had reached a junction in the dried-out bed of the stream he followed. Here where it split, the walls which miles back had been mere banks were now cliffs of red stone, rising sharp and sheer for hundreds of feet. The bed of the stream had seemed the easiest trail to follow, but now Garrison shook his head in disgust. It seemed unthinkable that the lie of the land could have changed so swiftly.

There had been green banks, a little water gurgling below, a gently winding, watery way to follow. Then the grass had become scrub as the banks grew boulder-strewn and steep, and finally the water had petered out. Then Garrison might have left the stream and headed for higher ground, but he had been tired or lazy or both, had failed to make the effort but simply allowed himself to drift on. And the banks had grown even steeper and craggier above a narrowing river gorge, until now at last the way divided, a cleft in the shade of the towering cliffs.

And now which way to go? Right or left?

Left would be the wizard's way, of course: the left-hand path. That would seem Garrison's natural choice, but . . .

The way seemed narrower to the left. He would hate to find the trail narrowed suddenly to an impassible crack in solid rock, and then have to come back all this way. The right-hand path seemed fairly wide; its dusky veil of gloom was parted here and there with shafts of light from above; there should be no baleful magics there to blight his course.

Suzy crouched closer to his back and whined ominously. Garrison frowned—edged the Machine forward right, then left, and paused—

cursed and set Psychomech down upon the cracked bed of the stream. He climbed down from the broad, now rust-tainted back of the Machine, Suzy jumping down beside him. Where its base stood upon hard earth the Machine's metal was actually scabbed with rust, some of it already flaking, and its hard plastic casing was showing cracks. Within, fraying cables were visible behind blistered tubes and blackened piping.

Garrison grunted. Better to leave the thing here and go forward on foot. Except that that would be like shooting an old horse just because he'd lost a shoe. Garrison grunted again and shook his head. No, it was worse than that and he knew it. A horse with a broken leg . . . or even a broken back!

But in any case he could not simply leave the Machine behind. No, for it had been there with him in his vision of the future, that agonizing vision of the parched desert glimpsed in the shew-stone of the circle of wizards. And so the Machine must go on with him, but along which path? If only he might glimpse the future again, see his way clear ahead . . .

"Richard . . . oh, Richard!" came the merest whisper of a soft female voice, fast on the heels of his fleeting thought.

"What. . . ?" Garrison fell into a crouch, gazed all about, first at the left-hand path, then the right. "Where? Who?" But Suzy, her coat bristling, knew no such indecision. No, the bitch stared straight into that well of shadows which was the left-hand path, and her growl was all the answer Garrison needed—for now.

"So that's the way, is it, girl?" he said, his eyes narrowing. *"And you heard it, too, did you?"* Suzy whined in answer, pressed closer to his knee.

"Richard, please!" came that woman's sigh again. "Please help me! Oh, please, please let me go!"

Help her? Let her go? What did it mean? Garrison's flesh crept. Wizardry? Witchcraft? A very black magic, certainly. And yet he knew, or had known, that voice. In some other place, some other time. He grasped at that last thought: some other time. Could it be, he wondered? A voice from his future, auguring some event yet to come? He had, after all, expressed his desire to glance once more beyond the veil of the present and into future time. And was this his answer?

He strained forward, his limbs shaking, his eyes already stinging from fathoming or attempting to fathom the vault of shadows which lay behind the entrance to the left-hand path. Did something move there? The figure of a girl, seen fleetingly, a wraith amongst the shadows? A girl, hiding, fleeing from shaded place to shaded place? Fleeing from whom? From Garrison? Possibly, for she had begged to be let go. Why, then, had she called on him for help? And if not fleeing from him, fleeing from—what?

Something else moved in there! Garrison's flesh crept again, violently, rippling on his limbs and body like the ripples on a pool. Cold sweat started from his forehead. Something moved, hanging from above, drifting, swaying along the zig-zag, flitting route taken by the girl. Several somethings. Trailing somethings—like tentacles.

The Other! That diseased evil insidious as cancer, gray as leprosy, warped as insanity. That vast octopus of evil from Garrison's dream within a dream! His enemy of enemies!

He waited no longer but clambered back onto the Machine. Suzy made no effect to mount behind him but raced beneath as he rode Psychomech into the gap of the left-hand path. In there was a deeper gloom than had been expected, a chill gloom and clammy as fog, but Garrison knew it for a psychic thing. The depression was in his mind, its external oppression springing from the heaviness of spirit within.

But now, too, he found that he must go cautiously; for here, where overhead the cliffs actually met in places—or rather where the upper strata remained but had been undercut by ancient waters—great stalactites depended to bar his way with their looming mass, forming columns where upthrusting spires had long ages since cojoined. And between and around these limestone relics he must drive the Machine, never knowing what lurked beyond or when it would strike, but ever aware that terror was here, breathing in the centuried stone.

Then, far down the cleft where the way grew narrower still—another movement!—a fleeting inkblot amongst the shadows, pressed low to the ground. "Suzy!" cried Garrison. "Wait, girl!" And her bark coming back to him, echoing with his own voice and dying into chill silence. But no, he must not call her back. She scouted the way for him and that was good.

He urged a little more speed from the Machine (in truth he merely exerted himself the more, for Psychomech was now worse than useless), and as his eyes grew more accustomed to the ever-deepening darkness bore along the old water-course, whose walls continued to close in on him. And thus, suddenly, from a claustrophobic realm into a wide, expansive elfland! Or perhaps a place of ogres . . .

So it seemed to Garrison as, bursting from the now completely arched-over tunnel, he entered through a portal into a huge irregular cavern of strange beauty and even stranger horror; and here he brought his Machine to a halt. Perhaps it was the sight of Suzy, cowering, that caused him to apply mental brakes; perhaps the sure knowledge that this was the subterranean lair of Evil itself. Oh, of shimmering beauty the cavern had its share, but so does the web of a spider.

The place had a domed, stone dagger-festooned ceiling, irregular perimeter columns of stalagmitic rock, a fairly even floor, though dotted here and there with weird mushrooms of dripstone, and the ghostly luminescence of the long-entombed: a firefly glitter that lent illumination and wonder to an otherwise lightless hole. Garrison skirted a column of massive girth which obstructed his way and his view, and came to where Suzy crouched, panted and whined. She immediately scrabbled up behind him, pressing to his back and shuddering as from a drenching in icy water.

And now Garrison saw the reason for Suzy's dread and understood his own. For without a doubt the Being which sat upon or floated over its stalagmitic throne at the far side of the cavern was that same Other of his inmost dream, the many-tentacled blasphemy whose nature was neither male nor female, neither black nor white, neither truly sane and human nor insane and inhuman but Other than these things.

Red-eyed, that horror, and glaring intently, searchingly—but not in Garrison's direction. No, for at the foot of that Being's throne here lay the phantom girl, whose sobbing was audible only as a distant sighing, whose shape and form were hidden in an ethereal glow or nebulosity from beyond the grave. And though Garrison could swear he knew or had known this creature, now he saw that she was indeed a wraith, a ghost; and knowing this he knew the Other for a necromancer, a wizard who raises up and questions the dead! But to what end, and how and why should it concern Garrison? In what way might the dead instruct the living, and how might Garrison possibly be endangered by such instruction?

With his flesh freshly acrawl, still he urged the Machine forward across the open floor of the cavern, and emerging from the shadows of encircling columns . . . was checked. He found himself shut out . . . beyond a certain point, roughly halfway, the Machine would not go, had seemed to come up against some invisible wall or impenetrable barrier. Garrison had met with such before and knew their breaking was impossible or at best most difficult. Weary and debilitated as he was through his fear, he could not summon the strength even to attempt such a breaking. How then might he help the ghost-girl or in any way interfere with the wizard's necromancies?

It seemed that he could not; moreover, slowly it was dawning on him that what he saw was not real, or at best some symbolic vision from an as yet inchoate future. Else why had the Other failed to detect him? The answer seemed simple: he had asked to see the future, the Other in that future had not asked to see the past. Garrison could observe but could not interfere.

His frustration knew no bounds. He must help the poor, shrinking luminescence, the ghost-girl of whom no single detail could be gleaned beneath her ethereal glimmer but whose whispered pleas had raised ghosts of their own, the ghosts of Garrison's memory. But how might he help? Too weary now even to think clearly, he could only look on as the tableau enacted itself beyond his and the Machine's and Suzy's range—but in another moment he held his breath at something else he saw.

For within the impenetrable area were not two figures but three, the third emerging with some stealth from behind a row of thin stalactites that arrased the upward curving far wall like a curtain—and Garrison knew the intruder. It was the Secret One, also from his dream within a dream, and clad in his Robe of Secrecy. An acolyte of the Other? Perhaps. But that did not explain the way he glided, silent and stealthy, now darting to place himself between ghost-girl and monster and drag her up and out of the clutches of that dread Being.

Across the floor of the cavern they fled, the Secret One bearing up her luminescent form where she lay half-fainting in his arms. And after them the now enraged Other, clearly bent upon their destruction, his many tentacles outstretched, with all their hooked sucker-mouths gaping and constricting in a frenzy of loathsome anticipation. For a moment it seemed that all would be well, that the pair might possibly escape—but then they came up against the inside of that very wall which kept Garrison out—and behind them the monster, leprous-gray and pulsating with rage!

"No!" Garrison cried out his frustration, his anguish. "No, this must not be!" And whatever part of him it was that issued forth from him at that moment to sear the wall—whatever ESP power he inadvertently unleashed, which attempted to transcend time itself and strike for the future—it seemed that it drained him utterly. For the moment, at least.

The Machine settled to the floor and teetered there an instant, then lay inert; and Garrison fell in a half-faint to sprawl across its broad back. Yet still he clung to consciousness long enough to see the Secret One straining forward through the weakened wall, and the ghost-girl bundled in his arms, and long enough to watch them make away, safe now from pursuit.

Then the darkness swept in upon him, and only with the greatest effort of will was he able to keep his eyes open and witness the final wonder: that

*of the Other in all his monstrousness, writhing
and raving and fading away, back into that future whence Garrison had drawn this strange and
inexplicable vision . . .*

It was not unconsciousness that claimed Garrison then but a psychic numbness, a spiritual exhaustion or weary lassitude; from which, with her
pawing and whining, Suzy eventually contrived
to rouse him. She knew, wise creature, that this
was no place to sleep, that they must be up and
about, away on their quest.

And surprisingly, for all the aching weariness
of his body, head and limbs, Garrison discovered
that he could now sit up; moreover that he could
lift Psychomech up from the floor and however
sluggishly guide the Machine from the great
cave. Where the Other had writhed on or over his
stalagmite throne there now opened a gloom-
shrouded tunnel, and far along its curving length
a glimmer could be seen as of daylight.

Slowly, yard by aching yard, man, dog and
Machine made for that glimmer, that glow of life
which grew and expanded with each passing
moment. Of the three Suzy seemed least affected,
merely eager to be out of the place. Garrison had
gone beyond tired, could only sway and nod and
groan where he sat. And the Machine . . . ?

Below Psychomech's belly a worn-through,
fraying cable dangled, and in the Machine's wake
lay frequent patches of red, fallen rust . . .

Chapter
15

AT 11:00 A.M., ON THE FOLLOWING MONDAY, CARLO Vicenti released himself from care. His doctor argued with him, likewise the nurses on his ward, but Vicenti's boys helped him dress and gave him what assistance they could to limp out of the place. Through the worst of it one thought made it all worthwhile: that when the Big Guy was finished with Garrison, then it would be his turn. Vicenti knew exactly what Mr. Garrison's fate was to be: concrete boots and a deep, very damp grave. And Garrison going down slow with a gag in his mouth, terror in his eyes and gaping, bubbling nostrils.

As for the subject of Vicenti's plan: as coincidence would have it Garrison left Dr. Jamieson's house in Haslemere at about the same time. Vicki Maler took his great silver Mercedes to pick him up, but from the moment she parked the car and got out of the driving seat she knew something was wrong. There was a sign she could hardly fail to recognize, one she had come to know all too well. Suzy was sitting outside the open front door of the house, her expression one of complete dog-despondency. The great black bitch had not been beaten or even chastised, Vicki knew that. It was simply that she had sensed a change in her master; this was how she was affected whenever one of Garrison's Gestalt facets took ascendence.

On this occasion that facet was Thomas Schroeder, and Vicki knew him as soon as he appeared with Jamieson in the open doorway. Oh, it was Richard Garrison's body and shape— though even these seemed strangely altered, so that at best his suit was ill-fitting—but the alien gestures and posture and voice, particularly the voice, quite gave him away. While the vocal cords were Garrison's, the accent and inflection could only be Schroeder's.

"Vicki, my dear!" he greeted her. "And punctual as ever. Thank you for coming for me." He took her hand like an old friend, which of course he was or had been, but there was a chill in his flesh and a feel to it that Vicki couldn't quite stomach. His kiss, for all that it was the merest peck, was almost unbearable. She knew exactly how Suzy felt and was glad when finally Garrison/Schroeder released her and turned to Dr. Jamieson.

"Just let me know what I owe you," he told him, smiling. "You shall have my check by return."

"Of course, Mr., er, Garrison." The doctor briefly took his hand and shook it, then turned to Vicki. "Now do take care of him, young lady, won't you? He's still not as strong as he should be, and—"

"And you fuss too much, my friend!" Garrison/Schroeder was smiling still, but his tone had grown harder, the German accent coming through a shade stronger. "I shall be just fine. I needed a little rest, that's all. Some peace and quiet—which you and your home provided most admirably. And for which you will be paid."

"Of course, of course," Jamieson was quick to placate him. "It's just a doctor's natural concern for his patient, that's all."

"Quite," Garrison/Schroeder nodded his head. "Well, thank you again, but now we must be on our way. Time is mistakenly thought of as a commodity—but none of us ever really has enough of it, and it is something we can't buy more of."

He led Vicki to the car, helped her into the front passenger seat and opened a back door for Suzy. The black Doberman whined as she jumped into the back to sit there, staring at him curiously, but Garrison/Schroeder merely smiled as he started the car and nodded a last farewell to the doctor.

Jamieson was still standing there as the car turned out of his drive and onto the country road beyond the gardens . . .

"Vicki," said Garrison/Schroeder when they had found a first-class road and were speeding for home, "you know of course who I am?"

"Oh, yes, Thomas," she answered, sighing, "I know."

He nodded, never taking his eyes from the road. "Very well, then know this also: I am not here through any ordinary resurgence of psyche. In future I will be here more often. Willy, too. He shall have his place. This is not a late recognition of status, more an *equality* of the same. True we all inhabit Richard's body, his mind, but not in the way I envisioned it when I was . . . before.

"We are, in a way, completely separate identities. But Richard's was the strongest identity—yes, I said *was*—and he would not relinquish control lightly. Despite my earlier generosity, he quickly grew jealous over his right of tenancy."

"Your generosity?" she broke in when he paused. "Are you talking about the money you left him? His right of tenancy? But you said it yourself: it's his body!"

"But *our* mind! We're all in here, Vicki. We share knowledge. Even suppressed, kept down, Keonig and I know when Richard is well, when he is unwell. Happy, unhappy. Threatened. Hurt! And we know that when—if—he dies, then we must die with him. Not only us, the three of us in here, but you, too. Oh, Vicki, Vicki child! You are resentful of us, Willy and I, but don't you see? We are your protection!"

"That's a . . . a side-effect, a spinoff," Vicki protested weakly. "Thomas, you were my father's friend, like a kind—a very kind—uncle to me. I appreciated that, but now I—"

"Now, now, *now!*" Garrison/Schroeder snapped. "Like it or not we are both of us, all of us, in the same boat!" His voice had risen in pitch, was harsh as chalk on a board. *"Mein Gott!—was ist los mit dir?"*

"Mit mir? Nichts!" she answered, her own heat rising. "But with you . . ? Is this the immortality you wanted, Thomas? What of our 'immortality' now?"

He was suddenly livid, Vicki could see that, but he made a concentrated effort to retain or regain his composure before answering. "Vicki, my dear, there are two flies in the ointment of 'my' immortality," he rasped. "You are one, the other is Richard himself. You because you interfere, Richard because he is the ascendant one: he is more often in possession. What an irony that of the three of us—myself, Willy, and Richard—Richard is least well-equipped to protect himself!"

"Is that why you're here? Now, I mean? To protect Richard?"

"To protect us all!" Garrison/Schroeder was calmer. "You know that the power is draining, Vicki. When it goes you will be the first to suffer. Don't you see how you will suffer? Blindness first, then death. You will . . . decay, Vicki! And very quickly. And like me, you have already been there once. You know what death is like . . ."

She shuddered. "Please don't!"—and turned to him sharply. "Thomas, I—"

He took a hand from the steering wheel, quietened her words before she could give them form. "Let me finish," he said. "The loss of power is not all. The plane was sabotaged, you know that. And so you must also know that an unseen, unknown agent is at work against us. Who? Why? Oh, I've had enemies enough in my time, but *that* Thomas Schroeder is no more. Likewise Koenig. And who would want to murder Richard, for what reason?"

"I . . . I don't know," she answered frowningly. "He's crossed people, I suppose, but—"

"—But murder? No, I think it goes deeper than a mere feud. That is merely its guise. We have become aware recently of another power in the Psychosphere, Vicki. An incredible, hostile power. That is the other reason I am here, the reason why I may yet have to call up Koenig in our defense. It is the sort of work Willy and I understand far better than Richard. So you see, there are problems enough without your adding to them with merely mundane, personal and emotional troubles of your own . . ." He looked at her shrewdly as her hand went to her mouth.

"You . . . know?" her eyes were wide, incredulous. And they were frightened.

"That you have started to doubt your love for Richard? Yes."

Now she sobbed openly, had difficulty controlling the ache inside her body, her soul. Finally she said: "I've tried to hide it . . ." She dabbed furiously at her tears. "But I knew that sooner or later you, he—all three of you—must read it in my mind. No, I don't love him!"

She had finally said it, was terrified of what

she had said, and now clutched at Garrison/ Schroeder's arm and wept harder yet. She buried her head in his breast, and as he pulled off the road and stopped the car on the grass verge, she said, "Oh, Thomas, Thomas—I can't help it! He *is* my life, but I don't love him. Yes, you're right, I have been . . . *there*. I have been dead. Oh, God!—and I fear it, fear it, *fear it*! But how can I love someone who must in the end kill me?"

"Vicki, Vicki!" he patted her shoulder, held her close and tight. "Don't, don't. Do you consider yourself a sinner? You haven't sinned. Were you disloyal? No, merely afraid. So you don't love Richard. Is that a crime? Not in my eyes—not even in Richard's, I am sure. What did you think he would do, will you out of existence? Is he— was he ever—that sort of man? Richard did not take lives, he saved them! He saved mine, for what it was worth . . ."

She looked up, dabbed at her tears; and for the first time it was as if Schroeder were actually here, that this was indeed that kind old uncle she used to know so very long ago. "He'll forgive me?"

"He'll be hurt, no doubt," Garrison/Schroeder answered. "He may not forgive you, not immediately. But is he a murderer? Is he a cold-blooded killer? Vicki, I Thomas Schroeder have killed men. I will not admit to murder, for those I killed or caused to die deserved it. Willy Koenig has also killed men, but for him I cannot answer. Still I tell you *nothing* could bring us to harm you. Why should we? And Richard—how could he? No, on that point you needlessly impale yourself."

"Oh, Thomas, if only—"

"My child, listen to me. We both fear death, you and I. Yes, for we of all mankind—and Christ, too, if you believe—have been dead and returned. Can you believe that while it is in my power to live I will suffer death again? You know I will not. But . . . someone wants to kill Richard. And however unwittingly, he would kill all of us with Richard. That is a terrible threat and my first task is to remove it. After that—" He shrugged, started the car.

"Yes?" she prompted him as he eased the Mercedes onto the road.

"After that I shall turn my attention to a much more difficult problem. Having removed the threat of immediate death, I hope to solve the riddle of eternal life. For I—we—are not immortal, Vicki, not yet. We lost that when Richard destroyed Psychomech. But the machine can be rebuilt, or a greater power may yet be discovered. Richard has dreamed, is dreaming even now, and his dream is a quest. He seeks that greater power."

"But what of me?" she asked. "Am I tied to him forever, without love?"

"I can't speak for Richard, Vicki," Garrison/Schroeder answered. "He may want to keep you, even without your love, but I doubt it. But whichever way it goes there is one thing I can promise you: while I live, you live. And, Vicki— you may believe that life is still very dear to me . . ."

* * *

At the house in Sussex Garrison/Schroeder wasted no time but took a heaped tray of food with him and locked himself in the study. He did not want to be disturbed. At midday a constable and police inspector called at the house, having driven up from Chichester to record statements. They had been requested to do so by the Metropolitan Police. Garrison/Schroeder emerged from the study for twenty minutes to offer them food and drinks and give them the statement they required. Vicki declined, saying that her experience on the plane had been more or less the same as his.

One thing Garrison/Schroeder did ask of the police was the names and addresses of the crew and hostess. During the outward flight to Rhodes the crew had only used shortened forenames, nicknames, and of course neither Garrison nor Vicki had known anything of their personal particulars.

When the police left, Garrison/Schroeder went back into the study. Before he locked the door, Vicki saw him take down a street map of London. A short while later she heard him using the telephone but could make out nothing of what he said.

He was in there for a further hour, finally came out looking pale and tired. His tray was empty and he was still hungry. While Cook prepared him a "proper meal" he sat and smoked, talked to no one. He ate his fill—not enjoying his food, simply stoking the fire, Vicki thought—then rested in the study, sprawled out at his ease in a great padded chair. At 4:00 P.M. he left the house, but before going he said to Vicki: "My dear, I'm not sure how long this will take. Do nothing out of the ordinary. Merely stay here and live as normally as you may. One of us will be back. Myself, Richard, or Willy."

Then he drove away in the big Mercedes, with Suzy (who appeared to be over her indecision about him) sitting beside him. Vicki waved them goodbye from the drive.

She would never see either one of them again . . .

At Gatwick airport Johnnie Fong used a public telephone to contact Gubwa. "Charon, I am at Gatwick. I followed Garrison here from the house."

"What's he doing?" Gubwa's interest was immediate.

"He appears to be waiting," Fong sighed. "He sits in the arrivals lounge with an airport magazine, but I do not think that he reads it."

"This is interesting," Gubwa answered, his excitement mounting. "Perhaps we are about to learn something new about our Mr. Garrison. He will be waiting for the Black brothers, a pair of common thugs. They are due in at seven o'clock. Now, Johnnie, I want you to watch most carefully what happens, and . . ." he paused. "No, better still, I'll watch it for myself—through your eyes. Let me know when the plane lands and position yourself so that you can see everything. After that—do nothing until I tell you. Understood?"

"Yes," Fong whispered. "But—"

"Yes?"

"There is something . . . strange."

"Go on."

"It is Garrison," said Fong. "I know of course that it *is* Garrison, and yet—"

"He seems a different person?"

"Yes. It is . . . strange, Charon."

There was a thoughtful pause before Gubwa answered. "Another of Mr. Garrison's more mysterious aspects, Johnnie. You are not the first to note his changeability, not by any means. I will wait for your call. One last thing: do not be seen to be interested. Don't get too close."

"Of course not."

"I trust you above all others, Johnnie. Your rewards will be great."

"My reward is great, Charon. I love you."

"Until later, then." And the Chinaman waited for the metallic *click* from the other end before he replaced the phone in its cradle . . .

Good as his word, Gubwa was watching through Fong's eyes when Joe and Bert Black passed through customs and emerged from the arrivals gate. They were tanned, seemed healthy enough, but their minds were patently preoccupied. They had tried to carry out a Mafia-contracted hit and had failed; their presence had been "requested" at the Big Guy's place tonight; and that would be more than sufficient to occupy or preoccupy anyone.

They spoke to each other in lowered tones, found a trolley for their luggage and made for the down-passage to the trains. But suddenly, as they reached the center of the arrivals hall, their footsteps were arrested.

Garrison had moved from his seat and was standing with his back to a pillar, his magazine held up before his face. There was no way the Blacks could know it was him, no reason why they should suspect him or anyone else to be waiting for them—but they nevertheless turned through ninety degrees, until they faced in his direction, and went up to him. And Gubwa saw that their movements had grown automatic, zombie-like.

Now Garrison lowered the magazine. Gubwa might have expected the brothers to flinch, attack, almost anything—but they merely stared, their faces strangely blank. Nothing was said, no movement was apparent. For thirty seconds, maybe even a full minute, the oddly frozen tableau held. Then—

As if they had not interrupted their exit from the hall, the brothers wheeled their trolley away and disappeared round a corner. Garrison watched them go, turned and began to follow the route indicated to the car park. He paused, leaned for a moment against a tiled wall, stood upright—but shakily—and finally continued walking.

GO AFTER HIM, said Gubwa in Fong's mind. FOLLOW WHEREVER HE GOES. REPORT WHEN YOU CAN, DAY OR NIGHT. BUT DON'T LOSE HIM.

"As you wish, Charon," the Chinaman whispered to no one, walking quickly after Garrison but keeping a good distance between himself and the man's back.

AND JOHNNIE, YOU MAY HAVE TO PROTECT HIM. I WANT HIM TO STAY ALIVE—FOR THE MOMENT, ANYWAY.

"Yes, Charon."

Gubwa withdrew and opened his eyes. He was seated at his desk in the Castle's Command Center, a Gatwick area Ordnance Survey map spread before him. He stared at the map thoughtfully, frowned, folded it carefully and turned in his seat to replace it in its rack.

His frown grew more severe as he tried to analyze what he had just seen. If it was what he suspected, then Garrison's strength was indeed incredible. He could of course check it out, could visit the minds of the Black brothers and discover what had been done to them, but that might be dangerous. Garrison could be maintaining a mind-link. That might account for his momentary weakness as he left the arrivals area: it could be the result of his continuing use of ESP following the initial surge when he had done to them whatever he had done.

No, Gubwa couldn't risk it. For one thing he did not wish to overtax his own powers, and anyway he had other things to do, other minds to monitor. Phillip Stone's, for instance . . .

Stone's car was parked on the hard-standing of a lay-by where the road climbed to a low hill half a mile to the west of Garrison's house. Stone sat in the driver's seat, a pair of binoculars hanging round his neck. He had seen Garrison drive away towards London, had seen a gray Jaguar pick up his tail as he approached the A27, but beyond that he had not been interested. He was simply following instructions. More than that was quite beyond him.

Oh, he could perform his normal functions, could talk, eat, drink, smoke and answer the calls of nature—anything, providing he did not stray from the mental course directed by Charon Gubwa. The awful thing about it was he knew what he was doing—or what he was not doing. For one thing, he was not protecting Garrison. No, he was waiting on Gubwa's command to snatch the man's wife, or mistress, whatever she was.

For what must have been the fiftieth time, Stone looked at his car telephone. All he had to do was pick it up, get his chief on the other end, put him in the picture. Or he might try digging a tunnel to Australia. An impossibility. He could think about doing it, want desperately to do it, but actually *do* it? No way. Gubwa had seen to that. A pretty thorough laundering of Stone's mind (done with an efficiency and speed that would have left the KGB in tears), a mind-block, and just to polish things off nicely a rather comprehensive list of post-hypnotic commands. These things were Gubwa's legacy to Stone: forming a governor on his mind like the governor on a car's carburetor or accelerator, limiting his performance. And until Gubwa's ends were served—until the albino had Vicki Maler to use as he would in the Castle—Stone would simply have to obey.

QUITE CORRECT, MR. STONE, said a voice in his mind, so clear and close that he jerked his

259

head round, fully expecting to see the hermaphrodite standing there, just outside the open door
of the car. NO, NO, said the voice, amused, YOU
CAN'T SEE ME, MERELY "HEAR" ME—AND OBEY
ME, OF COURSE.

Stone swallowed hard, took a sip of coffee from
the plastic lid of his thermos flask, thought:
What now, Gubwa?

JUST CHECKING. WHEN IT GETS DARK I WANT
YOU TO GO TO THE HOUSE. THERE YOU WILL
KEEP OUT OF SIGHT AND AWAIT FURTHER OR-
DERS. THERE IS A POSSIBILITY THAT YOU MIGHT
HAVE TO PROTECT THE OCCUPANTS. THERE ARE
OTHERS WHO SEEK TO BRING GARRISON DOWN.
I CAN'T WATCH EVERYONE AND I DON'T KNOW
EVERYTHING, BUT—

But it only seems that way? Stone's thoughts
were sarcastic.

YOU FLATTER ME—Gubwa ignored them—
BUT I DON'T WANT THE MALER WOMAN HARMED
IN ANY WAY. I'LL BE IN TOUCH. And he withdrew.

Left on his own, Stone was suddenly cold. The
sun wasn't down yet, the evening was warm, and
yet he was cold as . . . (he grinned mirthlessly)
stone cold. It had finally dawned on him that
Gubwa could do it. Mad he might or might not
be, but he could actually do it. He *could* conquer
the world. He *could* become Emperor of Earth.
He *could* refashion men in his own image. And
here was Phillip Stone—hard-man with fists of
steel, secret agent with all the resources of MIs
5 and 6 to back him up—and helpless as a newborn babe.

He finished his coffee, smoked a cigarette,

waited. As night began to fall, he locked the doors of his car and started off towards the house . . .

The London Mafia sat in extraordinary meeting. The Big Guy's "usual offices" were in a city center office block, on the tenth and top floor. The largest room, overlooking a busy London street, was the venue. There, about a table similar to the one at which another group had recently discussed Richard Garrison, was gathered The Coven, the Cosa Nostra's thirteen foremost London-based men.

At the head of the table sat the Big Guy, Joseph Maestro—a bullnecked, scar-nosed, hulking thug whose ugly, swarthy features and blocky frame seemed hugely incongruous with the immaculate cut of his suit—and from there down to the foot of the table sat his lieutenants in descending order of importance. Towards the foot sat Carlo Vicenti, quite clearly showing signs of wear and tear. One sleeve of his jacket hung loose; his arm was bandaged across his chest. One hand was swathed in bandages. His face showed severe bruising.

The meeting had been in session for a little over half an hour and it was now just after 9:00 P.M. Several minor items had already come up for discussion, clearing the way for the big one, but now it was Garrison's turn. The Big Guy had started it off and he was now almost through speaking.

". . . So it really would seem that this guy has an unbeatable gambling system. Hey!—not just one system but a system for every game. Now I don't have to tell you guys what that means . . . but I will 'cos I know a lot of you can't see past your fucking noses. If Garrison's methods get loose—if he lets this big cat out of the bag—in no time at all ten thousand Garrisons will be hitting our tables and machines and clubs. And a high percentage of our backing comes out of those clubs . . .

"On the other hand, if he tells *us* how he does it . . . well, there's a lot of clubs still belong to other people, yeah? So, that's why we're bringing the guy in. Hey!—and anybody who doubts how good he is only has to ask Mr. Vicenti down there how he lost his personal share in the Ace of Clubs, and I'm sure Carlo will oblige. And not only money, Carlo lost a lot of face. We don't like that, none of us.

"What it boils down to is this guy Garrison's a menace, but when we've finished with him and picked his brains a little he'll be a very thirsty menace—which is fine 'cos we figure to fix him up with a great big drink. Hey!—you think he can drink the river dry? Ha!"

"When?" Vicenti asked, his tone surly. "When are we bringing him in, Joe?" (Nobody called the Big Guy Joseph.) "See, I have a big interest in this bastard!"

"Yeah, yeah, we know. Stay cool, Carlo. Like I said before, he's yours when we're through with him. But being a democratic organization—and technically this being a hit, which it will be eventually—we need a vote. Ain't that why we're all here tonight? Sure! So, let's see a show of hands that we bring in this Garrison, that we get him to tell us his story, and then that we fit him up with concrete boots."

Along with Maestro's hand, eleven others were swiftly raised, Vicenti's more slowly and with a deal more effort. They were still in the air when the doors crashed open to admit Joe and Bert Black. Joe carried a levelled automatic, Bert's arm's cradled a folded-down Sterling sub-machine-gun.

"Now get the other arms up!" Joe's voice was cold.

"Up!" ordered Bert, the snout of his machine-gun moving to cover the entire meeting. All eyes were on that weapon, and all present knew Bert's reputation. The muzzle of the Sterling seemed to flare like some single obscene nostril in the face of a mythical beast. Before that beast could snarl they raised their other arms.

All except Carlo Vicenti. He pushed his chair back, made to stand. "You guys nuts?" he yelled. He mistakenly thought that they were here to pre-empt reprisals. "You come busting in here like . . . shit, you were *invited*! So you missed your hit, so what? It works out right. We want Garrison alive. We have no grudge with you guys."

While he talked Joe and Bert had moved to flank him; they pushed him down in his chair as he struggled to rise. Then, without another word—even as Vicenti continued to rage—Joe Black put away his pistol, took out a cut-throat razor, yanked back the suddenly shrieking man's head and slit his throat ear to ear.

Vicenti coughed, choked, made noises. The sounds issued from his gaping wound, not his gaping mouth; and a moment later, along with the sounds, blood in a crimson gush. Bert and Joe stepped back from him. He floundered in his chair, rose, sat, sprayed blood, clawed at his throat. He was drenched scarlet. He flopped face-down on the table, arms flailing. He slid off the table, leaving a spreading pool of blood.

While Vicenti died the Black brothers moved to the large casement windows. Now every living, bulging eye in the room turned from Vicenti's body to them. The Big Guy and his colleagues were on their feet, arms raised high. Maestro tried to speak but choked on the words.

"Compliments of Richard Garrison," said Joe, and for the first time the remaining occupants of the room noticed how vacant the faces of the assassins seemed. "And a warning, in case any-one else wants to try it on. This is to show you what he can do . . ." And the brothers turned on their heels and hurled themselves headlong through the closed windows, taking weapons, shattered glass and their spent lives with them.

For a moment no one moved, then there was a concerted rush for the door.

"*Hold it!*" Maestro found his voice as cries of horror began to float up from the street below. "Hold it right there. This place will be thick with filth in less time than it takes us to get out. And why should we run, eh? We're innocent bystand-ers, ain't we? If the Blacks want to cool Carlo and then jump, that's their business. As for us, we all tell the same story, okay?"

They all began to babble at once but Maestro held up his arms. Quick thinking was his forte. "*Listen*, for fuck's sake! We ain't carrying heaters, are we? The only prints on those guns down there are theirs, the Blacks! All we do is leave Garrison's name out. The rest of it we tell like we saw it. Shit, how should we know what was going down between Carlo and the brothers, eh?"

The rest of them looked at each other, nodded, began to relax. "Okay," Maestro continued, "so get your minds tidied up. Hell, we've seen worse than this."

As they began to gather into small groups and mull over what they had seen, the Big Guy called over Ramon de Medici and quickly took him to one side. "Ramon," he kept his voice low, "what you told me earlier—about Carlo being sure it was Garrison beat him up—that was straight-up stuff?"

"Sure Joe—except it don't look so silly now, eh?"

Maestro's face twitched. "This Garrison, I don't want him brought in anymore. I don't want to know anything about him. I just want him dead. I think he's safer that way."

De Medici nodded, "This we can do. We bugged his car while he was out of the country. A big silver Mercedes. Our technical boys can tell us where it is whenever we want to know. And Garrison is usually where the car is."

"Okay, as soon as they cut us loose from this mess, get somebody on it. Somebody reliable."

"You've got it."

"In fact, you better get the hell out of here now. Go out the back way and over the roof. Don't let anyone see you. I'll tell the guys to forget you were here, right?"

"Right," Medici nodded, taking his departure.

Outside, the mechanical *whoop, whoop, whoop* of police sirens was beginning to fill the air. Fists were already knocking on the external doors of the executive office suite, and authoritative voices demanded entrance.

A spider-splash of shadow, Ramon de Medici hurried over the dark roofs . . .

Chapter
16

GARRISON/SCHROEDER CAME OFF THE M1 AT Leicester and found a good hotel. He would have driven on but it was past 11:00 P.M. and he was weary to death. It was late for eating but he bribed reception to fix a meal for him; and while he was on about it he ordered an extra steak, raw, for Suzy. He took her supper out to the car and she gratefully wolfed it down. Then, leaving one of the Merc's windows open a fraction, he told Suzy to go to sleep and returned to the hotel. The bar was still open for residents.

Halfway through his fourth whisky the weasel-faced receptionist sidled up to him and asked if he would mind eating in his room; there were others here who had been refused food at this late hour. Garrison/Schroeder didn't mind, gulped down the rest of his drink, made his way to his room and ate his fill. Then, having made himself a coffee, he stretched out on his bed and opened up a magazine he'd picked up at Gatwick Airport.

That magazine—an airline throwaway full of advertising, duty-free offers and such, plus a couple of articles to occupy the passenger during his flight—was the principal reason he was here. He had picked it up off a table at the airport, used it for a shield to hide his face while he waited for Joe and Bert Black; but before then, as he had idly skipped through its pages . . .

Garrison/Schroeder's knowledge of the paranormal—not his experience of it, which was another thing entirely—was second to none. As Thomas Schroeder he had always been interested in parapsychology, especially in the nebulous region of prophetic dreaming. How such dreams worked he did not know, but he did know that he was here today as Garrison/Schroeder *because* they worked. It had been just such a prophetic dream which had helped convince Richard Garrison to accept his offer, his pact, and finally to become the host body and mind to *his* mind. Yes, his very reincarnation could be traced back to just such a dream.

And now . . . now there was this. This simple photograph in a magazine. Monochrome, not especially interesting, even dull. Dull, too, the text—boastful product of the British Energy Commission—but when Garrison/Schroeder's eyes had first glimpsed the full-page spread, then the paper had seemed illumined with some magical inner light.

The picture showed a valley, a dam, and in the background a range of great gaunt hills. The legend below said that this would be the biggest boost to the grid since the opening of the atomic power station at Dounreay. It also said that the dam, close to Glen O'Dunkillie, was due to go into production on Wednesday, the day after tomorrow, and that the Minister for Energy would be there for the opening ceremony. But Garrison/Schroeder had already determined to be there sooner, by tomorrow at the latest. His reason was simple:

This was that same valley and dam, the self-same wild hills that Garrison had seen in his dream. The Schroeder-facet had engineered that dream, had been "awake" while the Garrison-facet "slept" and had promoted the sleeping facet to probe the future—had even loaned his own natural, not inconsiderable ESP-talent to facilitate that probe—and of course he had shared the dream, he, too, had seen that part of their joint future.

Elements of that dream flickered once more like scenes from an old silent movie through the inner recesses of Garrison/Schroeder's mind. He saw the storm and the lightning, the six sprouting arcs of shining, steaming water, and felt the dampness in the air and spray in his face—and all superimposed over the photograph on the printed page. And down in the bottom right-hand corner of the picture, the bleak gables of an old house in the pines where once . . . where once had reared a golden dome!

In Xanadu did Garrison a stately pleasure-dome decree . . .

A pleasure-dome? Unlikely, unless "pleasure" represented the fulfillment of the ultimate dream, not really Garrison's this time but Schroeder's own: his lifelong dream of immortality. And hadn't that been the very purpose of Garrison's dream-quest? To seek out and seduce the Goddess of Immortality? Well then, the quest might soon be at an end. Garrison/Schroeder could sleep this night knowing that in the morning, no matter which facet took ascendence upon awakening—be it himself, Garrison/Koenig, or just Garrison—his journey would be completed. And that somewhere ahead, in a valley close by Glen O'Dunkillie, destiny waited.

For now he could simply sleep and dream his own dreams, except that he somehow knew they would no longer be filled with terrors. Or rather the One Great Terror: Richard Garrison's death, by natural causes or design, which must of course signal his own, Willy Koenig's, Vicki Maler's, yes, and Suzy's death too.

Vicki . . . Poor child; he thought of contacting her before sleeping, of finding and touching her mind, just to see if all was well, but—

The battery was leaking its energy into the great boundless Psychosphere. Energy which could not for now be replaced. Another good reason to sleep.

Garrison/Schroeder undressed, put out the light and got into bed . . .

* * *

Garrison's quest meanwhile continued.

He, too, sought the valley of the dome, but subconsciously, in a world which was grown more real to him now than any waking world.

Since that terrifying episode in the cave of the Other—the interrogation of the girl-wraith and her escape, aided by the one who wore the Cloak of Secrecy—Garrison had come far. He had skirted great green oceans, millpond calm, because he dared not cross them. Not with the Machine to weigh him down. The weariness was on him continually, and every furlong of the way seemed a mile. Even Suzy was weary—Suzy of the boundless energy—and spent a great deal of her time curled behind him, adding her weight to the general burden; but he would leave neither dog nor Machine behind. He must go on and they must go with him.

As for the Machine itself:

Psychomech's back was raw rust now, chafing at Garrison's thighs through tattered trousers. Cables trailed behind, their plastic sheaths eaten away, exposing dulled wire cores. Cracks gaped in the plastic body and flanks, and spots of corrosion marred even the gleam of chrome.

"A junkyard!" Garrison found strength for a feeble curse. "And still I carry you with me. Another folly of a fool upon a fool's quest!" But still he went on.

And where once he would have soared over the highest mountains, now he sought passes through them, making the way longer and his temper shorter. Forests of giant, twisted trees he would not enter for fear of what might lurk within, but had to skirt them; and remembering the circle of wizards and how they had gloated over their shewstone while he burned in the sand, he steered clear of all deserts.

Yes, and the memory of those wizards haunted him. He especially remembered the yellow, slant-eyed one. Indeed he could hardly forget him, for now it seemed that the Oriental mage followed him upon his quest, that wherever he turned his head the small yellow man would be there, distantly glimpsed, merging with trees or rocks or skylines the moment he was spotted. Aye, and possibly there were others on Garrison's trail, vague, furtive ghosts who disappeared at once if ever he tried to focus his eyes upon them too keenly.

Of sleep Garrison had had none, for he wished no more dreams within dreams; but it seemed to him his weariness was such that it transcended mere sleep, so that he could not even if he would. And in this condition, finally he crested a range of low hills and saw spread beneath him the Valley of the Mists.

Now, whether he actually "saw" it or not (he could not be sure for his senses were no longer reliable; his exhaustion was such that this might simply be a hallucination, a vision) he could not say, but certainly there was something very strange and ethereal about the entire valley. Its expanse lay parallel to and between the hills now behind him and an even lower range of foothills to the fore, and to the right and left the valley or low ground between these ranges stretched away and out of sight. And along its entire length the mists curled and eddied like vapor over a lake or moat of milk. And the silence there might be that silence which will come, one day, at the end of time.

This time Garrison did not hesitate. This was an obstacle beyond avoidance, which must be crossed. There were at least three good reasons. For one: it might go on forever, this misty valley, and not have a way round at all. Two: time pressed and Garrison grew weaker. Three: a storm seemed to be gathering, a doomful oppression of atmosphere manifesting in dark clouds that boiled in the sky all around and momently closed with the as yet clear patch of sky directly overhead. Also, the temptation to cross the valley was great; it did not seem wide; the foothills beyond seemed to beckon Garrison on.

And so, as these thoughts passed through his dully aching mind, he rode the maimed Machine down and into the sea of mist, and uncaring of the terrors it might conceal passed forward until the milky stuff closed above him and the external world was shut out beyond eerily drifting walls of white.

Lulled by the silence and veritable creep of Psychomech through the mist, and by Suzy's slow panting where she sat close behind him, Garrison's initial alertness gradually dissipated and he closed eyes already heavy from lack of rest and from peering ahead in this milky submarine realm—and at that very moment the storm broke.

Thunder smote like titan hammers and lightnings flickered down, their transient trails hissing through the mist and stabbing the sodden ground to steaming, lighting up the way in glow-

ing, blue-burning phantoms of rocky outcrops and shaly piles. And at any single moment one such bolt might have struck Garrison, or the metal of the Machine. But no, they were spared. Then, in the afterglow of a particularly vicious blast, Garrison saw, or thought he saw—

But no, in the booming confusion of thunder, the kaleidoscopic flicker of lesser lightnings and the blinding glare of that greater bolt, his eyes had deceived him—must surely have deceived him. He moved forward again, his flesh tingling, and not alone from the static electricity that plucked at his hair and the tatters of his clothing. And there it was again, but closer now and no longer limned by lightning. It was, could only be, a Machine like Psychomech . . . but no such Psychomech as Garrison might ever have imagined!

Huge, gigantic, the thing towered, until its uppermost parts were lost in the ceiling mist. Vast and squat it sat there, pipes and panels and bulkheads sprawling away until, on both sides, their outlines became dim and mist-wreathed. It would take fifty, perhaps a hundred, no, a thousand Psychomechs such as Garrison's Machine to fill the same volume! And deep within lights flashed and power surged, but silently, without the faintest hum of sound; and where the Machine should have had hard edges, they were instead blurred and indistinct; so that Garrison knew that in fact this was a vision, but of what strange place or event he could not say.

A vision, yes—a mirage such as men see in the desert—the mirror image of some distant thing or occurrence. Except that Garrison knew that the truth of this *mirage was not distant in space but in time. It had been sent, or he had willed it, as a sign that he pursued the right path, had not strayed from the course which might yet carry him to quest's end . . .*

He moved closer still, but carefully, unwilling even to disturb the air or milky mist lest the vision dissolve away. But a moment later he stopped again, this time with a gasp. The incredible MACHINE *had a platform—a raised central dais or bed beneath a pair of huge copper rods with knobbed ends, like vast electrodes—but it was the thing, the creature lying upon the bed, which caused Garrison to gasp.*

He knew instinctively what the creature was, even found a word for it squirming its way up to the surface of his mind. A word from another place, another world. Frankenstein! The thing on the dais was a monster, composite of corpses, an unnatural creature created by a crazed science. And as the lightning crashed again Garrison moved closer still for there was something here that he must discover, must see for himself. Something to do with this manufactured, composite creature.

He got down from his *Machine, approached the* MACHINE *until he stood in the shadow of its awesomely ethereal bulk, lifted himself up on tiptoe to gaze amazed at the monster spread-eagled upon the dais. It was in the shape of a man, yes, but a massive, powerful man. Garrison gazed along its length between huge, naked, callous-hardened feet, beyond which the trunk formed a horizon of flesh. He took a pace to one side, let his gaze follow the creature's thigh up above the knee to where a great fist lay loosely clenched. Relaxed, that fist, certainly—in sleep or death Garrison could not say—but there was that about it which mutely spoke of deadly dexterity. The hand of a killer.*

Garrison wondered at the sheer size and apparent hardness of the creature's limbs, which were huge even compared to its body. Upright and awake, with arms and legs, fists and feet like these, the monster would be walking death to any ordinary opponent.

And yet there was also a slyness about it, the suggestion of wily intelligence, like that of a fox. Where this idea sprang from in Garrison's mind was a mystery, but it persisted. This composite creature was made up of a brilliantly clever if morally suspect or even unscrupulous man, and of a simpler but definitely more brutal man—and of one other.

The thunder and lightning seemed to have moved on a little, lulling Garrison into believing that the storm had passed, but in the next moment he knew that he was mistaken. With a roar and a multiple crashing that near-stunned him, four great bolts, falling almost simultaneously, shredded the milky mist to tatters to strike at the MACHINE like hammers of Thor. In that one moment the entire MACHINE was bathed in flickering blue energies—Garrison, too, with his own nimbus of eerie fire—and in the next the lights burned brighter in the great engine's guts and a mighty pulse of power rocked its towering structure.

Then—several things—culminating in a sheet of flame and a rending explosion that hurled Garrison head over heels, skidding and tumbling until his back and shoulders came up against the rusty bulk of his Machine. And there he lay with reeling head and aching bones.

But before that tremendous blast . . . he would never be sure.

His senses seemed no longer reliable, were dulled from exhaustion and dazed from a succession of shocks. He had thought that the great copper rods with their huge electrodes had suddenly swelled up, as from an unbearable power gathering in them; and he had thought to see a lashing, streaming incandescence of energy unleashed between those terminals to cojoin and strike down at the naked monster. Then, finally, before the ultimate blast, he had thought that the entire body of the creature shuddered and jerked, and that he had smelled the reek of roasting flesh. And then with a shriek of absolute agony the thing had bent upright from the waist, glaring at him with mad golden eyes in a face which he had at once recognized—

—as his own!

Later (he had no way of knowing how much later), Garrison emerged from delirium to find himself on all fours, clawing uselessly at the rust-scabbed base of the Machine, Psychomech. Suzy was beside him, nuzzling his neck with a nose that was mainly dry, urging him back to his senses with little barks and whinings.

Of the MACHINE: no trace remained. Neither of

MACHINE *nor of monster. No trace—except in Garrison's mind. He remembered the monster's face,* his face, *and knew there must be a meaning. Doubtless he would discover that meaning at quest's end.*

Quest's end. Hah!—that was a laugh. For all Garrison cared it could end right here and now. And yet—

He set his jaw stubbornly. "Suzy, up, Girl!" His voice was cracked, throat dry. "You're not so heavy." She scampered aboard the Machine. Then he straightened his shoulders, took hold of a dangling cable, willed the Machine to float free of the ground. It did: one inch, two. But that was sufficient. Walking ahead, he led the Machine out of the valley like a man leading some strange lame prehistoric beast.

The stars of night were bright above. The gentle slopes of the foothills rose dark ahead . . .

Johnnie Fong sat in his gray Jaguar in the hotel car park and watched until the light blinked out in Garrison's first-floor bedroom. The man up there was in fact Garrison/Schroeder, but Fong didn't know that. To the Chinaman he was simply Garrison.

Fong waited a few minutes, left his car and found a public telephone. Moments later Charon Gubwa answered his private telephone in the Castle and was brought up to date. It was late but Gubwa had already slept. Precognition had told him that the upcoming hours would be busy ones.

Having quickly absorbed all of Fong's information, now the albino sent his mind out to Phillip Stone where he kept an eye on the Garrison residence. MR. STONE. GO BACK AND GET YOUR CAR. THEN BRING VICKI MALER TO ME.

Stone, a cigarette dangling from his lips, shielded by his hand in the darkness where he stood beneath trees not far from the house, jerked to attention. Or rather his mind did. He ground out the cigarette with his heel and looked around carefully in the empty darkness.

YOU STILL FIND DIFFICULTY IN BELIEVING, MR. STONE. PERHAPS YOU ARE NOT SO CLEVER AFTER ALL.

"How am I to get her to come with me?" Stone asked in a whisper, finding it too much of an effort to simply think his question. "And where to?"

It was as if he heard a chuckle. YOU ALREADY KNOW THOSE THINGS. YOU WILL REMEMBER THEM AS YOU GO, IMPROVISE AS REQUIRED. SIMPLY OBEY.

"Like shit!" Stone spat out the words—but already he was making his way back towards the spot where his yellow Granada was parked.

At the house it was easy. Stone found his mind whirling as his mouth ran on of its own accord—or of Gubwa's accord—as the simple fact of what he was doing triggered a stream of post-hypnotic commands which could not be denied. He was Phillip Stone from MI6, he told the Maler woman; Richard Garrison was now in the care of the Secret Service; it was believed that a second attempt on his life was in the offing; Garrison had asked that Vicki Maler be picked up and brought to him, for her safety. While Stone's mind might be in utter chaos, his words and actions were under a firmer discipline than ever he himself had mastered; and of course he carried proof of his identity. The woman had no choice but to trust him.

She had been preparing for bed but now she dressed, quickly packed a small case, gave the servants one or two cursory instructions and allowed Stone to take her to his car. Through all of this he wanted nothing more than to tell her to run, make herself scarce, phone the police—anything but go with him. Instead he smiled concernedly, told her not to worry, held the door for her while she got into his car after dumping her case in the boot.

And in a very short time they were on their way to London . . .

Meanwhile Gubwa dared do nothing. Word had already reached him of Vicenti's murder and the double-suicide of the Blacks, and he knew *who* was responsible if not quite *how*. But obviously Garrison was still a force to be reckoned with. A terrifying force.

Gubwa had taken a nail-biting chance when he had Stone pick up the girl; with powers such as Garrison commanded things still could have gone wrong. They still could, for which reason Gubwa would not rest easy until she was here, in the Castle, shielded by the mental blackout of his mind-guards. As for them: there were eight of them "on duty" now. Gubwa could take no more chances.

But with Garrison asleep and at a distance (though distance, as the albino had explained to Stone, made little or no difference) Gubwa had not been able to resist the opportunity to strike. Success was now well within his reach. The girl would know the source or secret of Garrison's power, and she would also know his weaknesses.

Meanwhile, in a dark car park not too far away, Stone would have parked his Granada. He would then have wound down his window and at his signal one of Gubwa's lieutenants would have stepped forward, broken the top off a tiny phial and splashed its contents into the car. A knockout gas, instantaneous, would then have put Stone and the girl to sleep. By now they were on their way to the Castle, and no power in the world could possibly follow their trail here . . . hopefully. That last because Gubwa knew, or strongly suspected, that Garrison's power was not of this world but of the Psychosphere. But at least every human precaution had been taken.

And for now it was simply a matter of waiting . . .

Ramon de Medici's call roused Joseph Maestro from an uneasy sleep. The Big Guy grumbled, switched on his bedside light, snatched the telephone handset from its cradle and checked the caller's identity. "Ramon? Okay, wait." Maestro turned to the girl in his bed and shook her awake. "You," he said, "out!"

"What?" she drowsily blinked sleep from her eyes, wrapped too-willing arms around him. He grunted and shrugged her off. She was very young and very beautiful—worthless, to Joseph Maestro.

"Wake up, dummy!" he snapped. "Go clean your teeth."

"But Joe," she mumblingly protested, "I already cleaned my—"

"Then take a shower. Just get the hell out of here. I have to speak to somebody. I'll call you when I'm through."

Grumblingly, she got out of bed, moved in the direction of the bathroom.

"Yeah," said Maestro into the phone, "what is it? You found Garrison?"

"Right," came the answer. "His car, anyway. He's not at home so we figure he's with his car."

"Where?"

"In Leicester."

Maestro frowned. "Leicester? What the hell is he doing in Leicester? Where in Leicester?"

"We don't know. Have to go up there to get a positive fix."

"So get on it."

"Tonight?"

"Right now!" Maestro snapped. "Hey!—we owe this guy. And not just for Vicenti. You ain't telling me you enjoyed last night, are you? Three solid hours in the beautiful company of the filth—and then spat out like so much stale gum? Now get on it. I want Garrison dead!"

"Okay, Joe, you got it. His car's not moving so we figure he's staying over somewhere. I'll go personally, take Carlo's boys with me. They'll enjoy it."

"Yeah, right," said Maestro. "That's good. The filth don't know you were there when the Blacks snuffed Carlo and jumped. If they do somehow figure out that Garrison was involved with that, they still won't be able to tie you in with it. You're in the clear. Okay, the job's yours."

"Right."

"Don't screw it up."

"I won't."

"You're a good guy, Ramon."

"Thanks, Joe."

Maestro put down the phone. The glass door of the bathroom was steamed up now and he could hear the *hiss* of the shower. It was hot tonight. He threw back the sheets, stretched and yawned. "Hey, baby? Okay, you can come back to bed."

She came out of the bathroom towelling herself down. He silently admired her breasts, the firm globes of her buttocks. "When you're dry," he told her, "you can do us both a favor and get your mouth round that."

She came over to the bed, wrinkled her nose, looked pointedly down on him. "Round what?" she asked without malice.

Maestro grinned. "So work on it," he said. "Hey!—I should keep a dog and bark myself?"

Chapter
17

WHATEVER FORCES OR CURRENTS THEY ARE
which circulate in or permeate the Psychosphere may never be known, but that Tues-
day morning at dawn they roused neither
Richard Garrison nor Garrison/Schroeder from
sleep but Garrison/Koenig; and it was this third
facet of Garrison's multimind which drove the
big Mercedes back onto the M1 heading north.
As fortune good or bad had it, de Medici and his
"boys" arrived seconds too late, just in time to
see the silver car making away into the distance. Then it was a case of turning about and
driving back to the M1, and of waiting there until their detector indicated that the Mercedes
was heading north once more.

As for Johnnie Fong: he stayed fairly close behind Garrison/Koenig until he was certain of the
route, then fell back to a respectful distance and

settled down to driving at the motorway's maximum of seventy miles per hour, which was the speed Garrison/Koenig was doing in the Mercedes. A man who held the law in some respect, Garrison/Koenig—when it suited him.

But having followed so close on his quarry's heels from hotel to motorway, Fong had given himself away. Richard Garrison would never have noticed him and neither would Thomas Schroeder, but Willy Koenig had been—still was, even as a facet of Garrison—a different kettle of fish entirely. As his beloved Colonel Schroeder had often used to say of him, Willy had an infinite capacity for thinking bad thoughts before others thought them. Whatever the circumstances, he invariably suspected the worst and prepared for it. And where trouble was concerned he was the most capable of men. Moreover, he was loyal to a fault. These were qualities which had earned him Schroeder's undying trust and friendship; yes, and Richard Garrison's too. Through them he had succeeded to a place in Garrison's Gestalt psyche. And right now they were qualities which made him by far the most worthy Garrison-facet to be at the wheel of the big silver Mercedes.

For upon spotting Fong's Jaguar in his rearview mirror, even though he had never seen him before (except perhaps in a mental "echo" of one of Garrison's dreams) it was Garrison/Koenig's nature to dislike and distrust his motives; also to begin to consider what steps might have to be taken to dislodge the Chinaman—perhaps permanently—from his tail. To this end he pulled in at a lay-by and went to the boot of the car. In there, where he had secreted them away some time ago while ascendant, were certain weapons. Now he placed these strategically about his person and closed the boot. As he did so the gray Jaguar sped by, its driver staring straight ahead. Perhaps Garrison/Koenig was worrying needlessly.

But fifteen minutes later the big Mercedes passed a cluster of lorries in another lay-by, and shortly after that the Chinaman was back once more on Garrison/Koenig's tail; he must have been waiting behind the lorries, waiting for Garrison/Koenig to pass. Very well, it was decided: the Chinaman in the gray Jaguar was a tail, an enemy. Now Garrison/Koenig could put it out of his mind—until later. But he had no doubt that there would be a later.

What neither Garrison/Koenig nor Johnnie Fong had noticed as yet was the powerful black saloon, almost a hearse in its design, sitting well back behind both of them but gradually drawing closer.

They would notice it soon enough . . .

8:15 A.M., and Charon Gubwa was tired. He had earlier taken a couple of uppers (though he was generally against using drugs of any sort personally, except perhaps as an aid to sex) and was now prepared to take more. Today would be crucial and he knew it. There were vibrations in the Psychosphere which were boiling towards a climax. That he himself would be involved he could not doubt, and certainly Garrison would be part of it. Garrison . . . or Garrison's passing.

For certainly the man must die. If there had ever been any question of that it existed no longer: he *must* die! And that was a thought which thrilled Gubwa as he had not been thrilled for a long time, and which at one and the same moment frightened him mightily. For he knew now that Garrison was not one but three men, and he further knew that he, Charon Gubwa, would never be safe until Garrison's multimind was utterly erased.

As for Phillip Stone and the Maler woman: they still lived. Gubwa had enough on his hands at the moment and they were neither a physical nor a mental threat. Vicki Maler's mere presence here was something of a threat, of course; but the mind-guards were in place, two to a cell, and the Castle had never been more mentally inaccessible from outside interference. Between Gubwa's mind and the outside world lay a great mental moat, a vacuum in the Psychosphere impenetrable to any but the most powerful mind. Not a two-edged sword by any means, for knowing the nature of his mind-guards Gubwa could direct his own probes outwards as easily as if the guards did not exist at all.

But let Garrison discover Gubwa—let him find a thread to lead him here, the smallest suspicious echo in the Psychosphere—and the huge albino had little doubt but that he could send *his* mind crashing in on the Castle, and that then all would be lost. This made him reluctant even to contact Johnnie Fong, and fearful of Fong's contacting him, as he sat alone in his Command Center and considered his course of action.

Gubwa knew now about Psychomech, almost all

there was to know. That it had been a machine dreamed up by Hitler or his scientific aides to create fearless supermen; built in England thirty-odd years later by the Nazi lunatic Otto Krippner, and used by Richard Garrison to rid his mind of elemental fears and boost his ESP-talents to an incredible degree. An experiment which had almost ruptured the Psychosphere itself! Gubwa knew, too, all about Schroeder and Koenig; how the sheer ego of the former had bent causality forces in the Psychosphere; how the defensive and destructive abilities of the latter had guided and protected Garrison through to that time when all three minds could meld into one.

But the machine, Psychomech! That wonderful machine!

So Garrison had destroyed the thing. Well, of course, he had—so that no man might follow him into the awesome flux of the Psychosphere. He had been jealous of his power. For in those early days he had been to the ESP ether what a black hole is to space and time: a complete disruption of psychic law and order, an insatiable feeder, a dark star of infinite gravity.

And what then? What had brought about the reversal, the decline, the power-failure? Gubwa had considered this and had come to the same conclusion as Garrison himself. A man is after all only a man. He has his span in which to do those things fate decrees. Even a superman's powers are finite, if only because as long as there *is* time he can never have enough of it to do all he is capable of doing. One cannot outlast time itself. Not even an immortal can do that.

And what if three men—three "facets," three brightly burning wicks—are feeding on the same fat? How much more rapid the waning of the candle then? Garrison, yes, and Schroeder and Koenig too, were simply burning themselves out! Garrison's mistake had been in the destruction of Psychomech, by which he might have revitalized himself. But Charon Gubwa would not make that mistake.

If he—*when* he—had Psychomech, he would make of the machine a god! It would stand in his innermost temple, and Gubwa would be High Priest. Yes, and when he hungered his god would feed him, and the Psychosphere would be his to command, and all would be possible, and he would live in power and glory forever! And—

—It seemed incredible, beyond belief, that this future Gubwa envisioned—this dream of infinite, eternal power—should lie in the hands and minds of one small perfectly normal-in-every-way human being. But it did. Not in Garrison, no, nor in Schroeder or Koenig or Vicki Maler. In a man whose name was Jimmy Craig—James Christopher Craig—the micro-electronic engineer whose skills had prepared Psychomech for Garrison's use. At present J. C. Craig was on the board of one of Garrison's companies, but soon he would work for Gubwa. And he would not have power of refusal. Under the twin pressures—irresistible pressures—of Gubwa's hypno-telepathic and narcotic controls, Craig would soon become little more than a puppet dancing to the albino's tune.

Oh, it would *seem* quite impossible that any

man, even the world's greatest electronic genius (and it was doubtful that Craig was that)
could remember all of the titan bulk of technical
information required for Psychomech's reconstruction. It would *seem* so . . . but falsely. Under the spell of Charon Gubwa's hypnosis he
would remember everything. Would recall the
most minute details, and soon Psychomech II
would be a reality.

But this time—ah, *this* time!—it would not be
any mere man whose mind the machine expanded. It would be a man whose powers were
already developed to an extraordinary degree.
Charon Gubwa would lay his obese and unnatural body down upon Psychomech's couch, but
it would be God himself who stood up!

And this thought also frightened Gubwa (not
of being God, for he already considered himself
a god of sorts), the thought that his dream, so
very close to becoming reality, could be oblit-
erated at a stroke. What if J. C. Craig should die?
At a stroke, an end to Gubwa's dream. What if
he were already dead?

Well, he was not, for Gubwa had checked up
on him as soon as he had his name. No, Craig
was alive and well. He worked for Garrison, as a
director of MME, Miller Micro-Electronics, to
which position Garrison had elevated him following Psychomech's success. Moreover Gubwa
had already issued those orders necessary to
bring Craig directly under his control. Within the
space of a day, two at most, the man would be
on his way here, kidnapped and drugged, to
wake up in the Castle and commence work at

once upon Psychomech II. And the soldiers Gubwa had assigned to this task were of his best and knew only too well the price of failure.

Nor were these the only arrangements Gubwa had made. He had twice "visited" Craig and on both occasions, brief though the visits had been, had inserted certain post-hypnotic seeds in the man's mind. And he had found Craig's mind very open to subversion; a talented mind, yes, but one lacking in personal conviction, which could be directed or re-directed by the very smallest of pressures. As to what Gubwa had actually done—what "seeds" he had planted, which would now blossom—that was simple:

He had generated within Craig the need to question Garrison's authority in the matter of Psychomech. Just what *was* this machine which had made Garrison so powerful? Why should Garrison alone benefit from Psychomech, when Craig himself had been so essential in the matter of the machine's reconstruction? Indeed, why should there not be an improved model, over which God-Almighty-Garrison would have no say or sway whatsoever? These were the questions Craig would now begin to ask himself—or which he would believe *he* was asking—and so, slowly but surely, his conversion to Gubwa's cause already had commenced.

But of course Craig was only one problem; there were others of far greater importance. Garrison, for example. What of him? How might his death be engineered without a direct connecting link to Charon Gubwa?

As if the thought itself had causality, Gubwa's

telephone purred; and on the other end of the line Johnnie Fong was waiting with what might be the answer to his albino master's problem. "Charon, Garrison is in danger from others!"

"Who? How many?"

"They have the looks of killers—Mafia, I think. Three of them, in a black saloon."

"Have they seen you?" Gubwa's pink eyes opened wide as his heart picked up speed.

"No, Charon. They are only interested in Garrison."

Gubwa sighed, relaxed a little, said, "Stay well out of it, Johnnie. Follow, watch, but do not interfere. Where are you now?"

"Still heading north, about an hour from Newcastle. Garrison has stopped to eat. I can see him from here, through the glass of the kiosk. He eats in the open air, at a wooden table in the sunshine. There are many people around him. He seems very tired, hungry. He did not breakfast in Leicester. And Charon—"

"Yes?"

"He has changed again. This *is* Garrison, but it is not the same Garrison. This one knows no fear. There is an arrogance about him, the strength and sureness of a great cat. Even weary, he looks dangerous. I am a master of the martial arts, as you well know, Charon, but even I would be wary with this Garrison now."

"And rightly so," said Gubwa. "Oh, this is Garrison, Johnnie, but it is also a man called Willy Koenig. When all is done I will explain—perhaps. But for now you may wish those Cosa Nostra dogs the very best of luck. They pursue a stag whose antlers are steeped in purest poison! Where are the Mafia now?"

"They stand near the exit from this place, which is a petrol station and restaurant. They are in shirtsleeves, leaning on their car. They drink beer."

"Does Garrison know they are onto him?"

"He appears preoccupied. He does not seem aware of anything."

"And yet he makes you wary?"

"Yes . . . yes, you are right, Charon. There is a tension about him. He is tired, but he cannot relax. He even eats quickly. He desires to be on his way."

But to what? Gubwa asked himself. *Where does Garrison think he is going? What is he doing?* "Follow," he repeated. "Where they go, you go. I will not contact you. Contact me when you can." He put down the telephone . . .

Phillip Stone had not been present at Vicki Maler's telepathic and hypnotic interrogation. When he had awakened, without a headache on this occasion, he had found himself alone in a room with two single beds, a chair—and a locked steel door. The place was much like a padded cell, with solid walls (metal, he guessed) beneath the padding. The door had a small barred window for observation. He had banged on those bars until they brought him his breakfast; and shortly after that, while he was still eating, the door had been opened again and Vicki Maler thrust inside with him. Food had been left for her, too.

Then Stone had explained all, and after initial doubts she accepted him and his assurance that from now on in he would do whatever was in his power to protect her; though that might not be a great deal. Finally, exhausted both mentally and physically, she had gone to sleep on the bed Stone had not used, and he had seated himself close to the door and calculated the odds against him, reckoning his chances and building up his anger. When angry, Stone had the reputation of being a very dangerous man.

Since then the hours had passed very slowly. At noon Vicki had awakened a little fresher for her sleep, had asked the guard outside the door for water to wash with and had received it. They had been given more food, left to their own limited devices. And with time on their hands, slowly but surely each had come to know the other's story almost as intimately as a well-read book. And with a future bleak as theirs appeared to be, literally no future at all, they did not hold back but talked with a frankness amazing to both of them in any other circumstance.

Long into the afternoon they had talked. Stone told her something of his life, loves and adventures; she in return advised him of her own far different background. She removed her contact lenses to show him the golden glow of her eyes, subdued now and seeming to have that varying brightness seen in a light bulb before the filament exhausts itself. And looking at her—her beautiful elfin features and perfect figure, which even her simple clothes could not completely conceal—Stone felt moved as never before.

"You know," he said on impulse, "this might seem sort of ungallant—I mean, I may feel this way because you might be the very last woman I ever get the change to talk to—but . . ."

"Yes?"

"Oh, hell, it doesn't matter." He shrugged angrily. "Yes it *does* matter. Damn it all, I got you into this. I mean I . . ." His words tapered off.

"What are you trying to say, Phillip?"

He sighed. "Just that it hardly seems fair, that's all."

"What doesn't seem fair?"

"Your life, mine. Yours because it's been—" again he shrugged, "rough on you. Mine because—"

"Yes?" she again prompted him.

". . . Because I had to wait until the end of it to meet you."

She managed a wan smile. "That is not ungallant at all. I think it very sweet of you. And I know what you mean. I too feel quite . . . quite small. I feel that everything is much too big for me, and that I am being swept aside in the rush of things."

Stone's anger—at himself—flooded over. He slammed his fist into the padding of the steel door. "I feel so bloody . . . *useless*! So *weak*!"

"You, weak?" She shook her head. "No, there's a great strength in you. It's being powerless that makes you feel weak. I'm the weak one, and growing weaker. Would you do me a favor?"

"Is it within my power?"

"Oh, yes. Simply sit here beside me and put your arms around me. After all, we have only each other. But this is a lot in itself. For such a long time now I have had nothing at all . . ."

* * *

By midday Garrison/Koenig was in Edinburgh, which was where his entourage lost him. That was deliberately contrived, and no man better equipped for the task than former Feldwebel (SS-Scharführer) Wilhelm Klinke. All one needs do is jump a couple of red lights (they seem somehow to stay red longer in Princes Street), turn a few corners with one's foot down and tear headlong into a multi-story car park. Garrison/Koenig did these things, parked the car ready for a rapid takeoff, walked to the open-air concrete balcony and looked down on the city.

Traffic was heavy. No sign of the gray Jag and black saloon. In a way it would be easier if there were. That way it would be over—one way or the other—that much sooner. He had spotted the saloon along the last couple of miles of A1 and had known why it was there. Revenge for Vicenti. It hadn't excited him; the Koenig facet was of an unflappable breed.

He waited until the middle-aged, tubby attendant came puffing up the spiralling ramp, red-faced and angry. "An' what the bleddy hell d'ye think ye're on, Jimmy?" he asked. "When ah lift the barrier ye pull up tae mah window an' pay—not come tearin' straight up here like a cock up a cunt!"

"I'm a stranger here," said Garrison/Koenig, letting his German accent come through as strongly as possible. "My apologies. Please accept this for your inconvenience." He handed over a crisp tenner.

"Oh! Ah see! Well, noo! Indeed! That's most kind . . ."

"Please don't mention it. Listen, I wonder if

you could do me another favor?" He crackled a second tenner between thumb and forefinger.

"Oh, aye, certainly. What is it, sir?" The tubby Scot's face was now wreathed in affable smiles.

"First you could send someone for a few sandwiches—ham, I think—and perhaps a thermos full of coffee? Oh, yes—and some raw meat, a steak perhaps, for the dog? I'm going to sit up here for an hour or two, maybe take a nap in the car. Also," (he took out a third tenner), "I would appreciate it if you could keep your eyes open for a gray Jaguar and a big black saloon. The Jag's driver is a Chinese gentleman. The saloon has three men in it, I think, probably Italians or some such. Mediterraneans, anyway."

"Oh, aye, sir—ah kin do they things, certainly. Er, friends o' yours, these gentlemen?"

"No," Garrison/Koenig smiled, shaking his head. "No, not friends. I would expect you to tell me before you let them in here. I would very much appreciate that. It would be well worth your trouble."

"Consider it done, sir!" the attendant cried. "Ye'll no be bothered, ah'll see tae that."

"Danke schön," smiled Garrison/Koenig. "I'm sure you'll do your best."

Under the Merc's dashboard the Mafia bug continued to send out its silent signals, and less than a mile away the black saloon nosed slowly through the city's streets, returning along its own tracks, covering the distance between . . .

"Charon!" Sir Harry's voice was sharper than the albino had ever heard it. "What's going on?"

"Going on?" Gubwa cursed to himself, wishing the man had chosen a more opportune time to call him. He himself did not know quite "what was going on," not right now. "Why, what do you mean, Sir Harry?"

"You know damn well what I mean! Garrison's gone missing, the Maler woman too. His servants got in touch with their local police. I found out from 'upstairs.' He wants an answer. Now what do I tell him?"

Gubwa relaxed a little. This was something he could handle. "Tell him nothing," he said. "Or if you must, tell him that Garrison is as good as dead."

"Explain."

"The Mafia are after him."

"Oh?"

"Revenge for Vicenti, among other things."

"Vicenti? That was Garrison?"

"He engineered it, yes."

Silence for a moment, then: "And Stone? What of him? He took the Maler woman and disappeared."

"Yes, and they will stay disappeared—always." Gubwa waited, smiled at the suddenly silent telephone in his hand. He could tell from Sir Harry's inability to frame another question that the man was stumped. "You wanted MI6 tied in with this, didn't you?"

"Yes, but—"

"Well, now you have it. Obviously Stone was on the Cosa Nostra payroll. That's what will be thought. He took the woman as Mafia bait for Garrison. All part of a feud between Garrison and the Mafia. For proof we have the Blacks and their bombing of Garrison's plane. And Vicenti, of course—and then the 'suicide' of the Blacks, which will now plainly be seen as the work of the Mafia, covering up the Garrison connection."

"Yes, yes, I see most of that. But Stone working for the Mafia—that's a bit strong, isn't it?"

"Do you think for a moment that MI6 is any clearer than your own outfit?" Gubwa laughed. "Well, maybe they are—but they too have their dirty washing, I assure you. Listen, how does this sound: Stone's body will be found in the river, weighted down, and there will be sufficient evidence hidden on it to clean the Mafia right out once and for all. Because you'll have advance knowledge, your branch will shine. You will make yourself directly responsible for any investigations. The very foundations of MI6 will be shaken apart. Now, how does that sound?"

Again the silence, then: "That sounds . . . fine. And when does all of this happen?"

"It is happening."

"Now? But you said six weeks!"

"I said a maximum of six weeks. I underestimated myself, that's all. It has worked itself out sooner—and without complications. By tonight Garrison should be dead, and by first light tomorrow you'll know where to start looking for Stone's body."

"Jesus!" Sir Harry's voice was a hiss. "That means I have things to do, and time is short."

"Then let's stop wasting time," said Gubwa. "I'm quite busy too, you know."

"Very well, but let's get one thing straight. It's

299

important that I know *the very minute* Garrison's dead. I can't be seen to act before the fact, but I will need to move pretty fast. Do you see any problems?"

"None at all. And you shall know Garrison is dead one minute after I myself know it. Is that satisfactory?"

"Yes, good man. But, Charon?"

"Yes?"

"I'd give my right arm to know how you've managed all this."

"Oh, I'm sure you would," Gubwa laughed again. "But that's a secret!"

Replacing the telephone, Gubwa found himself tempted to read Sir Harry's mind. He decided against it. Right now the man's thoughts must be in utter chaos; he'd make little of them. It was just that he felt a sort of niggling suspicion in the back of his own mind, like a bad taste at the back of one's throat. Sir Harry was, had always been, a man to watch. But Gubwa was tired and there was still much to do. Better to save his talents for now, hold them in reserve against a time in the very near future when their use might prove all-important.

That was Charon Gubwa's third error and probably his biggest. His first had been when he became interested in Garrison in the first place. His second had been to interfere, in any degree, with Vicki Maler. But this one? This failure to follow up his own instinctive hunch in respect of Sir Harry's immediate intentions . . . this was the beginning of the end.

For at the other end of the now dead line Sir

Harry's thoughts were anything but chaotic. They were crystal clear, as they'd rarely been in many a year. Gubwa had offered him two pots of gold at the end of the rainbow, but he was aiming at three.

Garrison was one, because he had already been given that contract. The London-based Mafia came next, because crushing them would fuel his rocket to fame and a position of even greater power. And Charon Gubwa himself, he was the third pot. Partly because he was a loaded pistol at Sir Harry's head—but mainly for the fun of it . . .

Chapter
18

JOHNNIE FONG RELOCATED THE BLACK SALOON AT about the same time that Ramon de Medici, Fatso Facello and Toni Murelli came to the conclusion that indeed Garrison was parked up and hiding in the multi-story. Their detector had indicated that he was stationary and close at hand, and the car park seemed the only likely place.

The Chinaman parked in a side street close by, got out of his car and watched what was going on from a safe distance. He kept himself out of sight, however, as Gubwa had ordered, which made the actual mechanics of the affair a little vague to him. What actually happened was this:

De Medici had driven up and stopped on the road opposite the entrance to the car park but without actually entering the drive-in lane. In effect he had blocked off both the drive-in and

-out lanes. Then Murelli and Facello had got out of the car, ducked under the barrier and gone to the booth. De Medici had watched from the driving seat of the car. Words had passed between Facello and the tubby attendant where he sat in his booth. For a little while the latter seemed a bit garrulous, waving his arms and reddening up a little, but he'd quietened down when Facello had gone into the booth with him. Murelli had then turned and given de Medici the thumbs-up, had disappeared up the ramp with his gun out and ready. Garrison had done them a favor; they couldn't have picked a better place for a hit if they'd chosen it themselves!

Garrison/Koenig was parked four floors up, almost directly above the entrance. He had finished his coffee and sandwiches the best part of an hour ago. It was time to move on. Except . . . there was something not quite right.

Too quiet, and Suzy strangely nervous where she sat in the back of the car.

Traffic sounds from below, but subdued somehow. Seagulls wheeling round Edinburgh Castle, their plaintive cries carrying on a breeze off the sea. A beautiful day—but the Koenig-facet was thinking his bad thoughts, and Suzy's restlessness must have a meaning.

Up on the castle ramparts they fired the One o'Clock gun.

Garrison/Koenig's head jerked round, eyes staring, his mind awash in psychic awareness. There was a flicker of movement in the Merc's rearview mirror. Toni Murelli had appeared up the entrance ramp, was crouching there, waving a gun in front of him, peering in the car park's dusty haze. Strong sunlight outside and gloom within. Murelli's eyes weren't quite accustomed yet.

He saw the Merc; its front doors were wide open, sticking out like comic ears. Creeping closer, Murelli saw the thermos flask still steaming where it stood on the front passenger seat. Empty sandwich wrappers lay opened out beside it. Murelli grinned. *That's right, Garrison baby,* he thought. *Take it easy. Have a break.*

Murelli was half behind the car, creeping up on its left. Now he could see that the driver's seat leaned back, in the half-recline position. His grin grew wider. He straightened up a little, covered the last three paces quickly, gripped the wrist of his gun-hand and thrust both hands into the car. His finger began to tighten on the trigger—but in the next second his grin slipped right off his face.

Garrison/Koenig stepped out from behind a massive square concrete support column and kicked the door of the car shut on Murelli's wrists. At the same time Suzy snarled and darted her head forward from the back of the car, snapping at the gunman's hands. Her deadly fangs ground together where they met through the bones of his right wrist.

Murelli's scream and the dull plop of his silenced weapon came simultaneously. Garrison/Koenig leaned his weight on the door, kicked Murelli in the groin where he flopped against the car. The gunman blew the rest of his air out in one great gasp. His gun fell from nerveless, ravaged fingers inside the car. Suzy had severed two of his fingers and was working on the rest. Garrison/Koenig let the door fly open, grabbed Murelli and waltzed him away, half-supporting, half-propelling him. He waltzed him towards the concrete balcony. Murelli, in agony and scared witless, saw it coming and made one last desperate effort. He whirled a bloody, torn fist at Garrison/Koenig's head. Cold-eyed, Garrison/Koenig ducked, grabbed the other's knees, lifted and pushed.

For a moment Murelli seemed suspended in air beyond the balcony. His white face puffed in and out, like that of some strange fish slowly sinking from view in bright water. And he was gone without ever mustering the sought-for scream. His body smashed down in front of the black saloon like one hundred and seventy-five pounds of lead.

For long seconds de Medici simply sat at the wheel of his car paralyzed, staring. His window was down and he had heard the sickening crunch as Murelli hit. Finally he gunned the engine, began to back away from Murelli's body—and at the same time heard the roar of the Merc's powerful motor as Garrison/Koenig's car came careening like some great silver beast down the out-ramp. Sparks flew where its metal sides jostled the ramp's low concrete wall.

Garrison/Koenig saw the bonnet of the saloon pulling back. He saw, too, Fatso Facello where he stood ashen-faced in the booth. There was no sign of the tubby Scot, but that probably would not have made a deal of difference. A grenade dangled by its ring from Garrison/Koenig's grinning teeth, its weight rolling a little on his chin. The metallic *chink!* was lost as he armed the grenade and tossed it into the booth. Then the Merc's nose crashed into the front couple of inches of the saloon and slammed it out of the way. At the same time Garrison/Koenig wrenched the wheel over, so that the combined action had the effect of throwing the Merc round the bend and into the street, its wheels skidding in Toni Murelli's blood. Then, tires screaming and throwing out smoke, the big car rocked on its springs as it hurtled away up the street.

In his rearview Garrison/Koenig saw Facello leap from the booth, the fat man's arms and legs an impossible blur of movement. Then—

The booth disappeared in a lick of white fire and smoke and deafening detonation. Facello was picked up, all eighteen stone of him, and tossed over the roof of the saloon. The blast blew in the saloon's nearside windows. That was as much as Garrison/Koenig saw, for in the next moment he was round a corner and applying his brakes, slowing down as he moved into a stream of traffic and picked up signs that aimed him towards the Forth Bridge.

He had killed one of them, possibly two, and with any luck the saloon would be out of commission. He must hope so. That would only leave the little yellow man to worry about, and Garrison/Koenig wasn't really the worrying type . . .

He did wonder momentarily what had become of the tubby car park attendant; he couldn't know that he had already been dead, knifed through the heart, in the bottom of the booth when the grenade exploded, and that a ten pound note was now flapping in the updraft on the concrete base of the car park's first-floor level, stuck there with blood and a little gristle.

It was only later, on the wide approach road to the bridge, when Garrison/Koenig stopped to examine the surprisingly small amount of damage to the Mercedes, that he thought of those powers he had neglected to use in his confrontation with the Mafia. He had known he had them, certainly, but their *use* had barely crossed his mind. Why take a machine-gun to swat a fly? And of course the power was not limitless; the well was rapidly running dry. Perhaps he had simply been saving what little was left.

What the hell . . . it wouldn't have been the same anyway.

At a little before 3:00 P.M. Johnnie Fong reported by telephone to Charon Gubwa, telling him all that had happened since his last report, especially detailing the incident at the car park. He phoned in from a garage high on a winding road overlooking a Grampian hamlet. Down there, at a second garage on the far side of the village, Garrison's Mercedes was undergoing a cursory inspection. On the nearside of the patchwork of lanes, fields, church and houses, the Mafia saloon sat at the side of the road with no movement visible. All of this Fong had seen through his binoculars.

"I do not know, Charon," he said, "how they got back on to his trail, but they did. And I, of

307

course, simply followed them. Now, however, I am obliged to stay well back for even if Garrison does not know I am here, it is very likely that they do."

"Then stay back," Gubwa ordered at once, "until after they have dealt with him. He must be weakening rapidly, Johnnie, for knowing they are there he should by now have disposed of them. He has powers, this Garrison, but they are leaking out of him like rats deserting a sinking ship. Still, I prefer not to take any chances. As to how the Mafia picked up his trail again: his car is bugged and they are carrying a tracking device . . . But tell me, what reason do you think he has for running north?"

"I think he is a fool, Charon. Brave, but a fool. The country grows wilder, the day wears on. His car has long been losing power. Perhaps the blast and collision caused it, I don't know. But I think that with the fall of night they must surely close in and kill him. If I had a rifle, I myself could kill all of them without ever being seen."

"*No!*" Gubwa snapped. "Through you he might yet find a way to strike at me. You must simply observe all that occurs. Observe and report."

"As you will, Charon. But for now I think I might get ahead of them. They are off the main road. I can go straight through the village and on into the mountains. Perhaps I can find a high place, watch and wait for them."

"Do it," Gubwa agreed. "I will give you one hour. Do *not* let yourself be seen. In one hour exactly I shall come to you, to your mind. In this I shall be at risk, you realize that?"

"You will be safe, Charon, I swear it."

"Good! You are a faithful servant, Johnnie."

"I love only you, Charon . . ."

When three of Gubwa's soldiers came for Vicki and Stone, both of them felt that this must be the end of the line. Stone could be of little use to the albino now, and under hypnotism Vicki had already surrendered all she had to offer by way of information. Stone might have made a fight of it (Gubwa's influence over him had only extended to the completion of his task) but he wasn't given the ghost of a chance. The three men, dressed in the Castle's uniform, were armed and very efficient. They quickly tied the captives into wheelchairs, and while two of them pushed, the third followed up the rear, a machine-gun cradled in his arms.

They were taken to the Command Center, where Gubwa had his own reasons for wanting them present during the coming hours. And in keeping with his nature, Gubwa's reasons were anything but pleasant.

The huge albino wore only a dressing gown and slippers, marking comfort as essential to any use of his powers as might become necessary. His face was lined but not yet haggard despite lack of sleep, and his captives saw that there was a sort of wildness about him now: that eager, barely controlled air of anticipation, the hysteria of mind and spirit which invariably marks the egomaniac or otherwise manic personality under pressure or in time of crisis.

"My dear Miss Maler," he opened, having sent

his soldiers away, "and Mr. Stone, of course," he nodded an exaggerated welcome. "And doubtless you're both wondering just why I've had you brought here."

"Not really," said Stone drily. "Since we're the only human beings in the place, naturally you'd want to talk to somebody. It must get hellish lonely amongst the freaks you call your servants and the zombies you use for guards!"

Gubwa smiled indulgently. "Not at all, Mr. Stone, on the contrary. I, too, am a 'freak,' remember? And as for my 'zombies': no general ever knew the obedience my word commands. Haven't you experienced that for yourself?" He let that sink in.

"But . . . I didn't bring you here for the sake of mere banter, however amusing."

"So let's not banter, Mr. Gubwa," said Vicki, finding a little iron to stiffen her voice. "Just why are we here?"

He stared at her and the false geniality slipped slowly from his gray-mottled face. His eyes became pink pinpoints. "Fire in your glance, Miss Maler. Fire in your heart. Admirable emotion. Enjoy its heat, for you'll soon be cold as these steel walls."

"We expected nothing more, Gubwa," Stone snarled. "We just wondered if it would be sooner or later, that's all."

"For the young lady, sooner," the albino answered. "If what she has already told me and what she believes is true."

"Richard!" Vicki at once gasped.

"Yes, your man Garrison," Gubwa nodded

gravely. "You told me that when he dies, you die. It struck me not long ago that this would be an admirable test: to have you here in sight, at the moment he dies. He will die, you see, in the very near future. I have seen to that."

Vicki hung her head, sobbed.

"You're a bastard, Gubwa, you know that?" Stone grated the words out, his face twisted with hatred. "A gray, slug-like, murderous, slimy freak bastard!"

"But tomorrow I shall be alive!" Gubwa cried, his eyes suddenly blazing. "And very soon I shall be a god!"

"You?" Stone sneered his derision. "A god? A freak god of a nuclear wasteland?"

"What?" Gubwa was raving now, strutting to and fro. "Don't you ever learn anything, man? What nuclear wasteland? Hasn't the girl told you by now all she told me?"

"I don't follow you at all, Gubwa," Stone spat disgustedly. "What the hell are you getting at?"

Vicki Maler was less slow. She had seen more, understood more than Stone possibly could from his short acquaintance with matters paranormal. *"Psychomech!"* she gasped.

"Aha! The girl knows!" Gubwa cried. "Explain to him, if you please, Miss Maler. Tell him my meaning."

She shook her head, not knowing where to begin.

Gubwa read her whirling mind. "Begin with Garrison," he laughed. "Before Psychomech."

"He was . . . just a man," she sobbed. "Oh, he was strange—he saw things, knew things others couldn't see or know—but he was a man. In a way he was little more than a boy, and a blind boy at that! Then . . . then the machine." She paused.

"Yes, yes!" Gubwa cried. "Go on, Miss Maler—you're doing so well."

"His powers were increased a thousandfold, almost infinitely. At first he was like . . . like a god! For a year or more. Then—"

"Then his powers began to fail him, and no way to replenish them," Gubwa cut in. "He had destroyed Psychomech, and the fool didn't know what was wrong! Only now, too late, has he recognized the truth. Now, as his ESP-talents ebb and he himself fails, he flees from enemies he would once destroy with a glance, with a thought! He will die—all three of you will die, and Garrison's alter-facets, too, tonight—but Psychomech shall live on. I have made arrangements. The man who built the machine for Garrison will be here tomorrow, and—"

"Jimmy Craig?" Vicki blurted. "You have him, too?"

Gubwa smiled delightedly. "Indeed! Mr. James Christopher Craig himself. I have him, yes—or will have him. Already I have visited him in his dreams and made certain . . . suggestions? Ah!—and how *susceptible*, our Mr. Craig."

"But Jimmy wasn't the builder," Vicki said desperately. "Psychometh was built by a man dead now or disappeared. Jimmy only improved on what was already there. He stripped away outmoded parts and replaced them. He—"

"I know all of that, Miss Maler," Gubwa cut her

off. "*You* told me, remember? Well, perhaps you don't," he shrugged. "Anyway, I have been in Craig's mind. I told him he has a mission, a Great Mission, which is to build Psychomech again—a mightier, more powerful Psychomech—and this time to build it for me. I told him that with the completion of this marvel, this Oracle, he himself will become a wondrous power in the world. I told him that he had erred in working for Garrison, and that Garrison was a great sinner! But I also said that I would strike Garrison down, and then that Craig—through his work for me—would be redeemed. And I told him that through Psychomech, one day he would communicate with the One True God himself. Yes, and I shall be that God!"

Gubwa chuckled and folds of fat heaved. "Do you see, Miss Maler, do you see?"

"Yes," she bowed her head. "Yes, I see. What Psychomech did for Richard, it will do a hundred times over for you."

"There!" Gubwa turned triumphantly to Stone. "And now do you understand?"

"You're mad!" Stone struggled with his bonds.

"And you are a fool!" Gubwa snapped. "Or utterly stupid. Man, you've seen what I can do without Psychomech. Just *think* what I shall do with it! Neutron bombs? Holocaust? No more, Mr. Stone. Genetic engineering? Unnecessary. With Psychomech's aid I shall simply command the things I desire—*and they shall be!*"

Gubwa's eyes gave him away. He was quite mad now, really mad. "*Homo Sapiens?* Oh, yes, indeed, Mr. Stone—but in a month's time, or maybe less, when Psychomech has made me God—*Hermaphro Sapiens*! Every man, woman and child, in the twinkling of an eye, at my command, in my own image, and I shall simply will it! Emperor of Earth? Of this one miserable planet? No, no! No longer, Mr. Stone, Miss Maler. My new plan is mightier than that. Why rule a mere world when the entire universe can be, will be mine? My titles? I shall tell you my titles:

"God of Earth and all the stars, Master of the Universe, and Lord of the Psychosphere! These shall be my titles!"

As Gubwa grew more and more animated, striding about the Command Center like some nightmarish, leprous windmill, gesticulating and gabbling, Stone turned his head to Vicki and whispered: "He's right over the edge. Just look at him."

"You are wrong, Phillip," she shook her head, and followed up quickly with, "Oh, he's insane in himself—but his reasoning is sound enough."

Stone's jaw dropped. "Sound reasoning? He thinks this machine, this Psychomech, can make him into a god!"

"The God," said Vicki simply. "Yes, it can."

"Vicki, I'm no believer, but that's a real blasphemy!"

"Oh, yes—yes, it is," she nodded.

"Out!" Gubwa suddenly shouted. "Out, out! Insane? Blasphemy? We shall see, we shall see." He pressed a button on his intercom. "Guards, in here now." The doors hissed open and a pair of Gubwa's soldiers entered. "Take them out. Let them wait in the corridor. I have something I

314

must do now. I shall call when I want them back. Quickly, quickly! I have much to do."

Vicki and Stone were wheeled out into the corridor and the doors hissed shut behind them . . .

Johnnie Fong had driven through the town and up into the Grampians. The road was narrower here and uneven, and the way not so easy for driving. There were steep slopes on the one hand and gorges on the other, with dark streams rushing below. At the end of the year, when the snows came, these would be among the first roads to go; villages like this one would be shut off from the outside world for weeks at a time. That was the kind of country it was: wild and beautiful. And dangerous. Fong knew that this was perfect ambush country.

The Chinaman had parked off the road up a narrow track where he could hide the car in thickly-grown pines. Then he'd climbed to a saddle between bald hills and seated himself upon a flat stone. From this vantage point he could once more train his binoculars on the village and see all that transpired. His timing was perfect; no sooner had he found the garage and the silver Mercedes than he saw a matchstick Garrison get into the car and turn its nose towards the mountains. Soon the car would be lost to his sight as it climbed into the pass, and then he would have to wait until it came round the contour of the mountain and onto the road directly below him, close to where he'd parked his gray Jaguar.

Charon Gubwa's timing was also perfect. He had said one hour and the hour was up.

Johnnie, the voice was the merest whisper in Fong's head, *is it safe?*

"Oh, yes, Charon!" the Chinaman never failed to be awed by his master's telepathy.

GOOD! NOW BE QUIET, LET YOUR MIND DWELL ON WHATEVER HAS OCCURRED SINCE WE LAST SPOKE. LET ME SEE IT. EXCELLENT! AND NOW LET ME SEE WHAT IS HAPPENING AT THIS VERY MOMENT—RIGHT NOW—THROUGH YOUR EYES!

Fong put his binoculars to his eyes and found the Mercedes where already it had climbed up along the winding road and into the foothills. Then he followed the road back where it ribboned along behind Garrison's car, finally focussing on the black saloon about a mile to the rear. Speed was dangerous down there, Fong could testify to that, but the saloon was leaving a trail of dust billowing in the summer air. The Mercedes was moving much more slowly and it would not be long before the saloon caught up. In a few more minutes the silver car passed out of sight; shortly after that the saloon, too.

WHERE DO THEY COME BACK INTO VIEW?

"Here, Charon," Fong trained his binoculars on the spot.

GOOD. I FANCY THIS RACE IS ALMOST RUN. WE SHALL WAIT AND SEE.

The road was steep round the mountain and through the pass. Very few cars were visible, with empty miles between them. It was almost twenty-five minutes before the Mercedes came into view, by which time the saloon should have been hard up behind it. But it was not. It was all of five more minutes before the shiny-black hearse-like car put in its appearance, and by then Garrison/Koenig had had all the time he needed.

Where the road made a sharp bend round a jagged outcrop of rock, hidden by the slate-gray mass and facing the road, there the silver Mercedes waited, its motor running and Garrison/Koenig at the wheel. Coming out of the pass and onto the straight, the occupants of the saloon couldn't possibly see the Merc until it was upon them.

But Fong and Gubwa saw it all.

FOOLS! the albino's mind cried out at the last moment. THEY DON'T KNOW WHAT THEY'RE DEALING WITH!

The silver Mercedes hit the saloon from the side, sending it skidding clean off the narrow road and into the shallow gorge. The black car fell, bounced, hit bottom and burst into flames. In moments the car was a blazing inferno. Garrison/Koenig got out of the Mercedes and stepped to the edge of the gorge. He looked down.

Then—

WHAT? Gubwa's mental cry was one of astonishment.

Garrison/Koenig threw up his arms and staggered forward, propelled by some invisible force. He went flailing over the edge and out of sight.

And in that same instant the sharp crack of a rifle echoed up to an astounded Johnnie Fong where he stood in the saddle between rounded peaks.

The Chinaman traversed his binoculars right, scanning the road, found what he was looking for. It was Ramon de Medici, emerging from behind a cluster of boulders, walking forward. He carried a rifle. For the first time in the Koenig-facet's life he had come up against someone whose capacity for bad thoughts was equal to his own.

As Fong and Gubwa watched, de Medici broke into a run. A moment later he stood looking down over the edge of the gorge. Down there the fire still blazed. Medici was satisfied, he turned away.

Gubwa, too, had seen enough. His mental voice rang in Fong's head, full of elation. JOHNNIE, IT IS OVER! STAY HERE. WHEN THAT ONE LEAVES, GO DOWN AND TAKE A QUICK LOOK— BUT TOUCH NOTHING. CONTACT ME LATER IF YOU CAN, AND IF THERE'S ANYTHING YOU THINK I SHOULD KNOW.

"Wait!" said Fong. "Look . . ." But Gubwa was already looking. De Medici had left the edge and was now examining the Mercedes. After a moment he seemed satisfied, opened the door and reached inside. With something of an effort he dragged out the limp black mass of—

GARRISON'S DOG, said Gubwa. DEAD! BUT OF COURSE SHE WOULD BE. SHE TOO ONLY LIVED BY COURTESY OF GARRISON. He was reminded of Vicki Maler. NOW I MUST GO. YOU ARE A GOOD AND FAITHFUL MAN, JOHNNIE FONG, AND YOU SHALL BE THE PRIEST OF THE TEMPLE.

"Thank you, Charon," said Fong, aware of the other's swift departure. Then, carefully, so as not to attract the attention of the man below, he began to make his way down the steep side of the hill . . .

Gubwa jerked alert where he sat before the suspended globe. "Sir!" an urgent voice was repeating. "Sir, sir?" Gubwa stood up, drew breath, swelled huge. The guard's voice, now worried, came once more over the intercom. "Sir, *sir!*"

Gubwa strode to the desk, said: "Bring them in."

The doors hissed open and Stone and Vicki were wheeled in. Stone was in tears, sobbing uncontrollably. The reason was Vicki. The faces of the guards were white, drawn. Something had seemed to age them. It was that same something which had "aged" Vicki Maler, but in her case the effect would be far more permanent.

She sat in her wheelchair like a wrinkled old mummy, her hair white and the yellow flesh loose on her bones. Senile, she mumbled and coughed; even as Gubwa watched she pushed out her tongue and a blackened tooth fell out of her mouth on a thread of yellow spittle. As Stone continued to sob she lifted an ancient hand from straps which were too loose now to contain the withered flesh and clawed at her face. Contact lenses fell to the floor. The eyes behind were fish-white, totally blind. She mewled like a kitten, beginning to drool. The smell of age and infirmity wafted from her . . .

"To see is to believe, Mr. Stone," said Gubwa, unmoved. "Garrison is dead and she, too, is dying—but it will get worse before the end. Soon she will begin to rot! Since you got on so well, you two, I would not deprive you of her company in these her final moments." He looked at the guards. "Take them back to their cell."

When they were gone he picked up his telephone and dialled Sir Harry's number . . .

Chapter

19

JOHNNIE FONG GOT DOWN THE HILLSIDE WITHOUT BE-
ing seen. As he had climbed down, so Ramon
de Medici had jacked up the front of the Mercedes and had been at work with a crowbar,
forcing the front-right fender and wing back
from the wheel. Now he had the job finished and
was climbing into the driver's seat. A moment
later the big engine roared into life.

Fong stood in the pines, peering out through
their branches. As de Medici backed the big car
away from the edge of the gorge and aimed it
back along the road south, a wheel went over
the body of the dog. Fong saw blood gush from
her jaws. But as the car pulled away he saw more
than that.

An arm came clawing up over the rim of the
shallow gorge . . .

Fong gasped his amazement, jerked his binoculars to his eyes. The distance was not great but he had to be sure. The arm stretched itself through dust and pebbles, its hand and fingers bloody and scrabbling. The hand found a hold and drew up a shoulder, a head and a face. Garrison's face, pale as a sheet, the red burn of a bullet scarring his temple into vivid contrast.

Fong blinked his eyes, quickly rubbed at the eyepieces of his binoculars and looked through them again. The top half of Garrison's body was now visible, face-down, and even as Fong watched the man somehow managed to drag his trunk and lower limbs up from the gorge. But it was Garrison's face which chiefly interested Fong, that white face with its red blaze . . . and its eyes.

Something about those eyes.

Now Garrison lifted his head and looked along the road at the cloud of dust which half-obscured the receding Mercedes, and again Fong saw that phenomenon which had caused him to doubt his own eyesight: that flickering golden glow, like a stirring of strange energies, flowing out from Garrison's eyes.

Garrison lifted an arm, pointed after the car. His lips formed silent words and for a single instant of time the golden glow suffused his whole face.

Then a brighter glow intruded, a white brilliance originating in the incandescent fireball which *had been* the Mercedes! Even at this distance the flash burned Fong's face. He dropped his binoculars, gasped his utter disbelief. He had been with Charon Gubwa many years, but never in all those years had he seen anything like this. Then the blast hit him.

As a red-blooming mushroom formed over the spot where the car had been, the Chinaman was snatched from his feet in a great fist of wind and tossed into the branches of suddenly whipping pines. For long moments the hot wind blew like the breath of some fire-elemental, then died away as quickly as it had come. Echoes of the blast came rumbling down from the hills, gradually receding. And finally Fong fell to the earth in a hail of pine needles and tangled, broken branches. Beneath him where he lay half-stunned, slowly the ground stopped trembling.

Fong climbed shakily to his feet. His Jaguar lay on its back. Several pines had been snapped off close to the ground and lay pointing away from the scene of the blast. The mushroom rose higher, white and writhing, like the cloud that forms above a nuclear explosion. The cliff face was coming down in great slabs of rock, filling the massive crater in the road. Automatically, all of his senses numb, Fong found his binoculars and looped their strap round his neck. But for the pines he might well have been whirled away and killed.

And now he understood something of his albino master's unusual caution where Richard Garrison was concerned. The man's powers were . . . Fong shook his head. Gubwa was awesome, but Richard Garrison was awful!

When Garrison/Koenig had fallen after being shot at, his unconscious body had thudded down onto a stony ledge some nine or ten feet below the level of the road. A small avalanche of dust and pebbles, falling on him, had hidden him from view from above, and the ledge had protected him from the heat of the car blazing below. He had only been out for a minute or two, following which consciousness had slowly, achingly returned. Another man might have taken hours to recover—might not have recovered at all—but there was that in Garrison which drove him on.

It was that same drive which had brought him through all the trials of his dream-quest, even the final trial of the burning desert. For such had been his dream—of the furnace wastes, of dragging Psychomech inch by agonized inch behind him, and of a desiccated, dying Suzy—when there had come that titan blast, that stunning physical agony of a searing, scarring bullet which had ripped Koenig's mind from its ascendency into unconscious oblivion and roused Garrison's mind up from nightmare.

And it *was* Garrison who had come awake and clawed his way back to the road above the gorge; not his alter-facets but Richard Garrison himself. It was Garrison now, picking himself up to stumble raggedly over to where Suzy's crushed body lay, sliding his hand under her faithful head. Life flickered in those black eyes of hers even now, but its light was quickly dimming.

Garrison cried. Cried burning tears from eyes already dim and robbed of most of their golden glow. His anger had robbed him—that anger expended in rending the Psychosphere in that great blast of vengeance—and power must pay for the waste. Useless now to attempt Suzy's resurrection. Once it would have been the very simplest business, but no longer. What psychic power remained in him would not run to that, not now. Even in the Psychosphere it was far easier to destroy than to create. But he must do something.

Garrison smiled through his tears as an idea dawned. He and Suzy were close, closer than any other animal and master gone before them. She was almost a part of him. Why not *make* her a part of him? He prayed he still had the power, the ability.

Gently he entered her mind, found a great love there and a great pain. Her tongue flopped loosely between bloodied jaws, licking his hand. SUZY, he said. STOP HURTING. GOOD! NOW, GIRL . . . COME INTO ME. COME INTO ME, SUZY . . .

Her eyes looked at him and went dim. Her head lolled lifelessly back. Garrison struggled wearily to his feet, the tears drying on his pale cheeks. He had many miles to go and the day was growing older. Which way now?

He knew the answer instinctively, with the instinct of a dog: along the road for a mile or two, then over the hill and . . . and *that* way, over there!

He smiled, however wanly, and began to plod slowly along the road. And in the back of his mind something bounded and barked joyfully, and he was not alone.

Behind him, the spot where the great black bitch

325

had lain was vacant now. Bright motes of dust spiralled and shone in the yellow sunlight . . .

Fong followed at a safe distance (was any distance safe?), keeping Garrison in sight but barely so, along the road and over the hills and for miles and miles across country rougher than any the Chinaman had ever known before. The man in front was weak and his pace had grown gradually slower, but still he pressed forward and never once looked back. Fong found himself trailing footprints in boggy peat, climbing steep inclines where shale slipped and slithered underfoot, digging his heels in down almost precipitous slopes and trudging weary miles through valleys of drear, boggy sedge. But while Garrison occasionally faltered, always he recovered and went on.

He had to, for he knew now that he approached quest's end. Somewhere to the west lay the picturesque Glen o' Dunkillie, but not far ahead was the reality of his dream within a dream. He had started his quest in the strange world of the subconscious, but he would finish it here—or it would finish him.

For a moment panic struck at Garrison. Night was coming on, true, but still it seemed darker to him, or gloomier, than the hour demanded. He knew the answer but dared not even dwell upon it, dared not admit of its existence. And yet he'd always known it: his eyes would be the first to go.

Garrison would dearly have loved to lie down and go to sleep (a mental rather than a physical

weariness, he suspected, despite the miles behind him and the ravaged state of his body) but
the very thought was out of the question. He was
not tired, could not allow himself to *be* tired. Too
much—too many—depended upon him. But
cresting a shaly rise onto a flat tableland, suddenly he knew that he would have to face up to
the worst. Not even the clouds of a gathering
summer storm would explain the darkness
creeping gradually across his vision. The battery
had almost run dry.

At that very moment, fifty yards to his rear,
Johnnie Fong made up his mind to act indepen-
dently of Charon Gubwa. The albino wanted Garrison dead, Fong knew that, and he also knew
that Garrison could die, almost had died. Very
well, this could not go on. The man ahead was
almost finished. He staggered, a silhouette
against the gray, troubled sky. A perfect target.
Fong lifted his pistol, took careful aim and
squeezed the trigger.

Garrison must have tripped at that very moment. His silhouette jerked out of sight simultaneously with the pistol's report. Fong believed
he had hit him but—

He held his breath, waited, half-expected destruction in a white-hot fireball. That would be
all right, nothing left of him to connect him with
his beloved Charon; but nothing happened. An
unseasonal chill was in the air and the clouds
were turning in the sky, but that was all. The
Chinaman began to breathe again, waited two
more minutes before climbing to the crest.

There was blood on the rocks where they

leaned out of shallow soil, heather and lichen. Fresh, wet blood. As for Garrison: a shadow moved ahead, stumbling over the tableland, arms pumping.

Incredibly, he was running!

It was 9:00 P.M. by Stone's reckoning when Vicki suffered her relapse. For an hour or two he had dared hope that . . . but in Stone's scheme of things hope had rarely been seen to spring eternal. He was a realist. For himself: he would take whatever chances came his way. He certainly didn't intend to go out without a fight. But Vicki? She was a woman with one hell of a handicap: her lifeline had just snapped. Richard Garrison was dead and Vicki Maler must soon follow him.

Stone didn't know her, not really, but he felt he had known her better than most. She had turned her heart out to him and he had listened. And he had held her in his arms—just that, nothing more—but they had shared. Now?

The thing lying on her bed wasn't Vicki Maler. It had been her once more, for an hour or two, but wasn't it of old renown that people brighten before they die? The flaring-up of the candle's flame before it flickers out. Well, Vicki's flame had flared up. The golden glow had not quite returned to her eyes, but some color had come back into her face and her flesh had seemed to firm out a little. She had even spoken a few words, telling Stone not to cry for her. Perceptive, yes. But he had also cried for himself, cried his frustration, his hatred. How very badly he wanted Gubwa, and how massive the odds against getting him.

Talk of the devil—or in Gubwa's case think of him—for at that moment the albino's face appeared at the barred window in the door.

"Ah, Mr. Stone—and so distressed! You surprise me. I had thought you harder." His pink eyes went from Stone, seated in his chair, to the bed where Vicki Maler's bundle of living bones lay wrapped in her now voluminous clothing. Her chest rose and fell with a slow, jerky, shallow movement.

Gubwa nodded, smiled at Stone. "She is fading. You may see the end, you may not. It depends how quickly she dies. You see, you only have forty minutes. When the night-shift comes on duty, Phillip Stone goes off duty—for good! I've promised Sir Harry that your body will be in the Thames in the morning, and it will be."

Stone stood up, moved to the barred window. His hands were huge white knots at his sides. "Some god, Gubwa, when you're obliged to keep your promises to scum like that bastard!"

"I shall do whatever is necessary, Mr. Stone, to maintain . . . a balance," he shrugged, "until Psychomech is mine. After that . . .

"Do you really think I have enjoyed my relationship with Sir Harry? Of course not. He shall be among the first to go."

Stone forced a laugh. "A god with a hit-list?" he sneered. "You get funnier by the minute!"

Gubwa maintained his equanamity. "But you would agree," he said slowly, "that gods do have the power of life and death, Mr. Stone. Why are they given such power, do you suppose, if not to use it?"

"In your case?" Stone answered. "I would say for the same reason a dog is given rabies! And funny, isn't it?—but 'God' reversed is 'dog!' How far is a rabid dog removed from Christ, Gubwa? Well, that's you, in my eyes—the Antichrist."

Gubwa scowled. He was tired of Stone now, but he could not leave without a parting shot. "I do not merely mouth words when I speak of life and death, Mr. Stone, though I will admit that my meaning is occasionally obscured—deliberately. But you see, what Garrison did I shall have the power to do one hundred times over. And there is one particular thing that he did which quite intrigues me." His smile was monstrous.

"Miss Maler was quite beautiful," the albino went on. "Garrison chose her for his mate and I consider his taste impeccable. So console yourself with this thought: I shall be merciful with her. She dies now, but when *next* she wakes she shall sit upon the right hand of God! *Hermaphro Sapiens*, yes—and she shall be the mother of the race, the mother of my children. What a Goddess she shall make, don't you agree, Mr. Stone? Why, even Jesus rose up only once!"

"You mad, mad bastard!" Stone hissed through clenched teeth. But Gubwa was already striding away down the corridor. His booming laughter came echoing back . . .

Garrison ran. For an endless time (it seemed to him) he ran and ran. He had lost a lot of blood, was losing more even now, but no longer cared or gave it thought. All sense of feeling was absent from his right shoulder where Johnnie Fong's bullet had passed through it, and his eyesight was three-quarters gone along with his physical strength, but still he ran. It was a race against time and he must run it to its end, even knowing that only willpower kept him going—and that even that was failing.

And somewhere back there a killer, and Garrison powerless to strike back. He ran until the earth fell away beneath him and he crashed headlong down a steep slope. The wall of the valley went down in dips, and it was one of these in which he found himself when his head stopped spinning. Wearily he sat himself upright in sliding scree, grit and coarse grass. Distant lightning flickered, firing his sight in its split-second duration. Garrison gasped, sucked on air, prayed. In answer the far lightning flickered again.

Dim as his sight was he could not mistake the vast bulk of the dam rising on his right, the dark mass of the solitary house where it squatted below. And now he knew. This was it, the valley of his dream within a dream. Only one thing was missing and for a moment it stumped him. Then he remembered.

The dam was quiet, its waters pent, the merest trickle bubbling from six great vents in its face. It would remain so until the official opening tomorrow. But everything else was here; and behind him, up there, the shadowy, looming spires of marching pylons. Oh, yes, this was it.

And with that knowledge, as the first stirring

of hope tightened his guts and heightened his awareness, Garrison also became aware of his pain, his weakness. Blind instinct had driven him before, the will to live, to survive. There had been no time, no room for pain or exhaustion. And there must be none now, not when he was so close, not with a killer on his trail.

Somehow he struggled on, and somehow, after endless ages of pain and weariness, he found himself at the foot of the path leading to the door of the lone house. Deserted, the place looked gloomy as its surroundings, as doomful as the great dam rising high above. Its roof had partly caved in, most of the windows were broken and the chimney stack was crumbling. These things Garrison could still see, but even seeing them his vision was blurring, the silhouette of the house merging with the dark valley and the darker horizon of valley-wall beyond.

Fear drove him forward in a surge he had not believed he could muster. He reached the door and found it locked. Sight was almost gone, but he could not tell how much of that was due to the night, the gathering storm. He sobbed, threw up his arms against the stout timbers of the door. He leaned against it and felt the contours of metal letters pressed against his forehead. The place had a name.

He traced the letters with his left hand, the hand with feeling: X-A-N-A . . .

Xanadu!

No one was late. Gubwa hadn't programmed his soldiers to be late. There were sixteen of them, double the normal requirement. Top ranker was Gardner, and he was in charge of the shift. Sixteen was the maximum the lift could take, else Gardner was sure there would have been even more of them. Something big was happening and the Castle's master was taking no chances.

The sixteen had arrived more or less individually, but at the hour appointed they had come together as a body in the underground car park at the access door to the lift. On their way here, on foot or in the city's transport, they had been articulate, at their ease, completely "normal" citizens; but now they were a crowd of zombies. That *was* in their program; for now, out of sight of the crowds surging in the streets above, they rapidly reverted to the human machines Gubwa had caused them to be. And that was a condition which left them particularly vulnerable to Sir Harry's attack.

He had arrived all of an hour earlier, him and six highly-trained operatives from the branch's Special Assignments Group. Killers all, they were utterly loyal to him; he had enough on each of them to guarantee their loyalty. Now, as Gardner counted heads, nodded and stepped up to the door, keys jangling, Sir Harry gave the agreed signal. This was simply his voice yelling *"Now!"* and the beam of his torch swathing the unsuspecting sixteen where they bunched in gloomy, concrete-cast shadows at the door. His agents did the rest.

Gubwa's soldiers didn't know what hit them. They were trained and conditioned for possible action *in* the Castle, not outside of it. They went

down like thistles under a scythe as the branch
men stepped out from cover and caught them
in a withering, short burst of intense fire. For no
more than five seconds the machine-guns yam-
mered, their insane chattering drowning the
echoes of Sir Harry's yell and bringing down riv-
ulets of accumulated dust from the concrete
ceiling. Then it was over, and in the stunned silence Sir Harry stepped forward and took Gardner's keys from fingers that were still twitching.
Moments later he was through the door, his men
dragging the bodies of the sixteen in after them.
Somebody outside threw down sand on the
blood and someone else swept it away into darkness. Then they were all through the door and
Sir Harry locked it behind them.

He stepped forward and pressed the button for
the lift. Far down below the empty cage jerked
and began its slow climb upwards. All unaware,
the men of the shift coming off duty were beginning to convene, moving towards the foot of the
shaft. Two of them had been assigned a special
duty—one which concerned Phillip Stone . . .

Garrison got in through a broken window. In doing so he cut himself badly, but he was far beyond caring about pain or loss of blood now.
Indeed his near-delirium sprang from these
sources, so that even he did not know how close
he was to death. But still he hung on.

The darkness was his biggest immediate problem. Inside the house he felt literally buried in
darkness, his near-blindness adding to his confusion. He found an open fireplace with crum-

pled newspapers already lying in the grate, brought out his cigarette lighter and struck flame. The paper, mercifully dry and crisp, blazed up. Garrison fuelled the fire with pieces ripped from an old, broken wicker chair—and sobbed his relief that he could still see, however dimly, the leaping flames.

The fire warmed his chill flesh, bringing comfort on the one hand and on the other a sure recognition of his condition, the fact that the life-force within him was ebbing. And yet there was something here—right here in Xanadu—which could yet save the day. Else all had been pointless. But what was it?

Stumbling about the room, one of three rooms on the ground floor, Garrison flopped into a chair and allowed himself to sprawl for a moment across a heavy wooden table. His hand came into contact with a table lamp, naked wires dangling from its flex. When the occupants, whoever they had been, left the house, they had taken the plugs with them. A pity, he could have used a little extra light . . .

Why not?

The thought spurred him on. The odds were all against there being any electricity, but he could at least try.

He half-fell from the chair with the rotten flex in his hand, found a socket in the skirting-board, shoved the naked wires in with fingers that shook so badly they seemed to vibrate. Then they *did* vibrate. He was holding the bare cores!

Even as the fact got through to his brain, Garrison was hurled across the room—but in that same instant of contact things had happened. Marvellous things!

For one thing his sight had returned, fully restored, however briefly. For another, strength had seemed to flow, however fleetingly, in veins and muscles and bones hollow as empty vessels. And finally . . . finally Garrison had remembered a dream. That dream in which a monster—the Garrison/Schroeder/Koenig monster—had been galvanized into life on the bed of the ethereal MACHINE.

Like the Frankenstein monster of youthful horror films, the Garrison-creature had been brought alive by Nature's own raw energies. By lightning. By electricity!

Now, blind again, he crawled back across the floor. The moment of contact had been too brief, had lasted for a single instant of time before his body reacted to the shock. This time it must be longer. It must be . . . as long as it took.

Weaker than ever, he clawed his way across the floor. Blood still flowed freely from his fingers, lacerated hand, scalp, perforated shoulder. He used the cracked nails of his hands to strip the age-brittled plastic from copper wires, wound them round his wrists, held them in his hands, found the socket and plugged the wires in, first one and then the other.

And where he had jammed himself between the heavy table and the wall, his body jerked and shook and fluttered—all of his limbs writhing, his hair standing out from his head, his eyes bulging—as his fingers smoked and blackened and the wires glowed red in his hands.

For five, ten, fifteen seconds he *sucked* energy from the socket. He would have gone on, continuing until something fused, but that wasn't to be. The vibration of his body increased in violence until, driving the huge wooden table before him, he flew once more across the room and the wires snapped.

Ah!—but now the battery was charged again. Not fully, no, not yet. But quest's end finally lay in sight and Garrison knew what he must do. He lifted his head from the naked floorboards and the entire room burned gold in the light from his eyes. A light which would suffer no barriers. A light which engulfed the entire house. A light which once, in a dream, Garrison had taken for the shining hemisphere of a stately pleasure-dome—or the temple of the Goddess of Immortality!

At the foot of the garden path Johnnie Fong stopped dead in his tracks, drew back, finally fled as the wall of that golden dome seemed to advance upon him.

Chapter

20

THE TWO SOLDIERS DETAILED BY GUBWA TO TAKE care of Stone arrived at his cell and opened the door. Inside the metal room Vicki Maler—or the thing she was now—lay sleeping or dead, completely hidden under a blanket Stone had thrown over her. The two men weren't interested in her, however, but in him. Youngish men, they were no longer dressed in their Castle uniforms but in normal street clothes.

Stone took them in at a glance. Smart and reasonably well-groomed, they would not look out of place as young executives in any of the city's firms or businesses. It seemed somehow unreasonable that they should be trained killers, working for a creature like Charon Gubwa. It also seemed unreasonable that he would have to kill them—which he would, quite cheerfully, if the opportunity presented itself.

They ordered him out of the cell at gunpoint and into a wheelchair. Then, as one of them held a pistol to his temple, the other prepared to strap him into the chair.

"Hurry it up," said the one with the gun, his tone urgent. "The cage will be down. They'll be waiting for us."

The other looked up as if to answer—but at the precise moment there came the loud rattle of automatic gunfire and whine of ricocheting bullets, interspersed with shouting and screams. It was exactly the chance Stone had been looking for. What was going on he couldn't say, but whatever it was he wanted to be part of it.

His two guards were momentarily startled; Stone didn't give them the least opportunity to recover. His arms shot up like pistons and he got a two-handed grip on the wrist of the one with the gun, deflecting it. At the same time he came to his feet like a coiled spring, his head smashing into the face of the man crouching over him. To complete the job on that one and without releasing his grip on the gun-hand of the other, he lashed out with a kick that pulverized the man's groin. The one with the gun had meanwhile started yelling and driving his free fist repeatedly into the side of Stone's head. Stone ignored the sticky, pulpy feel of a torn ear and brought his knee up and the soldier's wrist down in one sharp movement. The wrist snapped across his knee . . . the man screamed . . . the gun flew across the corridor and bounced off the wall. Before it could clatter to the floor Stone had whirled his agonized victim in a half-circle, crashing him headlong into the steel wall.

In the next moment the pistol was in Stone's hand and he fell into a crouch as a pair of combat-suited, woollen-helmeted men, armed to the teeth, came round a far corner. They could have been from MI5 or 6, could be more of Gubwa's soldiers, he had no way of knowing—until they began to sprint towards him, their weapons spitting fire. After that it didn't matter who they were.

Stone snapped off a shot and saw one man stopped in his tracks, spinning like a top as he fell. The other slowed down a little, then came on at a charge. Stone took cover behind the wheelchair, took careful aim, fired. As the chair was torn from his grasp by a spray of bullets, so Stone saw the muzzle of the machine-gun floating towards his face. Floating, yes, in a sort of slow motion. But the gun was in free-fall, its owner already sailing past with a neat red and black hole between his staring, dead eyes. Then things speeded up.

Stone snatched the machine-gun from mid-air, pocketed the pistol, stepped to the dead man's body and glanced at him. He'd seen him before, he was sure. Sir Harry's branch. Just like that treacherous, lousy, wonderful bastard! Stone snatched a magazine of ammunition from the man's belt, a couple of grenades, turned to the door of what had been his cell and shot the lock off. He went to snatch Vicki Maler from her bed and was surprised at her weight. Throwing back the blanket he saw her and his jaw dropped. She had firmed out again. She wasn't quite the youthful, beautiful girl he had briefly known, but she wasn't a hag either.

He thought to try and waken her, changed his mind and simply wrapped her in the blanket. Then she went over his shoulder in a fireman's lift, and a moment later he was back out in the corridor. Things were still chaotic in the Castle, but in the main Sir Harry's crowd had taken Gubwa by surprise. Grenades detonated somewhere as the invaders commenced a methodical destruction of the place, and there were still occasional bursts of fire and screams of agony and death.

Having no idea yet where he was going, Stone simply ran with Vicki bouncing on his shoulder.

Somewhere someone was shouting: "I want Gubwa, the big fat albino! I want him dead! I want all of these freaks dead! Wreck the place as you go but make sure you get every last one of them!" Stone recognized Sir Harry's voice. A long time since that pig had seen active service. Gubwa must have angered him mightily!

He reached a right-hand bend in the corridor at the same time as a member of Gubwa's harem came staggering round it. The transsexual's face was covered with blood which dripped from his chin. His heavy woman's breasts were scarlet with it. He carried no weapon.

"Don't shoot!" he cried in a falsetto voice. "Don't shoot . . ." But he was already crumpling to his knees, collapsing face-down on the floor's rubber coating.

More gunfire and screams, from close at hand.

Stone took a deep breath, threw himself round the corner with his machine-gun spurting lead. A combat-suited man took off in mid-air along the corridor as Stone's bullets chewed into him. He had been standing guard over a lift cage. Bodies littered the area, all of them dressed for the street. Gubwa's men, about to go off duty. Stone felt nothing for them.

He yanked the cage's latticed doors open, stepped through them—and as he did so heard the hiss of a door opening behind him. He whirled . . . and across the corridor stood Gubwa. The albino saw Stone, saw his gun, and he skidded to a halt in the middle of the corridor. His hair was wild, his pink eyes wide.

"In!" Stone snapped. "Now, before I change my mind!"

"Yes, yes, I'm coming. Please don't shoot, Mr. Stone."

"Shoot? Kill you? You have to be joking! If I shoot you who'll explain all this? And believe me you've got some explaining to do. And while you're doing it I'm going to sit there and grin. *And* I'm going to be able to tell them the right questions to ask!"

The cage was a big one. Gubwa got as far away as he could from the muzzle of Stone's machine-gun. His arms were in the air, trembling uncontrollably; his entire frame wobbled like jelly. "The button, Mr. Stone," he babbled. "Please press it. We have to get out of here—now!"

Stone became suspiciously aware of the other's urgency. It was understandable, of course, but . . . he hovered his finger over the lift's button, his shoulder supporting Vicki. "What have you done, Gubwa?"

"Press it, for God's sake!" the hermaphrodite gibbered, his hands fluttering. "The Castle is mined! I've set the detonation sequence in motion!"

"For 'God's sake,' eh?" said Stone mockingly—but he pressed the button. As the cage jerked and started upward, a tremendous explosion blew the debris of bodies along the corridor beyond the latticed doors. Then they were out of it, but beneath their feet they could still feel the concussions of further explosions. As the thunders receded, so Gubwa began to relax, his hands starting to fall towards his sides.

"Keep 'em up, fat thing!" Stone snarled. He took two paces forward, stuck his gun in Gubwa's belly, shoving hard through the towelling of the albino's robe. "Also, you can close your eyes—*close 'em*! And keep 'em closed. And let me tell you now: I only have to feel the tiniest tickle of an alien thought in my head, just one, and a second later you're going to weigh at least a pound heavier. And I'll love it!"

Through all of this a speaker in the ceiling had been droning Gubwa's recorded hypnotic orders, accompaniment to the pulsing of a blue strobe light. Stone, however, had not been conditioned to receive such orders. His lips twisted into a mirthless grin as he stepped back from the albino, lifted up the snout of his gun and fired off a burst at the speaker and strobe.

"There," he said as Gubwa's recorded voice squawked into silence and the light went out, leaving them in near-darkness. Once more he prodded Gubwa's belly with the smoking muzzle of the machine-gun. "That writes finis on that shit! And that only leaves you, mister. It only leaves you. And if you've any sense at all, you'll just stand perfectly still and do absolutely nothing . . ."

Garrison had lain quite still for some minutes, but while his ravaged body had rested his mind had been intensely active. First he had stilled the incredible pain in his limbs, trunk and head; which had required the merest effort of will, a simple command that the pain *would* stop. Then he had soaked up the essence of the house, the valley outside, the dam and surrounding countryside, over which a freakish summer storm was about to break in unprecedented fury. In doing so—in this systematic mental examination of his whereabouts—he had once more triggered memories of his prophetic dreams, stripping them of their mysticism until all that remained of them was the fact that they had been prophetic. Through them he had seen the future, a future, inalienable and unchangeable as the past.

The past was gone, but the future, as any future, began here and now. And however obscurely, the way into that future had been delineated. Garrison was powerful now but not nearly powerful enough to go that way, not yet. But how close the analogy had been, when he had likened himself to a battery leaking its power. And how easy and how terrible the solution. He had dreamed of a great MACHINE and knew now that this valley, this place, *was* that MACHINE. As for its power source—

Garrison reached out his mind to the dam and explored its mechanisms . . .

Johnnie Fong sat one-third of the way up the wall of the valley and stared at the golden glow of the dome. It had stopped growing, stood taller than the pines, enclosed what had been the entire garden of the house. Fong didn't know if it had substance and he wasn't ready to find out. But it was, must be, a manifestation of Garrison. About that the Chinaman had no doubt. If only Charon would contact him now, perhaps the albino would be able to tell him how to deal with things. Always his beloved Charon had the answers to such—

Fong jerked to his feet. The first warm raindrops were beginning to fall and the clouds were boiling madly overhead, but even the moaning of the wind could not drown out the new sound— the sudden, rapidly increasing roar of power unleashed. Fong's eyes went to the face of the dam, took in the spectacles of the six silvery trickles that ran down its concrete face erupting into gigantic spouts; and his ears heard the thunder of waters in chaos.

He backed away, turned and scrambled higher, not looking back until he no longer dared ignore what was happening behind and below him. Full fifteen minutes that climb, and Fong's limbs trembling with his exertion when finally he did stop and turn. But now he knew why he had fled, that it had been instinct which drove him up from the house and away from the dam. Instinct and fear.

Not fear of the rushing waters, no, for already his elevation had been such that they could not possibly reach him. Fear of the power which had *caused* those waters to rush, the Gigantic Unstoppable Power whose heart throbbed at the center of the golden dome!

Throbbed, yes, for the dome was unstable now. It pulsed with an irregular expansion and contraction like some vast alien beacon. It struggled with itself, or within itself, like molten lava in a volcano's cone, tossed by the turmoil below. And finally—it broke!

A figure—upright, manlike, golden, glowing, like some sort of anthropomorphic fragment of the dome itself—came through its wall and stood for a moment on the night wind, then rose up the slope of the valley directly towards the Chinaman where he trembled and gasped.

No part of that figure of golden fire touched the slope itself. Utterly suspended on air, it levitated itself a full two feet above the whipping grass and stunted shrubs; and as it passed close by Fong the truth of its nature, which of course he had known, made itself apparent. Namely that this was Richard Garrison, but shrunken, dried out, almost desiccated. It was Garrison, but devoid of life, or life as Fong understood it. Garrison, and yet less than Garrison, and yet greater, far greater.

He lifted his pistol as the figure passed, fired off shot after shot and knew that he struck the target each time; but the figure made no pause, showed no interest, paid no heed at all. And when Fong's weapon was empty, then it fell from his nerveless fingers; and still the mummied figure of Garrison sailed on, its eyes blazing, its skin a mass of golden wrinkles, its arms blackened stumps whose frayed threads hung in sticky tatters just below the elbows.

And behind it, down in the valley, the agonized fluctuations of the psychic plasma about the deserted house came to an abrupt end, the glow blinked out, and in the next moment the house went down in dust and ruin and the frenzied spume of the flood that rushed and roared down the old bed of the river.

Then, like an automaton, almost without knowing that his hands and feet bore him up, Johnnie Fong clawed his way to the crest of the valley wall, following the floating figure of Garrison as a moth follows a bright light. He had to know, had to see—even if it blasted him . . .

But even before reaching the crest Fong could hear the humming of the heavy-duty cables where they draped their loops between the pylons. They were drawing off power from the dam, power which Garrison required. And as Fong crawled exhaustedly up those last few yards of slope and emerged above the valley, so he became witness to the most awesome scene of all.

It was Garrison, a living cross of golden fire, the blackened stumps of his arms outstretched, floating in air between and beneath two of the pylons. And it was Garrison who, a moment later, received the tribute of the pylons—a massive, crackling bolt that smashed down, *was sucked down* from blazing cables, enveloping him and hurling him down to the ground. Nor did it stop there. The smell of ozone filled the air, and of burning flesh, as that lashing, living, weirdly snarling and snapping pulse of raw energy spent itself in Garrison . . . who now, impossibly, stood up and held himself erect, welcoming the very fires that consumed him!

And as if the storm itself knew Garrison's bizarre thirst, it added its own energies to that awesome, fearsome funeral pyre, sending down bolt after bolt from the madly wheeling clouds, each bolt absorbed at once into the crumbling skeleton thing which was Garrison.

Witless, tingling, himself glowing with the excess energies that filled the air and plucked at the hair of his face and head, Johnnie Fong knelt with jaws agape and rain streaming from his chin. The very elements seemed crazed now, and the undersides of the clouds were awash with St. Elmo's fire as the bolts continued to rain down. And all of his raw power focussing upon Garrison or what had been Garrison—and his megamind thirsting for more still!

More still—more energy to power the ultimate quest—more physical fuel for the psychic fire.

The megamind reached out, sought, discovered . . .

More than one hundred miles away at Dounreay the pile went crazy. Rods of uranium which would have lighted entire cities for weeks were consumed in seconds . . . and nothing to show for it. Throughout the length and breadth of

Scotland lights dimmed as the power was drawn off.

A magnificent aurora filled the skies. A shaft of fire split the heavens and lanced down, down, down, to Garrison, removing every last physical vestige of him from the world of men. Removing, too, Johnnie Fong.

But while the physical Garrison was dead the mental Garrison was newborn and borne up to penetrate, to become one with the Psychosphere . . .

As the lift slowed to an almost imperceptible halt, Charon Gubwa tensed himself. In fact Stone had done him a great favor by ordering him to keep his hypnotic eyes closed. Despite the apparent failure of so many of his plans, still there was the chance that he might yet achieve a final victory. With the Castle destroyed—which by now it surely was, beyond recovery, by plastic explosives and fire bombs which would have turned the entire interior to a raging inferno— Gubwa also would be thought to have perished, if or when the matter was looked into. But there were other places ready and waiting to receive him, and a car in the underground car park to take him to one of them. There would always be men he could buy or bend to his will, and Psychomech would still become a reality.

Moreover, Gubwa knew something that Stone didn't know: namely that one last bomb remained, located at the bottom of the liftshaft, and that its detonation would be triggered when the cage's doors were opened up here. Which was why the albino had ignored Stone's warning not to mind-read, an idle threat at best for Gubwa was a master of covert telepathy. Another telepath might have sensed him, but he had been in Stone's mind for all of five minutes without the slightest fear of detection. And he was still there when the lift cage slowed to a halt and Stone yanked the doors open. With his great arms held rigidly over his head, and with Stone's gun in his back, Gubwa was the first out of the lift—a split second before the bomb went off down below and its blast, channelled up the shaft, shook the cage like a terrier shakes a rat.

With his mind taking off at a tangent, and Vicki Maler in her blanket still balanced on his shoulder, Stone stumbled and went to one knee. Before he could recover, Gubwa's right arm came down at lightning speed and his great gray hand clamped like a vice on the stock of the machine-gun, wrenching it from Stone's grasp.

Demented but triumphant in his madness, the albino laughed as he turned the gun on Stone and ordered him out of the cage.

"It would appear, Mr. Stone," he said, "that even a god can err. I said you were intelligent—but even an idiot would have killed me when he had the chance!" He made a motion with the gun. "Put her down," he ordered, indicating an empty space amongst the stiffening bodies of his former soldiers. "Put her there with the rest of these corpses. Then we shall play a little game, you and I. I shall close my eyes and stand quite still, and you shall prepare yourself. Then, when you are ready, you shall attempt to take the gun back from me—or perhaps to take that pistol from your pocket and shoot me."

"Gubwa, you blackhearted bastard, I—"

"Of course you can't win," Gubwa cut him off, "because I shall know your move even as you make it. But surely it's worth a try? And to make the game more interesting, we'll limit its duration to fifteen seconds, after which I really must be on my way."

"In a hurry, eh, Gubwa?" Stone ground the words out.

"Oh yes, indeed! The Psychosphere is astir, Mr. Stone. It prepares to welcome a new Messiah. I feel its excitement, its psychic concentration. It beckons, and I must go."

He very deliberately closed his eyes and began to count: "One . . . two . . . three . . . four . . ."

In the matterless flux of the Psychosphere, three entities conversed. "Well?" *said Garrison.* "And are you satisfied?"

"I'm not sure," *Thomas Schroeder answered.* "It is, I suppose, equality of sorts. Not quite what I had in mind."

"You could hardly be my equal while you were part of me," *said Garrison.* "And so I have expelled you. Yes, and Willy too. How about you, Willy? Are you satisfied?"

Koenig's answer contained a shrug. "I think," *he said,* "therefore I am—I think!" *And he laughed.* "I'll get used to it."

"But what does one do?" *Schroeder asked,* "when one is unbodied, all-powerful and . . . immortal?"

351

"You do what you want to do," *Garrison answered*. "Do you want to go back to that blob of mud that spawned us? So go, make yourself a body—make yourself mortal! You can do it. You can do almost anything you can imagine."

"You're right, of course," *said Schroeder*. "So why don't we?"

"We?" *Garrison chuckled*. "You, maybe, but not me. I can always do that later, if I get bored. But I doubt it."

"Bored?" *Koenig queried*.

"Let me show you something," *Garrison answered*.

He showed them THE ALL—*or rather, he showed them something of it. To show them all of* THE ALL *would take forever.*

"You see?" *he said*. "Unbodied, all-powerful and immortal you may well be, but never omniscient. How can you ever know all of space, which goes inwards and outwards forever? Or all of time, which goes infinitely back and inexorably forward? Look again."

And they saw a sight whose beauty would be unbearable, blinding, blasting to mortal men. A sight which, in a dream, only Garrison had ever seen before them.

"That cosmic mote Earth?" *he laughed*. "Oh, no! If there's a place I would be, it's out there. Who would drink the waters of Earth when he can drink the wine of the universe? The ultimate quest, my friends—and the ultimate destiny! Make up your minds, for Suzy and I can't wait."

"Your battery ran dry once," *Schroeder cautioned*. "Remember?"

Again Garrison laughed, a ripple in the Psychosphere. "And who could thirst for energy in a great sea of suns?"

For a millimoment Schroeder was silent. "Very well," *he finally conceded,* "let the ayes have it."

And "Aye!" *they all three cried in unison.*

Then, soberly: "One moment," *said Garrison.* "First . . . there are several wrongs to right." *He let the Psychosphere wash over and through him, making small adjustments in its matterless structure. And,* "There," *he finally said . . .*

". . . Eleven . . . twelve . . . thirteen," said Gubwa, his eyes tightly shut, his smile a nightmare. Stone was reaching for his pistol, and the albino knew it.

"Oh!" Vicki moaned where she lay, throwing back her blanket as she came awake.

"Fourteen!" cried Gubwa, his eyes popping open as he turned to stare at her, then bugging in his leprous-gray face. His jaw fell open as the girl sat up, young, beautiful, green-eyed—fully alive.

Gubwa's face screwed up in an agony of terror. Someone else was inside his head with him. A terrible someone. *"Garrison!"* he screamed.

The machine-gun turned white hot in his hands, melting even as he dropped it from blistering fingers. Foaming at the mouth, his pink eyes seeming to stand out almost from his head, the albino floated free of the floor. He flew forward towards the steel doors, which opened before him. He passed through them out of sight, his last scream echoing back to Stone and Vicki where they hugged each other in that subterranean room of the dead:

"G-a-r-r-i-s-o-n!"

And up the spiralling concrete ramps went Charon Gubwa, doors crashing open at his approach and barriers lifting. Up and out into the night. Up and over the city. Up, up and ever up. His rate of ascent accelerating, his dressing gown leaping into flames along with his hair—only to be extinguished a moment later in airless space, where his friction-cindered shell popped open like a fried grape.

And then, because Garrison had named him for an abhorrence, the Psychosphere simply erased all trace of him.

Several things were erased, changed, rebuilt. For Garrison had been both right and wrong about time. Time is infinite, yes—but nothing is impossible in infinity.

Joseph Maestro and his gangsters were no more, had never been.

Likewise the less savory members of a certain branch of the Secret Service. They had never existed.

Oh, and several other things.

Several millions of things.

And when they were done the Earth became a better place to live.

Phillip and Vicki Stone certainly thought so, though they could not remember it ever having been different.

She looked out of the window of their Sussex home into the starry night sky and found a name on her lips. "Richard," she sighed—which was strange because she did not know, had never known, a Richard.

"What?" her wealthy, loving husband looked up from his book. "Did you say something, darling?"

But already she had forgotten. "I . . . I thought I saw a shooting star," she answered, feeling foolish.

"Then make a wish!" he smiled.

She stepped to his chair, leaned over and kissed him. "I believe I already have," she said . . .

Epilogue

ONE MONTH LATER . . .
 James Christopher Craig tossed and turned in his sleep. The weird dream was back, bothering his subconscious mind as always. The dream about a man he had never known—a man called Richard Garrison—and about an impossible, insane machine. A dream overshadowed by a commanding voice, the voice of a man dead now thirty days, whose every vestige had been erased with the sole exception of this one psychic echo. A voice like the voice of some strange, sinister god, demanding that Craig *remember*—and that he build the machine of his dream.

Craig's agitation increased. The dream was not frightening in itself; the source of his torment lay deep, deep down in forgotten recesses of his psyche. It lay in the darkest vaults of his subconscious mind, which should remain forever locked—vaults which now, at the post-hypnotic insistence of a dead man, were slowly but surely re-opening their doors to him.

And at last Craig stood before the final door, the *Sanctum Sanctorum*, the Room of Innermost Secrets. And even as he stood there, so the massive doors swung silently open. Within—

Craig saw a machine. *The* Machine . . .

He saw it—*and he knew its name!*

"Jimmy!" his wife, Marion, shook him awake. "Are you all right? What is it? Are you dreaming again?"

Craig sat up in bed, brushed cold sweat from his brow, trembled as he stared about the shadowy room. The luminous hand of his watch told him it was 2:00 A.M. The night was a cool, silent blanket all about the house. And the dream receding, fading, crawling back down and disappearing in deepest caverns of mind.

"You were shouting something," Marion told him, drawing him back down into the bed beside her. "One word, over and over again."

"Was I?" he sleepily mumbled, his mouth furry and tasting foul. "What was it? Do you remember?"

She told him what it had sounded like, then snuggled close and hugged him.

He lay in the darkness of their room thinking about it. He thought about it a long time before he finally went back to sleep. A strange word that, and yet it seemed to ring certain bells . . .

And drifting back into sleep, Jimmy Craig shuddered. Ominous, cracked, discordant bells were ringing in the back of his mind. They tolled a knell of horror and madness.

A strange, strange word.

A word to haunt him forever.

A word to haunt the whole wide world.

Psychomech.

Turn the page
for a Sneak Preview
of the exciting
conclusion to the
Psychosphere trilogy

PSYCHAMOK

*Coming in February 1993
from
Tor Books*

J AMES CHRISTOPHER CRAIG GLANCED AT THE OLD PEN-
dulum clock on the wall of his study and
checked the time. 6:15 P.M. Lynn was late, probably picking up some bits and pieces in Oxford.
The stores stayed open late Friday nights, so
that people could shop for the long weekend.
Craig got up and went to the window.

Situated on the Dome's perimeter, Craig's
study was a strange hybrid of old and new. The
"window" he stood beside formed an entire wall,
from which he could look out at the mighty
complex he had made his home; but the other
three walls were panelled in old English oak,
where books leaned in dusty rosewood shelves
and a lifetime's collection of objets d'art was
scattered on tiny tables and in carved corner
niches.

And side by side with the musty books, bric-àbrac and things of the old world, were those symbols of the new which seemed to Craig almost to bear his personal signature: a video-phone, a 3-D TV screen set flush in the middle of a wall full of antique books, and self-adjusting lighting which kept visibility in the study to that precise level of brightness best suited to Craig's eyes. It was rich, yes—but wasn't that only fitting for the man God had chosen as the instrument of His will here on Earth?

Almost all of PSISAC's employees had left the complex now. A couple of techs would be carrying out final checks on the main core—and of course Security would be there, guarding PSISAC through the night and weekend—but apart from them and the converter shift-workers the place was empty. The gate guard would let Lynn in when she came home, but before then Craig had something to do. It was time he checked on McClaren.

Only forty-five minutes had gone by since he talked to the man, and in that time he had given plenty of thought to their conversation. He had not liked the way it had gone. Too easy, somehow—like a forced smile. McClaren had seemed too eager too soon. And he had been nervous. Perhaps that was only natural, considering his attack earlier in the day. Perhaps—and perhaps not. Craig's call might just have tipped the scales one way or the other. If McClaren was going to run, then by now he should be running.

Craig crossed the floor back to his desk, picked up the handset of his video-phone and

keyed McClaren's home number. The phone rang
. . . and rang . . . and rang.

Craig's mouth tightened, his nostrils flaring.
He stared at the video-phone's flat, slender
screen where it sat atop his desk showing a
blank, swirling grayness. He knew of course that
McClaren did not have video—just an old-
fashioned telephone—but still the swirling grayness seemed somehow significant and strangely
permanent. And the phone in his hand went on
ringing.

Craig's knuckles slowly turned white where
they held the handset to his ear. He let the number ring for two long minutes, then carefully replaced the handset in its cradle and lifted his
hand to his furrowed brow. His face worked for
a moment, angry blotches of red showing on his
cheeks beneath the gray, swept-back tufts of his
temples. Then he smiled, however grimly and
lopsidedly.

He made his way to the elevator and was carried to the ground floor. There he passed quickly
and quietly through the garage area and into
Psychomech, the steel doors closing behind him.
Making his way towards the center, where the
throne's metal and polished leather gleamed
bright in Psychomech's pilot lights, he sighed
loudly and began to talk to himself:

"Lord, I have erred. I fear that one of my dis-
ciples—a man I myself chose to serve me, just
as I serve you—is a traitor. Woe is me, Lord, for
this is my Gethsemane. Ah, but have I not
learned from the trials of your own true son?

McClaren is not the first Judas, Lord, but certainly he shall be the last."

At the foot of the dais Craig bowed his head and remained motionless for long moments. Then he turned to one side, reached into the wall of machinery and drew out a computer keyboard on a swivel arm. He stared at it for a second or two, then tapped out information and a question on the white plastic keys:

ANDREW McCLAREN
HEADSET 12
LOCATION?

Dim lights began to glow in the heart of the machine, complementing the pilots, and needles twitched minutely on a thousand dials. There was the merest whirring as of tiny wings. A small screen flickered into life level with Craig's eyes. Psychomech was coming awake, searching. It would not take long.

Craig waited . . .

No sooner had the steel doors closed on Craig than his daughter's car purred quietly up to the Dome along the private approach lane from the main gate. A scanner read the car's number plate, checked the girl's face through the windscreen, and the metal garage doors pivoted up and back in a yawning welcome. As interior lights flickered on, she drove in.

She parked the car, got out and went to the elevator, tapped her personal code into its lock.

Inside the lock a latch clicked open, the door concertinaed to one side.

Moments later Lynn Craig stepped out of the elevator into the central area of the living level, calling out, "Dad? Dad?" She cocked her head and listened for an answer but none came. She hummed a tune to herself as she went through to her living room cum study and tossed down books, a string bag, daily newspapers and some small items of groceries into the wide lap of an easy chair. Then she stopped humming and pursed her lips.

It was unusual that her father wasn't here to meet her. He liked to see her off in the mornings and home at night. Perhaps he was swimming. She crossed to a renovated, refitted 19th Century roll-top bureau, pressed intercom buttons marked POOL, GARDENS and SOLARIUM, and said: "Dad? Are you up there?"

Silence . . .

The place was too quiet. Not unnaturally quiet, but after her hectic day (they all seemed hectic nowadays, and she liked it that way) it was as if she had suddenly been struck deaf. She switched on her 3-D TV, caught an item of the news—something about The Gibbering being on the increase again, about the introduction of new measures that required immediate reporting of all cases; apparently parents were loath to take action where their own children were concerned, had even started to hide them away—then switched channels to a quiz show.

That was when she remembered how earlier, when she had phoned her father from the institute, he had said something about an accident at the complex. Something about the main converter. She sighed. He was probably down there now with a gaggle of white-coated technicians, putting things back to rights. Why couldn't he work normal hours like ordinary men?

She frowned. Why couldn't he do *anything* like ordinary men! But no, that was unfair. He wasn't ordinary, that was why. He was J. C. Craig, Managing Director of PSISAC, and PSISAC was his life. And yet . . . there was something more than that. Something deep inside him, some secret thing. And just lately it had been far more apparent . . .

Suddenly the TV annoyed her: the gabble of voices engaged in quick-fire questions and answers. She switched it off.

It seemed warm in the Dome tonight, either that or she was just plain irritable. She frowned.

Funny how she always thought of this place as "the Dome." Her home for half of her life, still "the Dome" seemed more appropriate. She supposed she should consider herself lucky to live in such a place, in such luxury, but her frown deepened for all that. She had *used* to consider herself lucky—very much so and about many things—but that had all come to an end eighteen months ago.

Briefly, fleetingly, she allowed herself to picture Richard Stone as he had been then. But . . . that was no good. He wasn't that way now, would never be that way again. And as her father kept reminding her, she was very young and there was plenty of time for her yet.

Sighing, she flopped down on a huge recliner that dwarfed her spread-eagled figure. Plenty of time . . .

Time heals all wounds. And true enough, as the days went by she thought of Richard less and less. Or perhaps it was that the futility of her thoughts became more and more apparent.

She shook her head, clearing away the mood of cloying poignancy which suddenly threatened her, the loneliness creeping like a miasma from stagnant wells of memory. Angry with herself, she bounced to her feet and snatched up the groceries, whisking them away to the kitchen.

On the way she detoured and peeped into her father's study. There was an empty plate on his desk, a scattering of crumbs and a few small chicken bones; also, a mug with coffee grounds thick in its bottom. He wouldn't be wanting food tonight. Good! She wasn't hungry herself and relished not having to cook. But on the other hand she felt a little guilty; her father rarely ate a cooked meal these days.

Loneliness was creeping again. And the Dome wasn't just warm, it was clammy. She would take a shower! She put the groceries away, went back to her own rooms and into the bathroom. While the shower made its automatic adjustment to Lynn's personal preference of temperature, she slipped out of her clothes and gave her naked body a minute, almost clinical inspection in the bathroom's full-length mirror.

She was twenty years old but looked more like seventeen. Her figure was tall and slender, rounded where it should be. As befitted her youth, there was very little sag to her breasts; her buttocks were firm and taut. Richard (*again* Richard) had used to say she had a boyish bottom; and she had used to laugh and ask how the hell would he know?—or did he perhaps have some dark secret?

Again she forced him from her mind.

She gave her head a shake and her chestnut hair bounced on her shoulders; she smiled and the mirror reflected the darkness of her eyes, the perfect white of her teeth like a bar of light set in her tanned face. Turning, she looked back over her shoulder, checking that her tan was deep and even. Finally she was satisfied. She had lost weight since . . . over the last eighteen months, but was now putting it on again. That was something she must watch. It wouldn't do to look heavy and ungainly on the beach next summer.

The beach . . .

Suddenly she was bitter, snatching back the shower curtain angrily and stepping quickly into the hissing cascade, catching her breath in a gasp as the water hit her . . . but in the next moment relaxing gratefully and feeling her tensions streaming away from her along with the sweetly stinging water.

The beach. Actually, she wouldn't care if she never saw a beach again. It just wouldn't be the same. Not now . . .

After the car stopped, Stone had waited three full minutes before he moved. Minutes that seemed like hours, until he felt he *must* move or seize up altogether. Then, easing the boot lid up a couple of inches, he had checked that the garage was empty. The lights had gone out automatically as soon as Lynn entered the elevator, but still there was a little natural light in the place. Not much, sufficient that Stone could make out the outlines of the concrete support pillars. Sitting up, he waited until orientation was complete, then climbed stiffly, awkwardly out of the boot and eased the lid down until it clicked shut.

Less than thirty yards away, J. C. Craig stood with his head as yet bowed in the heart of the machine, but massive steel walls and doors separated the two men and neither knew of the other's proximity. And so, while Craig offered up silent obeisance before his oracle, Stone shuffled and stamped in darkness and flexed his aching muscles, allowing himself the luxury of a single, quiet groan as cramp momentarily threatened his legs. Then, gritting his teeth, he moved painfully to the front door.

Finding the driver's window open, he put his hand inside and fumbled around for a second until he found the keys. Pocketing them, he turned and picked his way carefully to the elevator. Now he would discover if anything else had changed while he had been . . . away. He had used to be a regular visitor here, had even had his own ID code by which the Dome had known him. Would it know him now, or had his code been erased? He paused for a single moment before the elevator. If his code was no longer acceptable, would the Dome see him as an intruder?

He tapped the number into the lock, sighed as he heard that once-familiar *click* and the elevator's door obligingly folded away.

Seconds later, ascending towards the living level, a nervous tic caused Stone's left eye to start jumping. He controlled it, tensing himself as the extra weight went out of his legs and the door sighed open. So far so good. Now the game was to find Lynn before her father found him. Most certainly before that! Stone had no proof but he had always suspected that J. C. Craig wasn't too keen on him. If he hadn't been called Stone, his and Lynn's friendship would have been stepped on before it ever got started. And now? What father would take kindly to an escaped lunatic come visiting his daughter?

Mercifully Lynn's and her father's rooms were on opposite sides of the Dome. If she wasn't in her rooms, Stone would simply hide himself away there and wait for her. If she was in, then they'd see what they would see. And if he bumped into her father first . . . Well, he could only keep his fingers crossed on that one.

Silently, listening to the pounding of his own heart, Stone made his way across deep-pile carpeting and into Lynn's rooms. She didn't appear to be there but her string bag and a collapsed stack of books lay on a chair, and the cushions on her huge recliner had been thrown about a little.

Stone passed down a short corridor towards her bedroom. The door was open, the room quiet and in darkness; but a light shone out from beneath the door of the room opposite. The bathroom.

Stone's heart pounded louder still. He could hear the hiss of the shower now, knew that she would be in there, arms upraised, curving her body and craning her neck to accept the soothing spray, letting the water touch every inch of her lovely body. He knew it because he had seen it, often. They had used to make love in the shower.

The thought of it was vivid, erotic, persistent. God, how they had used to make love! Like young animals coupling—wanting everything—tasting, feeling, lusting after everything. Since the first time, when both of them were just seventeen, they had never missed an opportunity. And nothing had been taboo. Here in the Dome on those rare occasions when her father was away; down at the house in Sussex; out in the open countryside, wherever the grass was long or the trees shady. And yet it had been more than just their youth and their lust, there had been something else.

Stone had known two other girls before Lynn, and both in the same summer, but with them it had been . . . well, it hadn't really been anything. With Lynn it was a fire, an inferno—it was love. Or it had been.

Stone's jaw tightened. Love? And how many times had he seen her since . . . since then? How many times had she visited him?

Was that why he had come here, to find out? A night's sanctuary was all he thought he wanted, wasn't it? Or was it that he really wanted to see a certain look in her eyes, a look which would write *finis* on all they had ever looked forward to and dreamed of doing together? *Finis* on the life they had planned.

No, that was too bitter. He *had* come here for sanctuary, yes—but there was another reason, too. And that was to tell her that there was hope yet, that he wasn't nearly ready to be written off. Something inside him told him there was an answer to all this, and that he was the only one who could find it. He wanted Lynn to know that, that was all, and he wanted her to wait for him. If he was wrong . . . the wait wouldn't be too long. But if he was right—

—Suddenly Stone reeled, clapped his hands to his head, drew breath in a hissing, agonized gasp. He ground his teeth together to keep from crying out, went weak at the knees as bolt after bolt of searing fire lanced through his skull. It was as if someone had slid a white-hot needle into his brain and was jiggling it about. Someone who tittered and sniggered and laughed demoniacally.

And not just one someone. No, for there were many of them, an army of them. Coming out of nowhere . . . dancing in his head like tiny imps . . . leaping and cavorting around his brain, stinging it with their barbed, burning needles . . . sacking the beleaguered city of his psyche.

And all of them gibbering, gibbering, gibbering!

Oh, Jesus—God—Christ almighty! Oh my great merciful God—not now! Please, not now!

But God was not listening, or perhaps the wrong god was listening . . .

Down below in the room of the machine, the screen before J. C. Craig's face was now filled with symbols and numbers. Some of the figures were static, unchanging, others were fluid as quicksilver and changed with each passing fraction of a second. Craig had studied the figures for many minutes, reading them as surely as the pages of a book. They told him that he had been right about Andrew McClaren.

Psychomech's lights were brighter, pulsing with strange colors, semi-sentient as they struck almost stroboscopic patterns. The machine seemed arched over Craig like a great indolent cat, stretching and purring for the moment but ready at a second's notice to snarl and spit and scratch. For, cruel as a cat, Psychomech had seen the quarry; the mouse was out in the open, but the machine was in no hurry. It would strike only when Craig, the master, commanded it.

Beads of sweat gleamed like iridescent pearls on Craig's brow as he watched the screen. His eyes were unblinking as he absentmindedly dabbed the beads away with a damp handkerchief. Oh, McClaren was running all right, scurrying north as fast as he could go. Well, it was his funeral.

Craig reached out a hand towards the computer keyboard, and with a nightmare grin on his clammy face he prepared to unsheath Psychomech's claws . . .

* * *

Edward Bragg's explanation of the headset's functions had been, if not a downright lie, deliberately vague and simplistic—as McClaren was about to discover. Certainly the sets were extensions of Psychomech, and what little Bragg had said of them was largely true, but he had not nearly said enough. He had *not* said, for instance, that even without use of the alert button on the headband, still each set was a microtransmitter, a "bug" whose signal Psychomech constantly tracked. And that was only one of the things Bragg had omitted to mention.

McClaren was not aware, for example, that the aberrant mental patterns of The Gibbering were different for every mind invaded—as different as individual sets of fingerprints—and that Psychomech recorded those patterns with better than photographic accuracy. Nor did he know that they could be reproduced. But indeed that was part of Psychomech's function: to drive the sick mind to the very brink of collapse, the edge of insanity—and then while it teetered and threatened to cave in, to shore it up and feed it those energies necessary to combat and overcome the mechanically-induced terrors of the id.

McClaren was now some sixty-eight miles north of Oxford, crossing Leicestershire and heading for Derby. Beside him on the passenger seat the headset jiggled and moved with the motion of the car, but there was other activity which was quite invisible. Tracking McClaren's tiny vehicle, locked-in on the headset, a needle-thin beam of energy from the skies had activated the micro-converters in the earphones, setting up between them a flux whose configuration was McClaren's aberrant pattern.

As the satellite-transmitted beam intensified, so the tiny cores of ultra-tough Herculite alloy were obliged to expand the flux until it overlapped the perimeter of the headset and began to permeate the entire interior of the car—including McClaren himself. And as if from nowhere, in his head, suddenly he heard the first distant tinkling of bells.

The start of the thing exactly duplicated his experience of the morning, so that he broke into a cold sweat as he applied the car's brakes, and pulled into a layby. There he switched off the engine and sat for a moment in comparative silence, tensely aware of his own blood's pounding, his eyes darting left to right in utter terror and hideous expectancy. And—

—Yes, there it was again, and louder now: the sound of the bells in his head, jingling on the pennants of the babbling mindhorde army where it marched to the attack! McClaren knew only too well how swiftly that monotonous clamor could expand to break down the walls of his psyche, letting in the baying warriors of lunacy, but still he took time to switch on the car's interior light and wind down his window.

Cool air rushed in and turned his fevered brow to ice. The roar of evening traffic on the dark, eight-lane motorway seemed strangely muted, drowned out by the rapidly rising tumult from within. Hope and pray as he might, McClaren could no longer doubt it. The thing was almost upon him.

He snatched up the headset, fumblingly found and pressed the button on the headband, fitted the device to his skull . . .

On the instant, Psychomech reacted, changed the configuration. A bland, harmless flux washed through McClaren's mind like a soothing salve laid gently on a raw wound. He groaned, sighed, drew deep drafts of air and finally sobbed—only to laugh, however shakily, in the very next moment. It worked! The thing really did work!

Then, as the exhaustion of all the day's tensions and terrors at last caught up with him, he lay back in his seat and wearily, shudderingly closed his eyes. How good it would be simply to sleep here, to stretch out in the car for an hour or two and let the world outside go roaring by, like the traffic on the motorway.

He stirred himself up. No, it wouldn't do to sleep. Not now. Not here. He must get as far north as he could, find a hotel for the night in Sheffield, maybe.

With the headset seated firmly upon his head, McClaren started up his car and pulled carefully out into the stream of traffic.

Under the night sky, the mouse was on the move again . . .

In the Dome, in the corridor between Lynn Craig's bedroom and her bathroom, Richard Stone slowly uncurled from his fetal knot and lay twitching and moaning where he had crumpled. The attack had lasted for mere seconds— maybe as little as half a minute—but it had been utterly savage in its intensity. And Stone had been helpless. Much longer and he knew he would have died. It had left him no room to fight, and he had had very little left to fight with. So perhaps God had been listening after all . . .

Anyway, it was over, done with for now, and Stone was left sick as a dog. His Adam's apple was working involuntarily as his gorge began to rise. Clammy in his own sweat and stinking of fear, he somehow got to his feet, opened and staggered in through the bathroom door.

Lynn was still in the shower, reluctantly finishing off. Her voice was low as she hummed some old familiar tune to herself, lost in the sheer pleasure of the hissing, laving water. The first she knew of his presence on the other side of the curtain were the animal sounds of his retching as he coughed and choked and heaved up his sickness into the toilet. Then the humming died on her lips and she held her breath, listening.

The water of the shower continued to hiss all about her but the other sound was gone now. Then there came a groan and Lynn was aware of movement beyond the curtain.

She queried: "Dad?" and drew back the curtain a little, poking her head out. "Dad, is that—"

Stone was stooped over a sink, its fountain jetting into his mouth, sluicing away vomit. He was a deathly gray, swaying and trembling uncontrollably when he turned his face to stare at her.

"*Richard!*" she gasped, her mouth falling open. "Richard? But how—?"

"Sh-*shower!*" he whispered hoarsely. He staggered towards the shallow well of the shower, arms outstretched. Lynn caught him instinctively, propped him against the wall.

"You want a shower?" Her wide eyes were questioning, trying hard to understand.

"Cold," he answered. "Tired. Hungry . . ." He lay back against the wall, let her hold him there, shivered like a leaf in a gale.

She stepped fully out of the shower and unmindful of her nudity tugged at his jacket, fought to get it off. He *was* bitterly cold, his flesh like ice. "Hungry? But you've just been sick!" she told him, helping him lower himself to the tiled floor.

"Sick, yes," he nodded, his eyes mud-colored in the pale dough of his face. "Sick from The Gibbering!"

She had him almost naked now, but stopped tugging at his clothes the moment he said those words. In that same instant the facts of what she was doing came to her. She was stripping naked a certified madman in her own bathroom; a man who by all rights should be dead now, and who must certainly be in the final, terminal stage of the mind-plague!

He saw the look on her face, managed a harsh, barking laugh. "Oh, yes," he growled, nodding. "All of that. But Lynn, I'm different. I can—" (he finally crawled free of his clothing) "—I can *beat* it! And here I am to . . . prove it."

"Beat it?" she stared at him incredulously, backing away now, aware of her stark nakedness—and of his. "Beat The Gibbering? But Richard, no one has ever—"

"But I *will*!" he cut her off. "I got this . . . this far, didn't I?" He used the bowl of the toilet to drag himself upright, stumbled towards the still hissing shower.

Again, instinctively, she went to him, helped him into the shower. If anything he was even colder now. Shock, she supposed. Reaction to . . . to what? Had he suffered an attack here? Again it was as if he read her mind:

"Yes," he nodded, his Adam's apple jerking. "A moment ago."

Then he was under the shower, gasping, clawing at the walls to hold himself upright. And in that moment Lynn gave up any pretensions to common sense and helped him sit down, then sat down with him and hugged him close.

Gradually his shuddering subsided, color creeping back into the marble of his face and form. "That was a bad one," he said, holding her tightly.

She laughed quietly, perhaps a little hysterically, into his shoulder. "You'd better start somewhere," she said, "and tell me all about it. Tell me everything."

He took her face in his hands, held her away from him, looked at her. He was seated in one corner of the shower well, his legs widespread. She kneeled between them, her hands on his shoulders. The water hissed down, streaming from their chins. "You believe me?" he said. "That I've beaten it?"

"You got this far, didn't you?" she repeated his own words of a few minutes ago. "I want to believe you. More than anything else, I want that."

He hugged her to him, his flesh tumbling as before, but no longer from the icy cold of shock. "You want me to tell you?"

"Yes—no! First let's get you properly warm and dry. Then tell me."

Both of them naked as babes, she helped him through to her bedroom and flopped him down still wet through upon her bed. She got him a towel and he managed to sit up, began towelling groggily at his hair.

"Hey," he said, "how about a sandwich? Maybe a beer?"

She shook her head to the last. "Fruit juice," she said. "But you have to stay right here—with the light out—till I get back. My father's not home right now, but he could be back any time."

He chuckled wearily and flopped back on the pillows. "I promise I won't move," he said. "Shit, I don't think I could!"

"I'll be two minutes," she said, putting the light out as she went.

She was five minutes, and while she got him food she worked some of it out. Back in her bedroom with the light on again, she said: "I thought the car was a bit sluggish tonight. And it was funny on corners, too. You were in that tricky boot, eh?"

He nodded. "What a waste, so late in the day: to discover a way you could have been smuggling me in all this time!" Then he sobered. "I didn't know how you'd react. I couldn't take any chances. And I needed somewhere to stay for the night." Between sentences he tore at a chicken leg and gulped at pineapple juice.

She shook her head in a fresh flood of wonderment, touched his shoulder almost as if she expected him to vanish, hardly dared take her eyes off him. "I'm not the kind who believes in miracles," she finally said. "You'd better tell me all about it."

"I do a trick with electricity," he began. "When it comes on—when I start to gibber—I give myself a jolt. The heavier the better—just so it's not a killer! That does it, knocks me out. Then . . . I dream. Hell, *weird* dreams! But somehow they mean something. I mean, they help me to see things, know things . . ." He shrugged. "So that's one way."

"I'm not sure I understand," she said, looking blank. "But go on anyway."

"Who understands?" he asked. "Okay, another way: I swear a lot."

"You what?" she thought he was joking.

"If the attack isn't too bad, I can hide it—bury it, sort of—under a barrage of curse-words. I do it in my head. I've found that if I make a lot of noise up there, my own noise, my swearing, it's like I don't leave any room for them."

"Them?"

"The voices. The chuckling, sniggering, idiot voices. The Gibbering . . ."

"Oh!"

"And I suspect there's another way. But this one's not so hot and I haven't tried it yet. And I don't think I want to." He frowned and turned his face away.

"You may as well tell me," she prompted.

"Violence!" he said. "I have this idea that sheer physical violence would be as good, maybe better, than the mental violence of my cursing. I think that's what makes them do the things they do—the gibberers, I mean. They try to work it off with violence, but they go over the top. That's why so many of them kill themselves . . ."

"Oh!" she said again, quietly. And then: "You know, I think I understand that."

"You do?"

She nodded. "The kids I work with. You've seen them. Sometimes when they hurt themselves—or when they can't make me understand something, when they're frustrated—then they become violent. Not all of them, but some. Afterwards, it's like they've worked it out of their systems."

"Yes, something like that," he said, rubbing at his eyes. "Jesus, I'm tired!"

"And you look it," she told him, taking his plate and glass and covering him with a soft blanket. "Why don't you get some sleep. But before you do, how did you get out of . . . out of that place?"

He turned his strange yellow eyes full upon her. "Damned if I know," he said, shaking his head. "It was during an attack. Afterwards I found myself outside the playground at the Clayton Institute. I only hope I wasn't . . ." He paused, chewed his lip.

"Violent?" she finished it for him.

"Lynn," he took her hands, "What I'm trying to do is important."

"Of course it is," she said.

He shook his head impatiently. "More than that, bigger than that. It's not just for me, or us. It's the world, Lynn . . ." Looking into his eyes, she knew he told the truth. At least as he saw it.

"Tell me more about it tomorrow," she said. And added: "I still love you, you know?"

"I hoped you would," he said, kissing her.

Gently but firmly she pushed him back until his head hit the pillows.

A moment later he was asleep . . .

In the room of the machine, J.C. Craig shook his head sadly and decided to end it. He had demonstrated to McClaren Psychomech's mastery over The Gibbering, had given the man plenty of time to think about it and every opportunity to turn back, and still the traitor fled north. Soon he would reach Sheffield and leave the motorway. It must be done before then.

Craig sighed and shook his head again; there was so little time now, else things might be different. But even as late as this, with the holocaust so close, still he could not take the chance that McClaren would remain silent.

For the last forty minutes Craig had been pacing the floor of the fantastic "tunnel" of machinery between the steel doors and the central dais, but now he paused and turned once more to the computer display screen. A single glance told him that indeed McClaren continued to race north.

He cleared a corner of the screen and typed up:

HEADSET 12
MAXIMUM LOAD?

Psychomech answered,

O.0000525 M/WAVE

Craig ordered:

TESTING:
IMPLEMENT OVERLOAD

Psychomech,

SPECIFY LOAD?

Craig, after a moment's thought:

WHAT LOAD WOULD CAUSE
DISINTEGRATION OF THE
CORES?

Psychomech,

O-0525 M/WAVE

Craig:

IMPLEMENT

The beam tracking McClaren's car immediately thickened, went from needle-slim to pencil-thick. Power sufficient to propel the car itself, if it had been equipped with a converter engine, surged into the cores at McClaren's temples. Under pressure a thousand times too great, they melted, disintegrated in a micro-second, and twin clouds of white-hot Herculite shrapnel were sucked into the suddenly seething flux—which of course had its center in McClaren's brain.

He was dead before his mouth fell open and said, "Ach-ak-ak-*ak*!" Dead before his body jerked ramrod straight and slammed the driving seat back, shearing its bolts and tearing it loose from the floor.

The car's engine roared as his dead foot vibrated where it drove the accelerator flat on the floor. His dead hands flopped from the wheel and played flutteringly with the air in front of his sightless eyes. Then—

—It was as if someone had dropped a bomb on the motorway.

The car seemed to give a leap, cut across from the third lane, into and across the fourth, bumped against and slid along the central barrier in a shower of sparks. A moment later it smashed into a stanchion, somersaulted into the south-bound lanes and landed right side up in the path of a pair of mighty night-freighters.

The giant articulated trucks were only allowed on the motorways at night, and then confined to the two outer lanes. Each one was twelve feet wide and a hundred long; their tires alone were taller than McClaren's car. Racing neck and neck, one was just about to overtake the other when the tiny blue weekender bounced down in front of them and skidded at them side-on. At a combined speed of one hundred and thirty miles per hour, they met.

The juggernauts shared McClaren's car between them. One took the front, the other the rear. They gobbled it up, dragged it under, tore it apart and set it explosively afire, and flushed it out the back in a confetti of blazing plastic and crumpled metal. Cars and trucks behind howled their protests in a blaring of horns and a screaming of brakes as flaming debris lit up the night. A lone tire went burning and bounding along the hardstanding, vaulted a fence and disappeared into an orchard.

The mouse had been taken; Psychomech's bloodied claws retracted into their sheaths; the paw was withdrawn.

Andrew McClaren, probationer disciple (failed), was no more . . .

Four years ago Harry Keogh, the Necroscope, aided by his son, known as Harry Wolfson or The Dweller in the Garden; the Lady Karen, a vampire noblewoman turned against her own kind; and the Szgany, or gypsies, of the vampire world, destroyed the great and terrible Wamphyri lords who had ruled the planet. Peace descended on the Szgany, peace and a new way of life . . .

L ARDIS LIDESCI'S HOUSE STOOD ON A RISE A LITTLE above Settlement, where the grassy, temperate but abrupt foothills of Sunside climbed towards rocky outcrops and steep, forested heights. He liked sitting in front of the house at sundown, to catch the last rays of the sun; likewise before sunup, to watch it rise. Unthinkable four short years ago (two hundred "days," or sunup-sundown cycles), and even now nerve-tingling: to be up and about, safe and sound, and the parent star itself not yet risen. Strange, too, to live in one place, in a house; though almost all of the Szgany did these days—certainly the majority of Lardis's prosperous, ever-increasing band.

The Szgany Lidesci: Lardis's people.

Oh, there were still a few families who preferred their hide-covered caravans along the valley trails, and those who dragged their scant belongings on travois from place to place, unwilling to rest, relax, rejoice in the fact that the scourge of the Wamphyri was a thing of the past. But in the main they were settled or settling now, while other tribes, clans, bands of Travellers were following suit, building their own places along the forest's rim, east to west down the spine of the barrier range.

Lardis's cabin was styled after The Dweller's house on Starside. Providing shelter for Lardis, his young wife Lissa, and not least their small son Jason, it stood a mile east of Sanctuary Rock. Lardis had chosen the spot himself, built the house, finally taken a wife and settled here, all in that period of twenty-four solar rotations following immediately upon The Dweller (whom some saw fit to call "the changeling" now, and others Harry Wolfson) sending the Szgany out of his garden on Starside. And while Lardis had toiled to construct his home here in the lower foothills, so his people had followed his example, felled trees and built Settlement.

Since the place was the first community of its

kind in more than two thousand years of wandering, Lardis found its simple name in keeping—if not the high, stout fence which the Gypsies had seen fit to throw up around it. With its catwalks, turret watchtowers and various defensive systems . . . perhaps after all "Fortress" would have been a more suitable name! But memories of hard times die hard, and Szgany dread of Wamphyri terror and domination was instinctive and immemorial.

The Wamphyri, aye!

Sitting here in the faint, false dawn light of Sunside, looking down on Settlement—with its tiny gardens and allotments, blue smoke spiralling from its stone chimneys, the first antlike movements in its cramped streets—Lardis wondered if the Wamphyri would ever return. Well, possibly, for they were like a recurrent nightmare which fades but not entirely from inner memory, bloating anew when least expected, resurgent in the night. But not, he prayed, in his time. Let it not be in his or little Jason's time.

It wouldn't be, not if he could help it.

And yet . . . it was reported that the vampire swamps were acrawl again. Creatures and ignorant, lonely men went there to drink, and came away more than creatures and less than men. Or more than men, depending on one's point of view: that of someone entirely human, or that of something other. Impossible and therefore pointless—and not least very, very dangerous—to attempt to quarantine, patrol or monitor those great boggy tracts sprawling west of the barrier range, those morasses of bubbling, festering evil. Their extent was unknown, un-mapped; no one fully understood the nature of vampire contamination, infestation, mutation.

How then to keep the threat at bay? The Szgany Lidesci could only do their best. Lardis's plan had been simple and so far had seemed to work:

West of the jagged barrier mountains, where the crags fell to earth, petered into stacks, knolls and jumbles, became foothills which eventually flattened into quaggy hollows, that was where the swamps began. Fed by streams out of the heights, the marshes brewed their horrors through the long, steamy sunups, released them into the gurgling, mist-wreathed nights. At least one tribe of Starside trogs, inhabitants of deep caverns far to the west of what was once The Dweller's garden, knew the danger well enough: they kept a constant watch for any doubtful crea-ture emerging from that region. And since all such were dubious, they destroyed them when-ever they could. Wolf, goat, man—it made no dif-ference—if he, it, whatever, came stumbling or stalking out of reeking, moisture-laden darkness into trog territory, then he was doomed.

Lardis had taken his cue from the trogs. One hundred and forty miles west of Settlement, where the mountains were less rugged and the green belt of Sunside narrowed down to some-thing of a thinly forested bottleneck, that was where the Szgany had always drawn their line of demarcation. In all Lardis's travelling days, he'd never taken the tribe across that line, neither him nor any other leader that he knew of. Apart from a handful of solitary types—lone wanderers who always kept themselves apart, perhaps for safety of body and soul—apart from these and the rare, nomadic family group, the territory beyond the line of demarcation was unknown to men, unexplored. But as for the line itself: now at least it was manned. And constantly.

There were two well established Gypsy communities west of Settlement: Mirlu Township only twenty miles away, and Tireni Scarp, three times as far again. Volunteers from all three of these "towns" took turns guarding the brooding vampire frontier. Even now two dozen men of the Szgany Lidesci were away from home, an entire sunup's march to the west. There they'd stay for four long days—and four fraught, eerie sundowns—until relieved of their duties by the Szgany Mirlu. Eventually it would be the turn of a band from Tireni Scarp, and so forth. This way, just as Starside's trogs kept a lookout for incursions into their territories, so the Szgani protected Sunside.

It was as much as could be done; Lardis had agreed all of the procedures with Anton Mirlu and Yanni Tireni; the Lidescis—because they were situated furthest from the boundary and so had farther to trek in pursuance of their duties—would seem to have got the worst of the deal. At the same time, however, they *were* the furthest away . . . but never to the extent that Lardis was out of touch. No, for he must always maintain his intelligence, keep up to date where and whenever vampiric outbreaks or manifestations were concerned . . .

Hunched in his chair in his small garden over Settlement, Lardis chewed over all of these things, considering what had been and wondering what was still to be; until suddenly, feeling a chill, he turned up the collar of his jacket. Not that this would warm him, for his was a chill of the soul—maybe. He snorted and gave an agitated shrug. At times he cursed the seer's blood in him; it told him things and gave warning, true, but never told enough and sometimes warned too late.

A thin mist was gradually (and quite naturally) rising out of the earth, up from the streams and rivers, advancing through the forests and gathering in the hollows. Already Settlement's walls were fading into the gray of it. Lardis didn't much care for mists; he'd seen too many which were other than natural; he remembered their clammy feel against his skin, what had issued them, what all too often issued *out* of them. But this one—

—He narrowed dark Szgany eyes and merely scowled at this one. Knowing its source he could afford to, for it was simply the dawn. In just a little while now the glorious, laborious sun would lift its rim up over the far furnace deserts, pour its light on fringes of scrub, crabgrass, savanna where they gradually merged into forest, until finally its golden rays would light upon Settlement and the barrier range itself.

Sunup, *soon!* The land knew it, stirred, breathed a moist breath of mist to wake birds and beasts alike, and cover the shimmer of trout in the brightening rivers.

Sunup, aye . . . And with the thought, all manner of morbid omens and imaginings slipped quietly from Lardis's mind. For a little while, anyway . . .

"Halloo!" The cry broke into Lardis's solitude, brought him to his feet.

Going to the front of the garden and looking down the zig-zagging, rudimentary stairway of stones which he'd wedged into the steepest part of the descent, Lardis saw two disparate figures climbing towards him, their feet swathed in a milky weave of ground mist. One of them, whose familiar voice had hailed him, was Nana Kiklu. The other—male, gnarled, and somewhat bent—was the mentalist Jasef Karis; or the "thought-thief," as most people knew him, except that was an unkind expression. Oh, the old Gypsy could get into your head right enough, *and* steal your thoughts if he wanted to! But that wasn't his way. Usually he kept his talent to himself, or else used it to the tribe's advantage as a whole.

After the slaughter at Sanctuary Rock and the period of sojourn in The Dweller's garden, when the tribe had returned to Sunside to build Settlement, then Nana had been given the task of caring for old Jasef; for there were no drones among the Szgany. Indeed, if circumstances had been as of old, then Nana would have been obliged to find herself another husband. And as for the old man: surely the day had long since dawned when the mentalist was no more. His rapidly shrivelling brain, desiccated bones and knotted ligaments must certainly have done for him by now, when during some nightmare raid from Starside—with neither wit to hide himself away, nor agility to flee—Jasef would have ended his days as fodder in the belly of a hybrid Wamphyri warrior. Except . . . that had been then and this was now, and things were very different.

Lardis continued to follow the progress of the pair as they climbed towards him, and his thoughts in respect of the aged Szgany telepath were neither callous nor calculating, merely honest:

Old Jasef, with his mind-reading abilities and what all: what he ate didn't amount to much, nor was he troublesome. In his lean-to adjacent to Nana's cabin, he lived out his time in what small comfort was available and was grateful. For he knew that in certain Szgany tribes he might not be so fortunate; he might even be put down, like his father before him, because there was something of the Wamphyri in him. It was very little and showed itself only in his mentalism, but in Lardis's eyes that made him valuable. Especially now that things were starting to happen again, albeit things which the Szgany could well do without.

Nana and Jasef had reached the top of the steps; Lardis took the old man, led him stumbling to his own chair and seated him there; Nana said:

"I could have come on my own but Jasef said no, he wanted to speak to you in person. Also, you have privacy here. Such things as Jasef would tell you are best said in private. He doesn't wish to panic the people."

"And you?" Lardis looked at her, giving the mentalist time to compose himself, catch his breath. "Has he told these things to you?"

She shrugged. "I look after him; he mumbles in his sleep; from time to time I overhear things."

"I mumble, aye," the old man agreed, showing his gums in a wry grin. "But ah, the substance of my mumbling!"

"Let's have it," Lardis nodded grimly. "What is it now, old man?"

Jasef made no bones of it: "The Wamphyri are back on Starside!"

Even though Lardis had feared as much, still he was aghast. He shook his head, grasped Jasef's arm. "But how can it be? Is it possible? We destroyed the Wamphyri!"

"Not all of them," said Jasef. "And now they've returned, Shaithis and one other, out of the Icelands. They plot against Harry Hell-lander, the Lady Karen, even the changeling. Their voices are in the wind over the barrier mountains, and in my dreams I hear them talking."

"Of what?"

"Of sweet Traveller flesh, of the blood which is the life, of bairns to roast like suckling pigs, and women to rend with their lust! All of these things, which they've missed in exile in the Icelands. Even now they inhabit Karen's aerie, flying out from it with their warriors invincible to raid on eastern tribes."

"Just two of them?"

"What?" Jasef's rheumy eyes peered at Lardis in wonder. " 'Just' two of them, did you say? 'Just' two Wamphyri Lords?" And of course Lardis knew that he was right. It might as well be an army. Except . . . armies weren't always victorious.

Jasef read his mind. "Aye," he nodded, "the Szgany Lidesci are protected: we have The Dweller's weapons! Those weapons in which he instructed us, at least. But what of the other tribes and towns? 'Just' two of them—for now! But do you think the Wamphyri won't take lieutenants? Do you think they won't breed, make monsters? Lardis, I'm only an old man whose days are numbered, and so I have very little weight in the world. But I'll tell you what I fear the most: that this is the beginning of the end for *all* of the Szgany."

Suddenly Lardis was desperate. He grasped Jasef's arm that much tighter. "How can we be certain that you've read aright? You aren't always so sure of yourself. Even *your* dreams are sometimes . . . only dreams."

"Not this time, Lardis," the old man shook his head. "Alas, not this time. Do you think I enjoy playing harbinger, bringer of ill omen, like a man whose very breath carries the plague? Believe me, I do not. But I *know* the Wamphyri, and especially Shaithis, who was ever the clever one . . ." He paused to issue an involuntary, uncontrollable shudder. "Aye, that one's thoughts are strong; they carry on the aether like cries across an echoing valley, and my mind the valley wall, which traps them for me to read."

Lardis turned this way and that in search of some unseen solution, but in the next moment hope lifted his voice. "What of Karen?" he demanded. "What of Harry Dwellersire? That one has powers, which he put to work in the battle for The Dweller's garden. And the pair of them—forgive me for saying it, for even thinking it—they are Wamphyri in their own right! I can't see them sitting still, doing nothing, while Shaithis regains his old influence, recoups his old territories. What? Unthinkable! We were allies before, we'll be allies again."

Jasef nodded, however tremulously. "Better the devils you know, eh, Lardis? But weren't you listening? Karen has *already* fled her stack! She's with the hell-lander at this very moment, in his son's garden. As for the changeling: almost certainly he'll side with them against Shaithis and the others. But tell me, what can a wolf do? Ah, he isn't The Dweller which once we knew!"

Lardis paced back and forth, to and fro. "Well, at least I know what *I* must do!" he said, finally. And turning to Nana: "Go back down into Settlement, speak with Peder Szekarly, Kirk Lisescu, Andrei Romani and his brothers. Tell them to report to me, and at once—with their guns! If Harry Dwellersire and Karen are in need of soldiers . . . I'll wait here and ready myself, until the five join me. We go to parley with them who defend the Starside garden, as they defended it once before. We go to offer our alliance, and to talk of war!"

Nana nodded. Silent all of this time, now words tumbled from her lips in a breathless gush.

"Lardis, do you think that I . . . ? Could you possibly . . . ? I mean to say . . . only that I should like very much to go with you!"

Astonished, he looked at her, frowned, tucked his chin in. "You? Starside? Are your wits suddenly addled, Nana? You, with two small sons to care for, and them only a year older than my own Jason? How could I allow such a thing—and why would you want it? Don't you know the danger?"

"I . . . of course I do," she looked away. "It was just . . . it was nothing but a whim."

"A damned foolish one, I say! And should I let a vampire Lord, even one such as Harry Dwellersire, lay crimson eyes on one of my own Szgany women? Such a fate could be yours . . . I would not wish it on a dog!"

But: *Ah!* she thought. *You don't know, you don't know!*

It was Lardis's last word on the subject, however, and Nana was left silently cursing her own tongue, which had so nearly betrayed her . . .

Returning downhill to Settlement was easier. As Nana and Jasef approached the last flight, where she would run on ahead with Lardis's message to his men, the old man panted, "Nana, that was a mistake back there."

While she, too, was short of breath, still she held it for a moment. "What was a mistake?"

"Forty sunups, thereabouts, a woman swells with her child," the old mentalist played at being thoughtful. "But four years ago," (he did not say "years" but continued to use terms suited to Sunside and Szgany time scales), "there were events of great moment, when no one was keeping count."

"What are you saying?" But she knew very well what he was saying, even before he answered.

"Hzak Kiklu died after the battle in the garden," Jasef mused at length (a completely unnecessary reminder, which proved what Nana had always known anyway: that old as he was, still Jasef wasn't the old fool which others believed). "But before he died he was still very much the man. Obviously so, for you have your sons! Ah, but a long, slow pregnancy that, Nana," he went on, "which lasted . . . what? Almost ten months?"

"Ten and a half," she muttered low. "But as you yourself have observed, no one was counting. Get to the point, Jasef."

"I was given into your care," he said, "since when you've been good to me. There are some who wouldn't have cared much one way or the other. What, an old thought-thief like Jasef Karis? As well forget to feed him, let him lie on his pallet, fade away and die. But with you, I've wanted for nothing . . . well, maybe a new set of pumps in this old chest, a couple of decent teeth, new knees! But of comforts I've all I can use. So, I have my own reasons for being fond of you, Nana."

"It works both ways," she answered. "You're not such a bad one. So?"

He was silent a moment, while they negotiated the final bend. But at last: "I saw you start," he said, "when I told Lardis that Harry and Karen were together in the garden. Those black eyes of yours turned hot as coals, Nana."

"Hot for a moment," she turned her face away. "But only a moment. His blood is in my children, after all."

He nodded, thought it over, and said, "What prompted you to keep it secret?"

"Common sense," she answered, "and maybe something other than that. There are a couple of women in Settlement who might have made much of it, and several who would have made *too* much! But at the time, when Harry lay ill in The Dweller's garden, I didn't think about him being a hell-lander. To me he was just a lonely man in a strange land, even as I myself was lonely. But you're right; a lot was happening; by the time the twins were showing, events were crowding fast. Everything became a blur in the mind's eye."

They were down onto the level. Nana released her charge's arm, handed him his stick. "And now, even if I would tell, I can't. Harry Hell-lander is Wamphyri! What would I gain from the truth? The best that could happen, my boys and I would be watched—always, and *very*, very closely—even in the best of times. And right now, with the Wamphyri back on Starside?" She shook her head. "When men are panicked, they are wont to stampede, Jasef. And then the in-nocent get trampled underfoot."

He nodded and watched her start away from him. "The innocent, aye," he agreed. And a little louder, as she put distance between: "My father paid the price in full! Impaled, beheaded, burned. But then, he was no longer innocent. Indeed, and as the vampire change took hold on him, he was no longer a man!"

She came to a halt, looked back. "But my babies *are* men," she said, slowly and dangerously. "And that's all they are."

"Of course, of course," Jasef waved her away. "On you go, Nana Kiklu! Be about Lardis's errand. Yes, yes, and we shall keep your secret, which no one else knows . . . Nor shall they ever . . . Only men, your babies, only men . . ." But to himself:

What, only men, Nana? Spawn of the Necroscope, the hell-lander Harry Keogh? And only men? Ah, I wonder. I wonder . . .

Two of the brothers Romani were off hunting in the forests; Kirk Lisescu was fishing; none of them returning to Settlement until mid-morning, by which time their movements were slow and tired. By then, too, Lardis had grown disenchanted waiting for them, and had come down from his house to discover for himself what was the delay. His arrival coincided with that of a weary, travel-worn party of terrified Gypsies from the eastern foothills—survivors of a Wamphyri raid!

That last took a little time to sink in, but when finally it did . . .

. . . Then the fact of it hit Settlement like a thunderbolt—stunningly! Even Lardis, who had received at least some prior warning, was shocked. And if in the past there had been times when he'd doubted the veracity of old Jasef Karis's telepathic skills, well, his doubting days were over.

Lardis talked a while with one of the seven survivors, a man of about his own age. Plainly he had been fit and strong, but now was mazed and mumbling. "When did they strike? When?" Lardis shook the other, but gently.

"Two, maybe three hours after sundown," the man answered, his face hollow and haggard. "Earlier, some of the children had wandered home in the twilight; they'd been chasing goats in the peaks; said they'd seen many lights in Karenstack. Perhaps we should have been warned. But it's rumored the Lady Karen is dead, and these were only children. They could be mistaken."

"Where were you? Where?" Lardis shook him again.

"Beyond the Great Pass," the other gave a start, blinked rapidly, "on a plateau under the peaks . . ." His eyes fastened on Lardis's, seemed for a moment to gaze into his soul, and in the next glazed over again. But somehow he managed to continue:

"Two years ago, we went into the heights and found a lake there. There was good fishing, goats in the peaks, game on the wooded slopes. We are—or we were—the Szgany Scorpi. Emil Scorpi, my father, was our leader. There were thirty of us . . . then. And now, only seven. We built homes for ourselves in the woods around the lake. Our boats were on the water. At night, under the first stars, we'd sit round our fires on the shore, cook our fish, eat together. Why not?

For there was nothing to fear. All of the great aeries lay broken on Starside: Wenstack, Menorstack, Glutstack—all tumbled and lying in ruins. Only Karenstack remained, and they said Karen was dead. Maybe she is, what odds? It wasn't the Lady Karen who fell on us . . ."

Lardis groaned and nodded. "Shaithis, aye."

The young survivor grabbed his arm. "Yes, Shaithis . . . and one other! I saw him! He isn't a man!"

"Not a man?" Lardis frowned. "No, of course not. None of them are. Wamphyri!"

"But even the Wamphyri were *once* men," the other insisted. "They are *like* men. Except this one . . . was not."

"What was he like?" Lardis asked.

The other's throat bobbed. He shook his head, failed to find words. "A . . . a slug," he finally gasped. "Or a leech, upright, big as a man. But ridgy as a lizard, cowled, and his eyes burning like embers under the hood. A weird worm, a snake, a slug . . ."

"His name?" The hairs had stiffened on the back of Lardis's neck.

The survivor nodded. "I . . . I heard what Shaithis called him. It was Shaitan!"

Shaitan! A gasp escaped Lardis before he could check it. Shaitan: first of all the Wamphyri! But how was it possible? Shaitan was a legend, the darkest of all Szgany legends.

"I know what you're thinking," said the other. "But I saw what I saw. One was a Lord, but there was also the great slug. I heard them conversing. Shaithis was the manlike one, whom I heard call the other—him, it, whatever—by the terrible name of Shaitan.''

After that: Lardis asked no more questions of these rag-tag remnants of the Szgany Scorpi, but went about Settlement seeing to its defenses. A guard from now on, on the catwalks and in the towers, and no more sending men west to man the vampire frontier. No, for now the threat was closer to home; and now, too, Lardis thanked whichever lucky stars shone down on him, that he'd been outvoted that time during the construction of Settlement, when the other council members had insisted upon huge weapons built into the very walls.

Catapults armed with boulders girdled in spiked chains; great crossbows to fire bolts hewn from entire trees outwards into the cleared area around Settlement; trenches covered over with tentlike frameworks of coarse hide, painted in imitation of small warrior creatures and supported by sharp-pointed pine stanchions. Any enemy warrior, spying one of these grotesque semblances, would attack at once and doubtless impale himself; and men, safe in the trench below, would leap out, hurl their oil, set fire to the monster where he writhed and roared!

While all of these devices were still in place, they nevertheless required attention. Frayed ropes to be seen to, and if necessary replaced; the great crossbows must be loaded, their launching tillers greased; children had played at climbing in the frames of the lures and broken them in places. All to be put back to rights.

So that as Settlement recovered from its shock, there was plenty of work for everyone.

It was like slipping from a tranquil dream into a living nightmare, the old horror resurgent after a brief respite. It was the Wamphyri! And sloth fell from the Szgany Lidesci like the shucked off skin of a snake, so that they emerged startled but fresh, alert, agile. And very, very afraid.

Lardis called a council meeting, revoked the powers of his fellow councillors, declared himself leader as of old. Councils are useful when times are peaceful, but in times of war a tribe needs a leader. None was better qualified than Lardis. In fact, since he'd never relinquished his position, this was simply his quick and efficient way of re-establishing his authority. And no one argued the point.

He made arrangements:

Two-thirds of the able-bodied men would stay in Settlement; the remainder and all of the women and children were to disperse into the woods to the west, far beyond Sanctuary Rock and even so far as Mirlu Township. Runners would meanwhile pass on the warning to the Szgany Mirlu, who in turn would relay it to Tireni Scarp. Lardis's own party of fighting men were to accompany him to the garden overlooking Starside, where he hoped to form an alliance with Karen and Harry Dwellersire.

Most of Sunside's "morning" of twenty-five hours' duration was used up by the time Lardis was satisfied with his arrangements. The "day" of seventy-five hours and "evening" of twenty-five would be consumed during the various phases of the climb and the rest periods between. For the trek into the mountains, along the high trails and through the passes, would be a long one . . . which was probably just as well.

For such as the three in the garden were, it was unlikely they'd be abroad during sunup . . .

Lardis called in at his house on the first leg of the trek. He told Lissa what was happening, kissed Jason, sent them off down to Settlement. There they'd join up with Nana Kiklu and her boys, old Jasef, and one younger, more capable man, before heading into the comparative safety of the forest.

Lardis watched wife and child begin their descent, studied for a moment the hivelike hustle and bustle of Settlement, finally turned to his five companions.

"Well," he said, "and so it's come to this. But we've all been here before, right? And this is nothing new to the Szgany Lidesci. However, if any one of you would rather stay with his family, take care of his own, let's hear it now. You know that it won't be held against you. Ours is a job for volunteers."

They merely looked at him, waiting.

And Lardis nodded his satisfaction. "That's it, then. Let's go."

Then, from the farthest reaches of the planet, the new vampires come, far more terrible than the old. Lardis Lidesci brings a warning to Settlement and the people he leads:

Attracted by a sudden commotion and surge in the crowd, Nestor Kiklu made his way through the milling people to discover what was going on. And he saw that he'd been right: it *was* Lardis Lidesci's voice making all the fuss. As for what it was all about: that remained to be discovered.

At the forward edge of the crowd, where the people who had come out to welcome Lardis home now held themselves back, shocked by their leader's outburst, Nestor felt himself swaying with an unaccustomed dizziness. Complementing the natural excitement of the night— that and his passion of a minute or two earlier, when he'd talked to Jason about Nathan and Misha—the Szgany wine was quickly going to his head. Reeling, he paused to lean against a cart, and became just one more slack-jawed witness in a sea of astonished faces.

For there at one of the old decoys Lardis stomped about in the tired, broken-down framework of torn, weathered skins and rotting wooden ribs—and raved! Ever faithful, Andrei Romani followed on behind his leader, trying to calm him down and imploring the crowd to hold back and not concern themselves; the old Lidesci was just worn out from the trek. But to Nestor and the rest, Lardis looked far less tired than . . .

". . . Crazy!" some woman muttered, close by. "He must have been dinking on the way in, and had a skinful. Why, listen to the man! Playing at being the Big Leader again, after so many years of doing nothing! What? But if his Lissa knew the state he was in, she'd be down here boxing his ears by now! But no, they have their fine cabin up on the knoll, well away from us common folk."

Old bag! Nestor thought. He didn't think much of Lardis, but old sows like that were far worse. All the same, what on earth was Lardis up to?

"Lardis!" someone shouted from the crowd. "Now what's all this about? Why, you sound like you've lost fifteen years out of your life, and gone back to the bad old days! As for these lures and all such rubbish: we abandoned their upkeep a lifetime ago. They should be stripped down for firewood. So what's all the fuss?"

Now Nestor began to understand, and to believe that maybe Lardis really was crazy; certainly he'd been acting strangely since they came back through the pass. In order to get a better idea of what was going on, he pushed himself upright and moved closer still.

Fuming and sputtering, with Andrei Romani still in tow, now Lardis stalked around the perimeter of the decoy. "What?" he snarled. "But look at the *state* of these lures! The skins are tattered and the timbers rotten. What could you impale on stakes as wormy as these? Nothing! They'd crumble at a touch. As for a warrior impaling himself, ridiculous! What creature would ever feel challenged by . . . by *this* mess?"

"Lardis," Andrei tried to keep pace with him, catching at his arm to slow him down. He kept his voice low but still Nestor heard what he was saying. "Lardis, you'll only excite the people, worry them, frighten them silly. Can't this keep, at least until you've rested? You have no proof, after all. I mean, you're not *sure*, now are you?"

Nestor's head felt light, even giddy. He wondered: proof of what? Not sure about what? Perhaps Lardis was tired after all—or sick, maybe? Even now he was looking at Andrei with burning eyes, turning his gaze on the muttering crowd, finally holding up a trembling hand to his sweating brow. But no, he wasn't sick, for in the next moment he was raving again.

"The stockade fence!" he shouted, heading in that direction. "You've cut doors in it, gates on all four sides. Except they've stood open for so long that they're warped and won't close any more. And just *look* at the great crossbows and the catapults!"

He went at a stumbling run, up the rickety wooden steps where they climbed the fence, to tug at the lashings of a catapult whose huge spoon of a head stood taller than his own. In a moment, rotten leather had fallen to mold in his powerful hands. Disgusted, Lardis let the dust trickle through his fingers and looked around. And his fevered eyes went at once to frayed hauling ropes where they dangled from the pivoting hurling-arm. Then, risking life and limb, he used these self-same ropes to slide back to earth.

"Oh, they take *my* weight, all right," he panted, landing. "But how do you think they'd stand the strain of hauling that bucket down against its counterweight, eh? Well, I can tell you that for nothing: they wouldn't!"

Lardis turned away to head for the South Gate.

Still following him, Andrei cried out: "Lardis, do you *insist* on being right? But man, you can't be! You mustn't be!" Sensing a drama, the crowd moved as one man to shadow the pair. But finally it seemed that something of Andrei's words had got through to Lardis. His footsteps faltered, stopped, and he turned.

And as Andrei caught up and went to him, pleadingly now, so Lardis hit him once and stretched him out. Then he turned and went more quickly yet—but crookedly, brokenly—towards the South Gate and the forest beyond. And this time the crowd let him go.

Nestor shook his head, partly in amazement and partly to clear it. The wine lay like a blanket in his brain and on his tongue. Alcohol: even as it deadened the senses and killed off commonsense utterly, still it generated passion and excitement. Drunk, Nestor was excited about what had happened, which must surely signal the beginning of the end for Lardis Lidesci, his decline and fall—and the rise of his weakling son, Jason? And he was passionate about . . .

. . . "Misha!" He spoke her name out loud, and turning bumped into someone. The other, a youth he knew, whose face was now a frowning blur, steadied him and said:

"Misha? I saw her earlier, heading for your mother's house, I think. But what do you reckon about—?"

But Nestor had no more time to waste here. Not waiting to hear the youth out, he thrust him aside and went stumbling in the direction of the houses huddled in the western quarter of the stockade, in the lee of the fence and the watch-tower. One of those houses had been "home" to him for as long as he could remember, but perhaps no more.

And the strong wine churning in his stomach, and likewise the thoughts in his fuddled head:

Misha at his mother's house . . . And who else would be there? . . . Why, none other than Nathan! . . . The two of them together, like lovers reunited after a long absence.

Well, Nestor knew what he must do about that!

With the murmur of the crowd fading behind him, he walked unsteadily through the empty streets of low cabins, store- and barter-houses, stables, beehive granaries; and with every thudding beat of his heart his resolve grew stronger and his course seemed more clearly defined. If what he planned was a crime, at least it would be justified. To Nestor, at least.

The west wall loomed, and there was Nana Kiklu's house, one of several built close to the fence: a long sloping roof of wooden shingles at the front, and a short one at the back, covering the stable and barn. Hanging open, the louvre-covers at the windows let out lamplight and the low murmur of voices. His mother's voice, Misha's tinkling laugh, and Nathan's stumbling stutter. Inside, all would be light and warmth.

Perhaps wistfully, Nestor thought about that: all light and warmth . . . but the narrow alley leading to the back of the house and the hay barn was as dark as his intentions. And suddenly he *knew* how dark they were; so that he might have gone straight to the door and entered, been one with the others, and woke up in the morning with a thick head, a sigh of relief and a clear conscience. But it was not to be, for at that precise moment he heard laughter and the door opened a crack, and he stepped back a pace into the shadows of the alley.

Then Nestor heard his mother bidding Misha goodnight, the door closing, and the lingering footsteps of two people coming towards him as they made for Misha's house. And when they stepped into view, and paused silhouetted, her arm hugged Nathan's, and the starlight gleamed on her smile. And Nestor was cold as stone again, but the fire inside him raged up hot as hell.

He felt his feet carrying him forward, had no control over them, or over the hand that made a fist and drove for Nathan's chin, striking him and rocking his head back against the wall. Misha had time for a single gasp as Nathan crumpled—time to stumble backwards, wide-eyed, away from his attacker, and gulp air to make a shout—which came out as a shocked exclamation as finally she recognized . . . "Nestor!?"

And as her eyes went wider yet he grabbed her up, muffled her mouth with his hand, and dragged her kicking and biting—but all in silence—along the passage to the barn door, where he lifted the bar with his elbow. Inside, the piled hay made a musty-sweet smell, and the inky darkness was striped with starlight filtering faintly in through a loosely boarded side wall.

Nestor was aroused now; with his free hand, he tore Misha's dress open down the front and fondled her firm breasts, and she felt him hard where he pressed himself to her. And the incredible became possible, even likely, as he half-pushed, half-fell with her onto the hay.

Misha has always known Nestor was strong, but the strength she felt now was that of the rapist: mindless, brutal, fevered and phenomenal! His breath was hot and sweet with wine, his kisses rough and lusty, and his hands even more so where they alternated between squeezing her breasts and dragging her legs apart, positioning her on the hay. And to accompany every move, each panting breath, he tore at her clothing, and at his own.

Now she fought him in earnest—raking his face, trying to butt him, bite him, bring her knee into his groin—all to no avail; in just a few seconds she was exhausted. Pinned down, breathless and gasping, her fate seemed certain. She drew air massively to scream, and Nestor brought his face down on hers, crushing her mouth. How she tossed and wriggled then, desperate to be rid of him as he threw her dress up over the lower part of her face . . . and a bar of starlight fell across her forehead and eyes.

Seeing the fear in Misha's eyes, Nestor flinched inside, in his guts. Perhaps for her part she felt the change in him, which came and passed in a moment. And: "Why?" she panted, as he completed the work on her underclothes. "Nestor, why?"

He began to come down on her, his hand behind and under her, opening her up. "When your father and brothers know," he husked, "they'll either kill me or see to it that we're married. Whichever, it will be decisive."

His mouth closed on hers; she felt his manhood throbbing, thrusting, searching her out, and wondered: *Married? Then why didn't you just ask me?* For after all, she had always known it would be one of them, Nestor or Nathan. She hadn't known which one, that was all. Now she did, and it wasn't Nestor.

But maybe she knew too late . . .

Nana Kiklu kneeled by her stone fireplace and chopped a few last vegetable ingredients into the stew bubbling in a copper pan. Her boys would be in soon, Nestor from the welcoming party and Nathan back from walking Misha home. They might have eaten already, but with their appetites it would make little difference. And home cooking was always best.

Nana smiled as she thought of Misha: that girl was rally smitten with her boys. But then, she always had been. Sooner or later she would make her choice, and Nana hoped . . . but no, she must be impartial, and certainly she loved them both and had no favorite. But Nathan, Nathan . . .

The smile fell from her comely face, became a frown, and she sighed. It not Misha Zanesti, then who *would* take Nathan? And if it *was* him, then what of Nestor? For they had grown up together, all three, so that whichever way it went the choosing would be painful and the parting of the ways hard.

And again Nana thought: Nathan, ah, Nathan!

Misha understood him and his ways; something of them, anyway. And as for Nana: she, of course, understood them only too well! She need only look at him to see his father, Harry Keogh, called Dwellersire, looking back at her. Fortunate that no one had ever noticed or remarked upon it; but times had been hard in those days, when people had enough to do minding their own business without minding the business of others. And Nathan's differences hadn't become really marked until he was five, in the year after the last great battle, which had destroyed his alien father along with the first and last of the Wamphyri.

On occasion, infrequently, Nana had seen Lardis Lidesci look strangely, wonderingly at Nathan. But even if he suspected, Lardis would never say anything. He had always been the strong one, Lardis: the protector. And anyway, he got along well with Nathan and liked him; that is to say, he got on as well as could be expected with someone who kept so far apart.

Nathan had always kept himself apart, yes, except from Misha, of course . . . And now Nana was back to that.

Finished with her vegetables, she sighed again, stood up, crossed to the window and looked out. Twilight was quickly fading into night now; the stars were very bright over the barrier range, and a mist was rolling down off the mountains and across the lower slopes. In the old days a mist like that would have sent shivers down Nana's spine, but no more. And her mind went back all of eighteen years and more to just such times—and one night in particular—in the Dweller's garden on Starside. What she had done then . . . maybe it had been a mistake, maybe not, but her boys were the result and she wouldn't change that.

Nestor and Nathan: they'd never known their true father; which, considering what came later, was probably just as well. But for all that Harry had been (and must now forever remain) a stranger to them, the one unknown factor in their young lives, still he'd left his mark on them, and especially on Nathan. Oh, Harry Dwellersire had marked both of her sons, Nana knew, but in Nathan it burned like a brand.

Burned! She sniffed the air and went back to the fire. For that would never do, to let her good stew burn. But in the pot, the water was deep, simmering, not boiling over at all. And so the smell must be something else entirely. A smell at first, and now . . . a *sound*, which Nana remembered.

Impossible!

She raced to the window. Out there, the mist was leprous white in moon- and starlight, undulating, thickly concentrated where it lay on the foothills and sent tendrils creeping over the north wall and through gaps in the stockade's inner planking. Nana had never seen a mist like it. No, she had, she had! But there are certain things you daren't recall, and *this* mist was one of them.

The *sound* came again—a sputtering roar—and a shadow blotting out the stars where it passed overhead. And drifting down from the darkness and the night, that nameless reek, that stench from memory, that impossible smell. *Utterly* impossible! But if that were so . . .

. . . Then what was the meaning of the sudden, near-distant tumult which Nana now heard rising out of the town? What was all that shouting? What were those hoarse, terrified, Szgany voices screaming?

No need to ask, for she knew the answer well enough. "Wamphyri! *Wamphyri!*"

And as the throbbing sputter of propulsors sounded again, closer, shaking the house, the one thought in Nana's mind was for her boys and the girl they loved: Nathan! Nestor! Misha!

She ran to the door and threw it open.

Nathan! Nestor! Misha!

The bellowing of warriors seemed to sound from every quarter, and the sickening stench of their exhaust vapors touched and tainted everything. Nathan! Nestor! Misha!

Something unbelievable, monstrous, armored, fell out of the sky, directly onto Nana's house. Along with the adjacent houses, her place collapsed into dust, debris, ruins, like a ripe puffball when you step on it. Shattered, the door flew from its leather hinges and knocked Nana down in the billowing dust of the street. But even as she dragged herself away from the hissing and the bellowing—and now the screaming, which rose up out of the smoking rubble of the nearby buildings—still she repeated, over and over:

"Nathan! Nestor! Misha!" And wondered, would she ever see them again?

* * *

Five minutes earlier, in the barn:

Misha felt Nestor beginning to enter her, and in desperation gasped, "Let me . . . let me help you."

He lifted his face from her breasts and stared at her disbelievingly. But then, as she reached down a hand between their bodies, he could only grunt an astonished, "What?"

Certainly Nestor could use help; not only was his drunkenness a handicap in its own right, he was also inexperienced. For all his swaggering and boasting among Settlement's youths, and his apparent familiarity with certain of the village girls, he was a virgin no less than Misha herself. Indeed, more so, for she at least seemed to know something.

She caught him up where he jerked and strained, and tightened her slender hand to a yoke around the neck of his pulsing member. As she began to work at him, he murmured, *"Ah!"* and rose up from her a little, to allow her more freedom. Never releasing him for a moment but continuing to gratify his flesh, she at once took the opportunity to roll him onto his back.

He was young and full of lust; her hand was a warm engine of pleasure, squeezing and pumping at him; it couldn't last.

Aching to touch her, tug at her, feel the warm resilience of her perspiring breasts, he reached out a trembling hand—but too late. And as his fluids geysered and splashed down in long, hot pulses onto his belly, so Nestor groaned and flopped back in the hay. But even lying there in a mixture of mindless ecstasy and empty frustration, still he sensed her straightening her clothing and drawing away from him. And as his tottering senses found their own level, suddenly he wondered:

How? How had she known what to do?

And trapping her wrist before she could stand up and run from him, his question was written there on his face plain for her to see. As was the answer on hers.

"Nathan!" he snarled then, as she snatched her hand away, got to her feet and backed off. He made to get after her, came to his knees. If she'd learned that much from his not-so-dumb brother, then obviously she knew all of it. And now more than ever, Nestor desired to be into her. If only for the hell of it.

Misha saw it in his face, shuddered her terror and flew for the door; he hurled himself ahead of her, slammed it shut. And moving menacingly after her where she stumbled in the dark, he huskily asked: "But why? Why with him? Why Nathan?"

"Because he . . . he *needed* someone," Misha's voice was a frightened whisper. "Because he needed something. But mainly because . . . because there was no one else who cared."

"Well, now there *is* someone else," Nestor growled, his head clearing. "Me! Except I don't care, not any longer. No, but there is something I need."

He caught her and lifted her skirts, and when his hand went to her throat she knew that this time she mustn't fight. But she could still protest. And: "Nestor, please don't!" she begged him.

"What you've done for him, you can do for me," his voice was choked with lust and fury.

"But we didn't . . ." she gulped as he pinned her to the wall and positioned himself between her legs. "We've never . . ."

"Liar!" he snarled. For in his mind's eye he'd seen them: Nathan and Misha, panting out their lust as the flesh heaved and shuddered. And hoarsely he ordered her, "Now do it, put me in. And after that . . . just pretend that I'm Nathan!"

It was like an invocation.

"B-b-but you're not!" said a stuttering voice from where the barn door now stood open. And it was Nathan, silhouetted against the night, one hand to his face, and the other a fist which was wrapped round the door's inch-by-three iron-wood bar.

Nestor half-sobbed, half-moaned as he thrust Misha aside and went for Nathan's throat—and ran head-on into the flat side of the other's iron-wood club! It smacked him in the face, shook his teeth and flattened his nose, struck him down like a swatted fly. He lay there groaning, clutching his face, while Misha stumbled towards Nathan where he stood with legs spread wide and feet firmly planted, and the bar held high for a second blow. Maybe he would do it, and maybe not, but Misha knew she couldn't let it happen.

And neither could Nathan. Even before she

could reach him, he'd turned away and let the bar fall.

At which point both of them heard the uproar swelling out from the town's crowded meeting place, and the throb of powerful propulsors overhead. If they had heard that ominous sound before, then they'd been too young for it to make any lasting impression. But still it was strange, frightening, evocative; as was the wafting stench which suddenly accompanied it.

They looked at each other, clung in each other's arms for the very briefest moment—

—Only to be wrenched apart as the roof caved in and the barn flew apart! Then, as their entire world collapsed in chaos all around them, the nightmare they had just lived through commenced its long spiral down from one dark level to depths more lightless yet . . .

Nathan drifted in a darkness shot with brief, brilliant bursts of violent illumination, scenes from the recent past:

Misha smiling where she held his arm tightly against her body . . . Nestor attempting to rape her against the wall of the barn, his voice husky with lust and fury, his hands hurting her with their fierce fondling . . . the ironwood bar from the door in Nathan's hand, feeling good and hard and solid there.

Then he had hit Nestor, hard! Following which something a great deal bigger had hit him, and harder! And now this claustrophobic darkness as his memories tried to piece themselves together and become whole again.

Nathan knew he wasn't dreaming; he was sure of that; his dreams were very special to him, and this wasn't one of them. No, it was the period between sleeping (or lying unconscious) and waking; the interval when the real world starts to impinge again, and the mind prepares the body for a more physical existence. It was him trying to remember exactly what had happened before the world caved in, so that he would know how to act or react when it all came together again.

And occasionally in such moments, those gradually waking moments as the mind drifts up from the fathomless deeps of subconsciousness, it was also a time for communication. Sometimes Nathan would hear the dead talking in their graves, and wonder at the things they said, until they sensed him there and fell silent.

It wasn't so much that they feared Nathan; rather they were uncertain of his nature, and so held themselves reserved and aloof. This was understandable enough, for in their terms it wasn't so long ago that there had been *things* in this world other than men, more evil than men, which had preyed upon the living and the dead alike; the former for the blood which is the life, and the latter for all the knowledge gone down into their graves with them. Things whose alien nature, whose *condition*, was neither life nor death but lay somewhere in between the two, in a seething, sunless no-man's-land called undeath! They had been the Wamphyri, who were known to spawn the occasional necromancer: one of the very few things that the dead fear. Which was why the Great Majority were wary of Nathan.

He knew none of this, only that he sometimes overheard them talking in their graves, and that where he was concerned they were secretive. He was like an eavesdropper, who had no control over his vice.

But in fact, and despite that he could hear them talking and might even have conversed with them (if they had let him), Nathan was no eavesdropper in the true sense of the word, and no necromancer. He *did* come close to the latter, however; very close—perhaps too close— though he wasn't aware of it yet. But the dead were, and they daren't take any chances with him. They'd trusted his father upon a time, and at the end even he had turned out to be something of a two-edged sword.

And so Nathan lay very still and listened neither maliciously nor negligently, but out of a natural curiosity, and in a little while began to hear the thoughts of the teeming dead in their graves: the merest whispers or the echoes of whispers at first—and then a great confusion of whispers—going out through the earth like sentient, invisibly connecting rootlets, and tying the Great Majority together in the otherwise eternal silence of their lonely places.

It didn't feel at all strange to Nathan—he'd listened to the dead like this, between dreams and waking, for as long as he could remember—but this time it was different. Their whispered conversations were hushed as never before, anxious, questioning, even . . . horrified?

For on this occasion there were newcomers among them—too many newcomers, and others who came even now—bringing tales of an ancient terror risen anew. Nathan caught only the general drift of it. But it was as if, along with a background hiss and shiver of mental static, he also heard the rustling of a thousand pairs of mummied hands all being wrung together. And so in the moment before they sensed him, he became aware that their fear was no nebulous thing but in fact very tangible.

This much he learned, and no more. For as soon as they knew he was there . . .

. . . Their thoughts shrank back at once, were withdrawn, cut off, and there was only a shocked, reverberating silence in the otherwise empty mental ether. It was as sudden as that, giving Nathan no time to probe any deeper into the problem; but at least he thought he knew *how* they had sensed him so quickly: because they had been alert as never before, almost as if they were expecting some . . . intrusion? The only thing that worried him about it, was how in the end he'd sensed that they identified *him* with the source of their terror!

And finally, before their withdrawal, there had been the *name* of that terror, which at the last was whispered from the tips of a thousand shrivelled tongues, or tongues long turned to dust: Wamphyri!

But why should that be—how *could* it be—that these long defunct legions of the teeming dead feared the Wamphyri, who were themselves dead and gone forever?

Nathan knew he would find no answer to that here, not yet, not now that the dead had fallen silent. And so he left them to return to their whispered conversations, and rose up from his dreams to seek the answer elsewhere . . .

. . . Rose up from dreams, to nightmare! To a memory complete with every detail of what had gone before, except the answer to the question: what had happened here? But in his first few waking moments Nathan knew he had that, too, for the dead had already supplied it.

It was a fact, all too hideously reinforced by the alien stench of warrior exhaust gasses, the rubble in which he lay sprawled, the distant screams of the dead and the dying, and other *sounds* which could only translate as inhuman . . . laughter? Unless all of these elements were figments of his imagination, and Nathan himself a raving madman, it could only add up to one thing: the Wamphyri were back! And they were here even now, in Settlement!

Which prompted other questions: how long had he been unconscious? Minutes, he suspected, a handful at most. And what of Misha, and his mother . . . and Nestor?

Nathan dragged himself upright, clambered shakily out of the debris of the barn—and back into it at once! For out there, maybe fifty yards towards the town center, he'd seen the incredible bulk of a warrior hurl itself against a barter house and reduce it to so much rubble. And overhead, a huge, kite-shaped flying thing had arched its wings as it came down like some weird leaf into the main street.

Someone moaned in the litter of timber and straw at Nathan's feet: Misha!

He tore at the rubbish, hurling it aside, and stared down at Nestor's face, all bruised and bloodied. He was stretched out flat, unconscious, three-quarters buried; but it was his moan Nathan had heard, not Misha's. And even as he looked at him, so Nestor moaned again. But there in the rubble beside him . . . a slender white arm. And this time it must be Misha!

Trying not to bury Nestor deeper yet, Nathan dug her out. He slapped her face, gathered her up in his arms, whispered her name urgently in her ear. She was wan, dusty, pale in the starlight falling through wispy smoke and gut-wrenching stench. He couldn't tell if she was breathing or not.

In the near-distance, the Wamphyri warrior roared as it moved inwards towards the town center. Nathan looked around. The stockade fence was buckled outwards behind what had been his mother's house. There was a gap there, where the great wooden uprights had been wrenched apart. And beyond the gap, the dark forest. The darkness had never seemed so welcoming.

Nathan saw how it must be, what he must do: first carry Misha to safety, then search for his mother, who was probably buried in the ruins of the house, finally come back one last time for Nestor.

He picked Misha up and staggered from the

ruins towards the break in the stockade fence. But halfway there he heard a panting and a patter of feet and looked back. A great wolf-shape—obviously one of Settlement's trained animals—had come from the direction of the main street and seemed to be making straight for him, seeking human company. All very well, but Nathan would have problems enough saving the girl he loved and his family, without having to worry about . . .

Nathan's eyes went wide, wider. The "wolf" seemed to be enveloped in a drifting cloud of mist, and one of its forepaws was bulky with something that made a dull glitter. More biped than quadruped—loping towards him at an aggressive, forward-leaning angle—it only went to all fours in order to sniff the earth and turn its great ears this way and that, listening. Worse: its eyes were scarlet and glowed like lamps in the dark, and to cover its hindquarters it wore belted leather trousers! And now Nathan saw that it wasn't coming *through* the mist, but that the mist was issuing from it!

He had heard all the campfire stories of the old Wamphyri—their powers, hybridisms, animalisms—and knew what he was facing. And of course knew that he was a dead man.

Canker Canison came loping, reared up snarling, as tall and taller than Nathan . . . !

Nathan tried one last time to stand Misha on her own two feet and shake her awake, to no avail. He held up a hand, uselessly, to ward the dog-, fox-, wolf-thing off. Canker came to a halt and leaned forward. He sniffed at Nathan, then at the girl in his arms, and cocked his head on one side, questioningly. And: "Yours?" he growled.

Nathan held Misha back from the monster; Canker laughed, caught him by the scruff of the neck and hurled him brutally aside, against the stockade wall. Unsupported, Misha crumpled to her knees. Canker caught her up, sniffed at her again, and snatched her rags of clothing from her in a moment.

And as Nathan slumped to a heap in the long grasses at the base of the damaged wall—even as his eyes glazed over and he passed out—he was aware of Canker's eyes on him and his writhing muzzle, and the spray of foam coughing from his jaws as he laughed again and said: "No, not yours—mine!"

What he did *not* see or hear, because he was already unconscious, was the scream of a terrified woman running through the streets: the way Canker let Misha fall to go chasing after her, and his grunted philosophy:

"Better a live one than one half-dead." And his half-bark, half-shout—"Wait my pretty, for Canker's coming!"—as he plunged after his doomed, demented victim . . .

The pain and the anger . . .

And not only inside, but outside, too.

It was an hour later and Nestor's turn to come awake—slowly at first, then with a sickening rush! And like Nathan before him, he too woke up from a dream to a nightmare. Except where Nathan had remembered everything, Nestor remembered very little: a handful of scattered, uncertain fragments of what had gone before. Mainly he remembered the pain and the anger, both of which were still present, though whether they sprang from dream or reality or both, he was unable to say.

Three-quarters buried in rubble, dust, straw, his body was one huge ache. His face was a mess and some of his teeth were loose; at the back of his head, above his right ear, an area of his skull felt soft, crushed. When he put up a tentative, trembling exploratory hand through the debris to touch it, agonizing lances of white light shot off into his brain. Something shifted and grated under his probing: the fractured bone of his skull, indenting a little from the pressure of his fingers.

He asked himself the same question that his brother had asked; what had happened? But unlike Nathan, he had no answer. Not yet.

He pushed at wooden boards pressing down on him, shoved them aside, choked as dust and stench fell on him from above. But framed in the gap he could see the stars up there, drifting smoke, and strange dark diamond shapes that soared in the sky. And he could hear a throbbing, sputtering rumble, fading into the distance.

Yes, and other sounds: faint, far cries . . . moaning . . . sobbing . . . someone shouting a name over and over again, desperately and yet without hope.

Nestor kicked at the rubble, extricated his arms, dragged himself into a seated position and shoved the clutter from his legs. He looked around, at first without seeing or recognizing anything; there was nothing here that his glazed eyes and stunned mind were prepared to take in. No, there was something: the tall stockade fence, which for a moment focussed his attention. But even that was different, gapped in places and leaning outwards a little.

He stood up, staggered, stepped from the debris. Whatever had happened here, his clothing seemed to have been ripped half from him! Automatically, fumblingly—like a man flicking dust from his cuffs after a hard fall—he made adjustments to his trousers, his leather shirt. And slowly, reeling a little, he headed for the town center, away from the rubble of his mother's house.

His mother's house?

Now where had that thought come from? And turning to look back at the freshly made chaos—at the black, jutting, splintered timbers and smoking mounds of debris, under a dark shroud of still settling dust—he slowly shook his head. No, for his mother's house had been a warm and welcoming place. Hadn't it?

In the near-distance, amid smoky, flame-shot ruins close to Settlement's east wall, a last lone flyer flopped up hugely onto a pile of rubble and craned its swaying head towards the sky. Pausing to watch, Nestor was vaguely aware of a rider in the saddle where the creature's neck widened into its back. But in another moment the flyer had thrust itself forward and aloft on powerful coiled-spring launching members, and rising up from the ruins it banked in a wide circle over the town and rapidly gained height. Feeling its shadow on him as it passed overhead, Nestor gaped at its massive diamond shape flowing black against the stars, and wondered at its meaning.

Then, slack-jawed, with his head tilted back at an angle and his half-vacant eyes still fixed on the alien shape in the sky, he continued his shambling walk through the reeking smoke and scattered rubble; until his path was obstructed and he felt something splash wet and warm against his torn trousers.

Sprawled at his feet, he saw the shattered body of a man whose face had been flensed from the bone. A dark red fountain was spurting in bursts from his savaged throat; but even as Nestor considered the meaning of this, so the crimson fountain grew spasmodic, lost height and gurgled out of existence. And with it the man's life.

But it had been only one life, and this was only one body among many. Looking around, Nestor could see plenty of others, almost all of them lying very still.

And so he came to the old meeting place, that great open space which stood off-center in Settlement, a little closer to the east wall than the west, and there discovered life in the midst of all this death.

Where tables lay overturned and the ground was strewn with the spoiled makings of a feast, a young man, Nestor's senior by five or six years, stood over the body of his girl and tore his shirt open, beat his breast, screamed his agony. She had been stripped naked, torn, ravaged, brutalized.

Stepping closer, Nestor stared at the man and believed he knew him . . . from somewhere. And a frown creased his forehead as he wondered how it was he knew so much yet understood so little. Then he saw the rise and fall of the girl's bruised breasts and noticed a slight movement of her hand. And as her head lolled in Nestor's direction, he saw a strange wan smile upon her sleeping or unconscious face.

He moved closer still, touched the sobbing man on the arm and said, "She isn't dead."

Wild-eyed, the other turned on him, grabbed him up with a furious strength, shook him like a rag doll. "Of course she's not dead, you fool—you bloody fool! She's *worse* than dead!" He thrust Nestor away and fell to his knees beside the girl.

Nestor stood there—still frowning, still mazed—and repeated the other's words: "Worse than dead?"

The man looked up, peered at him through red-rimmed eyes, and finally nodded. "Ah, I know you now, Nestor Kiklu, covered in dirt. But you're one of the lucky ones, born at the end of it. You're too young to know; you don't remember how it was, and so can't see how it must be again. But I *do* remember, and only too well! I was only six years old when the Wamphyri raided on Sanctuary Rock. Afterwards, I saw my father drive a stake through my mother's heart, watched him cut off her head, and burn her on a fire. That's how it was then and . . . and how it must be now." He hung his head and fell sobbing on the girl, covering her nakedness.

Nestor walked on, slowly, towards the high wooden catwalk. One of the men on the catwalk was shouting, his words carried over the open area loud and clear. And for all that they were hard words, still there was a catch and even a sob in his familiar voice:

"Too late now, you dullards!" he cried. "Didn't I try to warn you? You know I did. What? And you took me for a madman! And now . . . now I think I *am* a madman! But all those years of building, of being prepared, gone up in smoke, gone for nothing. And all this good Szgany blood, spilled and wasted, and unavenged . . ."

And at last Nestor remembered him: Lardis Lidesci, whom even the Wamphyri had respected, upon a time. And beside him on the catwalk, Andrei Romani; between them they'd wound back the loading gear of a giant crossbow, and manhandled a great ironwood bolt with a barbed, silver-tipped harpoon into its groove on the massive tiller. Men's work for sure, but they were men.

So were the others on the ground, whose names now sprang into Nestor's mind:

They were Andrei Romani's brothers, Ion and Franci, and the small wiry one was the hunter of wild boars, called Kirk Lisescu. Together with Lardis, these men had been legendary fighters in the days when the Wamphyri came a-hunting on Sunside and the Szgany dwelled in terror; even now Kirk Lisescu carried a weapon from those times, a "shotgun" out of another world.

But Nestor knew that except in dreams all such things were over and done with long ago.

Weren't they?

While he puzzled at it, the men had moved on towards the east wall. But up on the catwalk Lardis was shouting again and pointing at the sky— over Nestor! And now, shutting out the stars, a shadow fell on him.

He looked up, at the lone flyer where it sideslipped to and fro, deliberately stalling itself and losing height. For a moment it seemed poised there, like a hawk on the wing, before lowering its head, arching its membrane wings and sliding into a swooping dive. It was heading directly for the bereft young man where he sobbed over his ravaged love. And its rider was lying far forward in his saddle, reaching out along the creature's neck, directing its actions with voice and mind both.

Suddenly something snapped into place in Nestor's befuddled mind. For if this was a dream it had gone badly wrong. And if it was *his* dream, then he should have at least a measure of control over it. He started lurchingly back towards the ragged figure crouching over the girl in the center of the open area, and as he ran he shouted a warning: "Look out! You there, *look out!*"

The man looked up, saw Nestor running towards him, and beyond him the others bringing their weapons to bear, apparently on him! Then he glanced over his shoulder at the thing swooping out of the sky, gasped some inarticulate denial, and made a dive for the shallow gouge of an empty fire-pit. As he disappeared from view the flyer veered left and right indecisively, then stretched out its neck and came straight on—for Nestor!

Coming to a skidding halt, suddenly Nestor sensed that this was more than a nightmare. It was real, and the reality gathering impetus, rushing closer with every thudding heartbeat. He glanced all about, saw open space on every side and nowhere to take cover. From behind him someone yelled, "Get down!" And a crossbow bolt zipped overhead. Then . . .

. . . The flyer was almost upon him, and the underside of its neck where it widened into the flat corrugated belly was splitting open into a great mouth or pouch lined with cartilage barbs! Nestor turned, began to run, felt a rush of foul air as the flyer closed with the earth to float inches over its surface. And in another moment the fleshy scoop of its pouch had lifted him off his feet and folded him inside.

As darkness closed in, he saw twin flashes of fire from the muzzle of Kirk Lisescu's shotgun; up on the stockade catwalk, Lardis Lidesci and Andrei Romani were frantically traversing the great crossbow inwards. Then . . . cartilage hooks caught in Nestor's clothing, and clammy darkness compressed him.

Squirming and choking, denied freedom of movement and deprived of air and light, he breathed in vile gasses which worked on him like an anaesthetic, blacking him out. The last things he felt were a massive shuddering *thud*, followed by a contraction of the creature's flesh around him and its violent aerial swerving.

Then his limbs turned to lead as the flyer fought desperately for altitude . . .

BRIAN LUMLEY

☐ ☐	50832-7	THE HOUSE OF DOORS	$4.95
☐ ☐	51684-2	NECROSCOPE	$4.95
☐ ☐	52126-9	VAMPHYRI! Necroscope II	$4.95
☐ ☐	52127-7	THE SOURCE Necroscope III	$4.95
☐ ☐	50833-5	DEADSPEAK Necroscope IV	$4.95 $5.95
☐ ☐	50835-1	DEADSPAWN Necroscope V - *forthcoming October 1991*	$4.95

GRAHAM MASTERTON

☐ ☐	52205-2	CHARNEL HOUSE	$3.95 Canada $4.95
☐ ☐	52176-5	DEATH DREAM	$3.95 Canada $4.95
☐ ☐	52187-0	DEATH TRANCE	$3.95 Canada $4.95
☐ ☐	52178-1	THE DJINN	$3.95 Canada $4.95
☐ ☐	52183-8	THE MANITOU	$3.95 Canada $4.95
☐ ☐	52208-6	MIRROR	$4.95 Canada $5.95
☐ ☐	52204-4	NIGHT PLAGUE	$4.50 Canada $5.50
☐ ☐	52185-4	NIGHT WARRIORS	$3.95 Canada $4.95
☐ ☐	52199-4	PICTURE OF EVIL	$3.95 Canada $4.95
☐ ☐	51097-6	SCARE CARE *edited by Graham Masterton*	$4.95 Canada $5.95
☐ ☐	52211-7	THE WELLS OF HELL	$3.95 Canada $4.95

Buy them at your local bookstore or use this handy coupon:
Clip and mail this page with your order.

Publishers Book and Audio Mailing Service
P.O. Box 120159, Staten Island, NY 10312-0004

Please send me the book(s) I have checked above. I am enclosing $ _____
(please add $1.25 for the first book, and $.25 for each additional book to cover postage and handling.
Send check or money order only—no CODs).

Name _____

Address _____

City _____ State/Zip _____

Please allow six weeks for delivery. Prices subject to change without notice.

SPINE-TINGLING HORROR
FROM TOR

☐ ☐	50373-2	ADVERSARY *Daniel Rhodes*	$4.95 Canada $5.95
☐ ☐	51751-2	BLACK AMBROSIA *Elizabeth Engstrom*	$3.95 Canada $4.95
☐ ☐	52104-8	BURNING WATER *Mercedes Lackey*	$3.95 Canada $4.95
☐ ☐	51550-1	CATMAGIC *Whitley Strieber*	$4.95 Canada $5.95
☐ ☐	52112-9	CHILDREN OF THE NIGHT *Mercedes Lackey*	$3.95 Canada $4.95
☐ ☐	51773-3	THE HOUSE OF CAINE *Ken Eulo*	$4.95 Canada $5.95
☐ ☐	52505-1	NEXT, AFTER LUCIFER *Daniel Rhodes*	$3.95 Canada $4.95
☐ ☐	50350-3	OKTOBER *Stephen Gallagher*	$4.95 Canada $5.95
☐ ☐	52214-1	PLATFORMS *John Maxim*	$3.95 Canada $4.95
☐ ☐	52555-8	SILVER SCREAM *David J. Schow, editor*	$3.95 Canada $4.95
☐ ☐	50253-1	THE SUITING *Kelley Wilde*	$3.95 Canada $4.95